The Red Bird and the Devil

The Red Bird and the Devil

ROBERT E. LANHAM

Cardinal Press

Cardinal Press
Beaufort, South Carolina

ISBN (hardcover): 979-8-9862631-0-6
ISBN (paperback): 979-8-9862631-1-3
ISBN (ebook: 979-8-9862631-2-0

Printed in the United States of America
First Printing
Thank you to the Parris Island Museum for providing the cover image of Henry Woodward.
This is a work of fiction. Apart from actual historical persons, locales, and events in the novel, characters and events are products of the author's imagination. Incidents and dialogue involving historical figures are not intended to change the fictional character of the work. Any resemblance to living persons is coincidental.
Cover and book design by Tamian Wood, www.BeyondDesignBooks.com

PREFACE

...a small body of noblemen obtained a grant of sovereignty over an almost boundless extent of territory. With that philosophical spirit which might have been expected of an association of gentlemen who numbered in their ranks...Ashley Cooper, Earl of Shaftesbury... with a system of legislation supposed to have been devised by the genius of Locke...The native red man hovered about the settlements, and made it dangerous to quit the shelter of the fortress and their native ferocity was perpetually stimulated by the arts of the neighboring Spaniard...But there were other evils, which had their origin in their own hearts, and against these there was no hope....

(Inaugural Address of the South Carolina Historical Society, June 28, 1857, given by Prof. F.A. Porcher)

Originally, this novel was to be about a young seventeenth-century Londoner who had just completed his apprenticeship as a surgeon and was celebrating in a tavern where he made the mistake of bragging about it. He regained consciousness on a ship sailing for America, having been shanghaied as the new ship's surgeon. The ship sinks in a hurricane off the coast of South Carolina, he survives, is taken in by the Native Americans, and eventually joins a group of English settlers.

In the early stages of my research, I came across a mysterious figure in the penumbra of early South Carolina history, Henry Woodward, whose life had similarities to my fictional character. I realized he was going to be my protagonist, one with a life of far more import than that of my original trifling character. This novel is the result of five years of intense research and writing, and something much different than I envisioned when I began.

Henry Woodward (pronounced "Woodard" at that time) was arguably America's first frontiersman. Daniel Boone is often credited with this title; Henry was a hundred years ahead of him. Other explorers, Spanish and French, had visited America earlier, but they were only passing through; Henry made it his home. His exploits rivaled any of the explorers who came after him. At nineteen, he volunteered to live with the Native Americans in present-day Port

Royal, South Carolina, some 450 miles from the nearest English settlers in Virginia Colony, to learn about the area's suitability for a settlement. The enemy, the Spanish at St. Augustine, was much closer, 200 miles away. Less than a year later, he was a prisoner in St. Augustine until being rescued in a daring buccaneer's raid on the town. He spent the next year serving as a surgeon on a buccaneer ship in the Caribbean (voluntarily), sailing in the famous buccaneer Henry Morgan's fleet. Shipwrecked a year later (yes, in a hurricane) in a remarkable coincidence, he was rescued by the same person he had said goodbye to four years earlier in Port Royal, who was now the captain of the *Carolina*, which was on its way to establish the long-delayed Port Royal settlement. Joining the passengers, Henry thus became one of the first colonists in what became Charleston, South Carolina.

Henry was credited with saving the settlers from starvation in their first years by making a trade agreement with the Native Americans; he went on to become one of the most famous and influential Indian traders in America. Five years after he arrived, after trekking some 250 miles through the wilderness, he reached the Westo Indians' town near present-day Columbus, Georgia. There, amid rows of scalps hanging from lodge poles, he wrote to the philosopher John Locke about the spiritual beliefs of the Westo, who he said worshipped the devil, and the Escamacu who he had lived with and to whom the red bird (cardinal) was sacred.

Henry spent the next five years in the dark world of the Indian slave trade as the agent for Anthony Ashley Cooper, the Earl of Shaftesbury's, plantation. The Westo captured Native Americans living in present-day Georgia who were allied with the Spanish and delivered them to Shaftesbury's plantation to be sold as slaves in Barbados. Finally, a group of colonists, eager for some of the lucrative business, destroyed the Westo and took over the Indian slave trade. Using their control of the colony and its courts, they had Henry convicted of high crimes and misdemeanors; he sailed to London and received a pardon from Shaftesbury, as well as a broad commission to explore Carolina.

His final and greatest accomplishment was a trade agreement with the Creek Indians; although short-lived, the agreement ultimately was partially responsible for the expulsion of the Spanish from America.

This is a work of fiction, but, whenever possible, one with actual characters, events, and locations. Primary source information about the protagonist, Henry Woodward, is scarce; otherwise, this would have been written as a biography or historical narrative. There is no existing physical description of Henry, no records of any of his conversations, and virtually no details of his personal life. I have tried to follow the record of his life and times as closely as possible given the paucity of information and the goal of a readable novel.

In addition to incorporating known history, this book includes newly uncovered historical material not included in earlier writings. Because of the importance of his life in the earlier history of the American southeast, the author believes the reader, if he or she chooses, should have the opportunity to differentiate the imaginary parts of the novel from those based on fact. For that reason, extensive author's notes are included, making this distinction and referencing primary and secondary source materials where appropriate.

Several original letters and documents have been included in the novel; in the interests of clarity, they have been edited to varying degrees. Correspondence between family members is entirely imaginary.

This is a novel about seventeenth-century southeastern colonial America and is told from the viewpoint of its settlers (largely white males) and leaders (entirely white males). Reflecting the usage of that time, Native Americans are referred to as Indians, African people as Negroes, and enslaved persons as slaves. For familiarity and simplicity, some names have been standardized. For example, the Savannah River was not called the Savannah at this time. Many Native American names were in flux, depending on who was referring to them. This includes the Westo, Creek, and Yamasee. Charles Towne is of course modern-day Charleston. One confusing item is that the English were using the Julian calendar at this time which has March 25 as the start of the new year; the Spanish were using the modern-day Gregorian calendar. Where necessary, the year for dates between January 1 and March 24 is shown as 1683/84 for example, the first year being Julian.

Several people were indispensable in the creation of this novel. I cannot thank Professor James Farr at Northwestern University enough for his comments and corrections through multiple drafts of the novel. Also thanks to John Hiatt at Charles Towne Landing Park for details on the early days of the colony. A special thank you to my editor, Ericka McIntyre, and her skill in gently nudging me to make revisions I knew were needed but stubbornly resisted. Finally, thanks to my partner Sarah for her endless patience and support, as well as her editing.

FALLING CREEK, VIRGINIA COLONY

March 22, 1622

In the early morning hours of March 22, 1622, Good Friday, the devil appeared at Falling Creek in Virginia Colony. Fire and brimstone poured from the base of an ominous stone tower into the pristine morning air.

Christopher Woodward had moved here from England three years earlier to work on the Falling Creek blast furnace, set deep in the wilderness fifty miles from Jamestown. Half of the workers had died from disease; only with the aid of Powhatan Indians, cutting trees and making charcoal for the furnace, were the ironworkers able to finish it.

The furnace was finally ready for its first test. The men fired the charcoal at midday and engaged the waterwheel to power the bellows. The workers took off the rest of the day, leaving one man to watch the furnace; Christopher volunteered for the first shift—he never grew tired of the beauty of Falling Creek, especially at the end of the day when the other workers had gone home. Compared to the barren landscape of ironworks he had left behind, this was a paradise; the creek that powered the waterwheel was clear, flowing out of a forest filled with wildlife. He especially loved the red birds—their cheerful song seemed to portend good things to come.

Just after sunrise on Friday, the men gathered around the blast furnace. Christopher, as the oldest, was given the honor of opening the tap. He knocked out the plug at the tower's base; red hot molten iron flowed into the mold, and cheers rose from the elated workers' throats.

Turning to one of the workers, Christopher said, "Tommy, fetch the...." He stopped in midsentence when, to his horror, he saw Tommy slumping to the

1

ground, an ax embedded in his head and blood running down his face, one of the Powhatan men standing over him. Armed Powhatan braves poured out of the forest surrounding the blast furnace; within minutes, all workers were dead.

Christopher Woodward Jr. learned of his father's death and the deaths of more than 300 other colonists two days later. For once, he was glad he had left his wife behind in England when he had moved to Virginia Colony to join his father here. Once it was safe to venture out, he wrote her:

My dearest Margaret:

I begin tho plant spring crops, most of our livestock has been killed or taken, and we lack the manpower to rebuild.

The Powhatans have been trading with us, working in our fields and our homes, without incident. Our hopes that we could educate their children and teach them to adopt Christianity have been dashed; they are opposed to our very presence here. Many in the colony want to raid their towns and take revenge. I am undecided about what we should do. It is a matter of them or us, and few are willing to give up and go home. As a Christian, I cannot accept the idea of slaughtering them as they intended for us. But we cannot live together peacefully with them any longer. I know that we had earlier planned on you, William, and Thomas coming to Virginia once I became established, but I do not think it is safe at present. I could not forgive myself if harm came to you or our son here.

I still believe that our future lies here in Virginia, but the next year or two will be challenging.

I have not heard from Thomas for some time; the last I heard, he had finished Merchant Taylors' School in London and was looking for work. His son must now be about two. I know that my brother may wish to come here in hopes of joining attacks on the Indians to avenge our father's death. If so, do what you can to dissuade him. Please write me with more positive news than what I am telling you. I miss you and cannot wait until we are together.

Your loving husband, Christopher

Conditions were difficult after the raid; Christopher realized he had it better than many colonists as he only had himself to care for. Most crops had been destroyed, and there was no further trading with the Powhatan for food. He joined several raiding parties, burning Powhatan towns and destroying their crops, as they had done to the colonists, hoping for but not finding some satisfaction for his father's death.

2

LONDON

December 1646

Thomas Woodward was in a foul mood, even more so than usual. The Scots had taken King Charles prisoner, and the end now seemed in sight for the monarchy. It was time to reach out to his brother Christopher in Virginia Colony. As best he knew, Christopher now had a large family and had become a successful tobacco planter.

My dear brother Christopher,

I know that I have been remiss in not writing you, and we have a lot to catch up on. I have been appointed as the Assay Master of the Royal Mint. The pay is low, but I have little to do in that position, allowing me to pursue my other business interests.

As you may have heard, the war is not going well for the monarchy. Oliver Cromwell is a fanatic, and I fear he will ruin England if he takes power. Over my strong objections, my sons sided with Cromwell—John joined the cavalier army as a surgeon, and Thomas Jr. enlisted in the cavalry. Both have since seen the error of their ways, and we are again on speaking terms. I blame myself in part for the anger. You know that I have always been outspoken in my beliefs, but we must support our king who answers only to God, not to Parliament.

If the Parliamentarians take power, I will most likely lose everything I have worked for in London, including my position at the Royal Mint. If that happens, I may well fulfill my promise to emigrate to Virginia.

Turning to other topics, my son John and his wife had a second child, Henry, born in October. I can't recall whether your son William has yet married. He should be about John's age, who just turned twenty-one.

Last we spoke, you were doing well in Virginia Colony as a tobacco planter. Have matters finally been resolved with the Indians? I heard that they have been subdued and have pledged obedience to England. I still cannot forgive how they killed our father. He was a pious and godly man and believed that he could help to bring them into the light. It is unfortunate that they were unwilling to become Christians and accept the word of the true God.

If I am compelled to emigrate to Virginia, my family may go as well. There are few opportunities for ambitious young men in London, and if Cromwell and the Parliamentarians take power, there will be even fewer.

I promise to try to be a better brother and stay in touch with you in the future. I've always been difficult to get along with, and the civil war has only made me more so.

Your loving brother, Thomas

3

LONDON

April 1649

After visiting his last patient of the day, John Woodward returned home, a long walk from London's outskirts. Henry and John Jr. ran to the door and threw their arms around his knees in delight. Mary, kissing him on the cheek, said, "Your father came by this morning. He wants to have a meeting tomorrow with you and your brother. He said it was important but would not tell me about it."

John replied, "Knowing Thomas, I guess it was about King Charles' execution. He's been in a dark mood ever since."

Thomas was still at work when John and his brother arrived. Half an hour later, he stomped into the house and growled, "Some idiot in the melting house added too much copper to the mix and ruined an entire batch of sterling ingots." As the Royal Mint's Assay Master, he was responsible for the purity of its coinage, so his mood was understandable.

Thomas continued, "Sir Robert Harley called me to his office this morning and told me that he is resigning as Master of the Mint. My job would have been secure as long as he was there, but Parliament has already chosen his replacement, someone who I consider to be my enemy. I have no doubt one of his first acts will be to fire me."

After downing a glass of claret, he continued, "I have often thought about this day since it became clear that Cromwell was winning the war. The abolition of the monarchy gives me little choice—I have decided to emigrate to Virginia Colony. My brother Christopher is well settled there and has always said we are welcome there."

Refilling his glass, he continued, "As you know, your grandfather died in the 1622 Indian uprising. But my brother assures me that the heathens have been defeated and are now subservient to the colony. Any of you that wish to join me are welcome but know that life will be hard there at first. We will be starting fresh with no employment, no land, and few connections."

John spoke first. "This is no surprise to us. Mary and I have discussed what we would do if you left the Mint. Most of my income comes from treating injured workers there. Without you, I expect this would end; I wouldn't be able to support my family."

Thomas Jr. added, "And I would be fired from the Mint, too, as I am there only because of your position."

They discussed their father's decision late into the evening, the brothers agreeing that they could not continue to live in London without their incomes from the Mint. There were few opportunities elsewhere in England, and Virginia Colony seemed an attractive option. There was land available at low cost, tobacco plantations were prospering, and the colony's hard times were behind it. Other supporters of Charles I were also fleeing England for Virginia so Thomas could make political connections, and his brother Christopher could help them get settled. John's children, Henry and John Jr., were now three and five, old enough for the voyage. Thomas said he would be willing to loan his children funds to help them get established. By evening's end, they had arrived at a unanimous decision to leave that year.

⸺⧽∾∾⧼⸻

In early September, Thomas announced to his sons they would be leaving for Virginia Colony that month. "My friend Henry Norwood found a ship that can take us to Jamestown, *The Virginia Merchant*, a good-sized ship of 300 tons with thirty cannons. It will sail from Gravesend in mid-September. Norwood assures me that its Captain, John Lockier, is a skilled seaman. The passage is six pounds per person; as I promised, I will pay the cost."

4

VIRGINIA COLONY

1650

Thomas' friends were mistaken about Captain Lockier's competence. Not only had he failed to provision the ship with adequate food for the 200 passengers, but he also sailed it into two storms that almost sank it. By the end of the voyage, the passengers were reduced to eating rats, purchased from opportunistic crewmen, for sustenance. Fortunately for the Woodwards, Thomas could outbid the others to put broiled rats on their table.

Four months after leaving Gravesend on a voyage that should have taken no more than two months, *The Virginia Merchant* limped into Jamestown, its deck no longer crowded with passengers—sixty had perished from hunger, and twenty had been left behind on an island off the coast. The town's residents gathered in shock at the sight of the floating wreck, then quickly went to the aid of the passengers, carrying those who were too weak to walk. The Woodwards were able to disembark under their own power, although Mary, who had secretly been giving much of her meager portion of the food to her children, had to lean on John for support. Most of their possessions were destroyed, so they had little else other than the clothes on their backs.

Thomas shepherded his family to the Ship's Tavern and Inn and introduced himself to the innkeeper, "We just arrived from London on *The Virginia Merchant*. My brother Christopher Woodward was to leave instructions for contacting him."

The keeper replied, "You've not heard—your brother fell ill and died a month ago. His son William is taking care of his affairs; he lives at Shirley Plantation, thirty miles upriver."

This was unwelcome news—even though Thomas had never been close to Christopher, he had been their only contact in Virginia Colony.

Thomas had met his nephew William when Christopher's family visited London and thought he had seemed undisciplined; they had not gotten along.

Saying he had hit it off with William, John offered to write him a note explaining the family's situation.

After hearing from the innkeeper that there was no lodging available, Thomas asked, "If you had rooms, what would they cost?" Receiving an answer, Thomas placed a stack of coins, fresh from the Royal Mint, on the table, double the quoted price. Not only did the Woodwards now have rooms, but the innkeeper also agreed to deliver John's note to William at Shirley Plantation.

William greeted them two days later. After Thomas offered condolences for William's father's death, he asked if William would help them find temporary lodgings until the family could arrange for a permanent home.

William replied, "I heard you might be coming to Virginia and will help you to settle. My mother is still living in her home, and I live in a small cabin, so there is no extra space. But I have Colonel Hill's permission to use an empty house he owns on Shirley Plantation—you can stay there for now."

As they sailed up the James River on the rising tide, William pointed to the tobacco fields lining the riverbanks. "We recently finished tobacco harvesting, so the fields are empty; the tobacco is in the curing barns. At Shirley Plantation, we use indentured servants for our labor, but some other plantations also use African slaves."

Arriving at the family home, William introduced them to his mother. Although not yet over her husband's death, she greeted them graciously, inviting them for dinner.

Over dinner, the family discussed their options. William said, "As you saw yesterday, Shirley Plantation is far upriver from Jamestown and only exists to grow tobacco. We recently bought several hundred acres in the wilderness near Fort Henry some fifty miles to the north on the Appomattox River. I've thought of moving there someday as I have no desire to be a planter. My mother also owns a hundred acres along Pagan Point Creek downriver from here. It is not yet built up like Jamestown, but my father always believed it would be soon."

By the end of dinner, the Woodwards had agreed that John and his family would settle on the Pagan Point land; reluctantly, John said he would ask his father for a loan for the cost of building a home there and, in the meantime, would start building his surgical practice in the colony.

5

VIRGINIA COLONY

November 1652

In Jamestown to pick up some surgical supplies shipped from London, John saw his cousin William's boat tied up at the wharf and then found him eating a midday meal in the Ship's Tavern.

"Hello William, it's been some months since I last saw you. May I join you?"

After catching up on local news, William said, "I hear Thomas was appointed Clerk of Isle of Wight County."

John replied, "Yes, my father is prospering here. He's made important connections with fellow Royalists that also emigrated from England and is using his position as Clerk to buy up land."

William asked, "Are you also buying land?"

"No. I have no desire to become a planter, and there is little other reason to buy land here." John added, "I had hoped that my father's political views might become less extreme after we moved here. That is not the case; we often go for weeks without speaking to each other. His friends are no better—all they can talk about is tobacco and politics."

William then inquired as to how John's surgical practice was doing.

He replied, "It is going well; I can now support my family without borrowing money from Thomas. But I don't find it rewarding. I spend much of my time treating servant and slave injuries from tobacco harvesting, knowing full well they are likely to die from disease or overwork, and there's little I can do about it. Honestly, I miss my career, as brief as it was, as an army surgeon, where I was making life or death decisions every minute."

William looked down thoughtfully at his now empty plate and then spoke. "As you know, my wife and I also found life on a tobacco plantation tedious;

that's why we moved north to my land at the edge of the wilderness. We just finished our new home and Abraham Wood, who owns Fort Henry, hired me to work there. It's not an actual fort but a trading post. Indians bring deerskins and animal furs and trade them for beads, cloth, hatchets, knives, and the like. My job is to negotiate with them. Most are Powhatans; they are no longer a threat since the peace treaty. You and Mary could move onto our land; there is a lot of room, and we would welcome having neighbors. Perhaps Wood could find work for you at the fort. Also, there is a need for your surgical skills, even though there are not many settlers here."

John replied, "If it were only up to me, I would go back with you today. But I have three other mouths to feed, and the only way I know to make a living is as a surgeon. It was hard to do in London because there were too many other surgeons; even barbers could do surgery. Where you live, the problem is the opposite—there are too few patients."

William concurred but added, "We raise most of our food and get venison and other meat from the Powhatan; other than that, our needs are not great. You could do the same. If you're interested, you have an open invitation to visit us whenever you want."

William had planted a seed in John's mind that had turned into a flourishing plant by the time he arrived back at Pagan Point. Telling Mary of his conversation with his cousin, he said, "This would be a fresh start for us and far enough away from Thomas to stop his meddling in our affairs."

Mary replied that it sounded exciting but voiced the same concerns her husband had raised earlier. "John—the fort is in the middle of nowhere. You are a surgeon and need patients. It sounds like there's only a handful of people living there."

But he couldn't let go of the idea, and finally, after several days of listening to him, she agreed to visit and see first-hand what life would be like there.

⸺⧡⧡⸺

A month later, John and his family showed up unannounced at William's house. They had carved a cozy home out of the wilderness. There was a thriving vegetable garden in the front yard, complete with chickens scratching for bugs. A milk cow was tethered under an oak tree, contentedly chewing its cud. Four pigs rooted happily in their pen, and a pair of red birds were busily building a nest in a bush by the front door. Mary fell in love with the setting immediately.

William's wife said she needed to get to work to prepare enough food for them; Mary pitched in to help her, and John prepared a chicken that William killed for the meal. The meal was delicious, with cold milk from their spring-fed milk house for the children and fruit pie for dessert. Mary's concerns that they would be eating squirrel stew were unfounded.

William gave them a tour of his land the next day, saying he held over a hundred acres and there would be ample room for John to build his own home on if he so wished.

He then took them to Fort Henry, where they met Abraham Wood, who said, "I cannot tell you how pleased I am to have William working here. He has become invaluable by building a relationship with the Powhatan, and he is learning to speak their language."

William said, "My cousin John lives in Pagan Point where he practices as a surgeon. He is interested in moving away from the tobacco plantations, and I invited him to bring his family for a visit to see if he might be interested in living here. I told him you might even have work for him at the fort."

Wood smiled at John, "Your timing could not be better. One of my employees just announced he and his family want to be closer to Jamestown and are moving out within the month. William's word is good enough for me—if you want to take over his job, it is yours. It's not full-time and does not pay a lot, but living here is inexpensive, and you would be free to take patients as well if you can find any up here."

By the time John and Mary arrived at Pagan Point after the two-day boat ride down the river, Mary was as enthusiastic as John about relocating to Fort Henry. She felt that she and William's wife could become close friends; both families had young children, and she hoped to hear much less of John complaining about his father.

June 1654

Mary called the children to breakfast—bread, cornmeal mush, and milk. Johnny wandered in, sleepy-eyed.

No Henry.

"Johnny, get your lazy brother out of bed."

Johnny replied, "He's already up."

Mary: "Go find him."

He searched the yard and garden; no Henry.

Coming in after morning chores, John hadn't seen him either. "Perhaps he's at the neighbors." But they hadn't seen him since yesterday.

Midday, still no Henry. John went up to Fort Henry to ask his cousin William if he was there. No Henry. One of the traders said he had seen a young boy walking along the river near the fort.

John headed back home. For an eight-year-old, Henry was an accomplished woodsman and knew how to swim. Presumably, he would come home when he got hungry.

By early evening, Henry's parents were becoming genuinely concerned. He was a fearless and independent eight-year-old, but they could think of no reason for him to be gone for an entire day. Finally, just before dusk, William showed up at the house with Henry in tow.

Before his parents could speak, Henry blurted out, "I joined the Indians!"

William interjected, "Some Powhatan braves brought Henry to the fort an hour ago. He showed up midday at their town; eventually, they brought him back to the fort and left him with me."

Henry was unharmed and so happy that his parents could scarcely bring themselves to punish him. They told him he would have to go to bed without supper; he said he had already eaten at the Indian town.

Too excited to sleep, Henry told Johnny about his adventure: "I made friends with the Indians! I told a trader at the fort that my father was in their town, and he took me there. Some of them spoke English, and I asked if I could stay until my father returned. I got to play with some boys my age and shoot a bow and arrow. Then I got to help skin a rabbit. I'm going to ask father if I can go live with them. You can come and visit me."

Days later, Henry was still talking about his visit to the Powhatan town. His father explained that he was too young to leave home, and anyhow, there was a treaty with the Powhatan Indians that said settlers were not allowed to live on their lands. "But if you want, I can ask William if there might be a job for you at Fort Henry, helping with chores. "

Henry thought that didn't sound as much fun as living with his new Indian friends, but at least he could still see them sometimes.

His uncle did find a job for Henry. Wood gave him the task of sweeping floors and tidying up the warehouse. His uncle met with the Powhatan men who came to trade deerskins and conversed with them in a mixture of English and Powhatan. Henry would follow him around, listening closely; soon, he could welcome the men as they arrived at the fort, "*Chama wingapo*"—"Welcome friend."

After a few months, he was a favorite of the Powhatan traders.

One morning over breakfast, John and Mary told the boys over Henry's grumbling, "You are both now old enough to start your education. If we were still in London, you would be going to school. Since we have no schools, we've hired a tutor to give you lessons. He will also be tutoring your cousins. He will teach you grammar, Latin, and arithmetic three days each week."

Henry missed spending every day at the fort, but the tutor was exceptional. Henry found he had a knack for languages, so grammar and Latin came easily to him; his brother was better at arithmetic.

In addition to concentrating on lessons, the boys spent hours fishing on the Appomattox River with rods made from willow switches. One day, they returned home soaking wet.

Their mother asked, "What happened to you?"

Johnny replied, "Henry caught a huge sturgeon, as big as him. He couldn't land it and refused to let go of his pole. It pulled him into the water, but he still wouldn't let go. I had to jump into the river and save him."

If left up to Henry, he would have spent all his time at the fort. Taken by Henry's interest in his business, Wood gave him more responsibilities. Soon, he was proficient at sorting the deerskins by size and weight—a doe or young deerskin weighing about a pound, a buck's skin as much as three pounds—and grading them by quality.

Henry pestered his uncle with questions about the fort and the Indians who came there. "Why do they want our goods so badly? It must be a lot of work for them to catch the deer and prepare the skins to trade."

William replied, "Before the English came to Jamestown fifty years ago, the only tools the Indians had were made from stone, bone, or wood. To cut down a tree and hollow out a log for a canoe using only fire and a stone ax took weeks. Preparing animal skins was also hard. With iron axes and knives, they can make a canoe in days and prepare a deerskin in hours."

Henry was being tutored in Latin at home; at the fort, William became his tutor, teaching him the details of the Indian trade. "We only trade for dressed deerskins. After the men remove the hide, the women scrape off the flesh and hair, soak the skins in water and deer brains, and pound and stretch them to make them soft. Finally, they smoke them over a fire."

Later, Henry asked, "I understand why the Powhatan want to trade for our tools, but what do we do with all of the deerskins?"

William replied, "You've seen the big crates and barrels we pack the deerskins in. We ship them to London to make breeches, gloves, and shoes. There aren't enough deer there to meet the demand, so they buy deerskins from Virginia Colony. They also purchase beaver pelts from us to make hats."

⬧⬧⬧

In a few months, Henry was pestering his uncle to let him go back to the Powhatan town. William said that Henry could go to their town on his next visit if his parents and Wood approved. They had no objection; Henry practiced his Powhatan on his brother every night until he fell asleep, not even noticing that Johnny was usually already asleep.

William had arranged a meeting with the Powhatan elders to discuss trade for the upcoming year. Henry was up at the crack of dawn and at the fort before his uncle. As they walked to the town, Henry asked, "Uncle, how shall I address the chief? What if I get it wrong?"

William replied, "The chief is a kind man, but your place is to be seen and not heard." While William was conversing with the elder, Henry wandered outside and ran into several of the boys he had befriended in the town. When William finished the meeting and went to collect Henry, he found him in the middle of archery instruction with his friends.

That evening, Henry told his parents that he wanted to have his Powhatan friends come to his house to play.

His father said, "That wouldn't be a good idea—the Indians are not allowed on Virginia Colony's land."

Henry retorted, "Why not?"

Seeing an opportunity to give Henry a history lesson, Mary answered, "It is in a treaty with Virginia Colony. Borrow a copy of the treaty from Abraham Wood and give us a report on it."

Every evening for the following week, Henry labored over the document; when he finished, Mary asked him to explain what it meant. "It's awful. The colonists got all the lands between the York and the James Rivers. If any Indians came onto their land, the colonists could kill them. There was no penalty if the colonists went onto Indian land. The Indians could send messengers to Virginia Colony, but they had to wear badges to identify themselves."

Henry said that the treaty did not seem fair.

Mary explained that the English had defeated the Powhatan after the battle in 1646. Some of the Virginia Colony leaders wanted to drive out the Powhatan from the area entirely; others, including Abraham Wood, wanted to continue trading with them. "Your grandfather Thomas sides with those who want to drive out the Indians, but you must remember that the Powhatan killed his father in the 1622 attack, and he has never forgiven them." She added, "We live many miles from Jamestown and pay scant attention to the treaty."

But it was still not a good idea to have his Indian friends visit him at his home.

7

THE BATTLE OF BLOODY RUN

Virginia Colony, 1656

Busy with his chores outside the fort, Henry did not see the approaching stranger until they almost collided. He was not Powhatan, wearing unfamiliar garb, lacking the required striped cloth badge, carrying a gun, and speaking a language Henry had never heard. Henry greeted him, first in English, then in Powhatan, but received only a shrug from the stranger. As they tried to communicate, several of the stranger's companions emerged from the woods, also armed, two with bundles of beaver pelts on their backs. The first pointed to the pelts and then to the ax Henry was carrying. Henry realized that whoever they were, they had come to the fort to trade.

Motioning for them to stay, he ran back to the fort and told his uncle of his encounter. They found the strangers where Henry had left them. Again, William greeted them in English and Powhatan, getting a response he did not understand.

One of them finally spoke: "Parlez-vous Francais?" William, who knew basic French, replied, and they exchanged a few words. They came from far to the north, where they had traded beaver skins with French fur traders. Their tribe had just moved to this area and wanted to do business with Captain Wood. William told them that he would take one of them back to the fort if he left his gun behind.

With William's help, Wood and the brave could carry on a conversation of sorts. The Indians were from the Erie Confederacy hundreds of miles to the north. Seven hundred of them had left their home and settled on the James River, north of Fort Henry. The Powhatan were calling them the Rickahocan.

They had heard of Captain Wood and wanted to become trading partners with him—furs and skins for English goods, including guns. Wood said he would welcome a trading agreement with them but had to clear it with the Virginia Colony Council.

The following week, the Virginia Council ordered Wood to attend a meeting about his request. Wood quickly realized that the new governor, Edward Digges, an English barrister, understood nothing of the Indian trade. Several council members were skeptical of trading with Indians not subject to the 1646 treaty and thought this new settlement was too close to their plantations.

When the meeting finally adjourned, Wood returned to the fort in a dark mood and asked William to see him. He said, "Not only did the council refuse to approve my trade request, but they also passed a resolution that the new arrivals, the Rickahocan, not be allowed to settle anywhere near the colony. Worse yet, the governor ordered Colonel Hill to raise a party of one hundred men from the militia and one hundred Powhatan warriors to remove the newcomers, peacefully if possible. He also ordered that I meet with the Rickahocan but not tell them of this meeting."

After hearing that, all William could say was, "Let's hope for a peaceful resolution."

Wood replied, "That's unlikely. Colonel Hill fancies himself a soldier, not just a planter. Hill's father, like your grandfather, died in the 1622 massacre, and, to this day, Hill hates all Indians. I see bloodshed as being the likely outcome of the council's order."

Colonel Hill immediately called up the Colonial Rangers; Henry's father was among them, serving as the volunteer militia's surgeon. Hill then sent a Powhatan brave to Rickahocan town with a message asking them to meet at Fort Henry to discuss a trade agreement.

Five unarmed Rickahocan elders appeared at the fort's outskirts several days later. Hill had stationed ten armed Colonial Rangers inside the fort. At his command, they burst out and opened fire on the elders, killing them all.

Immediately following the massacre, Hill ordered the Rangers, reinforced by a hundred Powhatan warriors, to march north to Rickahocan town, kill the men, and capture the women and children. Henry's father, taking his surgeon's bag and medical supplies, and concealing his dread of what was about to unfold, kissed Mary goodbye, saying, "I will probably be absent several days. I can't tell you more than that."

Two days later, John returned, his clothes encrusted in dried blood. Mary rushed out to meet him. "John, are you injured?"

"It's not my blood." But even though he was unhurt, she had never seen him this badly shaken. When she pressed him for details, he promised to tell her after cleaning up and having a warm meal.

That evening, after the children were in bed, he told her about the battle:

"Hill led about a hundred of us, all armed, as well as a hundred Powhatan warriors, to Rickahocan town. The Colonel told us that we could expect them to flee when we approached with such a strong force. But that is not what happened. Hill sent the warriors ahead of the militia. About a mile from the town, suddenly, the forest ahead of us was filled with the sound of gunfire. We knew it was not from the Powhatan, as they had only bows and arrows. The Rickahocan must have heard about us killing their elders and, expecting us to follow up with an attack on their town, ambushed us. Several of us urged Hill to have our men engage them, but he panicked and did nothing. Finally, when the gunfire had quieted, he sent a ten-man party ahead to reconnoiter. Not long after that, we heard more gunfire, and then it was quiet."

John stopped and was unable to continue his narrative for some time. Finally, collecting himself, he resumed:

"About half an hour later, two of the militia returned, one wounded, and told us that several hundred Rickahocan, armed with guns, had ambushed and killed all of the Powhatan warriors, scalping many of them. They also attacked the militia scouts killing all but the two who had escaped. There were so many dead that the stream ran red with their blood. When the Colonel heard this, he ordered an immediate retreat."

Hearing this, all she could say was, "Are they going to kill us next?"

John replied, "I can't say what will happen. We can only hope that the Rickahocan understand this was not Wood's idea. It would be wise to stay home for a few days and see if things settle down."

John and Mary had not noticed Henry had crept into the room after his parents thought he was in bed—he had heard everything.

AN UNHOLY ALLIANCE

8

Virginia Colony, 1657

A month after the failed attack on the Rickahocan, which the colonists had taken to calling the Battle of Bloody Run, Wood saw his trade with the Powhatan come to a near standstill. The battle had cost the lives of many of the warriors and their chief. Feeling betrayed by the colonists, they had pulled back from dealings with Virginia Colony, including trade with Fort Henry.

Wood called a meeting at the fort with his employees to look for ways to stay in business; he opened the meeting, saying, "The battle may well have been the end of our reliance on the Powhatan as trading partners. We need to look elsewhere if we are to continue the Indian trade."

William agreed, saying the Powhatan now distrusted all the colonists, including himself and others at the fort.

Wood continued, "The Rickahocan came to us looking for a trade agreement. Instead, we killed their leaders. But we have seen that they are the fiercest and most skilled fighters in the region, and Virginia Colony lacks the power to defeat them. I suggest that we go back to them to see if it still might be possible to trade with them."

One of the traders interjected, "It is more likely that they would kill us as well. They will never trust us after Colonel Hill's perfidy."

Wood replied, "They are going to need us just as much as we need a new trading partner. I suggest William and I go alone and unarmed to their town to meet. I would make it clear that we are not friends with Hill and had nothing to do with his attack on them."

Wood followed through on his plan. That week, he and William, unarmed and carrying packs filled with trade goods from the fort, headed out to the Rickahocan town. Several miles before reaching it, two warriors stopped them at gunpoint. Wood showed them that he and William were unarmed and pointed at their packs and a beaver pelt William had brought with him. The warriors escorted them to the town and their chief, who could converse with William in French.

When they had finished, William summarized for Wood, "This is Paytah, their new chief, replacing his father who Colonel Hill killed. I explained that Fort Henry was still interested in a trade agreement for skins and furs. He is not as angry as I expected him to be and does not blame you for what happened. His people live in a constant state of war, killing many of their enemies and losing many of their men. He said his father was old and had become soft and should never have met with Hill as he did." William continued, "He said they are still willing to become trading partners with Abraham Wood but want nothing to do with the rest of Virginia Colony."

Wood instructed William to tell Paytah that he would still need to get permission from the Virginia Council to trade with them. Giving the chief the trade goods as gifts with a promise to return soon, the two returned to Fort Henry.

Wood's meeting with the Virginia Council and the new governor received a mixed reaction. Predictably, the members who wanted all Indians driven far away from the colony were strongly opposed. But Samuel Matthews, who had just replaced Digges as governor, was more knowledgeable about dealing with Indians and also more pragmatic, said, "We did not authorize Hill's attack on the Rickahocan, and we cannot blame them for defending themselves. In any case, since we know we cannot defeat them, we must live with them. Also, now that the Powhatan have been badly weakened, they are not as valuable to us as a buffer to protect us from attacks from more distant tribes. The Rickahocan could fill that role."

After several hours of heated wrangling, the council finally reached an agreement. The governor announced, "Wood is authorized to make a trade agreement with the Rickahocan as he has with the Powhatan. They will be allowed to stay in their town, but they can only trade at Fort Henry in groups no larger than ten men and not come into the colony's lands."

Wood went back to the Rickahocan town to finalize their trade agreement, similar to the one he had with the Powhatan. Paytah agreed but added a request Wood had not considered, asking that he also trade for firearms. Wood had not been allowed to provide the Powhatan with guns and had not thought to bring up the issue with the council. When he told him he was not allowed to trade with anyone for guns, Paytah replied, "We traded for guns with the French before coming here, and guns are now a part of our life. We cannot live without them."

After conferring with William about this impasse, Wood told Paytah, "You have many guns now. If our agreement is working in three months, I will return to the council and explain why they should allow me to trade guns with you. That is the best offer I can give you."

Paytah, knowing he had little choice, agreed.

By year's end, Wood calculated that his trading profits were still down. The Rickahocan provided Wood with more beaver pelts than the Powhatans had, but fewer deerskins, which were his primary source of income. It was time for another meeting at the fort.

Wood told the assembled group, "Unless we can increase the fort's income, I can't keep all of you on. I have begun growing tobacco for more income but cannot find enough affordable labor to work the fields. Regardless, Fort Henry is a trading post, not a tobacco plantation."

No one had a helpful idea for improving business, and the discussion came back to tobacco and the labor shortage.

One worker said, "My father-in-law has used Indian slaves captured in skirmishes with the colony as workers in his fields. It was hard to prevent them from escaping into the wilderness, but they cost him nothing. Someone else mentioned that he knew a grower who had traded with the Powhatan for several Indians they had captured from other tribes. They cost far less than either indentured servants or African slaves and, if they ran away, he paid the Powhatans to track them down and return them."

Wood adjourned the meeting with no resolution to the fort's financial problems. That evening, he thought about what he had heard. Perhaps he could supplement his trading business by selling captive Indians as slaves, in addition to skins and furs. He knew that many tribes had a long history of capturing Indians in battle and bringing them into their communities as slaves. Possibly the Rickahocan could capture Indians from other tribes to trade at the fort. They were fierce fighters and had enough guns to overcome any resistance. After thinking it over, he saw some potential problems – Indian slaves working in the tobacco fields would escape if possible. It would be bad for his reputation if he sold slaves who ran away at the first opportunity. Also, it seemed imprudent to have the Rickahocan capture Indians who lived near the colony, creating discord with the tribes that the colony had spent decades soothing. Captives would have to be from Indian towns distant from Virginia Colony.

He knew he would need permission from the Virginia Colony Council and the governor for this plan that went far beyond the right to trade for skins and furs granted in his original contract with the colony. Some council members might oppose the idea of enslaving Indians, but the council was always open to generating revenue, especially with tobacco prices being down. Offering the colony higher taxes for selling captives than he paid for skins and furs might work.

Wood went back to the Rickahocan's town and met with Paytah to discuss his proposal. He told him, "I need you to supply more deerskins to make our trade agreement worthwhile for me."

Paytah replied, "Before we moved here, we trapped beaver and only killed deer for food. We do not have enough people in our town to prepare more deerskins."

Wood asked, "Have you ever considered capturing Indians from tribes which are your enemies and selling them to the colonists to become slaves?"

Paytah said, "No. When we captured our enemies in a battle in our old home, we killed them or made them slaves in our towns. The French and English traders there did not have slaves, and nobody would have wanted to buy ours."

Wood explained to Paytah, "In Virginia, we grow tobacco. Most of the workers are servants from England. Some planters have begun using slaves from Africa, but they are expensive and hard to come by. Would you be willing to make war on Indian towns and bring the captives to Fort Henry to sell to us? It would be more profitable than trading skins and furs with us. The Rickahocan are the best fighters I have ever seen; if you attack towns that do not have guns, there should be little risk."

Paytah said, "We have never taken captives from other tribes that we were not at war with. I do not know if it is honorable to attack peaceful towns and take their people prisoner so that we can sell them to become your slaves."

Wood replied, "Then you will need to provide us with many more deerskins, or we will need to find other tribes to trade with as well. At present, I am not making enough profit to keep Fort Henry in business."

Paytah said he would need to talk Wood's proposal over with the other elders in his town and let him know their answer.

Wood replied that he would also need to get permission from the Virginia Council as his contract only provided for trading skins and furs.

At the council meeting, Wood introduced his proposal to deal in captive Indians to be sold as slaves on the tobacco plantations. Some members wanted nothing to do with the Rickahocan, the Battle of Bloody Run still fresh in their minds. Several others voiced moral objections to enslaving Indians; to them,

Wood replied, "Virginia Colony allows African slaves to work on the plantations. What is the difference?" Answering one planter's comment that Indian, unlike African, slaves could easily run away, Wood responded, "If they were taken from distant towns, it would be harder for them to escape and easier for them to be recaptured. We could even pay the Powhatan to bring them back."

Finally, after a full day of heated debate, the council approved Wood's proposal with the conditions that no Indians could be taken within fifty miles of the colony and a twenty percent tax on each captive sold would be paid to the Virginia government.

Wood went back to Rickahocan town and met with Paytah. "The Virginia Council gave me permission to buy captive Indians from you, but you cannot take them from nearby tribes."

Paytah replied, "I have already met with the elders, and they have agreed to your proposal."

Both Wood and the Rickahocan were experienced traders, but no one had ever exchanged Indian captives for English goods before. They finally agreed on a price—a young adult male would have the same value as seventy-five deerskins, less for women and children. Deciding where the captives would come from was more difficult. Paytah said they did not want to raid towns to the north of the colony as they were skilled warriors. He told Wood, "I have heard there are towns to the south along the coast that we could raid. They are peaceful farmers and should be easy for us to attack. But they are a month's travel from Fort Henry, and it will be difficult to bring prisoners that distance."

Wood and Paytah parted with the understanding that the Rickahocan would move ahead with the plan, both of them knowing it might not be feasible.

⚬⚬⚬

It worked better than Wood had hoped. In the first two months alone, the Rickahocan had delivered sixty men and women to the fort. They were raiding towns along the coast to the south; the inhabitants were indeed peaceful and easily captured. Wood found a ready market for the captives on the tobacco plantations and was making a handsome profit, more than trading in deerskins and furs had provided.

But the Rickahocan still did not trust the colony not to attack them again, nor did the colony trust them being so close. Late in 1658, Paytah asked Wood to meet about their concerns.

He began, "My people do not feel safe living near Virginia Colony and the Powhatan. We do not go onto their land, but they often behave in a threatening way to our women and children when they come near our town. Our elders are talking about once again moving to a place where we would feel safer."

Understanding and agreeing with Paytah's concerns, Wood asked if he knew where they might go.

Paytah replied, "We want to live far from any English settlements and away from tribes who are powerful enough to threaten us. We came from the north and cannot go back there. So, it must be to the south, but we do not yet know where."

Wood asked if they still planned on trading with him.

Paytah replied, "We do. We would like to move closer to the towns we are raiding. We are so far from them that it is hard to plan our raids. If we move to the south, it will be easier. I will suggest that we should follow the Indian Trading Path south until we find a place where we could put our new town."

By the early summer of 1659, the entire Rickahocan town had packed up and started the long trek south along the Indian Trading Path. Wood heard nothing further from them for the rest of the summer.

9

PARADISE LOST

Virginia Colony, 1658

Henry's relationship with his Powhatan friends had been strained ever since the Battle of Bloody Run. Several of them no longer wanted anything to do with him, blaming the colonists for the deaths of their fathers or uncles at the hands of the Rickahocan. Daily life at Fort Henry was now more subdued, and the surviving Powhatan traders less friendly.

A large part of the fort's income now came from the Indians captured by the Rickahocan. Their hands and feet bound, the captives were transported downriver by boat to Jamestown to be sold to tobacco planters. Henry saw little of the braves; they stayed to themselves at the fort, took payment in guns, ammunition, and other goods, and quickly departed. Sometimes wearing war paint, their appearance was frightening, but William had assured him that they were no threat to the fort's employees, whom they depended on for trade goods.

John and Mary sensed that Henry had been deeply affected by the aftermath of the battle; he had become withdrawn and uncommunicative. They agreed that it would be best for him to spend less time at the fort, at least for a while.

That evening, John told him, "I'd like for you to start accompanying me on my patient rounds; you would be my surgeon's apprentice."

"Father, couldn't I spend my time at the fort? I can still learn a lot from Uncle William about trading."

"I know that you enjoy being there, but it's time we start thinking about how you will make a living. I believe you can do better as a surgeon than as an Indian trader."

Henry, having no actual say in the matter, was soon learning how to treat the diseases common to the colony, pull teeth, stitch wounds, and even helping to saw off an occasional limb.

⁓

Even bigger changes awaited Henry, now twelve, and his brother, Johnny, now fourteen. It was summertime, 1658; the boys were outside playing.

Mary told her husband, "We need to talk about something I've been thinking a lot about recently—I believe that it's time we move back to London so Johnny and Henry can get a proper education. They have reached the limits of what they can learn from the tutor, and there are still no schools in the colony. I know that some of the other families are moving back to England for this reason."

"I don't see how we can afford to move back," John replied. "I would have to start up my practice yet again; we would have to pay rent as well as tuition for the boys."

Reminding him that his father Thomas had once offered to pay for their education at the Merchant Taylors' School in London, she said, "there are few opportunities, apart from raising tobacco, for the boys to make a living here. With an education, at least they would have the choice whether to move back here or seek their fortunes in England."

He had to agree his wife was right and said he would have to think about it.

⁓

After mulling it over for weeks, John traveled downriver to his father's house and brought up the idea of returning to London and enrolling the boys in Merchant Taylors' School.

Thomas was enthusiastic. "My student days at Merchant Taylors' were some of the happiest times of my life. We were drilled in the Bible, Latin, and rhetoric eight hours a day. The school produces responsible, God-fearing citizens. Not only will I gladly pay for their tuition, but I will also pay for your family's passage to London and loan you the funds to get established there."

John cringed inwardly when he heard this but made a show of pretending to agree with his father's view of the school and thanked him for his generosity.

When their parents told Henry and Johnny of their plan to move back to London, the boys were downcast for days. Johnny had only faint memories of the city; Henry had none, so they had no way of knowing how different London was from Virginia Colony. They loved their life here and had no wish to change it but had no say in the matter.

Ending the discussion, their parents told them they would be students in London the following spring.

LONDON

1659

John and Mary were true to their word. The family packed up, left Virginia Colony, and arrived in London in the spring of 1659. Unlike their four-month voyage on *The Virginia Merchant*, this trip was an uneventful six weeks at sea.

London was as they had left it ten years earlier—crowded and reeking from the ankle-deep sewage, horse manure littering the muddy streets. The family rented a small house on Suffolk Lane a few blocks from the Merchant Taylors' School. In Virginia Colony, they had free lodging and food; now, they had to pay for both with no income and little savings. The funds that Thomas had given them would not last long at this rate.

Mary insisted that John enroll the boys at Merchant Taylors' before they had a change of heart. "Once you've done that, I'm sure we will feel better about our situation here, and you can focus on re-establishing your practice."

John went to the school the following day; introducing himself to the school's secretary, he told her they had just moved back to London and wished to enroll their two boys. The secretary told him he would need to meet with the headmaster, who was expected back any minute.

A short while later, a gentleman in his late fifties came into the hallway and introduced himself as William Dugard, the headmaster.

John said to him, "We're originally from London and just returned after ten years in Virginia Colony. I would like to enroll our two boys in your school."

Dugard responded, "I'm sorry, but we just filled our enrollment quota for the year and are not accepting new students."

This was not what John wanted to hear, but he remembered his father Thomas telling him to mention Thomas Woodward's name if he had any trouble. He did, and the headmaster's demeanor changed immediately.

"We know him well. He is one of our alumni and has made generous gifts to the school over the years. There is always room for any of his grandchildren."

John was simultaneously relieved and irked—once again, his father's money had saved them—but managed to say, "Thomas is living in Virginia Colony; he always spoke very highly of your school and said he spent some of his happiest days here."

Dugard answered, "And we will be pleased to have your children here. Tell me about them."

John explained that there were no formal schools in Virginia Colony, but a private tutor had taught the boys; they were literate and knew Latin.

Dugard replied, "We have high academic standards here, and they may well be unable to keep up with their peers. But why don't we give them a chance to see how they perform? They can start on June first."

⸻ ❧ ⸻

The following week John paid a visit to the Royal Mint to inquire if there might be any work to treat Mint employees. He returned home, downcast, telling his wife, "I met with the Mint Master; unfortunately, he still remembers my father's outspoken support of Charles I. He was polite but made it clear there would be no patients for me from the Mint."

Almost forty, with a family to support and no connections in London, John was adrift. Renting a small space west of the Tower, he mounted a red and white surgeon's pole at the entrance and soon had a steady stream of patients. Most were sailors and dock workers with toothaches and the like. They were poor and could pay little, but after two months, he was earning enough to pay for rent and food for his family.

⸻ ❧ ⸻

In May of 1660, Parliament restored Charles II to the throne. London was abuzz about their new king—not only his mistresses who he openly paraded in court but also his generous rewards to subjects who had supported him or his father, Charles I.

When John heard that many who had lost their jobs under Cromwell might be rehired or given pensions, he had a thought—*perhaps I could ask for father to be reinstated as Assay Master at the Mint.* He brought up the idea to his wife.

"Now that Charles II is on the throne, Thomas should be back soon. If I can get the King to give Thomas his job back when he returns, I can again treat Mint employees as I did before.

"John, that is a good idea, but doesn't that depend on Thomas first returning to London? What if he doesn't?"

John thought about it for a moment, then said, "I understand that some positions at the Mint are hereditary. Perhaps I can ask that, as his son, I fill the position until my father returns. If by chance, he never does, perhaps I could keep the job. It only pays sixty-six pounds per year but includes the use of a home on the Mint property. Thomas always said the job took little of his time; if that is the case, I could continue to see patients as well."

The next day, John filed his petition with the crown. The clerk told him he would have to be patient—hundreds of people were filing petitions asking for their old jobs back; he expected it would take at least a year.

—◦◦◦—

Johnny and Henry had just finished their first day of classes at Merchant Taylors' School; over dinner, Mary asked them what they thought of it.

Henry blurted, "I hated it. The classes were really boring, and we had to pray three times during the day. I already know more Latin and grammar than the other boys my age. The class is so big that the students mostly just listen to the teacher and don't talk. It's so hot and stuffy and so dark that it's hard to stay awake."

"Well, Johnny, what did you think?"

A boy of few words, he replied, "I thought it was stupid, and nine hours in that classroom was torture."

Their father chimed in, "I know it's very different than having a tutor in Virginia was, but perhaps it will get better after some time. Try to make the best of it."

School did not get better, and the boys continually complained about it. Mary told her husband that he needed to meet with the headmaster and find out what was going on.

Dugard, the headmaster, told John that the boys were very different from the other students. "I was concerned that, because they were starting at Merchant Taylors' School later than many of our students, perhaps they would have difficulty keeping up. I was mistaken; they are both ahead of most other boys their ages. Also, most of our students are the children of London merchants and grew up here. Johnny and Henry grew up in a very different world in Virginia. It sounds remarkable, and I'm a little jealous of them."

"So, what do you suggest that we do with them?"

"I don't say this very often, but I'm not sure that Merchant Taylors' is the right place for your boys. Trying to force them to be like our typical students will most likely only harm them. I suggest that, after the end of a full year here, if they are still unhappy, you withdraw them."

Mother, if we have to continue at Merchant Taylors' School for one more day, I will run away and become a pirate," Henry exclaimed one morning over breakfast.

Mary, smiling, replied, "Henry, you might be a bit too young."

Johnny chimed in, "Knowing my brother, that wouldn't stop him. We talked about this on our way home—you and father agreed to see how we liked school after a full year. It's been a year, and we both hate it more than we did when we started."

As the headmaster had suggested, John and Mary did not enroll their children for the following school year.

Now the boys were at loose ends, and Mary was adamant that they somehow continue their education. "Why don't we get them another tutor? The boys loved their tutor in Virginia; I expect we could find someone as good here."

John replied, "I can't argue with that idea, but we just can't afford it. My father paid their tuition at Merchant Taylors' School. If we tell him the boys hate it there and ask him if he would instead pay for a tutor, with his love for the school, I fear what he would say."

"That's true. We could try schooling them at home, but they already know more than I do about most of their subjects. Let's see what happens with your petition to be Assay Master at the Mint; if you get the job, that will change our financial situation. In the meantime, I'll do my best to tutor them here."

❧❧❧

The royal clerk who had accepted John's petition to be Assay Master of the Mint was optimistic when he said it could be a year for a response. It was the end of 1661, more than two and a half years later, when a royal messenger delivered a letter to the Woodward residence while John was at work. Mary could scarcely resist opening it immediately but decided to wait until the evening meal.

She dished up supper for herself and the boys and put the letter, but no food, on John's plate. He was puzzled until he saw the royal seal. Reading it as Mary and the boys watched, his face broke into a smile, and he handed the letter to Mary:

November 1661, Petition of John, son of Thomas Woodward, to the King

To be put into possession of the house and office of Assay Master of the Mint, held by his father until the late troubles, when John Bradshaw, the so-called President of the Council of State, on the 23rd of October, 1649, dismissed him for refusing obedience to the usurper's power and put in Samuel Bartlett. On this, his father repaired to Virginia with a public declaration never to see England again till His Majesty's return; is forthwith sending him the joyful news, and wishes to keep the office until his return, or if he be dead to have a grant of it himself.

Grant with survivorship to Thomas and John Woodward, on surrender of Andrew Palmer, of the office of Assay Master of the Mint within the Tower; fee, 100 marks per annum.

John was elated—he would be the new Assay Master, with the same sixty-six pounds salary that his father had received and would have the job until his father returned. The grant also included the Assay Master's residence inside the tower walls. He had heard from his father earlier in the year who wrote that he was doing well in Virginia and had no intention of returning to London, so the job would be John's for as long as he wanted it. His family's financial worries were over.

***

The first thing John and his wife did was find a tutor for the boys; having them underfoot every day was putting all of them on edge. John left it to Mary to interview for the new tutor. Finding one who could appreciate the upbringing her boys had in Virginia proved difficult, but she finally found someone who at least approximated their Virginia tutor. They arranged for him to work with the boys for twenty hours each week.

After working with them for the first few days, the tutor congratulated Mary on how well she had done with them. "I'm used to working with pupils to help them catch up in classes; your boys are ahead of where they would be if they had stayed at Merchant Taylors' School."

The Woodward family settled into a comfortable routine. Mary loved their home on Mint Lane. Within the walls of the Tower of London, it was safe and secure; she had planted a garden and, though they could now afford to buy their food, she enjoyed harvesting her own vegetables. The boys, especially Henry, still missed Virginia Colony but had made friends with some of the Mint worker's children.

Taking them out of Merchant Taylors' School and hiring a tutor had been a complete success; John had finally written to his father telling him what they had done, and that Thomas would no longer need to pay for their education. Thomas had not responded. John was able to continue his surgical practice in addition to his job at the mint; Henry often accompanied him and was becoming a proficient surgeon in his own right; Johnny, more mechanically inclined, was working part-time in the Mint.

One summer day in 1664, when Henry and Johnny arrived at their tutor's home, he handed a pamphlet to Henry, saying, "I know you're still interested in the Indians who live at Virginia Colony. You might like this; it's about a recent expedition along the coast south of Virginia, written by a sea captain named William Hilton. He talks about the Indians he met at a place he calls Port Royal. It just came out this June and is making quite a stir among my friends."

Henry read the cover page, *A Relation of a Discovery Lately Made on the Coast of Florida, By William Hilton Commander*. He thanked the tutor and, when he returned home, put it in his room to read later.

12

THE SHIP RAT AND THE FLEA

London, 1664

Late in 1664, a ship just in from Amsterdam unloaded its cargo of cotton bales at the Pool on the Thames. As evening set in and the sailors and dock workers left, ship rats scampered down the hawser lines onto the wharf, joining their brethren from a hundred other ships at anchor. One rat, lagging behind its comrades, made its way ashore, crawling into a pile of sacking in the corner of a warehouse. After its heart stopped, the last flea, who had faithfully stayed with it for weeks, finally deserted it for a larger two-legged warm body.

It was late evening, two days before Christmas. Matthew Phillips said goodnight to his fellow stevedores at the Pool and trudged in the dark across London to his home in St. Giles in the Fields. He was exhausted after twelve hours of unloading cotton bales and cold as well; someone had stolen his coat earlier that week. At least the cold, along with the itching from flea bites, helped him stay awake. It had been a frigid winter; the Thames was iced over and barely navigable; the ground was also frozen, saving him from having to slog through mud and sewage in his worn-out boots. But December had been a good month, with enough work for him to save a few extra shillings to buy a chicken for Christmas dinner.

He hoped to find his wife Abigail better—she had been feeling poorly for a week and had been unable to rise to make him breakfast that morning. When he arrived at their simple cottage on Drury Lane, there was no fire in the hearth. The dwelling was cold, with an icy wind blowing through gaps in the walls, a single candle guttering. Their three young children were huddled together in tears.

Abigail was still in bed, her eyes closed, her breathing labored. He touched her forehead. She was burning with fever, and there were more of the small red bumps covering her chest. There were now swellings on her neck as well.

It was too late to fetch the local apothecary. The following day, after lighting a fire and preparing a simple meal for the children, he went to Dr. Boghurst's shop, the White Hart, and told him of his wife's symptoms.

Boghurst, hiding his concern, picked up his bag and set off for the Phillips cottage. He was too late—Abigail was dead. A brief examination of her body confirmed Dr. Boghurst's fears—buboes, swollen lymph glands, were present on her neck and under her arms, an unmistakable sign of the plague. He had seen other cases over the years; now it was back.

The authorities locked up the Phillips cottage with the family inside, painted "Lord have Mercy on Us" in red on the door, and posted a guard to keep anyone from leaving. As was the custom, the parish paid Mr. Phillips five shillings for his family's support and paid for his wife's simple wooden coffin.

By mid-April, several more plague deaths in St. Giles in the Fields had been listed in London's Bills of Mortality. The authorities were not overly concerned—London's walls, combined with the cold weather, should prevent the plague from entering the city. But a month later, it had wrapped around the city, and the first death was reported inside the walls.

As the death toll rose, so did the number of quack treatments and cures for the plague. The *Intelligencer* was filled with advertisements for them. For the rich, there were expensive concoctions of plague waters and potions. The College of Physicians suggested one treatment for the poor—pull the feathers from the tail of a chicken and hold its beak against the patient until the bird died from drawing the poison out of the patient's body. Coaches and wagons clogged the streets as London citizens who could afford to do so fled to the countryside.

⁂

In mid-July, a Royal Mint foreman asked John Woodward to examine one of his workers who had fallen ill. It was apparent to John that the man was suffering from the plague; he ordered that the worker be sent home. In the next several days, he was called on to visit several citizens in the Tower neighborhood who had fallen ill. Henry, as he often did, accompanied him as his assistant. All of them had the plague, and John had to tell their families there was little he could do for them—they would either get better on their own or die.

13

LORD, HAVE MERCY ON US

London, 1665

July was a busy time at the Royal Mint; John had spent the entire day working in the hot, noisy building. By afternoon, he felt unusually tired. Attributing it to the summer heat, he decided to take off the rest of the day. Greeting his wife who was preparing their evening meal, he said that he was tired and wanted to take a short nap before supper.

"You look flushed." Placing her hand on his forehead, she added, "I think you have a fever. Get some rest; I'll call you for dinner." Half an hour later, she said, "The boys are home, and dinner is on the table." Receiving no response, she went into their bedroom and found him soaked in sweat, delirious, and unable to rise.

All he would say was, "Do I have tokens?"

She was puzzled until she remembered him saying that was the name for the red bumps on the plague victims' bodies. Unbuttoning his shirt, to her horror, she saw his chest covered with hard red spots.

"Johnny, Henry, come in here now!"

Henry examined him—he also had an irregular pulse, high fever, and buboes on his neck. All they could do for him was try to get him to drink tea or water and give him sponge baths.

His condition worsened. He never regained consciousness. On Sunday, four days after first feeling ill, he passed away.

Hearing of his death, the Mint Warden immediately ordered their home sealed and no one allowed to leave. The family was not even permitted to attend his burial the following day at St. Giles Cripplegate.

For the next two weeks, the Woodward family was quarantined in their house, Mint workers leaving food and water at their door. They began to be hopeful that they would escape the plague. But then Johnny came down with the same symptoms as his father. Henry and his mother could do nothing as his symptoms worsened. Three days later, he was dead, mercifully quick compared to many others. Henry placed his body outside their door, and it was taken away to join their father at St. Giles.

A few days later, both Henry and his mother fell ill. Within a single day, neither of them was strong enough to care for the other or even themselves. The food and drink left at their door went untouched.

Finally, both drifted into unconsciousness.

Henry opened his eyes several days later. He was too weak to get out of bed, but his fever was gone. Calling out to his mother, he got no answer. By afternoon, he had mustered enough strength to crawl to her room, where he found her body.

Opening the front door of their house, Henry saw a mint worker who backed away when he saw him. Later that day, two men came and took his mother's body away. He asked one if she would also be buried at St. Giles; he replied that there were so many deaths that they were burying the bodies in mass graves at St. Botolph Aldgate.

Henry was now utterly alone in London. He had survived the plague but lost his entire family in just a few weeks. He was too weak to do anything other than retrieve the food and water left by the Mint workers at the door.

Finally, the quarantine on the residence was lifted. In the Tower courtyard, Henry asked a worker about the plague's progress.

"It has worsened; thousands are dying every week. The King has fled the city, the shops are closed, and the streets are empty," the man grimly replied.

As Henry slowly regained his strength, all he wanted was to get out of London. By the end of the week, his mind was made up—there was nothing for him here; he would return to Virginia Colony, where his grandfather Thomas lived. He knew that Thomas and his father had not been close in recent years, but he hoped Thomas would not hold that against him. Henry took stock of his situation—he had a few clothes, and there was just over ten pounds sterling in the family's savings box.

He said goodbye to his few friends, packed up his clothes, a few books, and his father's surgeon's bag, and went to the Pool to seek passage to Virginia Colony. Shipping was at a standstill; no boats were allowed in or out of London. He tried leaving the city on foot. However, the authorities had blocked the roads and turned him back.

But an idea came to him. He changed into his best clothes and proceeded down a different street. When stopped again, he drew himself up to his full six-foot height. With surgeon's bag in hand and looking older than his nineteen years, he said in an authoritative voice, "I am a surgeon and have been called to attend Samuel Pepys in Woolwich."

He was allowed to pass with an apology from the guard. In the next town, he found a local boatman willing to take him downriver to Gravesend.

It was not a cheerful time in Gravesend—the London quarantine had brought commerce to a standstill. Ships clogged the port, waiting to offload their cargo to smaller ships bound for London, and idle sailors and laborers filled the taverns.

Finally, Henry found a ship ready to depart for Virginia Colony but lacking a surgeon. Henry offered to serve as one in return for his passage. He did not mention that he was not a real surgeon and hoped the captain was desperate enough not to inquire. The captain, eager to get underway, decided it was an offer he could not refuse and welcomed Henry aboard.

The ship sailed the following day.

CAROLINA COLONY

1665

After a six-week crossing with favorable winds, no storms, and no seriously ill or injured crewmen, Henry's ship was sailing into Chesapeake Bay. Leaning against the railing, watching the fields and forests come into view, he thought to himself, *I don't want to see my grandfather and have to tell him what happened. Perhaps I'll visit my Uncle William instead.*

Fort Henry was just as he remembered it. Abraham Wood was still running it and didn't recognize Henry at first. Offering his condolences for Henry's loss, Wood said, "William is no longer at the fort. He is now an official translator for the Powhatan's dealings with Virginia Colony."

Wood continued, "Business is good. You may have been too young at the time to remember the Rickahocan—after the Battle of Bloody Run, the tribe became my main trading partner. They moved, five hundred miles to the west, and are bringing me a steady supply of Indian captives that I sell to the planters as slaves."

Wood's comments about the Powhatan prompted Henry to visit the nearby Powhatan town, unsure what to expect after six years away. It was very different than he remembered—his former friends, now adults, were guarded and distant. One of them said that he made his living tracking down and returning slaves who had escaped from the plantations.

By the end of the day, he realized that the tribe was now subservient, unhappily so, to Virginia Colony. Any thoughts of returning to his idyllic childhood of days spent with his Indian friends were an illusion—that world no longer existed.

Henry, realizing he couldn't put off seeing his grandfather any longer, made his goodbyes to Wood.

As they parted, Wood asked, "Would you be interested in coming to work for me, taking your uncle's place?"

Henry replied that his life was still far too unsettled to make any commitments but would consider it.

Catching a ride downriver, he chatted with the captain, who knew his grandfather. The captain said Thomas had recently moved south from Pagan Creek to the mouth of the Chowan River on Albemarle Sound; the only way there was a two or three-day journey by boat.

Thomas and his wife did not recognize Henry when he knocked on their door; he was only thirteen the last time they saw him. They had not yet learned about the deaths of Henry's family; the news devastated them. Henry's father and grandfather had been virtually estranged, but both grandparents had been close to his mother, and Johnny had been the favorite grandchild.

It was several days before Thomas could bring himself to talk about his life in Virginia. "Two years ago, King Charles granted all of the lands south of Virginia Colony to eight men who had helped him regain the throne. He called the new province *Carolina*, which you must have learned in Merchant Taylors' School, is Latin for 'Charles.' The eight men are the lords proprietors. One of them is my friend Sir William Berkeley, governor of Virginia. They divided Carolina into three counties; Berkeley appointed me surveyor and secretary for Albemarle County. He also awarded me 5,000 acres of land."

Thomas continued, "People are moving here from Virginia, seeking fresh soil for tobacco as well as more political freedom. I have a better life here than I ever did in England, and I have no intention of leaving."

Knowing he needed to stay on Thomas' good side, Henry replied, "You have done very well for yourself here."

Thomas replied, "With my connections here, I could get you a good job. You could settle down, marry and raise a family here."

But, aside from having no desire to settle, it seemed to Henry that Albemarle County would soon be little different from Virginia Colony's tobacco plantations. He would be better off accepting Wood's offer to work at Fort Henry. He replied to Thomas, "Thank you for the kind offer, but I need time to decide what I want to do with my life before settling somewhere. I have no wish to return to England and, for now, I would like to find work away from Jamestown and the plantations."

Thomas replied that he could get him a job as a surveyor's assistant in Carolina. "Other than the settlers here in Albemarle and a small settlement on Cape Fear, Carolina is wilderness, with nothing but heathens, wild beasts, and forests."

A job surveying in the wilds sounded ideal to Henry, far away from people and the horrors of the last months. He could tell his grandfather seemed disappointed that he did not want to settle down, but Thomas promised that he would let him know when he could start as a surveyor's assistant.

15

SIR JOHN YEAMANS

Barbados, 1664

It was a comfortable April day in Barbados on the patio of Nicholas Plantation where John Yeamans enjoyed an after-dinner drink with his friend and fellow plantation owner Thomas Modyford. Modyford remarked, "I never tire of the beauty of your home; I believe it is the most magnificent in Barbados."

Yeamans heard this often, but it still made him wince. Everyone knew the home had been built by his former business partner, Benjamin Berringer. Also, everyone knew the story that went with the home—he and Berringer had both courted Margaret Foster, a local preacher's daughter. She chose Berringer; they married and had three children. Their marriage was not a happy one, and they separated in 1661. That same year, Berringer suddenly and mysteriously died. Yeamans and Margaret were charged with poisoning him, but the Barbados Council, where Yeamans had supportive friends, cleared them. The two married only ten weeks after Berringer's death and moved into a far more elegant home.

Yeamans congratulated Modyford on his recent appointment as governor of Jamaica and asked when he would start.

"This June, but I have some matters to clear up here first."

Yeamans added, "Whatever happened to the proposal you made to start a new colony in America?"

"I don't know if you heard about it, but a year ago, Charles II granted a large portion of America to a group of his supporters, who call themselves the lords proprietors. Named Carolina, it includes all of the lands southwest of Virginia Colony. When I heard about the grant, I sent a proposal to the proprietors that I be allowed to establish a colony there, and I also hired a ship to survey its coastline to seek a location."

"That was the ship that sailed from here last summer?"

"Yes, the *Adventure*, captained by William Hilton. He spoke favorably of an area in the southern part of Carolina called Port Royal." Modyford continued, "Shortly after receiving my proposal, the proprietors wrote to me that they support it and are eager to move quickly. But only a few months later, as you know, I was appointed governor of Jamaica, so I will not be pursuing it."

Yeamans was intrigued. He was always looking for new opportunities, especially if they increased his wealth. He asked Modyford if he thought the proprietors might be amenable to him stepping in to take over Modyford's proposal.

Modyford replied, "We can certainly ask, and I'll be glad to recommend you. Why don't I have my man send over Hilton's report and the correspondence. You should act quickly if you're interested—I understand that someone else is also considering setting up a colony in Carolina."

A change of scenery might be what he needed, Yeamans thought. His wife's children were stirring up ill feelings toward him over their father's death, and Barbados was becoming increasingly uncomfortable. Also, a plague of caterpillars had ravaged the island's cane fields for the past two years. Not only was there no cane to harvest, but he now had to pay to feed his slaves as the worms had also devoured their gardens. He had no idea if a settlement in Carolina could succeed. Still, it would be a change from his current troubles, especially if he could convince the proprietors to use their funds to establish the colony.

Yeamans received the Carolina documents the next day. Hilton had stayed with an Indian tribe at Port Royal, in the southern part of Carolina, and said only glowing things about the area. The soil was good—the Indians were able to grow two or three crops of corn a year, as well as melons and pumpkins. He reported that they were healthy, the air clear and sweet, and the country very pleasant. Hilton concluded his report by saying that any Englishmen looking for an excellent place to settle would do well to move there.

The letter from the lords proprietors to Modyford was even more encouraging:

Thomas Modyford, Peter Colleton
August 30, 1663
Sirs:

> *We find by a letter from Thomas Modyford that several people of Barbados wish to settle and plant in some part of the province of Carolina, whom we desire by all ways and means to encourage. To that end, we have enclosed a declaration and proposals for you to send to all persons who are*

interested and to assure them that what we propose shall be timely per-formed. We hope that the problems the settlers at Cape Fear suffered will not discourage your people. They settled at the wrong time of the year and not in the area recommended by Hilton. We conceive it will be advanta-geous to the King, his people, and particularly to your Barbadians to go on with the settlement where we are informed the air is wondrously healthy and temperate and the land proper to grow such commodities as are not yet produced in other plantations. This is so because England spends great sums of money on wine, olive oil, currants, raisins, silk, etc., from other countries. If these are grown on your plantations, the funds will be kept in the King's domains. Also, by planting these commodities, your settlement will not compete with other plantations presently growing sugar, tobacco, ginger, cotton, and indigo. We expect your people to want a more formal proposal and greater assurances from us, which we shall willingly give. Also, we can appoint a governor now if you wish, and if you have any other requests that do not cause a loss to us, we shall consider them.

George Monck, Duke of Albemarle

It seemed to Yeamans the proprietors would be open to someone other than Modyford heading up a settlement, as long as the settlers were willing to plant the crops suggested by the proprietors. Yeamans decided to ask some of his friends in Barbados if they would sponsor a settlement at Port Royal. In short order, he had a list of over eighty men, mostly small sugar planters.

By the summer of 1664, Yeamans had decided to proceed. In England, his son William could negotiate directly with the proprietor; Yeamans gave him instructions to tell the proprietors that he planned to settle Carolina according to the proprietors' earlier agreement with Modyford.

William's efforts were successful. That January, the lords proprietors appointed Yeamans as governor of the proposed colony and, as a bonus, also had Charles II appoint him as a Knight Baronet; henceforth, he was Sir John Yeamans. The proprietors committed to supplying guns, ammunition, and supplies to build a fort there. For his part, Yeamans was to provide two ships to transport settlers by the end of the coming September.

William wrote his father that another settlement in Carolina was underway, headed by John Vassal. It seems Vassal had heard of Modyford's proposal for a settlement in Carolina and decided to beat him to the punch. In May, Vassal landed at Cape Fear, south of Virginia Colony, and, without a formal agreement from the lords proprietors, established a small colony they named Charles Town. At the same time that William was negotiating with the proprietors, Vassal's brother was also in London, seeking approval for his settlement. But William was the shrewder negotiator and had the advantage of adopting Modyford's earlier proposal, already blessed by the proprietors. The proprietors agreed to Yeamans' proposal, telling both parties there would be no further support for the Charles Town settlement.

Thus, Carolina Colony's first English settlement, cut off from further funding from England, died with a whimper.

16

CAPE FEAR

Carolina Colony, 1665–1666

Yeamans acted quickly before the lords proprietors had a change of heart. He purchased a 150-ton flyboat, naming it for himself, the *Sir John*, and added a small frigate of his own. His Barbados supporters donated a sloop, making a fleet of three.

The fleet left Barbados in early October of 1665, heading for Carolina Colony. Off the coast of Cape Fear, the ships were caught in a storm, the frigate losing its masts. Almost immediately, a second storm ran the *Sir John* aground, with the loss of all the weapons and most of the provisions. Limping into the Charles Town settlement on Cape Fear, the expedition was now a fleet of one.

In the meantime, having been cut off from further aid by the lords proprietors, Charles Town was in dire need of food and supplies. Even though Yeamans was indirectly responsible for their plight, he could not let them starve, so he ordered the sloop to sail north to Virginia Colony for provisions.

It had not yet returned by Christmas, and Yeamans had run out of patience. Calling the remaining men together, he said, "I feel bad leaving the expedition, but I have business in Bermuda. Robert Sandford, the Secretary of Clarendon County, has agreed to serve as the expedition leader in my absence." With that, he sailed off in the newly repaired *Sir John*, leaving the remnants of his venture stranded at Charles Town.

The agreement with the proprietors to settle Port Royal had a tight deadline, so before Yeamans left, he had hired a ship presently anchored in Charles Town, captained by Edward Stanyon. If the sloop did not return soon, Stanyon would complete the voyage to Port Royal with the settlers. He was already scheduled for a trip to Barbados but would be back in time for the voyage if necessary.

The sloop was trying its best to get back to Charles Town with the badly needed supplies. But the expedition's bad luck continued. A storm drove the sloop ashore at Cape Lookout in the middle of the night, with the loss of two lives and all the supplies. The survivors managed to refloat the ship and get it back to open water, where they realized there was no choice but to return to Virginia Colony, repair the ship, and reprovision.

After two days of limping north, another ship came into view and anchored alongside. Its captain hailed them, "Do you need assistance?"

The sloop's crew gratefully accepted the offer of help, resetting the mast and patching leaks. One of the new ship's crewmen introduced himself to the sloop's captain, "I'm Henry Brayne: I hear you've sailed from Charles Towne. I must say, if you're planning on taking this wreck to Jamestown, you're not going to make it."

He was correct—even with the repairs, the sloop was taking on water as fast as the crew could bail. He added, "There's a small settlement at Albemarle Bay, halfway to Jamestown. You might be able to make it that far."

The sloop's captain, quickly realizing that Brayne was a more competent seaman than any of his remaining crew, asked if they could hire him, at least until they got the sloop to safety.

Brayne was agreeable, especially after hearing what the captain was offering to pay. "I've sailed this part of the coast before. As long as we don't sink first, I can get you to Albemarle Bay."

Limping into Albemarle Bay, they finally reached the Chowan River and tied up at the settlement's dock. The crew set about trying to repair the sloop, but it was beyond saving—the timbers were rotten; another storm would sink it.

The captain and crew were at wit's end; Brayne again proved he was a resourceful man. "The only option I see for you is to wait for a ship bound for Jamestown, buy or rent another ship there, resupply, and return to Cape Fear."

—⁓⁓⁓—

Thomas Woodward, hearing that a disabled ship had landed at the mouth of the Chowan, strolled down to the wharf to investigate. Among the ship's crew was a familiar face, Henry Brayne, who he had met before in Virginia. "Brayne! What in the world are you doing here?" Thomas exclaimed

He started to explain; Thomas interrupted, "Why don't you tell me over dinner?"

Having eaten little since joining the sloop's crew, he was more than happy to accept the invitation. "I was returning to Jamestown when we came across a ship barely afloat and in distress. We stopped to assist them, and I joined its crew to help them reach safety. They told me they are part of an expedition from Barbados planning on settling on the Carolina coast north of St. Augustine at a place called Port Royal. The rest of the group is presently at Charles Town on Cape Fear."

Thomas interjected, "May I ask who is in charge of the expedition?"

"I understand that John Yeamans from Barbados put together the expedition based on a report by a sea captain named John Hilton who had earlier explored the area."

Henry, just back from a week of surveying in the wilderness, perked up when he heard this. He left the table and returned with a pamphlet he handed to Brayne. "This is John Hilton's report; it was the talk of London before I left—he says Port Royal is a new paradise."

Brayne replied, "I don't know about that as I was only hired a few days ago. I know that the venture is off to a bad start—the sloop we just arrived in is unseaworthy, and its other two ships were badly damaged in a storm, and most of their supplies were lost. The expedition was supposed to build a fort for defense against the Indians there, but all of the guns and ammunition are now at the bottom of the sea."

After dinner, before Brayne returned to the sloop, Henry took him aside and said to him, "My parents and my brother died in the London plague last year; I barely survived and left England to come here. Thomas is all the family I have left. He found a job for me as a surveyor's assistant, but I don't want to stay here. I want to get as far from my old life as possible; Virginia Colony is not far enough. Do you know if there might be room for me in the expedition? "

"It's not for me to say, but I do know that the sloop is shorthanded as two men were lost when it wrecked. You could probably join the crew and ask at Charles Town about joining them."

Weeks later, the crew finally found a ship for hire to take them to Virginia Colony for supplies and then back to Charles Town. In early February, they returned to a cold and hungry settlement with much-needed food and supplies and Henry Woodward. They had expected to find Captain Stanyon and his ship waiting for them, as previously arranged. But Stanyon was not there, nor was John Yeamans, who had left for Bermuda, leaving Robert Sandford in charge.

The Port Royal venture, now without a fleet, or even a single ship, was stranded in Charles Town with nothing to do but wait for Captain Stanyon to return from Barbados to take the tattered expedition to Port Royal. Weeks passed with no sign of the captain.

Food for Sandford's crew members was again running low; the Cape Fear Colony could barely sustain itself, let alone the additional mouths.

Trade with the local Indians had come to a standstill after settlers had taken Indian children from several nearby towns into their homes, where they were forced to work as unpaid servants. Relations had deteriorated so far that settlers were attacking and killing Indians, who retaliated by killing several settlers and stealing their cattle.

Henry took it upon himself to approach Robert Sandford about the crew's predicament: "Mr. Sandford, I spent almost ten years at Fort Henry in Virginia Colony, trading with the Powhatan Indians. I know how Indians feel about the English and believe I can reach an agreement with the Indians here to trade for food."

Sandford was skeptical as relations seemed beyond repair but, seeing Henry as expendable, authorized him to speak to the Indians as a representative of the expedition.

Wasting no time, Henry headed north into the forest toward the nearest of the Cape Fear Indian towns. Before it was in sight, two men confronted him, bows drawn and pointed at him.

Knowing they spoke some English, Henry said, "Hello, I come in peace."

The taller of the two replied, "the English are not welcome in our town."

Heeding Sandford's words that he could only negotiate on behalf of the expedition, not the settlement, Henry said, "I am not from the settlement, and those people are not my friends." This seemed to be the right thing to say, as both lowered their bows.

"We are here only long enough to find a new ship and leave. I am friends with Abraham Wood in Virginia and the Powhatan there. I would like to trade English goods with you for food."

The two men invited Henry back to their town, Necoes, where he met their chief, who offered him food and tobacco. Henry said they were going to Port Royal to the south; the chief replied they were related to the Indians there.

The chief agreed to trade food for hatchets, knives, cloth, and beads. The crew survived on food from this agreement for the next two months, and Henry became a respected crew member.

Finally, in mid-May, Stanyon's ship arrived, minus Captain Stanyon, with a crew of only two men and a boy and a tragic story. After departing Barbados, they had been caught up in contrary winds and blown far off course. Captain Stanyon, overcome with fatigue and worry, suffered a nervous breakdown, threw himself into the sea, and drowned. The contrary winds finally abated, and the ship, now far off course and lacking a navigator, was somehow able to complete the voyage.

The Port Royal venture now had a ship but no captain or experienced seamen. Sandford, a Barbadian with a checkered past and no nautical skills, was determined that the adventure continue even though the supplies and weapons for a fort had been lost. He knew they could not establish a settlement at Port Royal, but he did not wish to tell Yeamans the expedition was a total failure. Perhaps it would count as a partial success if one of his crew stayed behind with the Indians at Port Royal. He could learn their language and customs and pave the way for a later expedition.

～

Henry Woodward seemed to be the logical choice to leave behind—he was the only one who had any experience with Indians and had no immediate family—nobody would miss him if he came to an unfortunate end at Port Royal.

Sandford approached Henry and said, "As you know, we're not in a position to establish a settlement at Port Royal. We have no ship of our own, no weapons, and few supplies. John Yeamans and the lords proprietors will be very unhappy if we don't make some effort toward a settlement. I know of your experience with the Powhatan in Virginia and how successful you were trading with the Indians at Charles Town. Also, you seem to have memorized Captain Hilton's report about Port Royal. Would you be interested in staying there, learning the Indian's language and customs until we can come back with a larger expedition?"

Henry was intrigued. He had taken the job as a surveyor's assistant to get as much distance as possible from his former life or what was left of it. This would be a considerable step beyond even that. He knew from the Hilton report that Port Royal was as remote a place as one could find. He would be the only Englishman on the entire continent south of Virginia Colony. St. Augustine was a week's journey to the south, but he didn't know if the Spanish there were friends or foes.

He replied, "That is an interesting proposal. You may not know my full story—my family died last year in the London plague. I survived and left for Virginia Colony and my grandfather Thomas as soon as I was able. My former life is gone; all I want now is solitude until I decide what to do. Port Royal would certainly provide that, but it might be too distant even for me."

Sandford responded. "I am sorry to hear about your family; that must have been a terrible time for you. I know I am asking a lot from you and cannot promise that it will not have enormous risks. I could not tell from Hilton's report whether the Indians at Port Royal would treat you well or not; he said he had problems with them. All I can offer you is that we leave you with what supplies we can spare and that I will do my best to see that an expedition returns shortly, whether to settle or to bring you back. If we settle in Port Royal because of your efforts, you will have the gratitude of John Yeamans and the lords proprietors."

Sanford and Henry agreed that they would decide whether or not Henry would stay behind once they saw how the Indians received them in Port Royal.

17

PORT ROYAL

Carolina Colony, 1666

Nine months after leaving Barbados, the Sandford expedition had lost three lives, several ships, and most of its provisions and supplies. By contrast, Captain Hilton had safely completed the same journey in seventeen days.

The remnants of the expedition set sail for the last leg of the voyage—Port Royal, 250 miles to the south. They immediately ran into foul weather, and the shallop, captained by Henry Brayne, was separated from the ship.

Sandford, without Brayne to guide the way, quickly became lost. He anchored at the mouth of a large river to get his bearings where a canoe carrying two Indians approached the ship. They spoke no English, but Henry, who had learned some of their language at Cape Fear, understood them to say this was the country of Edisto and their town was nearby.

Introducing Sandford, Henry said, "He is our leader and would like to meet with your chief."

Several hours later, the two men from the canoe returned, accompanied by a long line of Indians. They lifted Sandford onto their shoulders and carried him like royalty across the creeks and marshes to their town; Henry walked. The men took Sandford and Henry to the town's meeting house, a large circular structure, where the Edisto chief, who they called their cassique, and his wife were seated on a tall bench. Lower benches were filled with men, women, and children; a fire, surrounded by clay statues, was burning in the center of the building.

The cassique motioned for Sandford to sit next to him. Other members of the tribe greeted Sandford by giving him animal skins and stroking his shoulders with their palms while sucking in their breath.

Sandford looked to Henry in puzzlement. Henry said, "This is their welcoming ceremony. It would have been better if we had gifts for them, but we can give them later."

The Edisto people treated them graciously, with a meal of fish, oysters, and turkey, and lodging for the night. The following day, Sandford asked Henry to arrange another meeting with the cassique. At the meeting, Sandford broke a twig from an oak tree, handed it to the cassique, and gestured for him to plant the twig in the ground. Looking as puzzled as Sandford had the previous day, he complied. Sandford then gave him some beads and cloth and said, "I hereby claim all of these lands for Charles II and the lords proprietors."

Henry asked, "What are you doing? We can't simply take their land, and we're not yet at Port Royal in any case."

"It's called the ceremony of turf and twig; Yeamans told me to perform it."

"But the cassique has no idea what it means."

"That's not my problem; besides, the King claimed all of this land for England years ago."

When the cassique realized that Sandford was scouting for a future settlement at Port Royal, he told him that Edisto was a much better location and urged him to settle there instead of proceeding to Port Royal. Sandford was noncommittal.

⚬⚬⚬

Henry stayed behind at Edisto town after Sandford went back to the ship. He watched as the men played a game on the field in front of the meeting hall—teams of two took turns rolling a stone ball down the long field and then throwing heavy six-foot poles at it. The team with the pole closest to the ball won a handful of beads. As a youngster in Virginia Colony, Henry had played games with Powhatans but didn't recognize this one, which seemed a cross between boules and javelin throwing. He asked to join in and quickly found the game was more challenging than it looked. The playing field was long, the poles heavy, and the late June noontime sun hot. After an embarrassing performance, Henry rejoined the spectators on the sidelines.

Later that day, a group of men returned from a hunting trip; one of them greeted Henry in nearly perfect English. "My name is Shadoo, a captain of the Edisto people. Who are you?"

Henry introduced himself and explained they were trying to get to Port Royal.

Shadoo said, "That is where Captain Hilton visited two years ago. He then took me to Barbados, where I learned the ways of the English before returning here."

Henry replied, "We are trying to follow Hilton's route to Port Royal but were separated from our other ship in a storm and are now lost. We hope to establish a settlement at Port Royal someday."

"The Escamacu at Port Royal are our neighbors. Their town is only a day's journey from here."

Finally, thought Henry—*we will get to Port Royal alive.* As Sandford prepared to leave for Port Royal, the cassique once again tried to persuade him to settle at Edisto, promising a deep harbor for ships, a friendly welcome, and trade opportunities. Sandford told him that he must first continue to Port Royal to the south and asked the cassique to accompany him as a guide; he agreed.

⁓⁕⁓

Even with the Edisto cassique as his guide, it took Sandford three days to sail the twenty miles from Edisto to Port Royal. The ship narrowly avoided being driven onto the shoals numerous times by the strong currents; Henry again found himself questioning the wisdom of volunteering for the expedition, which so far had been an endless string of disasters.

On July 4th, they reached a river flowing into Port Royal Sound; the cassique said it was where Hilton had anchored. A canoe filled with Indians was waiting for them at the river's mouth and led them to a town on its bank. Waiting for them at the Escamacu's town was the missing sloop; Henry Brayne hailed them as they arrived. Once ashore, one of the Indians from the canoe introduced himself as Nisquesalla, the cassique of the Escamacu people. A younger man introduced himself in English as the cassique's son, Wommony.

Henry asked how it was that he spoke such good English; Wommony replied, "Captain Hilton took both Shadoo and me to Barbados; we learned English there."

⁓⁕⁓

With Wommony serving as translator, the cassique performed a greeting ceremony for Sandford, much like what he had received in Edisto town.

Sandford then told him, "I represent an important man who wants to establish a settlement at Port Royal and make a trade agreement with you. We are looking at different places to see where might be the best location."

When his son explained this to him, Nisquesalla asked if Captain Hilton was the chief that Sandford worked for.

"No, it is a man from Barbados named John Yeamans."

"Captain Hilton was not a good friend to us; he took some of our people, including my son, prisoner."

To which Sandford replied, "We are here to be your friends and to trade with you."

The cassique responded, "We would be most happy to have you as our neighbor. We have the best harbor for English ships, open land for crops and livestock, and will trade with you for all the food you need."

At Sandford's request, Nisquesalla spent the following day showing Sandford their town and countryside.

Henry took the opportunity to explore the town on his own. It was similar to Edisto, with a large round meeting house at the end of an open playing field. One difference was that a large wooden cross stood at the other end of the field.

Wommony said, "The Spanish left it, and our people pay no attention to it." He showed Henry the remains of a stone fort and added that the Spanish had also built it, but they moved away many years ago and settled at St. Augustine.

After several days, Sandford, satisfied that Port Royal would be a good location for Yeamans' settlement, was eager to return to Charles Town. As he prepared to leave, he said that they would be back.

Nisquesalla asked, "Will you return in three months?"

"Three months is too soon; we will be back within ten," he replied, knowing that, in reality, they might never return.

As they were preparing to sail, Nisquesalla came on board with a young man in tow who he introduced as his nephew. "Will you take him with you and teach him your ways as Captain Hilton did with my son?"

Sandford remembered that he was going to propose leaving Henry Woodward behind when they left, but it had slipped his mind. The following day Sandford said to Henry, "The cassique wants me to take his nephew to Barbados, as Hilton did with his son. I want to tell him that, in exchange, you would remain here. Are you still willing to stay for ten months?

Henry had found the Escamacu people peaceable and hospitable; he was also eager to leave Sandford's expedition and its endless bungling behind. "Yes, I will stay."

Accompanied by Henry, Sandford went back to the town and asked the cassique to gather his people. In their presence, he said, as Wommony translated, "I wish to take the cassique's nephew back to Barbados with me and teach him our ways. Do you approve of this?"

The townspeople answered as one: "Yes."

Sandford then said to the cassique, his second in command, and their wives, "I am placing this man, Henry Woodward, in your care until I return."

The townspeople's reaction was joyous; Nisquesalla seated Henry alongside him on his throne. Next, he took Henry to a large field of corn and told him it would be his. Finally, he introduced a young woman as his niece and said, "I am giving Henry Woodward my sister's daughter to tend, feed, and be careful of him so that her brother will be better treated."

Sandford stayed a few more hours and, before departing, said to Henry, "I give you possession of this land to hold as a tenant at will of the lords proprietors." He also left Henry with English trade goods for gifts to the Indians and a promise to return in ten months.

HENRY AMONG THE ESCAMACU

Port Royal, Carolina, 1666

When Henry awoke, it was early dawn, and for a moment, he had no idea where he was. A woman who he did not recognize was sleeping next to him. She rolled over, smiled at him, and spoke words he did not understand, so he replied, "Good morning to you."

She pointed at herself and told Henry her name, Dehhewamis.

Arising, wearing very little, she began preparing breakfast for him. He could not help but stare. She was exquisite; he decided to give her an English name reflecting her beauty. He would call her Bella. He pointed to each of them, said his name, and then her new name.

Despite being from two different worlds, Henry and Bella quickly fell into a routine. He was determined to learn as much of her language and culture as possible in the next ten months, so, each morning after breakfast, he had her tell him the names of everything around him. Bella's laughter when Henry mispronounced her words made the lessons enjoyable. Within a month, he knew the plant and animal names around the town and could converse with her in simple sentences.

Henry soon understood that he was an honored guest with no duties or responsibilities. The townspeople treated him with kindness and respect, especially when he addressed them in their tongue. His only job was the assignment Sandford had given him—to learn their ways during his time here. Once he knew enough of their language not to be a nuisance, he began accompanying the men hunting and fishing. His childhood fishing and rudimentary archery skills from Virginia Colony were helpful, but he lacked the stealth necessary for hunting.

Henry had settled into a comfortable daily life by the end of August. Bella indeed took care of his needs as the cassique had promised. She made some simple buckskin clothing for him as the clothes he had arrived in were impossibly hot. Fishing, hunting, and vegetable gardens provided ample food for the town with little effort, leaving the men free much of the day. As far as he saw, the women had little free time. The younger men played the same version of boules he had tried in Edisto town. Vowing to improve on his previous performance, he never turned down a chance to play and could hold his own against all but the strongest men after a few weeks.

Henry and Wommony had become friends; once he was somewhat fluent in their language, Henry began conversing with his father as well. The cassique was especially eager to learn about the plans of the English for Port Royal; Henry had no idea if there were any such plans but did not want to admit it. Instead, he said, "My grandfather Thomas at Albemarle Sound is an important person and a friend of the King of England. The English are looking at different places in Carolina to establish a colony but have not yet decided where it would be. When Sandford comes back in ten months, I will tell them my opinion of Port Royal."

Nisquesalla seemed disappointed when he heard this, believing that Sandford was returning to settle here, not just to retrieve Henry.

⁓✦⁓

By that fall, Henry sensed something had changed between him and Bella. Not only her, but all of the townspeople seemed more reserved. He finally asked if he had done something wrong; her response was evasive.

Wommony was as vague as Bella but finally told him, "A tribe armed with guns that we call the Westo is attacking nearby towns, killing the men and taking away women and children who are never seen again. Some people believe they are cannibals who eat their captives. The raids are getting closer to our town; we have only bows and arrows and are no match for their guns."

Henry, hearing this description, realized they were the same tribe that was providing Indian slaves to Abraham Wood at Fort Henry, where they were called the Rickahocan. Recalling how they had slaughtered the Powhatan warriors at the Battle of Bloody Run, he understood Wommony's concern.

Wommony continued with his story, "We hoped that the English would establish a settlement here to protect us against the Westo. We now understand we cannot depend on them to do this. The town's elders have decided that it is no longer safe here and that the entire town will move to St. Catherine's, an island closer to St. Augustine, where the Spanish will protect us. In return, we will have to provide workers for St. Augustine. We are not happy with this decision, but the alternative is slavery or death. We are waiting for their permission to move."

Henry now realized why Nisquesalla seemed eager for Sandford to settle here and had tried to convince him to return in three months rather than ten. He also understood why Bella and his friends in the town had cooled toward him—they had realized the English could not be counted on to protect them, and Henry was therefore of little use to them.

Nisquesalla received permission from the St. Augustine governor to move his people to St. Catherine's. After talking to Wommony, Henry realized he would not be invited to accompany them. The town elders knew that the English and Spanish were not on good terms and did not want to hurt their relationship with St. Augustine's government by bringing an Englishman into their backyard.

⌘

Henry realized his situation was desperate—his lifeline was Sandford's promised return. If the Escamacu moved before then, Sandford would find only a deserted town. Henry had no way to contact Sandford, his grandfather, or anyone else for that matter. Charles Town, the closest English settlement, was far to the north. The expedition had barely survived the journey from there by ship; he had no wish to attempt a return journey on foot. If he stayed, he would be an easy target for the Westo. He knew from his time in Virginia Colony that they did not hesitate to kill English and Indians alike.

After considering his situation, Henry hatched a bold plan—ask the Spanish at St. Augustine to retrieve him. He knew that there was a Catholic priest at St. Catherine's. He would write him, saying that he was a Catholic surgeon abandoned by the English at Port Royal and wished to come to St. Augustine to live. Would they please send a ship to rescue him? Henry knew this would be a golden opportunity to gain valuable information about the Spanish and the other Indian tribes in the area. Then, when he had learned enough, he would ask them to send him home, wherever that might be.

Henry decided he could safely confide in Wommony about his plan as his cousin was in Sandford's hands, and Wommony and Nisquesalla would want to ensure he would be well treated. Wommony agreed to deliver his letter, which Henry drafted in Latin, to the Spanish priest.

Realizing his time with Bella was running out, he spent more time with her learning their language and with Wommony learning about the other Indian towns along the coast. One day, as he and Bella were walking near the town, they came across a pile of red feathers on the path. Henry said, "It looks like a fox got that unfortunate red bird."

Bella picked up several of the feathers and blew them into the air. "What was that?" Henry asked.

"Whenever we see feathers of the red bird, we do this for luck. It is a sacred bird for us; we believe that, after the great flood, there were only two survivors. They found the feathers of a dead red bird and blew them into the air. Each feather created a new tribe; that is how the Escamacu came to be."

SAINT AUGUSTINE, LA FLORIDA

1667

In late December, a ship flying the Spanish cross of St. Andrew sailed into Port Royal and anchored at Escamacu town. Wommony told Henry it was from St. Augustine. As the townspeople gathered to watch, several men, including two clad in armor, rowed ashore. One introduced himself as the captain, saying they were here to plan for the town's move to St. Catherine's and take Henry back to St. Augustine as he had requested.

Nisquesalla and the Spanish captain spent the next day discussing the details of the tribe's relocation. The governor had set aside land for their new town at St. Catherine's, north of St. Augustine, where they would be under the protection of the Spanish. They could take the elderly on their ships, but the rest of the townspeople would have to make their way there by canoe or on foot.

Henry put on his English clothes for the first time in months, gathered his few possessions, and said his goodbyes to friends, not knowing if he would ever see any of them again. Bella accompanied him to the water's edge and watched as he was rowed out to the Spanish ship. He had grown fond of her and would miss her. She had been a good companion and provider and a patient teacher of her tribe's language and ways.

His final words were to her: "Goodbye, Dehhewamis," honoring her with her given name. "Thank you for caring for me. I will miss you."

❧

None of the crew spoke English, nor he Spanish. Trying Latin to no avail, he gave up trying to communicate and concentrated on memorizing the coastline if he ever came this way again.

They had reached St. Catherine's by evening, where they would spend the night. Henry overheard the Indians talking among themselves, but they spoke a different language than the Escamacu, so he could not understand them. He saw the captain give the chief some cloth and iron tools and, in return, receive maize and squash. It surprised him to see the Spanish trading for food; it seemed the Spanish would be self-sufficient.

Arriving at St. Augustine, the ship anchored next to a dilapidated wooden structure with several cannons pointed out to sea; the only clue it was St. Augustine's fort.

Henry had expected a warm welcome as a Catholic abandoned by the English. But instead, he was taken to a small room with a single barred window and a locked door. The only furnishings were a wooden bench and a bucket. As daylight was fading, he heard a key in the lock, and two men entered his cell, the soldier he had seen earlier and his superior. The soldier handed him a plate of hominy and squash, a mug of water, and left without a word. Henry spent an uncomfortable night with nothing to sleep on other than the hard bench.

⌁

The following morning, the soldier reappeared, this time with a priest who addressed Henry in Latin, "I'm Father Sotolongo, the Catholic priest at St. Augustine. I have the letter you wrote requesting that we bring you here. Governor de la Vega asked me to find out who you are."

They spoke for some time, Henry finding the father to be a kind person but no fool. He congratulated Henry on his excellent Latin but added that he did not believe Henry was a Catholic, as claimed in his letter. Henry had to admit that he was not but stayed with his story that the English had abandoned him at Port Royal and said he feared for his life.

Sotolongo said, "The governor knows about your King Charles granting much of the lands of La Florida to his noblemen. He believes you are an English spy sent to learn about St Augustine."

Uncomfortably close to the truth, this was not what Henry wanted to hear. All he could think to say was, "If that is what he believes, he can put me on the next ship from St. Augustine. I will leave knowing as little as when I arrived."

The father said he would propose the idea, but the governor was very suspicious of the English.

Henry's days in confinement dragged on. As Sotolongo had warned him, the governor refused to send him away. Sotolongo visited Henry often and asked him about his life in London and Virginia and how he had ended up in La Florida. The father was kindly, but Henry could tell he was being interrogated. One day he brought a man into Henry's cell who introduced himself as Joseph de Prado from Mexico City. He spoke with Henry at length in Latin before conversing with the Father outside his cell and then leaving.

Letter from Joseph de Prado, Royal Treasurer in Mexico City, to the Spanish Crown, upon his visit to St. Augustine:

> *In this Presidio, I found an Englishman called Henrrique, a native of London, his age about twenty. He was brought by an English ship in the month of October, year of sixty-five and about seventy leagues north of this Presidio; they put him ashore and left him among the heathen giving him trade goods of the kind the Indians use to please them and support himself among them in order that he might learn their language and that the following year they would return. He was expecting them and seeing that they were delayed, he wrote a paper in Latin (in which he excels) to a missionary in a province called Guale which was thirty leagues from the place where the Englishman was, telling him that he was a Catholic and a surgeon and that they might take him from where he had been for more than a year. The governor, learning of this, sent an officer with ten men in December of last year, and he arrived here in January, and it appeared that he is not a Christian. And in view of the above circumstances, he should be questioned to learn his designs.*

Finally, Sotolongo told him that the governor had decided his fate; Henry feared the worst.

But rather than declaring that he was to be executed as a spy, he said, "The governor has decreed that you cannot leave St. Augustine. But if you agree to work as a laborer, you will be released from confinement. If not, your imprisonment will continue."

Henry, seeing he had little choice, said yes.

He was assigned to work with the Guale Indian laborers and African slaves, cleaning streets, digging ditches, and repairing the ramshackle government buildings, working twelve-hour days in the searing St. Augustine sun. He slept on the dirt floor of a thatch-roofed wooden shack shared with other workers. Meals were scanty, mostly corn, beans, and fish. Always hungry, he became thinner and weaker by the day. Two of the slaves had died within the last month; Henry believed he would soon follow.

Every evening, Henry concocted escape plans before falling into a fitful sleep. Every morning, he saw how hopeless they were. The Guale Indians, whose towns extended for miles in every direction, were loyal to St. Augustine. If he tried to escape on foot, they would capture and return him. The only ships were Spanish, destined for Havana, and regardless, there was no way for him to sneak aboard. Perhaps he could ask Father Sotolongo to get him transferred to a less demanding job.

He did not get the opportunity. The next day, the brutal heat finally too much for him, he collapsed. Seeing him lying on the ground, one of the workers called out to the overseer, "Enrique está muerto!"

The overseer, prodding his body with his boot, thought he saw signs of life and ordered that he be carried to the poor persons' hospital, a wooden shack with pallets on the floor where the slaves and Indian workers were sent, as often as not, to die.

The laborers laid Henry on one of the pallets; an African slave woman, a healer who ran the hospital, placed her hand on his chest. His breathing was shallow, and his heartbeat rapid. She saw these symptoms often—too much sun and not enough water. Spreading wet clothes on his body, she forced sassafras tea between his lips. By the next day, he could sit up and eat some food.

Father Sotolongo, hearing that Henry was ill, stopped at the hospital to check on him and immediately instructed the healer that he be moved to the royal hospital, Nuestra Señora de la Soledad. When Governor de la Vega learned of this, he berated the father, telling him that he was wasting scarce resources on an English spy.

Sotolongo, who answered only to the church, not the crown, replied that Spain and England were presently at peace and the English might be unhappy to learn that one of its subjects had died from ill-treatment at the governor's hands.

❧

Reluctantly, the governor agreed to move Henry to the other hospital. It had two rooms rather than one and beds, rather than pallets on the floor. It also had a surgeon, Pierre Piques, who examined Henry and confirmed that the healer was correct—he was suffering from overwork, exhaustion, and heat, not from disease. Pierre spoke Latin almost as well as Henry, and they chatted briefly. He said he was French and had been St. Augustine's surgeon for only a brief time.

Pierre told him that the labor performed by the African slaves and Guale laborers was so grueling that half of them died within two years. He and Father Sotolongo constantly complained to the governor about it, to no avail.

He said to Henry, "You can stay in the hospital for another week, but de la Vega will insist you return to work after that. If you continue as a laborer, you will be dead before the year's end. I will talk to Father Sotolongo to see if we can persuade the governor to assign you to a less demanding job."

Pierre asked him more about his training as a surgeon.

Henry replied, "I haven't completed a formal apprenticeship, but I often worked with my father, who was a surgeon in London and Virginia Colony before he died."

Pierre explained his job as St. Augustine's surgeon—he was responsible for the health of the Guale Indians who had submitted to Spanish rule, but most of them did not trust Spanish medicine and would only see the African healer. His main job was treating the fort's soldiers and the townspeople, but there was never enough money for medicine or supplies. In St. Augustine, the death rate was high—poor diet, disease, and hot, humid summers took the lives of many workers and soldiers, even the townspeople.

"I need an experienced assistant; would you be interested if I can get Sotolongo to go along?"

Henry, of course, agreed.

Sotolongo explained to Henry that the governor might be opposed to the idea but, because the church provided much of the funding for St. Augustine's two hospitals, he had an equal say with the governor.

20

PIERRE PIQUES

St. Augustine, La Florida, 1667–1668

The patient lay on a rough wooden table, his leg shattered by a falling beam. As Pierre prepared the tools to amputate, Henry spoke up. "I saw my father save the leg of a man with the same injury. Perhaps we can save this leg."

"Henry, even if I set it instead of amputating, it would become infected, and he would die."

"I agree that is what would usually happen, but my father applied a poultice from an African healer to the fracture. Perhaps the healer at the poor hospital might have something similar."

Examining the patient, the healer spoke to Pierre in Spanish—she also thought the leg could be saved. Asking for a pitcher of clean water and a knife, she pulled out bits of wood and dirt from the wound. When she continued cleaning and scrubbing the injury, Pierre asked what she was doing. She told him the dirt in the wound harbored evil spirits that had to be expelled for the leg to heal. She then spread a poultice over the injury, explaining that it was a mixture of aloe vera and honey, which the healers in her village used to keep the spirits out as the wound healed.

When she had finished, Pierre set and splinted the leg. The healer told him that the wound had to be kept clean and that she would return to apply more poultice and change the bandages.

Two months later, the patient was walking, much to Pierre's surprise. After that, he often asked for the healer's assistance in treating patients. He also began keeping wounds clean and using the healer's poultice liberally.

By the fall of 1667, Henry had settled into his life of involuntary servitude even though he still dreamed of escaping every night. Pierre placed him in charge of the poor hospital even though they knew the healer was the one who ran it. The two became close; Pierre reminded Henry of his uncle William at Fort Henry.

One October evening, celebrating his twenty-first birthday with a bottle of rum, Henry told Pierre his story—his family's death from the plague in London, coming to Virginia, staying with the Escamacu at Port Royal, and finally coming to St. Augustine to escape the Westo.

In turn, Pierre told Henry his. "I was a surgeon on a ship commanded by a French corsair, or as the English call them, a buccaneer, named l'Olonnais. He knew his way around the Caribbean and had captured several Spanish treasure ships. From my share of the loot, I sent funds to my family in France. But the fates turned against us in 1664. We were sailing off the coast of Campeche when our ship was struck by a storm and capsized. We made it to shore, but a group of Spanish soldiers was waiting for us. They slaughtered most of the crew and took the few survivors, including myself, as prisoners. They transported me to Havana and told me that if I renounced the life of a corsair and swore allegiance to Spain, my life would be spared, and I would serve as an unpaid surgeon. I agreed and served in Havana's hospital for several years. In 1666, they sent me here to serve as the official surgeon. I am here against my will and have little hope of ever seeing my family again."

As they finished the bottle of rum, Pierre said half-jokingly that their only chance of escape would be for l'Olonnais to raid St. Augustine and free them. "If he knew about the silver bars in the treasury, he would be here tomorrow."

"What silver bars?"

Pierre explained, "About ten years ago, a Spanish treasure ship, *Las Maravillas,* was bringing a cargo of silver and gold back to Spain when it sunk in a storm. The water was shallow, and the Spanish recovered many large silver bars. Over one hundred of them are stored in the treasury here."

Seeing that Governor de la Vega disliked Henry almost as much as himself, Pierre suggested converting to Catholicism. Father Sotolongo protected Pierre from de la Vega's worst impulses; he should be able to do the same for Henry. Pierre said the father was eager to make converts and suggested bringing Henry to next Sunday's mass.

Father Sotolongo was happy to see him there and, after the service, invited both of them to dinner. Henry expected that the father's meals would be better than what he ate, but the food was surprisingly plain. The only difference was that it was brought to the table by an Indian servant.

After dinner, the father said to Henry, "I know that, when you came here, you said you were Catholic. You've since admitted to me you are not. Have you considered converting?"

Well coached by Pierre, he replied, "I have had time to reflect on my life since arriving here, and yes, I am now interested."

"For you to be baptized as a Catholic, you will need religious instruction; I'll be glad to instruct you."

Henry, contrary to his expectations, enjoyed his meetings with the father. He was a quick study, so they spent much of their time discussing other topics. Sotolongo, who spent endless hours listening to the townspeople's tedious and unimaginative confessions, relished the chance to talk about his life in St. Augustine.

"I was sent here from St. Augustine earlier this year; I believe it was at the behest of my superior who I did not get along with. Few of us, including our governor, are here voluntarily. The crown no longer believes that St. Augustine is useful for protecting the Spanish treasure ships. If it wasn't for you English challenging Spain's ownership of these lands, I think the government might remove all of the soldiers and turn it over to the church."

⌘

As unhappy as Henry was with being held prisoner in St. Augustine, Pierre was even more so. The governor never missed a chance to demonstrate his dislike for Pierre and let him know he would die of old age here. Unlike Henry, Pierre had a family in France. Paid a pittance for serving as surgeon, he could not send even those small sums home.

In February, Pierre confided to Henry that he had a plan for getting out of St. Augustine. "The governor is a thin-skinned man who can easily be pushed into a rage. I will deliberately antagonize him until he cannot stand the sight of me. With Sotolongo to protect me, perhaps the most he could do would be to send me back to Havana. There, I would have a better chance of escaping to Tortuga and eventually back to France. Even if I didn't escape, my life in Havana would be preferable to this."

By March, Pierre had so antagonized the governor that he would no longer speak to him and had stopped paying his small salary. When one of his children fell ill, he asked Henry, rather than Pierre, to tend to him. Finally, de la Vega became so incensed in front of Sotolongo and others that he struck Pierre across the face. Pierre knew his plan had succeeded.

Henry's conversion scheme had also succeeded; on Holy Saturday, Father Sotolongo baptized him as a Catholic.

The following Monday, Pierre approached Henry with a grin. "The governor just informed me I am to be sent back to Havana a week from now."

Later that day, the governor sent word for Henry to see him. Henry had no idea what to expect—was he going to be sent away as well?

But the governor was unusually cordial, although Henry thought it seemed forced.

"I am sending Piques back to Havana. I have been unhappy with his work and can no longer tolerate his disruptive behavior. Until Havana sends me a replacement, you are now the official surgeon."

The frigate from Havana arrived in early April with food and supplies. It left two days later, with Pierre as a passenger. Henry and Father Sotolongo were the only ones to say goodbye to him as he boarded the ship. When they had a moment alone, Pierre said to Henry, "If I ever have the chance, I will do everything I can to help you escape from here." As the ship left the harbor, Henry saw the only person in the world he considered to be his friend leave with it.

21

REVENGE

St. Augustine, May 1668

It was one in the morning. Henry had just fallen asleep, having been in the hospital until almost midnight when the sound of shouting and gunshots awoke him. His first thought was that the fort's soldiers were holding a midnight rum-fueled celebration. Then he heard screams and someone cursing, not in Spanish, but in English. He knew he was the only person in St. Augustine with that skill.

Pulling on his clothes, he stumbled outside to the sight of a gang of roughly dressed men armed with muskets and cutlasses chasing the town's residents down the street. They were not soldiers and were indeed speaking English. It dawned on him that they were buccaneers.

Hands raised, he approached one of them: "Don't shoot me; I am English."

To his amazement, the man replied, "Be you Henry Woodward? We're looking for you."

The buccaneer took Henry to the harbor where a Spanish ship was anchored. It was dark, but Henry thought he saw a familiar figure.

The figure spoke. "Bonjour, mon amie!" It was Pierre Piques. Embracing Henry, he exclaimed, "I promised I would come back for you."

Henry was hopelessly confused—Pierre was standing next to a boat that Henry recognized as the harbor pilot's launch, flying its Spanish flag. But several English buccaneers were standing on its deck. Pierre said, "I am here to rescue you; the buccaneers are here for the silver bars. I will explain later. Now, we need to help the ship's surgeon tend to the injured."

Buccaneers were already carrying the wounded to the wharf where Pierre and Henry set up some planks as an operating table, with light from a lantern. Their first patient had been struck by a musket ball, shattering his lower leg. Assuming they would set and bind it as they had done in the town's hospital, Henry began to clean the wound. Then he saw Pierre remove the bone saw from his bag.

Pierre said, "There is no time for an injury such as this—the leg will have to be removed."

He gave the injured buccaneer a mug of rum and placed a rag between his teeth. He had Henry hold the buccaneer down as he cut back a flap of skin to cover the stump, sawed through the leg, cauterized the exposed blood vessels with a hot blade, and sewed the skin flap over the stump. The operation took less than fifteen minutes. They laid the now unconscious buccaneer on the wharf, threw a bucket of seawater over the bloody planks, and prepared for the next patient. This was a different kind of surgical practice than Henry was used to; he remembered his father telling him about his days as a surgeon in Cromwell's army where such amputations were the norm.

Gunfire, shouting, and screaming continued through the night, and more wounded were carried to the wharf. The buccaneers began bringing groups of men, women, and children, mostly in their nightclothes at gunpoint. Pierre said they would be held hostage for ransom.

The following day the buccaneers searched the town, house by house, for valuables they carried to the ships, along with more prisoners. There were now almost a hundred captives from the town, including the treasurer. The governor and other officials had holed up in the fort, which resisted repeated assaults by the buccaneers despite its decrepit condition. After heavy losses, they gave up and continued sacking the town.

Now soaked in blood, Henry looked up from the makeshift operating table when he heard a familiar voice. It was a stunned-looking Father Sotolongo, escorted by a buccaneer to the wharf. When he saw Pierre and Henry working together, he had realized that Pierre was in league with the buccaneers and that Henry was not their captive. He knew Pierre had been miserable in St. Augustine but had not suspected Henry might be of a like mind. Putting aside his feelings of betrayal for the moment, he told Henry that he was volunteering himself as a captive to protect the women and children from the buccaneers. Henry and Pierre returned to tending the injured, Henry thinking that Sotolongo was either the bravest person in St. Augustine or perhaps the foolhardiest.

⸺◦◦◦⸺

During a lull, Pierre told Henry how he came to be back in St. Augustine barely two months after he left. "A week after leaving St. Augustine, just north of Havana, we were attacked by buccaneers flying the English flag. Hopelessly outnumbered, we surrendered. There was little of value on board as we were returning empty from St. Augustine. I feared the buccaneers might kill or throw us into the sea as angry buccaneers often do. I told one of them that I was French and being held as a prisoner and wanted to talk to their captain. They took me to his ship, the *Cagway,* where he introduced himself as Robert Searle. I knew of him—he often sailed with Henry Morgan, the most famous of the English buccaneers.

"I told him that I had been a surgeon on l'Olonnais's ship and one of the only survivors when the Spanish killed its crew at Campeche. Since then, I had been held captive by the Spanish and forced to serve as St. Augustine's surgeon. Searle knew l'Olonnais by reputation; they shared a common hatred of the Spanish.

"Searle told me that several days earlier, they had captured a Spanish brigantine, the *Nueva España*, on its way to St. Augustine with food and supplies and added it to their fleet of two. The ship had few valuables, so they were looking for new targets.

"I realized this was the kind of opportunity we often dreamed of at St. Augustine. If I could persuade Searle to go along, I could rescue you, get revenge on the Spanish, and become wealthy with my share of the silver bars. I would then return to France and find my family."

Before Pierre could continue, an injured buccaneer approached them. His arm appeared broken, but he seemed unconcerned about the injury; all he wanted was a mug of rum, which he knew was only given to the wounded during a raid. Pierre told him they needed to tend to his arm; the buccaneer agreed only after Henry gave him his rum.

Pierre then returned to his story. "Searle invited me to supper in his cabin on the *Cagway.* I told him about my idea, that there was a large stack of silver bars in the St. Augustine treasury from the *Las Maravillas*, as well as valuables in the homes of the town's wealthier citizens. I explained to him that during my time in St. Augustine, I studied its defenses—the fort was dilapidated and protected by only a few cannons; there were about a hundred ill-trained and poorly fed soldiers to defend and no warships."

"I told Searle that the *Nueva España* he had captured would be manned with his crew and sailed into Matanzas Bay under cover of darkness. From there, we would launch an assault on the town, retrieve that silver bars, and sail away. I told him that I knew the protocol and signals to enter the harbor without being challenged by the fort's guards."

"If the plan succeeded, I would share in the booty for telling Searle about this opportunity. I told Searle that I had three other conditions: that the town not be burned to the ground as was customary, that the townspeople not be tortured to reveal hidden possessions, and that my English friend and fellow surgeon, Henry Woodward, who was being held against his will, be rescued. I told Searle he could do as he pleased with the governor.

"Searle was intrigued by my plan; his crew was becoming unruly, and he feared a mutiny; he was also angry with the Spanish for a recent unprovoked attack that had killed some of his friends."

Pierre and Henry were interrupted again when Searle asked them to treat an injured townsperson. Usually, prisoners were treated last after all of the wounded buccaneers had been cared for, if they were treated at all. But Searle told them he was wealthy and would fetch a good ransom, so he wanted to keep him in good condition. It was a simple cut, and Henry bandaged it.

Pierre continued, "The plan worked perfectly. The buccaneers had captured the harbor pilot's boat when he sailed out to greet them and forced him to give the proper signals to the soldiers at the fort. As a result, we were able to land by surprise. You know the rest."

⸺◈⸺

By the next day, the buccaneers had removed 133 silver bars from the treasury, looted the wealthy citizen's homes, and stripped the church of valuables. They began transferring the prisoners, including Sotolongo, to the two larger ships, now anchored at the fort.

Searle freed the remaining prisoners but kept the Indians he had taken. Sotolongo argued that they were not slaves but free men. Searle was unmoved, claiming that his letters of marque from the governor allowed him to keep them to sell in Jamaica as slaves. Sotolongo was insistent and refused to leave the ship until the Indians were freed; Searle finally had to remove him forcibly.

The *Cagway* was ready to sail for its home port, Port Royal, Jamaica. As a parting shot, before putting him ashore, Searle told Sotolongo they would be back to capture the town and make it a base for buccaneers. They departed, taking depth soundings as they left, which would be helpful if they did return.

Henry was a free man for the first time since arriving in St. Augustine almost two years earlier.

22

JAMAICA

1668

Searle's fleet headed south to Jamaica; at the last minute, Searle decided to go to Port Morant rather than Port Royal, the hub of buccaneer activity. Strictly speaking, the St. Augustine raid had not been conducted according to the terms of his commission from the governor, and Searle saw no need to draw undue attention to himself. At Port Morant, he divided the St. Augustine haul among the crew. Pierre's share of the loot was ten sixty-pound silver bars and a stack of pieces of eight; he was now a wealthy man.

Port Morant was a far more sedate town than Port Royal, but that did not stop the buccaneers from doing their best to spend their gains as quickly as possible. Their celebration did not last long. Governor Modyford, hearing of the St. Augustine raid, had issued a warrant for Searle's arrest. Having earlier crossed the governor for illegal attacks on the Spanish, Searle decided it would be prudent to move on. He had planned to sell the Indian captives at the Port Royal slave market; instead, he sold them to a local planter at a reduced price. The fleet then set sail for the island's west end to lay low until things had quieted down.

Pierre told Henry he planned to make his way to Tortuga and catch a French ship sailing for home. He had not seen nor heard from his family for almost eight years. His children would be grown, and he feared that his wife would have remarried, assuming he was dead.

"What are your plans, Henry?"

Henry confessed he had none. Sandford had no way of knowing what had happened to him in Carolina; his immediate family was dead and going back to his grandfather Thomas in Virginia Colony was not an option he wished to pursue. As difficult as his confinement at St. Augustine had been, he had a routine there, albeit an involuntary one.

Pierre, flush with his share of the *Las Maravillas* loot, rented rooms for the two at a local inn. Dinner at the inn was sumptuous compared to the food in St. Augustine—beef and fresh vegetables, washed down with tankards of ale.

⸺⟋⟋⟍⸻

The following day, over breakfast, Pierre said, "I've thought about what you said yesterday. After working with you in St. Augustine, I've realized you know as much as most ship's surgeons. Why don't you sign on with a buccaneer ship?

Henry was silent for a moment. Finally, he said, "I must admit the last weeks have been exciting, but I'm not qualified to be a ship's surgeon."

Pierre replied, "It's not that difficult. You already know how to treat common ailments. The rest of the job is treating wounds. Buccaneers are a hard-hearted lot. They know their life is dangerous and short and have little fear of death. If you can't put a bandage on an injured limb, you saw it off, and he lives or dies. Nobody will blame you if he doesn't live."

Henry and Pierre had been in Port Morant for a week when they heard that Governor Modyford had arrested Searle, seized his fleet, and confiscated the silver bars.

Pierre said, "We were the only winners in the raid—St. Augustine was sacked, and its governor humiliated; Sandford lost his ships, the treasure, and many crewmen. I have a stack of silver bars, and we both gained our freedom."

⸺⟋⟋⟍⸻

Pierre decided it was now safe for them to go to Port Royal. From there, he would sail to Tortuga and back to France. Henry was undecided what he might do.

Henry knew that Port Royal was the main port for English buccaneers, reputed to be a lawless collection of taverns and brothels. It was not what he had expected. The wide streets were clean sand, laid out in an orderly grid, unlike London's narrow, twisty, and muddy lanes. The shops were tidy, clean, and prosperous. There were numerous taverns, but most of them looked safe. Walking along the wharf, Henry and Pierre were surrounded by vendors offering everything from fresh fruits and vegetables to arts and crafts. There were buccaneers everywhere, many staggering drunk but in good spirits.

Food and lodging were expensive, prices driven up by the cash-flush buccaneers. They finally found rooms on the edge of town, away from the taverns' noise, and spent the following day looking for a ship sailing to Tortuga. Pierre met a French corsair in one of the taverns; this was his first chance to converse in his native tongue in years, and the two were soon deep in conversation.

Henry joined a table of English buccaneers. When he told them his story of imprisonment at St. Augustine and rescue by Searle, the men, temporarily wealthy from a successful raid, insisted on buying him rounds of drinks. They knew of Searle's raid and were optimistic he would be released quickly since Governor Modyford was Henry Morgan's silent business partner, and Searle was one of Morgan's lieutenants.

Henry asked, "Is this the same person who was a sugar planter?"

"Yes, he's been getting rich as governor for the last four years."

Henry knew of him—Modyford was the Barbados planter who gave John Yeamans the idea to establish a colony in Port Royal.

Hours later, Pierre and Henry left the tavern, less than sober. Pierre had found a ship leaving for Tortuga in two days. Henry had mixed emotions about the news. He knew that Pierre was eager to return to France, but he also knew he would never see his only friend in the world again.

The next day they went shopping. Awash in Spanish gold and silver, Port Royal was the wealthiest city in the English colonies. There were goldsmiths, jewelry stores, fine French clothing stores, and expensive taverns in a two-block stretch of the main street. Even though Pierre knew that his wife probably thought he was dead and might have remarried, he purchased a gold necklace and several silk scarves to take back to France. He also insisted on buying Henry a new set of clothing.

That evening, they dined at the most expensive tavern Pierre could find and reminisced about their time in St. Augustine, so different than Port Royal that it scarcely seemed real.

After dinner, Pierre dropped a leather pouch on the table. "For you," he said. It was filled with Spanish silver dollars.

When Henry protested that it was too much, he said, "You earned it—you were a prisoner in St. Augustine almost as long as I was. And, you cannot begin your new life as a pauper. This will help you get back to England or whatever else you decide to do."

≈≈≈

The next morning when Henry arose, Pierre, not wanting to face another goodbye, had already left. Henry was now truly alone, but he was free and had money in his pockets. He spent the next few days exploring Port Royal. The town was perched on the very end of a long sandy cay between the open ocean and a large bay; its buildings were shoulder to shoulder, extending to the water's edge. One strong storm could sweep it into the sea.

Henry told a shopkeeper that he was a surgeon newly arrived in Port Royal. Was Port Royal perhaps in need of one?

The shopkeeper replied, "There are already a fair number in town. Also, this is a hard place to live—food and lodging are expensive. Most men come here to become buccaneers. If I were younger, I would be one myself."

Henry asked if it was true that Henry Morgan and Governor Modyford were friends.

"Yes. Charles II appointed him governor to put down the buccaneers. Instead, he has gotten rich from sharing the spoils with Morgan. Between them, they now control all of the buccaneers based in Port Royal."

Thanking him for the information, Henry adjourned to a nearby tavern to ponder his future. Jamaica seemed a fine place, but Port Royal was too crowded and busy for him, even if he could find work there. Perhaps Pierre's suggestion that he sign on as a surgeon with a buccaneer ship was a good one.

The best way to do so would be through Henry Morgan from what he had heard. He and Modyford were business partners; Modyford was friends with Yeamans; Henry could claim at least some connection to Yeamans. He needed to find a way to meet the governor. He spent the rest of the week in the town's better taverns, buying drinks for the local merchants and planters, and learning all he could about him.

It only took Henry a few days to tire of Port Royal. When he asked a tavern-keeper he had befriended if there was anywhere quieter and less expensive where he might find a room, the keeper said, "Pay a visit to Spanish Town. Mostly planters live there, with no buccaneers."

Although Spanish Town was just across the bay, getting there was not easy; Henry had to wait hours for a wherry to take him. Although not nearly as ragged, the town looked more like a prosperous St. Augustine than Port Royal. Unlike the broad, straight Port Royal avenues, its streets were narrow and irregular. Many of them were not even named.

On one such street, a handwritten sign in a window advertised "room for let." Henry asked a woman working outside about it. She was the landlady and invited him to view it, and they agreed on a rent of five pieces of eight per month. This was a third of what he was paying for much worse lodgings in Port Royal. Leaving his new lodgings, he stopped at a nearby tavern, the Spanish Town Coffee House, for a meal. Unlike Port Royal's taverns inhabited by buccaneers, it was bustling with planters and government workers drinking coffee, not rum, and discussing politics, not conquests. At his table was a dog-eared copy of *The London Gazette.* Henry had never seen it in London and asked the proprietor about it.

The proprietor said, "It started in 1666, after the plague, and carries official government news."

Even though it was several months old, Henry had heard nothing other than gossip from England since leaving London three years ago. He spent the next hour avidly devouring its contents, along with his meal. One article caught his eye—the Merchant Taylors' School, where he had spent an unhappy year, was reopening after the Great Fire had destroyed it two years earlier. Henry had heard nothing of a fire in London. The proprietor told him that half of London had burned in the fall of 1666. On the heels of the plague the year before, it was a terrible blow, but the city was recovering.

The next day, Henry shaved, put on his best clothes, and set out for King's House, the governor's official residence, a few blocks from Henry's new home. He told the guard who stopped him that he had information for the governor. The guard told him to wait. Half an hour later, an officious clerk bustled into the room and introduced himself as the governor's secretary.

Henry explained who he was and why he needed to see the governor, embellishing on his connection to John Yeamans and the matter's importance. The secretary said that Modyford had some free time before his next appointment, and perhaps he could see Henry. Indeed, it was only a few minutes before he was escorted into the governor's quarters. Henry introduced himself, and Modyford invited him to be seated. He was in his fifties, overweight, with dead-fish eyes, fat lips, and a ridiculous wig. "My secretary told me you are an English surgeon and that John Yeamans sent you to explore the Carolina coast for the lords proprietors. Is that true?"

Henry explained that it was and added that he had since been held prisoner by the Spanish in St. Augustine, only just freed by Robert Searle.

"Ah, yes, I know about that. I'm still holding Searle for violating the terms of his commission for the raid. But I'll release him shortly; I had to arrest him to keep London happy."

When Henry began to recount his stay in Carolina, Modyford made it clear that he no longer had any interest in it. He added that Yeamans, presently in Barbados, might still be interested.

He then asked, "What can you tell me about the Spanish?"

Henry began to tell him about St. Augustine, but again Modyford interrupted—"that's too far from here to be of interest to me. What can you tell me about Havana?"

When Henry admitted that he knew very little, the meeting was over. But before leaving the room, Henry said, "When Searle rescued me, I was the official surgeon at St. Augustine. I'm interested in becoming a buccaneer ship's surgeon here. Could you perhaps put in a word for me?"

Waving it off as a matter of minor importance, Modyford told Henry to have his secretary arrange it before dismissing him.

23

A BUCCANEER'S LIFE

1668–1669

Crossing the bay to Port Royal, Henry saw ten new ships at anchor. One was the *Oxford*; Morgan's fleet had finally returned. Buccaneers crowded the streets, boisterous, unwashed, drunk. At the Three Crowns, a favorite tavern of buccaneers, Henry struck up a conversation with one who was still somewhat sober. Insisting on buying Henry a drink, he said they had just returned from a successful raid of Portobello, Panama, with at least 250,000 pieces of eight. "We will all be rich," the buccaneer boasted.

Henry thought to himself, *for a week or two, perhaps.*

Henry waited for several days before returning to King's House to ask about a position as a ship's surgeon. To his surprise, the secretary had news for him. One of the ships on the Portobello raid, the *Dolphin*, needed a new surgeon, and Morgan would recommend Henry to the ship's captain, John Morris.

Henry asked for permission to board the *Dolphin*, a medium-size ship of Spanish design, carrying ten cannons. Morris, about fifty, was striking in appearance—tall and lean, bearded, with a piercing gaze.

"Morgan told me about your St. Augustine adventure. I know Robert Searle well; both of us bought our ships from Morgan after he had captured them from the Spanish. My surgeon made enough money from the Portobello raid to finally retire, so I need a new one."

Asked about his experience, Henry admitted that he had never served as a ship's surgeon but had been the chief surgeon for St. Augustine until Searle had rescued him. Morris seemed satisfied and told Henry he would welcome him as his new surgeon.

"We're going to be in Port Royal until Morgan plans a new expedition; you'll need to be on call to treat crew members. You may be busier than at sea as my men will be trying their best to spend their loot in the taverns and brothels."

Apart from treating the crewmen for a host of ailments, from French pox to alcohol poisoning, shipboard life was dull and uncomfortable while the *Dolphin* was in port. Port Royal was hot and humid onshore; it was even worse in the confines of the ship. Henry's cabin was small and dark; the bed and surgeon's chest took up most of the space. The odor of unwashed bodies in close quarters was almost more than Henry could bear. He slept on the beach some nights, where he found the mosquitos only slightly less unpleasant than his cabin.

⸻ ✿ ⸻

Finally, in early October, Morris took him aside. "We'll be leaving port shortly. Morgan has ordered the fleet to set sail for Isla Vaca; it's a small island near Hispaniola that he uses as a staging area. You will love it."

Isla Vaca was the most beautiful place Henry had ever seen—white beaches lined with coconut palms, coral reefs teeming with fish, and freshwater streams. A herd of cattle from the days of the Spanish roamed the island, hence its name.

Most of the ships' crews set up small camps along the beaches, with simple palm-thatched lean-tos. Next to his campsite, Henry built a covered area to treat patients. But he was less busy than he had been in Port Royal. The buccaneers stayed in good health with ample fresh fruit, fish, and beef and Admiral Morgan's ban on alcohol.

Henry swam in the crystal-clear aqua ocean in his free time, something he hadn't done since he was a child in Virginia Colony. On occasion, curious dolphins joined him. He became friends with other ship's surgeons, including a Frenchman named Alexandre Exquemelin and Morgan's surgeon, Richard Browne. Alexandre was his age and, like Henry, had no formal training.

In his spare moments, Exquemelin was always scribbling in a journal. When Henry asked him about it, he said, "I'm writing a book about my adventures. I'm thinking of calling it *The Buccaneers of America*."

Time stood still for Henry that fall. His duties as ship's surgeon only took up an hour or two a day. He spent the rest of his time exploring the island, reading from a small library Captain Morris kept and chatting with other crew members.

A ship flying the English flag anchored at Isla Vaca in early December. It was the *HMS Oxford*, a recently decommissioned Royal Navy ship given to the Jamaican government to help put down the buccaneers. But the ship's captain also carried secret instructions giving Governor Modyford the right to use it against the

Spanish as he saw fit. Rather than employing the vessel for its intended purpose, Modyford refitted it and sent it to join Morgan. At seventy feet with twenty-six cannons, it was bigger and more powerful than anything in Morgan's fleet, and he immediately commandeered it as his new flagship.

By late December, the buccaneers were becoming restless and thirsty for action. Finally, in early January, Admiral Morgan called a war council to meet on the *Oxford* to plan their next adventure. The ships' captains agreed that Cartagena de Indias would be their next target. It was the most heavily protected port on the coast, but a raid could equal the earlier Portobello haul. At noon, Admiral Morgan ordered fifteen of the *Oxford*'s guns fired to celebrate their decision.

Henry was sitting in the shade of a palm tree, having just finished his dinner. He looked up briefly at the sound of the firing cannons and went back to reading *Dox Quixote*. Suddenly an enormous explosion knocked him over. When his head cleared enough to look around, he saw a cloud of smoke over the bay. Where the *Oxford* had been anchored minutes earlier, there was now only floating rubble.

Despite the complete devastation, there were several survivors. Admiral Morgan had only a minor leg wound. His surgeon, Richard Browne, was brought ashore unharmed, as was Captain Morris. When the rescue effort was completed, only twenty crewmen were found alive.

After Browne had bound the Admiral's wound and he and Henry had seen to it that he could do nothing more for the remaining survivors, Henry had a moment to talk to him.

Browne said, "When the cannons were fired, a group of us were on the quarter-deck, eating our dinner. I heard a great rushing noise, accompanied by fire and smoke, and was pitched into the sea by the force of the explosion."

The following day, seeing that Exquemelin was hard at work on his journal after the disaster, Henry asked him if he was writing about the explosion of the *Oxford*.

Exquemelin replied, "My book is going to make Henry Morgan the most famous pirate in history, and it will sell so well I will never have to go to sea again." Waving his arm over the bay where just a day earlier, the *Oxford* had been anchored, he said, "The public wants to hear about cruel, bloodthirsty, drunken pirates, so that is what I will give them." To make his point, he read aloud from his journal. "After the loss of the *Oxford*, Captain Morgan commanded the bodies of the miserable wretches who were blown up to be searched for, as they floated on the sea; not to afford them Christian burials, but for their clothes and attire: and if any had gold rings on their fingers, these were cut off, leaving them exposed to the voracity of the sea."

Henry commented, "That will certainly get the readers' attention."

Exquemelin replied, "My torture scenes are even better. I make out Morgan and his crew to be the most depraved men ever to sail the seas."

Henry finished their conversation by saying it would be wise to keep the journal to himself for the time being.

———◦◦◦———

Morgan's fleet now lacked the manpower for its planned attack on Cartagena. After several days, it set off to cruise the Spanish Main coast, looking for new targets but finding none. Discouraged, three of Morgan's ships left the expedition, leaving him with only six.

After several fruitless weeks, the fleet anchored at Saona, near Isla Vaca. Even more beautiful than Isla Vaca, it was a popular gathering place for English and French buccaneers, so Morgan's fleet did not have it to themselves. One evening, as they shared dinner and drinks with a French crew, their captain suggested that Morgan consider Maracaibo, on the north coast of Venezuela, as a target. He said he had been on the l'Olonnais raid of that city three years earlier, and it was wealthy and poorly defended. If Morgan was interested, they could join forces.

This was Morgan's favorite kind of target, especially with his now greatly reduced fleet, and he accepted the French captain's proposal. Stopping in Aruba to replenish supplies, they reached the mouth of Laguna de Maracaibo two months after the *Oxford* was lost. But there was a problem—there was now a large stone fort with cannon dominating the channel, erected after l'Olonnais' raid three years earlier. As Morgan's men landed to attack the fort, its guns began firing on them. The skirmish continued until nightfall when suddenly the cannon fell silent. The buccaneers cautiously approached the fort and found that its troops had fled. Searching the fort, Morgan found the cellar filled with gunpowder with a lit fuse leading to it. They extinguished it only minutes before the fort and his men would have gone the way of the *Oxford*.

Morgan's men spent a week in Maracaibo, plundering anything of value, taking hostages, and drinking its wine and spirits.

As the fleet left the Maracaibo lagoon for the open gulf, it suddenly came under fire from the previously abandoned fort—a Spanish fleet, looking for Morgan's buccaneers, had arrived in the meantime, manned the fort, and placed its largest ship, the thirty-eight-gun *Magdalena*, in the middle of the channel.

Morgan's fleet now had no way out of the lagoon other than smashing through the Spanish fleet. After a week of preparation, Morgan sailed his fleet with one vessel, previously a merchantman, and now converted to a flagship, leading the way. It sailed directly at the *Magdalena*; at the last second, the sailors on the flagship threw grappling irons on the *Magdalena*'s deck, binding the ships together. Then Morgan's crew jumped overboard into waiting canoes and paddled away. As the Spanish sailors swarmed onto the ship, it exploded into flames, and within minutes the wind blew the fire onto the *Magdalena*. The *Magdalena*'s powder magazine exploded, killing most of the crew, a replay of the *Oxford*'s earlier fate.

Morgan had completely outfoxed the Spanish captain. He had refurbished the Cuban merchantman to only look like a flagship as a ruse. In fact, he had converted it to a fireship stuffed with gunpowder; the last buccaneer to abandon the ship lit the fuses before jumping into a canoe.

The remaining Spanish warship, the twenty-four-gun *Marquesa*, sailed toward the fort, but Morgan's men, overpowering its crew, captured it.

Led by his new flagship, the *Marquesa*, Morgan's fleet arrived at Port Royal after two months of pillaging Maracaibo and Gibraltar. Their haul was more than 250,000 Spanish silver dollars, plus the value of the hostages being held for ransom and slaves to be sold in Port Royal. He had lost the *Oxford* after only two weeks, but the *Marquesa* was every bit as fine a flagship. Privateers' lives were short and cheap, so the loss of 200 men when the *Oxford* blew up was not held against him.

After the haul had been divided up, the buccaneers once again began the ritual of disposing of their newfound wealth as rapidly as possible. Henry retreated to his residence in Spanish Town, feeling very satisfied. Between his share of the loot and the funds Pierre had given him, he had more than his father had made in three years as a London surgeon. Also, a buccaneer's life was far more exciting than being a surgeon on land.

But Morgan's glory days were near their end. Spain and England were once again at peace. As Henry and his buccaneer friends enjoyed a meal at the King's Arms in late June, they heard drummers marching down High Street. They were followed by the town's crier announcing that England and Spain were now at peace and all letters of marque against the Spanish were null and void. Any buccaneers engaging in further hostilities against the Spanish, on land or at sea, would be severely punished.

One of the buccaneers, holding up his mug of rum, exclaimed, "Well boys, looks like we're out of business. We might as well get drunk."

24

SHIPWRECKED

At first, the government's prohibition against the buccaneers had little effect on Port Royal's economy. Morgan's buccaneers, still flush with loot from the Maracaibo raid, kept the taverns, brothels, and merchants busy. But by mid-July, many buccaneers turned to other pursuits as their pockets emptied. Some went to work on Jamaica's plantations; others simply drifted away. Governor Modyford even offered the Spanish, his erstwhile enemies, Morgan's fleet to attack French ships and settlements in the Caribbean. Unsurprisingly, the Spanish governor rejected the offer.

Henry had paid for his room in Spanish Town several months in advance and returned after it became clear there would be no new raids. He now had enough funds to live for several years without working if he chose. But, after a few weeks, he was bored.

In late July, while dining at the King's Arms in Port Royal, one of his shipmates from the *Dolphin* approached him with a proposition.

"My friend, Captain Allen, owns a fifteen-gun ship, the *Sea Eagle*; he missed out on the Maracaibo raid and needs money. He has an idea of how to make it. Three years ago, Modyford issued him a commission to attack French ships. Since Modyford had just offered the use of Morgan's fleet to the Spanish to attack French targets, Allen sees this as an invitation for him to go after French shipping. He has a crew of thirty men but still needs a ship's surgeon. Interested?"

Captain Allen welcomed Henry aboard the *Sea Eagle*. He had spoken to Captain Morris, captain of the *Dolphin* that Henry had been on at Maracaibo. Morris had lauded Henry's skill as a surgeon.

"The job is yours if you want it, but you would have to be ready to sail now."

Henry left Spanish Town with his surgeon's bag, a change of clothing, and most important, his savings.

On August first, the *Sea Eagle* hoisted anchor in Port Royal harbor, heading east on a thousand-mile voyage to Guadeloupe to hunt French merchant ships bringing goods to the sugar plantations there. As they passed Isla Vaca the weather was perfect—clear skies and a light breeze. But off the coast of Guadeloupe, the weather began to deteriorate. Sunshine changed to high gray clouds, and the breeze strengthened. By the end of the day, waves had grown to ten feet, and the wind was so strong that the crew lowered the sails, leaving only the foretopsail and jib. Within hours, waves broke across the deck, and crew members had to lash themselves to the mast to avoid being swept overboard. Heavy rain pelted the ship as the wind speed increased.

That evening, Captain Allen announced the storm was a hurricane; they would ride it out in the open sea rather than put in at Guadeloupe, where they could expect to be imprisoned or hung. By nightfall, it was all he could do to try to keep the ship pointed into the waves; further headway was impossible. Below deck, conditions were miserable. The bilge pumps could barely keep up with water pouring into the ship, and crew members were thrown about in the darkness. Several crew members who had been in hurricanes before said this was the worst they had ever seen.

Suddenly, there was a loud crash—the mast had broken and landed on the deck, killing the captain. Any chance of control was gone, and the *Sea Eagle*, now parallel to the waves, rolled onto its side. A wave crashed over it, shattering the hull. Most of the crew were killed instantly; a few were pitched into the seething waters to face a slower death. Henry was one of those few and the only one who could swim. But swimming in these conditions was impossible. As he tried to stay afloat, a timber struck him. He wrapped his arms around it and concentrated on drawing a breath in the few moments when he was not underwater.

Then the wind and rain stopped, and the sea grew calmer. Henry looked up and could see the stars overhead. It was utterly still, with no sounds from the hurricane or other crew members. Henry knew he was alone.

Twenty minutes later, the hurricane's eye had passed overhead, and the wind and waves were even stronger than before. All Henry could do was hang on to a piece of rigging attached to the floating timber. As the night dragged on, he became colder and weaker. He tried not to think about his chances of survival, which seemed remote. Then he felt nothing.

NEVIS

Fall 1669

Henry was waist-deep in the Appomattox River, holding on for dear life to the sturgeon he had caught; he couldn't understand why his brother Johnny was trying to drag him to shore. He tried to raise his arm to push him away but could not.

Then he heard a voice, "I believe he is dead."

He thought, *So this is what death feels like. It's not so bad.* When he felt his shoes being taken off, he finally lifted his head and opened one eye.

The voice turned into two young men who leaped back in surprise when Henry stirred. They untangled him from the rigging of a broken ship's spar and helped him sit up.

When he could finally speak, he asked, "Where am I? "

One of the men replied, "I'm Jim. This is Charlestown on the island of Nevis."

"What day is it?"

Jim replied, "Tuesday, the 17th of August. Did you come from the ship-wreck?"

It all came back to him; even though it had only been a single day since the hurricane struck, it felt like an eternity. "I must have. Where is the rest of the crew?"

"You're the only person I've seen. I'm sorry for trying to take your shoes, but I was sure you wouldn't be needing them."

When Henry had regained enough strength to stand, Jim helped him across the beach to a nearby tavern, where he introduced Henry to a man seated at a breakfast table. "I work at a nearby sugar plantation; this is its owner, Richard Gibbes."

Seeing Henry's condition, Gibbes ordered a meal for him as well. Henry told him all he remembered of the storm and the loss of his ship; Gibbes said that the island had been hit by a hurricane yesterday, pieces of ship wreckage had washed up on the beach, but there were no signs of survivors other than Henry.

Henry said, "I was a surgeon on that ship, the *Sea Eagle*, out of Port Royal with a commission to attack French ships." He wasn't sure how Gibbes would respond to this, knowing that planters often did not have kind feelings toward buccaneers.

But he need not have worried. Gibbes said, "My nephew was killed in an attack by the French several years ago; he was about your age. Why don't you come back to the plantation with us until you get on your feet?"

Henry readily agreed. The only thing he now had in the world was the clothes, now in tatters, on his back. His savings were at the bottom of the ocean. He was worse off than when he had been rescued from St. Augustine, where he at least had his surgeon's bag.

—∞—

The four rode in Gibbes's carriage to his plantation several miles from Charlestown. Gibbes gave Henry the use of a cottage where he promptly fell asleep.

He awoke to Jim once again prodding him. "You've slept for an entire day."

Ravenous, Henry devoured the breakfast laid out for him. For two days, he ate and slept.

Finally, when he felt himself again, Jim gave him a tour of the plantation. He said, "I started here four years ago, first in the cane fields and then in the mill. Last year, the foreman died of fever, and I got his job." Waving an arm across the fields, he said, "This is a small plantation; we only have fifty acres of cane. Our neighbor has over two hundred."

Seeing a group of slaves working in a cleared field, Henry asked what they were doing. Jim said, "They're replanting where rats devoured the cane shoots; we had to burn off the field to kill them. It's our slow time now; we do most planting in the late fall. Next spring, we'll harvest the cane."

Henry asked why the fields looked like a giant checkerboard.

Jim replied, "We plant in ten-acre lots over several months, so some cane is taller than others. This spreads out the harvesting time to keep the workers busy." He added, "It's hard and dirty work. The workers cut the cane with a long knife, often almost cutting an arm or leg in the process. Also, the cane rats will attack the workers if their nests are disturbed, so rat bites are common."

Jim showed Henry the mill where the workers processed the cane into sugar. Pointing to a machine in the center of the building, he told Henry, "This is a three-roller vertical mill. We use oxen to turn the rollers. The workers feed the cane stalks between the rollers, and the cane juice is collected in this trough."

He pointed to an ax leaning against the mill. "Feeding the roller mill is dangerous. It's easy to get a hand caught in the mill and be sucked in and crushed between the rollers. The ax is so someone can cut off the worker's arm to save him."

The boiling house was next to the mill, with four large copper kettles hanging over a furnace. Jim explained, "The juice from the roller mills is piped to the boiling house and into the cistern. A worker ladles the juice into the largest kettle. When it has boiled down, the syrup is ladled to the second, then the third and fourth as it boils down. When it becomes syrup, he moves it to the cooling cistern."

He continued, "After twelve hours, it becomes solid light brown sugar. We pack it into clay pots in the curing house. Molasses drains from holes in the pot bottoms; we sell it to the distillery in town to make rum. When the sugar is finally dry, it is packed in hogsheads to send to England. This brown sugar is called muscovado. In England, it is refined into white sugar."

Jim showed Henry round scars on his arms—"Ladling the sugar in the vats is almost as dangerous as feeding the roller mill. If you get any of the hot syrup on your skin, it sticks to your flesh and causes terrible burns."

Henry thought that perhaps Jim was trying to make it sound more dangerous than it was until he saw some slaves working outside the mill, their arms and legs covered with cane knife and burn scars.

When Henry commented that life on the plantation seemed hard, Jim replied, "For everyone except the owner. Most of the slaves live only a few years."

⚬⚬⚬

Henry had been a guest at the plantation for a week when Gibbes invited him to dinner, telling him there was something he wanted to discuss with him. Afterward, the two retired to the veranda, where a servant brought them brandies. Gibbes started the conversation by saying, "Jim is quite impressed with you. I could use someone like you with surgical skills to treat my workers, and I also need someone who can read and write to help me with the books and correspondence."

Henry pondered the offer. He couldn't go back to being a privateer ship surgeon in Morgan's fleet as Modyford had canceled his commissions. He was destitute and couldn't afford ship passage anywhere, even if there was somewhere he wanted to go. This sounded like an excellent chance for him to regroup. He asked Gibbes if he could think about it overnight.

The following day, he accepted Gibbes's offer. He quickly adapted to his new routine. The plantation had thirty slaves, two indentured servants, the overseer's and Gibbes's families, far fewer people than he had looked after in St. Augustine. It was the slow season for cane harvesting and processing. The slaves were mostly hoeing the fields for weeds, so there were few injuries. Unlike a buccaneer ship, there was no scurvy or French pox to treat. Soon, he was spending most of his time working with Gibbes managing the operation and finances of the plantation.

The plantation's finances were quite simple. The biggest expense was purchasing slaves to replace those who died or, in a few rare cases, became too elderly for the brutal work in the fields. Gibbes complained daily about this. "The Barbados planters get the first choice of the best slaves. Modyford and his friends in Jamaica get the next best, and I get the leftovers but have to pay more for them."

Gibbes said that the big planters on Nevis were squeezing out the small growers like himself. They could deal directly with the sugar buyers in England and could afford better equipment. The same thing was happening in Barbados and Jamaica as well. Soon there would be only a handful of large growers left. He told Henry he hoped to sell out to a bigger planter and retire.

—◦◦◦—

By the end of November, Henry's comfortable routine had become one of tedium. He treated the slaves for tropical diseases that he didn't understand and couldn't cure. On a buccaneer's ship, amputating a limb took his full attention and was a life-or-death event. Here, he knew that the field workers faced an early death from disease and overwork, and he could do nothing about it. He found the business side of the plantation almost as depressing. To make a profit, the plantation owner had to drive his slaves as hard and as cheaply as possible since he had little control over the price he got for sugar. Henry remembered, as a child, how much he had disliked Virginia Colony's tobacco plantations. Sugar plantations were even worse.

NEVIS

December 9, 1669

I n town to pick up a load of rat traps for the cane fields, Henry noticed a cluster of townspeople on the pier. Joining them, he could make out several sails on the horizon, drawing nearer to town. For days, Charlestown had been buzzing with rumors that the Spanish were planning an attack in retaliation for Morgan's recent raids. No ships were scheduled to arrive for several weeks—were these friend or foe?

Finally, a sharp-eyed onlooker cried out, "They're flying the red ensign." The relief was immediate—they were English civilian ships. Within the hour, the largest tied up at the town's pier, passengers crowded on its deck. Coming ashore, one of the sailors addressed the crowd: "I'm the master of the ship *Carolina*, just arrived from Barbados. Where may I find the harbormaster?" He was clearly unfamiliar with Charlestown, which was too small to have a harbormaster.

Henry thought the person looked familiar, and hearing the ship's name, *Carolina*, got his full attention. He finally recognized him—it was Henry Brayne from the Port Royal expedition more than three years ago.

"Brayne, what in the world are you doing here?"

Taken aback, Brayne finally replied, "Henry Woodward! I can't believe it's you! We thought you were dead. How do you come to be in Nevis?"

Henry replied, "That is a long story, but first, tell me why you are here."

Brayne said they had been caught in bad weather three days out of Barbados and forced to land for repairs. He was too busy for further conversation; they agreed to meet that evening to catch up on the last three years.

The two met at the Copper Kettle, Henry's favorite tavern. He thought Brayne seemed a different man since he had last seen him—more confident, harder. But, he thought, that could probably be said about himself as well. Henry told his tale of how he had been taken from Port Royal by the Spanish, held prisoner in St. Augustine, rescued by Robert Searle, served as a buccaneer ship's surgeon, and shipwrecked on Nevis four months earlier.

Stretching the truth slightly, he added, "I was saving enough money to be able to return to London and tell the lords proprietors what I had learned about Carolina, but I lost everything in the shipwreck."

Brayne then filled Henry in on his news since Port Royal. "The Great Plague and the Great Fire the following year distracted the proprietors from a settlement in Carolina. But Sandford wrote a report that promised Port Royal to be a new Eden. After reading it, they outfitted a second expedition to settle Port Royal."

Brayne continued, "They bought three ships, the *Carolina*, of which I am the master, the *Albemarle*, and the *Port Royal*, stocked with enough food, supplies, and weapons to be able to settle two hundred people at Port Royal."

Henry asked whether Sandford was involved with this expedition. To him, Sandford had seemed a pompous fool, primarily responsible for the Port Royal disaster.

Brayne replied, "He is no longer in the good graces of either the proprietors or Yeamans after Port Royal. He returned to Barbados, and no one has heard from him since."

Brayne continued, "We sailed from England and reached Barbados in October with a hundred passengers. There we were to recruit more settlers for Port Royal. But the curse that lay over us on the last expedition had not left us. In Bridgetown, a storm destroyed the *Albemarle* and damaged our other two ships. The lords proprietors loaned us a smaller ship, *The Three Brothers*, to replace it. Finally, we were able to depart in early December."

He added, "God is surely watching over you, Henry Woodward—after we left Barbados, another storm forced us to make landfall for repairs. We thought we were landing on Saint Kitts but were mistaken and landed here, only to find you."

Before they went their separate ways for the evening, Brayne said that Yeamans was on the *Carolina*, along with a friend of the proprietors, Joseph West, who had been appointed temporary governor and commander of the fleet. Brayne did not doubt that they would want Henry to join the settlers.

"Would you be interested? We will be sailing as soon as we have repaired the ships."

Henry replied he would let him know first thing in the morning.

—⁂—

Henry slept fitfully that night, pondering Brayne's offer. He could pick up where he had left off three years ago on the Sandford expedition. Then, he had little to offer the expedition; now, he knew more about the Indians and the Spanish in Carolina Colony than any other Englishman. There was little to keep him here—life on a sugar plantation had little appeal for him, and, with England and Spain at peace, he could not go back to being a buccaneer surgeon.

But he was unconvinced this expedition would be successful. Even though Sandford was no longer involved, one of the fleet's three ships had already been lost, and the other two damaged, akin to what happened to the Port Royal expedition. In his time with Henry Morgan's fleet, Henry had learned a lot about sailing, and Brayne's description of their progress so far gave him little confidence in its success. When he had been left at Port Royal three years earlier, Brayne had little experience in open sea sailing; now, he was the master of the *Carolina*, the flagship of the small fleet. Henry didn't know anything about the other two ship's masters or Joseph West, who had been appointed commander and acting governor. Whether or not a settlement at Port Royal would succeed was a risk he was willing to take; what concerned him was whether he would live long enough to get there. He and Brayne had more to discuss before he could decide.

—⁂—

The following day, Henry returned to Charlestown and met Brayne, overseeing repairs to the *Carolina*.

Henry told him, "Your offer to join the fleet is tempting, but after what happened to the Port Royal expedition, I'm reluctant. You've already lost one ship, and you're still a long way from Carolina."

Brayne replied that it had probably been a mistake to set out during hurricane season, but it was now behind them, and they expected good sailing the rest of the way. He added, "Captain West is an experienced officer who served in the Royal Navy in the West Indies. He will be a far better leader than Sandford was. Also, we have more people, support, and provisions than last time."

While he was not entirely convinced joining the expedition was wise, staying no longer seemed an option. He said, "I will be here tomorrow, ready to sail."

Back at the plantation, Henry told Gibbes that he had an unexpected opportunity to return home on a ship leaving the next day. Gibbes was not happy with the short notice and did not offer to settle Henry's wages. But that was a small price for escaping the monotony of plantation life.

He packed his few belongings, said goodbye to Jim, his only friend on the island, and left on foot for Charlestown.

Henry found Brayne onboard the *Carolina*, preparing for departure. He told Henry that, after learning of Henry's experience in Carolina and St. Augustine, West wanted him to sail on *The Three Brothers* rather than the *Carolina*. *The Three Brothers'* captain, John Baulk, while a skilled seaman, had no familiarity with the Carolina coastline. If the ships separated, Henry's knowledge would be invaluable for guiding them to Port Royal safely.

THE VOYAGE OF *THE THREE BROTHERS*

December–February 1669

The three ships left just before noon. A crowd was once again on the pier, this time to watch their departure—it was a slow time of the year on Nevis, and the fleet was the biggest event of the month.

The Three Brothers was overcrowded with thirty passengers, in addition to supplies. Apologizing for the conditions, Brayne told Henry that the *Albemarle,* which *The Three Brothers* had replaced, had been a larger ship, and they had also taken some passengers from the *Carolina.* "But the weather will be good this time of the year, and we should be in Port Royal in two weeks."

Only two days out, Brayne's promised smooth sailing came to an end when the passengers awoke to a strong northeast wind and ten-foot waves. Over the next few days, conditions worsened and blew the ships south despite their best efforts to maintain the course.

Captain Baulk said, "We've run into what we call the Christmas Winds. I've experienced them before, sailing from London. They can reach forty knots, making sailing almost impossible and may last for days."

Conditions were miserable on *The Three Brothers.* Waves broke across the deck, and it was pitching so severely that most passengers were seasick. The evening meal was cold as it was unsafe to light a fire. By morning, neither the wind nor the seas had abated, and *The Three Brothers* was now alone—there was no sign of the *Carolina* or *Port Royal.*

Baulk said to the passengers, "The wind has blown the ships off course in different directions. If we continue south at this rate, we'll end up in Caracas, not Carolina, but I know how to deal with the wind." He showed the crew how to build a sea anchor out of wood, sailcloth, and metal from the ship's stores. When it was deployed, the ship's speed slowed to a crawl.

Baulk commented to Henry, "We're not getting closer to Port Royal, but at least we are not getting farther away. If the other two ships don't know how to deal with the Christmas Winds, we're unlikely to see them any time soon."

Finally, the wind subsided, and *The Three Brothers* corrected course, making for Port Royal a week behind schedule. Despite the crowded conditions, the voyage was now pleasant as Brayne had promised it would be.

—⁂—

Henry had gotten to know some of the other passengers; one, in particular, caught his attention. She was striking—tall, although not as tall as Henry, with long brown hair and captivating brown eyes. When he finally got a chance to strike up a conversation with her, she smiled and said, "I wondered when you would introduce yourself."

Henry blushed, something he didn't know he could do. He introduced himself; she did the same. Her name was Margaret Tuder; she had left London on the *Carolina* with her guardian, Dr. William Scrivener. "My parents died in the plague, and I had no other family in London. My guardian told me he was emigrating to Carolina and asked if I wanted to accompany him. I just turned twenty-one and don't need his consent to go or to stay in London, but I do need his financial support."

Henry told her of losing his own family and that he also had decided to leave England for a new start. In the few brief moments he had spent with her, he felt a bond he had never experienced with anyone before. He learned her father had been a schoolteacher and her mother a tutor. Margaret was fluent in Latin, even more so than Henry, and had read all of the classics. He wished *The Three Brothers* was not so crowded—it was impossible to have any time alone with her. As one of the only single women on the ship, the other men pestered her continually. But with a quip and a smile, she made them realize she was not interested. Henry was pleased that she did not do so with him.

—⁂—

By the time they were nearing the Carolina coastline, Henry had told Margaret of his recent adventures, living with the Indians at Port Royal, his sixteen-month captivity in St. Augustine, his rescue, and his time as a surgeon on a buccaneer's ship. He felt foolish to be talking about himself so much, but she seemed genuinely interested in hearing it or did a convincing job of appearing to be.

A month after the fleet had sailed from Nevis, *The Three Brothers* was in sight of the coast. Captain Baulk had done a masterful job getting the ship back on course, and Henry had little trouble directing him to the mouth of Port Royal Sound. The ship dropped anchor in the exact spot where Henry had arrived with Sandford. They were the only ship in the sound; apparently, they had made better time than the *Carolina* and the *Port Royal*.

Baulk, Henry, and several of the crew went ashore to scout. There was no sign of the Escamacu town where Henry had lived; even the wooden cross left by the Spanish was gone. Henry called out, knowing if there were any Indians within earshot, they would come to investigate. Indeed, two men soon appeared, carrying bows and arrows. They spoke the same language as the Escamacu, and Henry said to them, "I am Henry Woodward; I lived here with the Escamacu three years ago. We were traveling with two other ships and were to meet them here. Have you seen them?"

They had not. They told Henry they were Edisto, from the next town to the north, and confirmed the Escamacu had moved to St. Catherine's several years earlier. After that, the Westo Indians burned the town. It had been deserted since then.

⎯⎯ⱺⱺⱺ⎯⎯

Food and supplies on *The Three Brothers* were low; most had been lost on the *Albemarle* when it sank in Barbados. Baulk calculated that they had about a week's supply of food left. If the other two ships had not arrived by then, they would have to reprovision, probably in Virginia Colony, 400 miles to the north. Henry said that the last he knew, his grandfather was living at the mouth of the Chowan River in Albemarle Sound, a hundred miles closer than Virginia Colony. He was well-connected and should be able to help them.

The week passed slowly, with lookouts posted for the two missing ships. Henry spent time with Margaret, away from the crush of passengers he had endured on *The Three Brothers*. It felt strange, spending time with her in the very spot where he had lived with Bella, the cassique's niece, three years ago. He had not mentioned her to Margaret and decided it would be best not to.

Finally, Baulk told the settlers they could not wait any longer for the other ships. Leaving the settlers with Henry as a guide, he set sail for Albemarle Sound, Henry making sure they steered clear of the treacherous coastline that had almost undone the Sandford expedition.

Henry left Baulk at the river's mouth and headed to his grandfather's house, not knowing what kind of reception to expect after four years gone. Thomas had wanted him to settle in Virginia and become a responsible citizen. He doubted if his grandfather would approve of how he had spent the last few years.

It took his grandparents a few moments to recognize him, but they greeted him warmly. When Thomas asked how the Port Royal settlement was faring, Henry realized that the last time they had spoken was when he left in 1665 to join the Port Royal expedition. It seemed a lifetime ago. Making no mention of buccaneers, he told them of his adventures since then. He said that they now had over a hundred people to establish the Port Royal settlement, and he was here for food and supplies. He would bring Captain Baulk to the house the next day to discuss where they might get them. When he made his way back to *The Three Brothers* the next day, he found Baulk had already bought food and supplies. Henry recalled what a disaster it had been trying to do the same thing with Sandford.

Perhaps this time, the expedition would succeed.

ST. CATHERINE'S

Port Royal was just as they had left it two weeks before. *The Three Brothers* passengers were still there, hungry and unhappy, wondering why they had ever left England. There was no sign of the other two ships.

Captain Baulk called a meeting of the passengers and crew to discuss their options—"The other two ships must have been blown far off course. But even so, they should be here by now. We can either stay and start our settlement without them or return to Barbados."

Maurice Mathews, one of the passengers, said, "The *Carolina* has most of the provisions and supplies we need to settle. Also, John Yeamans is the only one with authority to decide if we settle here; he was on the *Carolina*. I believe we have no choice but to return to Barbados."

Lacking an official leader, the settlers put it to a vote whether to stay or leave. The majority voted to leave.

So, once again, *The Three Brothers* weighed anchor and left Port Royal, arriving in Barbados in early March after an uneventful voyage. Baulk had predicted the *Carolina* and *Port Royal* would already be in Bridgetown. They were not, but John Yeamans was and asked Baulk to meet with him.

Yeamans explained, "Shortly after we left Barbados, we were blown off course and separated from the other two ships. Finally, the wind stopped, and we continued toward Port Royal. But we were low on food and water, so we stopped in Bermuda to reprovision. I had to return to Barbados for important business; before I left, I appointed William Sayle as governor of Carolina in my stead with instructions to proceed to Port Royal. I have seen no sign of the third ship since we first left Barbados."

When Henry heard about Yeamans leaving the expedition in Bermuda, he thought, *That is what he did on the first expedition—when we ran into difficulties, he put Sandford in charge and returned to Barbados. Whoever and wherever Sayle is now, I hope he's more competent than Sandford was.*

Expecting that the other ships would be at Port Royal, Yeamans instructed Baulk to turn around and go back one more time.

It was almost a month before they were ready to depart; Henry finally had time alone with Margaret. Most of the passengers on *The Three Brothers* who could afford it took rooms in Bridgetown. Dr. Scrivener, Margaret's guardian, found rooms for himself and Margaret.

Margaret asked him, "Why are you staying on the ship? It's awful."

Henry, embarrassed, told her, "All of my money is at the bottom of the sea at Nevis; I don't have a penny."

"Henry, why didn't you say so? I'm not wealthy, but I inherited a comfortable sum from my parents. I insist that I loan you some of it."

Henry said, "I can't possibly. You should not have to take on the burden of my bad luck."

Margaret replied, "You haven't yet asked me, but we both know you and I will marry after we reach Port Royal. I'm going to be quite angry with you if we can't share some of this money now."

Henry was taken aback—Margaret always seemed to be one step ahead of him. He had been looking for a chance to propose to her, but there was no privacy on *The Three Brothers*. All he could say was, "Yes, I intend to propose to you, and no, I don't want you to be angry."

Henry dreamed of them sharing a room in Bridgetown, but Margaret made it clear that would not happen until after they were married; they spent their days together but nights apart.

After thoroughly exploring the town, Henry suggested one of his favorite activities—touring the countryside. He asked Margaret, "Do you know how to ride horseback?"

"I grew up in London. The only horses I've ever been near were pulling carriages."

But she was a quick learner, and they spent most of the month riding in the Barbados countryside. Margaret found it charming, but it reminded Henry of Nevis—endless cane fields. An old-timer told them that the island was covered with forests not long ago, cleared to plant cane and fire the boilers to make sugar.

Margaret was eager to talk about their future in Port Royal; Henry found there was not much he could tell her. "Port Royal is entirely swamp, forest, or river. There are some small Indian towns; the nearest English are in Virginia Colony, hundreds of miles to the north. I don't know how I will make a living—I served as a ship's surgeon, and before that, the surgeon for St. Augustine. But I don't want to go back to that unless there is no other choice. Perhaps I can become an Indian trader."

Margaret asked, "What is an Indian trader?"

"Mostly, they trade English goods such as cloth, beads, and tools for deerskins and other animal furs. The skins and furs are sent to London to be sold."

Margaret said, "It sounds like a wonderful adventure. I can't wait to get there."

⎯⎯⎯⎯⎯⎯

After *The Three Brothers* left Barbados, following Yeamans' instructions, it stopped in Bermuda on its way to Port Royal to see if there was any news about the two other ships.

There was; Baulk told Henry what he had learned: "After Yeamans left Bermuda, several bedraggled souls arrived on a ship cobbled together from bits and pieces. They were the survivors from the *Port Royal*, which had also been blown off course and shipwrecked in the Bahamas. They finally reached Barbados and reunited with the *Carolina*. After finding a replacement for the *Port Royal*, the two ships left for Port Royal in late February."

The Three Brothers also headed back to Port Royal, for the second time. The winds were against them, and the journey went slowly. By the time they saw the Carolina coastline, food and water were low.

Captain Baulk told the passengers, "I expect we will find the other two ships at Port Royal, but we cannot count on them having enough provisions even for themselves, let alone the thirty of us. I suggest that we return to Chowan Creek and reprovision before going to Port Royal."

Henry thought *That would mean seeing my grandfather yet again; I'd rather not.* Then he thought of an alternative and told Baulk, "I have an idea that will save us days of difficult sailing to Chowan Creek. The Escamacu Indians I lived among at Port Royal have since moved to a place not too far from here called St. Catherine's. They are my friends and would be eager to trade with us for provisions."

The Three Brothers anchored at St. Catherine's the next day. Several canoes approached the ship and called out to them.

105

Still fluent in Escamacu, Henry replied, "Hello, I am Henry Woodward and used to live with you at Port Royal. We are returning there and wish to trade with you for provisions."

Several of the Indians remembered Henry. He asked about Dehhewamis, Bella; she had married and moved to another town. Wommony, Bella's cousin and his friend, was still there.

On May 17th, a man, part Indian, part Spanish, appeared with a gift for Captain Baulk, saying, "We have pork to trade with you for English goods."

Baulk, having learned that the provisions from the Escamacu would be mostly fish and vegetables, jumped at the chance of real meat. The next morning, he, along with one of the passengers, John Rivers, and four others, went ashore to trade for the promised pork, saying they would be back on the next tide. Two servants also went to cut firewood.

Margaret said to Henry, "I'm going to go with them and wash some laundry. Do you want to go with me?

Henry replied, "I'm meeting Wommony today, so I will stay and wait for him."

Seeing they had a moment to themselves, Margaret planted a kiss on an unsuspecting Henry. "Well, I'll see you later then."

By late afternoon none of them had returned.

Henry was back before sunset. Immediately seeing that something was wrong, he asked Maurice Mathews, "What happened?"

"The Spanish took Baulk and others, including Margaret. We've had no word from them since they left this morning."

Hearing this, Henry called back Wommony's canoe, still within earshot. They joined Henry in a search until it was pitch black, without success.

Fearing the worst, *The Three Brothers* posted a watch that night; there was still no sign of them by early morning. Henry, standing every watch, did not sleep.

At ten in the morning, to the sound of a drum, four Spanish soldiers armed with muskets appeared on the shore. Waving a white flag, one of them announced, "We are holding your captain prisoner. We demand your surrender."

Assuming command in Baulk's absence, Maurice Mathews answered, "Return our people, and we will depart in peace."

The soldiers responded with a volley of musket shots, arrows from their Guale allies, and a command, "You must send people ashore to meet with us."

Instead, Mathews sent a boy who swam to shore with a letter, asking for free passage to leave.

Their answer came half an hour later in the form of another demand that the ship come ashore and surrender all passengers. Mathews stalled, telling them that there was no wind for them to sail to shore. The reply was another volley of gunshots. The *Three Brother's* muskets were distributed to the passengers who found themselves in a pitched battle with the soldiers.

Finally, taking advantage of a timely breeze, *The Three Brothers* sailed beyond the reach of the Spanish guns and anchored. The ship's sails were riddled with bullet holes, but nobody had been injured.

The heavily armed soldiers were still on the shore the following morning; any attempt to rescue the captives would be futile. Finally, admitting defeat, *The Three Brothers* raised anchor. The other passengers had to restrain Henry from jumping overboard and swimming to shore.

When Henry suggested that they stop at St. Catherine's for supplies, he had not known that the Spanish now regularly patrolled the Guale coast, awaiting Searle's promised return. *The Three Brothers* had the misfortune to be discovered by one of these patrols, backed by Guale Indians loyal to the Spanish.

As they sailed toward Port Royal the following day, four men in a canoe approached the ship and identified themselves as Edisto.

Henry introduced himself and said, "We are going to Port Royal to meet up with two other English ships there. Have you seen them?"

One of them said, "There are no ships at Port Royal. I will have Shadoo come to your ship and tell you more."

Henry recognized Shadoo from his earlier visit to Edisto when he had asked him directions for Port Royal; now, he was doing the same thing again four years later.

If Shadoo thought this odd, he said nothing about it. "The two English ships you are looking for were at Port Royal two months earlier but are now at Kiawah. It's only a few hours north of Port Royal. I can take you there tomorrow."

Henry asked, "Do you know anything about the Spanish seizing some of our people at St. Catherine's?"

Shadoo replied, "We heard from our friends that the Spanish and Guale Indians attacked an English ship there, but I don't know anything more than that."

29

ALBEMARLE POINT

Carolina Colony, May 1670

With Shadoo guiding the way, *The Three Brothers* picked its way north along the coast to the Kiawah River, a half-day journey.

A shallop flying the English flag was anchored in the river's mouth. Pulling alongside, Mathews spoke with its captain, who said it was the replacement for the *Port Royal*, shipwrecked in the Bahamas. The shallop guided *The Three Brothers* two miles up the river, where the *Carolina* was moored along the bank of a smaller creek.

As Henry came ashore, Brayne called out, just as he had done on Nevis five months earlier—"Henry Woodward! I can't believe it's you! We thought you were dead."

Henry replied, "Brayne, we've spent months looking for you. Where in the hell have you been?"

Taken aback, Brayne replied, "We've been here since early April and thought you must have been lost at sea."

"But why are you here instead of Port Royal?"

Brayne replied, "That wasn't my choice; you need to ask William Sayle, the new governor."

"What happened to Yeamans?"

"He left us in Bermuda and returned to Barbados. He appointed Sayle as his replacement when he left."

Changing the subject, Henry said, "We lost ten of our people to the Spanish; we need to rescue them."

Brayne replied, "I don't know how we can. Since the Searle raid, the Spanish are guarding the coast. You need to talk to Sayle about it."

Brayne arranged a meeting with the governor for the next day. Henry had heard that Sayle was elderly; that was an understatement. He looked to be at least eighty and in poor health. Henry told him what had happened at St. Catherine's.

Sayle replied, "Yes, I know about it. We're working on a plan to get them back. For now, we need to be patient."

He added, "I understand you are upset that we did not settle at Port Royal. We spent several days there and met with the Kiawah cassique. He told us that the Spanish have been expecting us at Port Royal ever since Searle's raid. It is a better port but too dangerous—Spanish ships could anchor in the middle of the river, beyond the reach of our small cannons, and destroy it. So, we chose to settle here at Albemarle Point, which is better protected."

Henry could not argue with Sayle's observation, especially since he knew he was in part responsible for it. Pierre Piques had convinced Searle to raid St. Augustine to rescue him, in addition to looting the town; the Spanish had been humiliated and have long memories.

Not knowing what else to say, he asked Sayle, "Why are you calling it Albemarle Point?"

"We named it after George Monck, the first Duke of Albemarle. He is one of the lords proprietors."

❧❧❧

The new settlement was a sorry sight—a clearing of some ten acres hidden away on a small peninsula surrounded by marshland. The settlers had erected crude palm-thatched huts on small plots and were busily clearing trees, planting gardens, and building a palisade around the settlement.

Henry asked Brayne, "How were the plots of land decided?"

Brayne replied, "The settlers who arrived on the *Carolina* and the shallop were each given a plot. We didn't set aside plots for you and the others on *The Three Brothers* because we thought you had perished. But don't forget that we each get 150 acres outside of the settlement."

Henry was annoyed for a moment before deciding he wouldn't want to be crowded inside the palisade walls with a hundred other settlers. He would find somewhere else to live for now.

30

SILVER AND PEARLS

Carolina Colony, June 1670

Henry had been at Albemarle Point for a week. He blamed himself for the loss of Margaret and the others at St. Catherine's and could think of no way to rescue her. And he was almost completely cut off from the other settlers. With four years of experience under his belt, he was the only person at Albemarle Point with knowledge about the Indians, the Spanish, what crops could be grown here—all information critical to the colony's survival. But the settlers had chosen the colony's location without him, and some of them blamed him for the disaster at St. Catherine's. Finally, Henry Brayne, the only person he counted as a friend here, had just sailed for Virginia to get supplies, not expected to return for weeks.

This was not the life he envisioned when he left Nevis on *The Three Brothers* six months before. He had expected to be someone important in the settlement; instead, he was alone, penniless, and without a purpose.

There was work to be done—cutting trees, preparing lumber, building a meeting house, and completing the palisade walls. Henry did not feel inclined to participate and began spending much of his time at the nearby Kiawah town. But he found he was not an honored guest there as he had once been in Escamacu town in Port Royal; the townspeople, sensing he had no power in Albemarle Point, were pleasant enough but distant.

He decided to start exploring further away from the settlement and asked the Kiawah cassique about other tribes in the area.

The cassique told him, "The Westo Indians to the northwest are cannibals, to be avoided. The Guale are peaceful farmers and fishermen and are friends of the Spanish. Their lands are between Port Royal and St. Augustine. There are other small towns along the coast from Port Royal to Cape Fear, most of them are related to us, and we speak the same language."

Henry asked, "What about the Indians who live to the north?"

The cassique replied, "We seldom travel there, but four days away are tribes who speak different languages than we do. Some of their towns are large, and one is said to have buildings covered in pearls and silver."

This was all Henry needed to hear; he was going exploring for silver and pearls. He said, "I would like to visit them. Could I take some of your men as guides?"

"None of us know these lands well enough to guide you, but our Sewee neighbors do. You should ask them."

Returning to Albemarle Point, Henry told Governor Sayle he wanted to explore the lands to the north of the settlement and asked for some trade cloth and beads to make trade agreements with the tribes there.

Sayle reluctantly agreed—"I'm unhappy with what happened at St. Catherine's. Please be careful not to make that kind of mistake again."

Henry replied, "The town I am visiting is far from St. Augustine, and the Spanish have no presence there. If Albemarle Point is to succeed, we will need to have good relations with our Indian neighbors so they will be our allies against the Spanish. I am the only one with the experience to make trade agreements with them."

The next day, he paid a visit to the Sewee cassique. "I am going to travel to a town several days to the north, said to have pearls and silver. I heard you are familiar with those lands. Could you provide me with a guide?"

The cassique introduced Henry to two men, one an interpreter. They knew the town Henry spoke of—it was the home of the Cofitachequi, on the Indian Trading Path. Henry recalled the Trading Path from his time at Fort Henry—it started at the Fort and ended at the Westo's town, far to the south.

⁓

Henry and his guides set out north on the Santee River path in late May. He found it difficult to match his guides' pace, even though they carried all the supplies and trading goods. The journey was exactly what Henry needed to forget his troubles. Set in pristine wilderness, live oaks festooned with Spanish moss bordered the riverbanks; the magnolias were in full bloom with their magnificent white flowers as big as his hand. When they finally stopped, Henry spent his most restful night since his buccaneer days on the beaches of

Isla Vaca. The sounds of the frogs lulled him to sleep; he dreamt of Margaret and himself living in a small cabin, far from Albemarle Point.

⁓⁓⁓

The following day, they were visited by Indians who introduced themselves as Santee. Henry's guides told them he was from an English settlement near their town and exploring the countryside. At the Santee's town, an elderly man introduced himself as the chief. He told Henry he had never met an Englishman before and insisted they spend the night, giving Henry their best lodge. In turn, Henry gave him beads and cloth and said he could trade iron tools for deerskins and furs. The chief readily agreed although Henry knew the town was not large enough to be an important trading partner.

The next day, he gave Henry a tour of his town. Henry pointed to several small buildings on stilts, completely sealed with clay. The chief responded to his inquiry by scraping away some of the clay and opening a small door—the building was filled with corn. The chief took out an ear and mimicked a rat chewing on it; Henry tucked away the idea of rodent-proof storage, to take back to Albemarle Point, which was already having a problem with rats.

Henry then asked about the earthen mounds scattered around the town, the largest at least twenty feet tall. The chief explained that these were ceremonial burial mounds. The largest mound was reserved for the leaders; this was where he would be buried someday. Smaller mounds were for warriors and other important persons.

Bidding farewell, Henry and his guides continued along the Santee River. As word of their arrival spread, they were greeted by more and more Indians from small towns along the river—the Congaree, Wateree, and Waxhaw.

In the Wateree's town, Henry spent an uncomfortable night in a dark, smoky dwelling; the following morning he found he was covered with flea bites and missing some of his trade goods.

The next town was the home of the Waxhaw. Their dwellings were spacious, light, and clean. They were the tallest Indians Henry had ever seen, but their most remarkable feature was their flat foreheads. Their chief explained to Henry that the infant children were bound to a board that was loosened as the child grew. The result was that the Waxhaw had tall, straight bodies. As a result of their flat foreheads, their eyes were widely spaced, which they believed gave their hunters better eyesight.

That evening Henry and his guides feasted on barbecued meats, stewed peaches, and corn—the best meal Henry had eaten since arriving at Albemarle Point.

As they continued north, in each town, their chief insisted they spend the night, and often the next day as well. Almost two weeks had passed, and he had not reached Cofitachequi town.

Soon the landscape began to change—swamps giving way to low hills and valleys with red soil and scattered rocks. One day they were stopped by several warriors—tall, almost Henry's height, and armed with bows. Taking away the guides' bows and Henry's musket, the Indians led them several miles to a large town. This was the fabled city of the Cofitachequi.

The men escorted Henry to the chief's dwelling, who summoned an interpreter after trying to communicate with them.

Henry said to him, "My people have settled near the Kiawah town and wish to trade with your town. We can supply you with iron goods, beads, and cloth in trade for deerskins and furs. I have heard you also have pearls and precious metals; we could trade for them as well."

He had hoped to reach a trade agreement, spend the night dining and conversing with the chief, and head back to Albemarle Point. But, while the chief gave him a warm welcome, he would not discuss trade. Instead, he took Henry on a tour of the town, telling him how powerful the Cofitachequi were—the men of his tribe were superb warriors; even the Westo were afraid of them.

The town's lodge was magnificent. Built next to a large earthen mound, it was adorned with thousands of pearls and metal pendants.

Henry had heard the pendants were made of silver but, he could see that they were only copper. He asked the chief about the decorations on the building.

"We gathered pearls from our rivers for many years. The copper comes from mountains far to the north."

When Henry asked if they had more pearls, he found he had touched on a sensitive topic.

"We once had many baskets of pearls and decorated our homes with them. But long ago, Spanish soldiers on horses and wearing armor raided our town, stole the pearls, and took away our empress as their prisoner. Their leader called himself de Soto. They returned several times, attacking our people and taking more pearls. They have not been back in my lifetime."

The chief continued, "We were once an even larger empire but suffered many deaths from illness after the Spanish had arrived. We are now only a few thousand, although the smaller towns to the south are still subservient to us."

Henry was well-treated as a guest for the next two days. However, he could not get the chief to discuss a trade agreement; he was a more sophisticated negotiator than those in the smaller towns he had passed through. He did learn that the Cofitachequi tribe had skilled hunters and traded deerskins and furs with the Indian tribes along the coast for salt, fish, and oysters and that they could still harvest pearls from their rivers if they wished. Henry did not doubt that they would welcome the chance to trade for English goods if the chief would only agree.

Finally, understanding that the chief knew he was not an important person and wanted to meet with the settlement's leaders, Henry invited him to visit Albemarle Point. He suggested that the chief bring deerskins and furs to trade.

Having read a copy of the Fundamental Constitutions of Carolina on the journey from Nevis, Henry knew that the lords proprietors reserved for themselves all pearls, ambergris, and precious stones found in Carolina. He decided that he would keep the information about pearls to himself for now and find a way to return to England to tell the lords proprietors directly, rather than informing Sayle about them.

As Henry was preparing to leave for Albemarle Point, the chief told him he had just learned that morning from an Indian passing through their town that an explorer named John Lederer had recently been at the Indian town of Occaneechi, about two hundred miles east on the Indian Trading Path. He had been sent by Abraham Wood at Fort Henry in Virginia Colony to explore the mountains. While Lederer was there, the Occaneechi killed five Westo Indians who were visiting the town. The chief said that the Westo were bad people and did not blame the Occaneechi for their deaths.

Giving the rest of the trade goods to the chief in return for his promise to visit Albemarle Point in the near future, Henry departed in good spirits. At last, his luck had changed—he would get the credit for bringing an important trading partner to Albemarle Point, and he would personally tell the lords proprietors about the Cofitachequi pearls.

HENRY WOODWARD, INDIAN TRADER

Albemarle Point, June 1670

Back from Cofitachequi town by the end of June, Henry found that the *Carolina* had not yet returned from Virginia with provisions for the colony. But there was even more disturbing news—while he was gone, Governor Sayle had sent *The Three Brothers* back to St. Catherine's to seek the release of the settlers taken by the Spanish.

Maurice Mathews told him what had happened. "We met with the Spanish friar there and asked him to return our people. He told us they had been taken to St. Augustine, where they were guests, not prisoners. When we asked what that meant, he said they were not being held in cells and were free to walk around but could not leave. Then he refused to let two of our men return to the ship, saying that he needed to communicate with St. Augustine first. After three days, we heard that three ships were sailing from St. Augustine to seize our ship. We had no choice but to return to Albemarle Point, leaving yet two more of our men in the hands of the Spanish."

Henry knew what the Spanish meant when they said they were guests, not prisoners, in St. Augustine. He had been their "guest" for almost a year and a half before escaping.

Henry was beside himself. Barely able to contain his temper, he demanded of Governor Sayle if he had any further plans for rescuing Margaret and the others.

Sayle told him, "One of the people taken prisoner when you were there was Mr. Rivers, a relation of Anthony Ashley Cooper. As you know, he is the most important of the Carolina lords proprietors. I will ask him to use his influence

115

with the crown to arrange for their release directly with the Spanish government, bypassing the St. Augustine governor."

Henry said, "That will take at least six months, if not longer."

Henry realized he had lost the only person in the world he cared for. Knowing it was largely his fault made it feel worse. Losing his family to the plague in England had been devastating but beyond his control. Losing Margaret was something he could never forgive himself for.

❧

Henry had noticed that work on the settlement had slowed almost to a standstill. Rather than clearing trees and building cabins, the indentured servants spent most of the day resting in the shade. He asked Governor Sayle about it.

He replied, "We're running out of provisions; rations have been reduced to one pint of peas a day. The servants can't work with that little food. The *Carolina* was to bring provisions from Virginia, but it's long overdue. We've planted potatoes, corn, and squash, but they will not be ready to harvest for months."

Henry responded, "There are enough fish, oysters, deer, and turkeys to feed everyone. Why is there no food?"

Sayle answered, "Most of the settlers are from English cities or Barbados sugar plantations; few of them know how to hunt or fish."

From his childhood in Virginia, Henry remembered stories of the early settlers in Jamestown starving because they didn't know how to feed themselves. The settlers at Albemarle Point were in a similar predicament. Unless the *Carolina* showed up soon, they would need to trade with the Kiawah for food. Henry knew he was the only one that could arrange this—he spoke their language, had a good relationship with them, and knew how to trade. This would also be a golden opportunity to establish his position in the colony better.

He said to Governor Sayle, "I believe I can make a trade agreement with the Kiawah for enough food until the *Carolina* returns. They are farmers and fishermen; we have the kinds of trade goods they want—hoes, hatchets, knives, and beads."

Two days later, with permission to make a trade agreement, Henry met with the Kiawah cassique and laid out his proposal. He knew that the Kiawah had never traded with Europeans before and that they might even think him foolish to offer valuable iron tools for something they could easily grow or catch. So, he made what seemed to him a one-sided offer, asking for enough corn, squash, and turkey to feed all of the settlers for the next month. In return, he promised the cassique three axes, two hoes, five knives, and ten handfuls of glass beads. The cassique agreed without hesitation.

Henry asked him, "How will you have enough food for your people if you trade for this much food?"

The cassique replied, "We will use some of the corn and squash from our stores and trade with our neighbors for the rest."

The settlement's food shortage was now behind them. Henry even got Governor Sayle's approval to make a similar agreement for the following year. By the beginning of August, he had agreed with the Kiawah cassique to deliver three tons of corn over the coming twelve months.

With their bellies now full, the settlers quickly forgot about the St. Catherine's disaster, and Henry was, at least for the moment, the most famous person in Albemarle Point. Several of the townspeople even began calling him "Dr. Woodward."

32

THE VERY SHORT BATTLE OF ALBEMARLE POINT

August 1670

Henry was in Kiawah town, meeting with the cassique to settle up the month's trading when they were interrupted by two Indian scouts from St. Helena. The cassique excused himself, saying he needed to talk to them.

When he returned, he told Henry, "The scouts said there are 200 Spanish soldiers and 300 Guale Indians traveling toward Kiawah from St. Augustine. They also heard that three Spanish ships were coming as well. The captain of the Spanish soldiers said they were going to attack the English settlement here and destroy any Indian towns that supported them."

Henry rushed back to the settlement and told Governor Sayle of the impending invasion. He told Sayle, "I am no soldier but, from my time in St. Augustine and serving on a buccaneer ship attacking Spanish targets, I'm familiar with their tactics. I can help plan a strategy for the settlement's defense."

Despite his advanced age and poor health, Sayle rose to the occasion, putting Joseph West, one of the only settlers with actual military experience, in charge of organizing an impromptu militia. Based on the Kiawah scout's report, it would be several days before the Spanish could launch an attack. The first order of business was to strengthen the settlement's defenses. Fortunately, the settlers chose the site because it was defensible, not because it was an ideal location for commerce. A marsh surrounded two sides of the settlement, and another side opened onto a creek. The soldiers and their Guale allies would have to attack across the narrow neck that separated the town from the rest of the land.

West ordered the completion of a wooden palisade across the neck—trees were felled, trimmed, and dropped into postholes, creating a ten-foot-high wall. Cannons were placed along the wall; the rest of the cannons pointed at the Ashley River. West, who had been a captain on an English warship, doubted these small guns were a match for the firepower of three Spanish ships, but this was all the settlement could muster. The late August weather was brutally hot and humid, and the men fortifying the defenses were suffering, not used to hard labor in such weather. Henry, dusting off his medical skills, was kept busy treating them for heat exhaustion.

Kiawah scouts made daily reports of the enemy's progress. The Spanish soldiers and their Guale allies were presently several miles from the settlement, poised for attack; their ships were anchored offshore from the Ashley River, well out of the reach of the settlement's cannons.

West was confident that they could repel any attack by land if the enemy was only armed with muskets and bows and arrows; the scouts had seen no cannons in the Spanish encampment. The biggest threat would be from the Spanish ships anchoring within cannon range and bombarding the settlement. If the settlers fled into the woods, they would be massacred by the waiting soldiers and their Guale allies.

⁓∿⁓

Long overdue, the *Carolina* was approaching the mouth of the Ashley River, three months since its departure for Virginia to bring back provisions for the settlement. Brayne had spent two of those months in Virginia Colony, visiting old friends and getting married. He had spent the last few days thinking of excuses to explain his prolonged absence.

Waiting for the rising tide, he saw a group of Indians gathered on the riverbank. Curious, he launched a boat to investigate. His Kiawah guide told him they were Guale, not Kiawah, and were not friends. As Brayne and his guide came ashore, one of them approached. The guide motioned for him to lay down his weapons before coming closer. Appearing to do so, he suddenly pointed his bow and arrow at the guide but fled when Brayne aimed his musket at him.

Another began waving a white flag, motioning for Brayne to approach. Brayne recalled Maurice Mathews telling him this was what had occurred at St. Catherine's when the Spanish and their Guale allies captured Captain Baulk and the others from *The Three Brothers*. He hastened back to the *Carolina* and weighed anchor. The Spanish soldiers opened fire as they sailed away, but the ship was out of musket range.

Arriving at the settlement, Brayne rushed ashore to warn the colonists, only to find they were already on full alert. The *Carolina's* three-month absence momentarily forgotten, West called a meeting to decide how the ship could be used to bolster the settlement's defense.

Brayne said, "Navigating the creek from the Ashley River to the settlement is difficult. I expect the Spanish ships will anchor in the river instead."

Henry added, "When I was in St. Augustine, they had only lightly armed small ships. If these are the same ships, they would be too far away to inflict serious damage."

West said, "If they launch small boats from their ships to attempt a landing, they will be easy targets for our guns and cannons. Mr. Brayne, please anchor the *Carolina* in the creek and aim its cannon out toward the river."

Now there was nothing to do but wait for the Spanish to attack. Thinking back to his buccaneer days, Henry asked himself what Henry Morgan, the master of illusion, would have done in this situation. He finally came up with a plan.

He said to West, "Let's not wait for the Spanish to attack. Instead, let's launch an illusory attack on the soldiers and Guale Indians massed across the clearing in the forest. Aim the cannons on the palisade wall into the forest and load them with grapeshot; aim the *Carolina's* cannons into the woods. Then, at dawn, fire all of them for half an hour. The noise will panic the Guale, who have no experience with guns, let alone cannons. They will most likely flee, leaving the Spanish soldiers alone. They would have to cross the open field without the Guale as a shield. Our weapons would cut them to ribbons before they reached the palisade wall. Rather than attacking, I expect they will probably retreat and return to St. Augustine."

West added, "Then we would only have the three Spanish ships to deal with. If they stay anchored in the river, they are little threat to us. Also, they will soon be running low on food and supplies, and it will be them, not us, who will be going hungry."

Governor Sayle agreed that there was little to lose, other than some ammunition, by adopting Henry's plan. The following day, at first light, the settlement's cannon began firing. The noise of the cannon fire and the sound of grapeshot tearing through the forest was terrifying.

After half an hour, they ceased firing and waited for word from the Kiawah scouts who had been watching the enemy massed in the woods. Henry's idea worked—the scouts said the Guale Indians had fled even before the cannon fire had ended. Shortly after that, the Spanish soldiers had packed up and began to retreat toward home.

After two days, the Spanish ships weighed anchor and sailed for home, having made no attempt to attack the settlement. The short battle of Albemarle Point was over before it began.

33

HENRY AND LORD ANTHONY ASHLEY COOPER

1670

Henry had selected his 150 acres of land awarded to him but could not afford to pay for even one indentured servant and had no desire to clear trees on his own. Still spending most of his time in Kiawah town, he now turned his attention to how to let the lords proprietors in England learn about the Cofitachequi's pearls. One of the few people he trusted in Albemarle Point was John Jones, a Barbadian and John Yeamans' agent who had been on *The Three Brothers*. John was the only settler who had helped Henry, who had arrived at Albemarle Point utterly destitute.

Henry told him about the Cofitachequi and that he had made an important discovery that he could only reveal to the lords proprietors, but he did not feel it proper to write to them directly.

John said, "I think you should write to John Yeamans about your visit to the Cofitachequi, but not mention your discovery. You should also tell him how you helped save the settlement from starvation. I will also write Yeamans, praising your accomplishments here."

He took John's advice, writing to Yeamans and not mentioning pearls.

Albemarle Point in Kiawah, September 10, 1670
The Right Honorable Sir John Yeamans Knight Baron in Barbados
Honorable Sir,
Please excuse my tardiness in not giving you an earlier account of our proceedings and transactions since you have departed for Barbados. It has been my fortune to have gone on a 'discovery of the Cofitachequi and the

fruitful province where their Emperor resides. I have discovered a country so delicious, pleasant, and fruitful, were it cultivated doubtless it would prove to be a second paradise. It is northwest from us fourteen days travel in the Indian manner of marching. While there, I contracted a league with their Emperor, as well as with all of the petty chiefs between them and us. A few weeks after my return, the ship Carolina had not yet returned from Virginia, we ran out of provisions, and had it not been for myself, Mr. Jones, and a few others' diligence in procuring provisions from the Natives, it would have gone very hard with us. During this time, we received a warning from the St. Helena Indians to the south that Spanish ships and thirty canoes of Spanish and Indians were planning on attacking us. It seems that they were expecting the arrival of the Carolina and intended to sink our ship to deprive us of supplies and force our surrender. It pleased God that our ship arrived safely with much-needed supplies. The Indians were terrified at the firing of our cannon. The Spanish, being frustrated in their plans to starve us, cowardly retreated to St. Augustine, having not attempted anything against us but threatened to destroy the St. Helena, Cumbahee, and Edisto Indians, who are our friends.

This is the state of our general affairs. As to our family necessity, I suppose Mr. Jones has made your honor fully acquainted as to my particular wants. I am most beholden to your honor's agent, Mr. Jones, here than from anything from the public, although I must confess that they have made honorable recommendations of me in their letters.

I shall endeavor by the next to send your Honor some of our American rarities, our troubles at present not permitting me the opportunity to explore the country. Most of my business is waiting in town and giving an account of what information the Natives bring us from the south or the north. Least I seem long-winded, I rest my recitation of services presented to your honor and pay my respects to Mrs. Marvel Carter and the rest of your Honorable family and relations.

I rest your Honor's most obliged servant,
Henry Woodward

John Yeamans' lengthy battle over the ownership of his Barbados home, Nicholas Plantation, had finally come to an ignominious end. The court awarded ownership to his stepchildren, lending further credence to the belief that he and his wife had murdered her former husband so they could marry. Opinion was now firmly against them, and they could not appear in public without disapproving stares and muttered comments. By November, they decided to leave Barbados and move to Carolina. Yeamans wrote to Anthony Ashley Cooper that he planned to be there the following year, asking that he be appointed to some position in the government. He noted that he was sending twelve cedar planks from Carolina, optimistically describing them as "the first fruits of that glorious Provence."

Enclosing Henry's earlier letter, he added,

> *Woodward has made a very large discovery in the colony but is much unwilling to declare it to the Government there being desirous to be sent for to make it out to your lordships which if granted will redound much to the prejudice of the settlement, he being the only person by whose means we hold a fair and peaceable correspondence with the natives of the place. But I expect by my arrival there to have a full and perfect discovery from him of all his proceedings and so send it for your lordship's satisfaction.*

As Yeamans' letter made its way across the Atlantic, one from Ashley Cooper to Joseph West crossed its path. He mentioned in passing that the Spanish ambassador had assured him the prisoners from *The Three Brothers* being held in St. Augustine would be released. In the same sentence, he accused the Carolina settlers of finding a large quantity of ambergris and concealing it from the lords proprietors. The thought that the settlers were cheating him was more important than losing twelve of them to the Spanish. He closed by telling West that the river at the settlement was henceforth to be called the Ashley River and that Albemarle Point was to be called Charles Towne.

❧

The following spring, months after Yeamans' letter, Ashley Cooper belatedly wrote to Henry.

> *Besides the correspondence you manage for us with the neighbor Indians, I hear you have been fourteen days' journey up in the county with a great emperor there with whom you have made a league and where you have discovered things which you think not fit to reveal to any but us ourselves. You have done very discretely in that silence, and I wish that the condition of our people there did not yet a while need your stay among them. For the keeping up the friendship and commerce with our neighbors*

with whose language and customs you are so well acquainted.... We must therefore for some time yet deny ourselves the satisfaction of those discoveries you reserve for us till you come to England and desire you would not leave our Plantation till the Indians and our people are grown into so good an acquaintance with another as not to need an Interpreter between them.

Henry realized that his hopes of establishing a pearl trading enterprise with the Cofitachequi and the lords proprietors were dashed, at least for the time being. But the letter also said that the proprietors were giving him 100 pounds credit that he could use to buy goods or indentured servants and Ashley Cooper was personally contributing another twenty pounds in recognition of his value to the colony. This was welcome news as he had arrived with only the clothes on his back. Even more promising were Ashley Cooper's further instructions to him:

If those inland countries have given you any knowledge or conjecture of mines there I earnestly desire you not give the least hint of it to anybody whatsoever for fear our people being tempted by the hopes of present gain should forsake their plantation and so run themselves into certain ruin which has followed all those who formerly have marched into this county of search of gold and silver. Pray, therefore, if there be any such thing, keep it secret to yourself alone, but if it should be convenient, as perhaps it may, to give me some hint of it in letters to me. Pray call gold always antimony and silver iron by which I shall be able to understand you without any danger if your letters should fall into other hands.
I am your very affectionate friend, Ashley.

Henry was ecstatic after reading this. Lord Ashley Cooper, the most important of the lords proprietors, had singled him out from the other settlers, given his blessing to his explorations, and asked him to communicate with him directly and secretly about his finds. He had no way of knowing that this letter would be the beginning of a future linked to one of England's most important political figures, a man who would be the guiding figure in the early days of Carolina.

34

WOODWARD'S SECRET MISSION

Summer 1671

Mid-July in Charles Towne, it was the hottest day Henry had yet seen. He was resting under the shade of an oak dripping with Spanish moss when a man approached him, dripping equally with sweat, and introduced himself as one of Sir John Yeamans' servants. Yeamans, recently arrived from Barbados, wanted to see him on an urgent matter; he would not say what. But everyone knew that he was in a bitter dispute with Joseph West over which of them should be the colony's next governor; Henry suspected it had something to do with that.

Yeamans was in a bad mood when Henry arrived at his home. "Joseph West claims he is now governor after Sayle died in March. I appointed Sayle as temporary governor in my absence. I am now here to resume my duties as Carolina's governor."

Henry, unsure what this had to do with him, asked Yeamans why he had been summoned.

Yeamans said, "I want you to carry a letter to Governor Berkeley in Virginia Colony. West cannot know of this, so you must make the journey in secret by land, not ship."

Henry was taken aback—there was no easy way to travel from Charles Towne to Jamestown by land. It would be a journey of at least 500 miles through the wilderness and potentially hostile Indian tribes. He had never heard of anyone other than Indians making the journey on foot.

But, since the 1665 Port Royal expedition, Henry's efforts to impress Yeamans had come to naught; helping Yeamans win the battle for the governorship would change that. Also, Yeamans was wealthy, and Henry was destitute. Finally, he said, "This would be the most dangerous and difficult thing I have ever done. I would be gone for at least two months and may well be killed. If you want me to do it, it will cost one hundred pounds, in advance."

Without hesitation, Yeamans replied, "Done."

Henry added, "I want someone to accompany me. You know James Needham, recently arrived from Barbados; he is my choice if he is willing. I also need Indian guides and trade goods for the Indian towns along the way."

Again, Yeamans agreed and said, "If you are back with Berkeley's response by the end of September, I will pay you an additional fifty pounds."

Yeamans gave no further details regarding the purpose of the trip, but it was apparent he was seeking Berkeley's support in his bid for the governorship. Berkeley, the governor of Virginia Colony, and the only one of the lords proprietors living in America, was potentially an important ally.

Henry's journey would be on the Indian Trading Path running from Guale country to Fort Henry, outside Jamestown. As he recalled, it was about a month-long journey. To impress Yeamans with how dangerous the journey might be, Henry told him that since he might not survive the trip, he would make his will before leaving, making Yeamans his sole beneficiary.

July 17, 1671
To all Christian People:
I Henry Woodward now resident at Ashley River in the province of Carolina being now minded to journey northward of the said River and in respect, the same may be very hazardous and dangerous I do make my will and testament; what lands I have as one of the first settlers to Hon. Sir John Yeamans Baronet. Item, whatsoever goods may or shall arrive on my behalf either from the said proprietors or any of my relations to the above Sir John Yeamans and until such time as the certainty of my death or return be known, I do constitute and appoint the aforesaid Sir John Yeamans my attorney.

Henry knew that the will was an empty gesture as Yeamans was a wealthy man; he was not and had no intention of dying on the journey, which would be difficult but not as dangerous as he had portrayed.

Needham, finding it difficult to adjust to life in Charles Towne, jumped at Henry's proposal, especially when he learned he would be paid for the adventure. The two left with their weapons, food, and trade goods, first stopping at the Sewee's town, where Henry asked if the two scouts he used the year before were available to guide them. Only the translator was available but said his brother could accompany them.

The previous year, following this same route north along the Santee and stopping at the Indian towns along the way, it took Henry two weeks to reach Cofitachequi town. Now, on a tight schedule, they briefly greeted the various towns' chiefs along the way, gave them the obligatory gifts, and moved on, reaching their destination in only eight days.

Henry told the Cofitachequi chief they were traveling to Fort Henry along the Trading Path. Apologizing for not staying longer, he asked if he could hire two of his men to accompany them as the Sewee scouts were not familiar with the route.

Leaving Cofitachequi town, the four men headed east on the Indian Trading Path, through gently rolling hills. Crossing the Yadkin River, they stopped at the town of Sara, where they spent the night and were well treated and fed. The chief warned them to be careful in the next town, Occaneechi, four days ahead—the people there were bothering travelers on the Trading Path and had recently killed several Indians.

Occaneechi town was on an island at the head of the Roanoke River. The current was too swift for them to cross, and as they sat on the riverbank, several Indians approached them. They seemed unfriendly, asking Henry what his business was.

Henry replied, "I have an important message from the leader of Carolina to the leader of Virginia."

After hearing the purpose of his trip, the men arranged for a canoe to take Henry and his party across the river to the island.

The town was large, well laid out, and more prosperous than the previous towns. Their dinner of bear and barbecued venison was a welcome change from turkey.

At dinner, a man introduced himself: "I am the chief in charge of hunting and fishing; our other chief is responsible for the town's defense." He continued, "We settled here twenty years earlier to escape raids from the Iroquois to the north. We have become middlemen in the trade between Virginia Colony and tribes to the west."

Recalling his earlier conversations about the deaths of the Westo/Rickahocan at the hands of the Occaneechi, Henry asked the chief if they ever had trouble with them.

The chief replied, "Anyone who passes our town bringing trade goods on the Trading Path must pay us. The Rickahocan were bringing captives from Guale along the Path to Fort Henry and did not want to pay us. We met with them to resolve the dispute but did not reach an agreement."

Henry, glad he had not mentioned that he was friends with Abraham Wood at Fort Henry, said, "We've no business with Fort Henry; we are delivering an important message to the Virginia governor."

As Henry and his party prepared to depart for Virginia Colony, the chief, saying it was a ten-day journey across scrubby land with little food except for turkeys, gave them a supply of barbecued venison for the trip. The final two hundred miles were monotonous but went quickly; on several days, they traveled thirty miles or more. Henry had been thinking about Needham's interaction with the Occaneechi chief; James had been brusque and impatient with his long speeches. Henry realized that having grown up on a Barbados sugar plantation, James was unfamiliar with their culture. He explained to Needham that they were guests in the Indian towns and needed to follow their rules of etiquette. Needham promised to do better in the future.

⸻ ◌◌◌ ⸻

Thirty-four days after leaving Charles Towne, they reached the end of the Trading Path at Fort Henry. At first, Abraham Wood did not recognize Henry, who now had long hair, a beard, and was dressed in buckskin.

Catching up on the last five years, Wood said, "Business is good -- the Ricka-hocan are bringing a steady supply of Indian captives from Guale for me to sell to Virginia planters. I make more profit from them than from deerskins and furs."

Henry replied, "In Carolina, the Rickahocan are called the Westo, and the local tribes are very afraid of them and believe they are cannibals. Could you per-suade them to leave the Carolina Indians alone? They are important allies for us."

Wood said he would tell them, but they were not good at taking instructions from anyone.

Over the next few days, Henry quizzed Wood about what he was paying the Rickahocan for deerskins and furs, as well as captives from Guale, not mention-ing that he was considering becoming an Indian trader himself.

After two days of resting, eating, and drinking, Henry said, "We need to be on our way and see Governor Berkeley. Have you ever met him before?"

"I have; I suggest you get haircuts and new clothing before you see him. And remember, there is always a job as Indian traders waiting for both of you."

"You cleaned up pretty well for a frontiersman," Henry told Needham. "But we can't sleep on the ground in these clothes. Let's use some of Yeamans' money and take rooms here."

Spending more of Yeamans' money, they hired a coach for the journey to Green Spring, Governor Berkeley's plantation.

This was the first time Henry had been to Green Spring; as a boy, he had only seen it from a distance. It was a massive brick building on two thousand acres of fields and orchards, the most magnificent home in the colony. The coach deposited them at the entrance where a Negro servant, better dressed than either of them, greeted them and ushered them into the waiting room.

When Berkeley's secretary asked them what their business was, Henry said, "I have a letter from Governor Yeamans in Carolina Colony for the governor."

"Leave it with me; I will give it to him."

"My instructions are to deliver it to the governor only."

Frowning, the secretary said, "Wait here."

Two hours later, he reappeared and said that the governor would see him. His reception of Henry was brusque: "Who are you, and what does Yeamans want from me?"

"My name is Henry Woodward; Governor Yeamans gave me this letter to deliver to you. I don't know what it says."

Berkeley was still frowning, so Henry, handing him the letter, added, "Thomas Woodward is my grandfather."

Berkeley didn't comment, but he stopped frowning as he opened and read the letter; Henry could not interpret his expression.

"Come back tomorrow, and I'll have a response for you."

Henry thanked him and said, "I was admiring your plantation earlier. Do you mind if my partner and I look around before we leave?"

Berkeley said, "Ask my plantation manager; he will arrange it for you."

Henry was disappointed with their reception—he had heard that the governor was a just and reasonable person, but he seemed as unlikeable as Governor Modyford had been in Jamaica.

The plantation manager was friendly, giving them a guided tour of the estate. There were hundreds of fruit trees, vineyards, mulberry trees for silk, and fields of cotton, flax, and hemp, but no tobacco.

The manager said, "Governor Berkeley has spent years trying to find crops to replace tobacco, which is destroying the land and our economy. Many of the plants they had tried grew well. We now produce wine and send Charles II hundreds of pounds of silk. But the crown won't support our efforts, and the governor has finally given up."

Henry and Needham thanked the manager for the tour and accepted his offer of a carriage back to Jamestown.

The next day, they were again greeted by the servant who handed them a letter from Berkeley to deliver to Yeamans. The governor was done with them.

CORN

Fall 1671

Now experienced travelers on the Trading Path, Henry and James' return trip went quickly. The only excitement came two days south of Occaneechi town, where they met a Westo trading party returning to Fort Henry with twenty Guale captives. Their guides urged them to get off the trail and let them pass. But Henry had been intrigued by the Westo ever since he was a boy at Fort Henry, where they were known as the Rickahocan. Handing Needham his musket, he proceeded alone up the trail to greet them—ten men, with faces painted black, all carrying guns.

Henry greeted them in English, "I am a friend of Abraham Wood and am returning from Fort Henry to my town of Charles Town in Carolina."

One of the men replied, also in English, "Wood is also our friend; we are taking these captives to him."

Henry, recalling what he had heard about the Occaneechi killing the Westo men visiting their town, asked him about traveling the Indian Trading Path.

He replied, "It is harder than when we first began using it. The Cofitachequi and the Occaneechi demand payment from us for using the Path. We now have to bring more warriors to protect ourselves from them."

Before they parted, Henry told them that he was considering starting a deerskin trade. "It would be easier for you to trade with me than with Wood. Your town is 400 miles from Fort Henry and only 150 from Charles Towne, so you would save weeks of travel on the Path. Also, while you would still have to pass the Cofitachequi town, you would be far from Occaneechi town. If you are ever interested, send a messenger to Charles Towne and ask for Henry Woodward."

131

—⦿—

Henry and Needham were back in Charles Towne on September 7th, ten days ahead of Yeamans' deadline, having traveled over a thousand miles with no significant incidents. Yeamans took Governor Berkeley's letter, opened it, and read it. Cursing, he tore it in half and threw it in the fireplace. Whatever answer from Berkeley he had been hoping for, he had not received it. Without explanation, he dismissed him. Henry didn't ask about the promised bonus for their early delivery of Berkeley's response.

Through no fault of his own, Henry's plan to get in Yeamans' good graces was again a failure. To make matters worse, he learned that the Cofitachequi chief had stabbed him in the back. When he and Needham passed through the chief's town, he told him they were traveling to Jamestown and hired his men as guides for the journey. He heard from Henry Brayne that the chief had visited Charles Towne while he and Needham were traveling the Trading Path and invited Charles Towne's leaders to visit his town and make a trade agreement. When Henry stopped at Cofitachequi town on his return to Charles Towne, the chief had said nothing of this visit. Brayne said the chief also told Joseph West, now the acting governor after Sayle's death, that Henry had been seen near the Virginia border. West was angry at both Yeamans and Henry and said he would write a letter to Ashley Cooper about it.

—⦿—

Charles Towne upon Ashley River Carolina
September 3, 1671

May it please your Lord,
Sir John has privately sent Dr. Woodward away to Virginia by land without any knowledge, which when I heard I was very much concerned at it for many inconveniences attend it. We want our Interpreter. I had sent for him to come back, but he had gone too far for me.
Your most faithful humble servant,
Joseph West

—⦿—

Henry considered the results of his trip for Yeamans—he was not in Yeamans' good graces despite risking his life for him; Governor West was upset with him for siding with Yeamans and leaving Charles Town without permission; the goodwill he had with Ashley Cooper was at the very least tarnished; and finally, the Cofitachequi chief had used his absence to cut him out of any trade agreement with Charles Towne. The one hundred pounds Yeamans had paid him seemed small compensation for what the journey cost him.

He had been spending little time in Charles Towne since his arrival; now, utterly dispirited, he spent even less, retreating to the solitude of a small hut he had built along the Ashley River. Margaret was never far from his mind; almost every night, he awoke in a cold sweat, reliving the St. Catherine's disaster.

Making matters worse, three weeks after his return, he saw a proclamation posted on the town's meeting house wall:

At a meeting of the governor and council September 27th, 1671:
The governor and council, taking into their serious consideration the languishing condition that this colony is brought into by reason of the great quantity of corn from time to time taken out of the plantations by the Kussoe and other Southward Indians. They refuse to live peaceably and threaten our lives, and they invade our plantations in the nighttime and have said they intend to work with the Spaniards to cut us off in this place. Ordered and ordained that an open war shall be forthwith prosecuted against said Kussoe Indians and their co-adjudicators and that commissions are granted to Captain John Godfrey and Captain Thomas Gray to prosecute the war.

Henry was appalled. The governor and the council had made poor decisions before, but this was the worst. Henry had an agreement with the town's government that he would be consulted in Charles Towne's dealings with its Indian neighbors. He had heard nothing from them about this, and as far as he knew, there had been no serious problems with the Kussoe.

The governor had announced an all-out war against the Kussoe simply because some had stolen corn from colonists' fields. Any threats the Kussoe might have made to join with the Spanish and drive out the English was bluster if they had been made at all—none of the Indians around Charles Towne were friends of the Spanish. The town's militia probably could defeat the Kussoe, a small tribe armed only with bows. But this would infuriate neighboring tribes who were allies of the Kussoe. Charles Towne was not strong enough to simultaneously fight all of them and, if it did come to open warfare, then at least some of the tribes might well turn to the Spanish who were always looking for a chance to drive out the English.

Henry knew that he was not in good standing with Governor West and the council, so they would likely not heed his advice. But perhaps the Kussoe would. He didn't know their cassique well, but he hoped his reputation with the other towns would carry weight. He needed to act immediately before Charles Towne could organize its militia.

After a half-day journey to Kussoe town, Henry introduced himself to their cassique and told him of the council's order to wage war on them.

The cassique replied, "We traded so much of our corn to the Kiawah to give to your settlement that we do not have enough to feed ourselves. Some of our people have gone into the settler's fields at night for corn to feed their families."

Henry recalled that he had negotiated an agreement with the Kiawah last year to deliver three tons of corn; the cassique had told him they would be trading with neighboring tribes for much of it. He realized he had not considered the agreement's impact on their ability to feed themselves, but he could do nothing about it now.

He told the cassique, "I agree with your position, but Charles Towne feels strongly about the matter. In England, if someone took corn from a field, he could be imprisoned or even killed. The settlers here feel the same way. I suggest you seek peace and promise not to take any more corn from the fields."

The cassique replied, "My people do not understand how the English can claim to own our lands. We have lived here for hundreds of years, and the English tell us it is now their land to grow crops and raise cattle. Many of my people believe that they have as much right to the crops as the English."

Henry said, "You have a better argument about your lands than do the English. But they have guns and believe they have God on their side. Unless you are willing to move away from Charles Towne, you should offer to pay a fine of deerskins and promise to leave the colonists' fields alone."

The cassique grudgingly agreed to talk to the other elders about Henry's advice.

The next day, Henry tracked down John Godfrey, assembling the militia for the attack. Knowing that Godfrey was less of a hothead than some of the other council members, Henry related what he told the cassique and asked if he would pass it on to the governor. He suggested that, in the meantime, it would be wise not to take any steps to begin a war with their neighbors, who they needed as allies.

On October 2nd, the council issued its order:

> *It is resolved and ordered by the grand council that every Company which went upon that expedition shall secure and maintain the Indians they have taken till they can transport the said Indians, but if the remaining Kussoe Indians do in the meantime come in and make peace and desire*

the Indians now prisoners, then the said Indians shall be set at liberty hav-ing first paid such a ransom as shall be thought reasonable by the grand council to be shared equally among the company of men that took the Indians aforesaid.

The Kussoe took Henry's advice, came to Charles Towne, entered into a peace treaty, and paid a fine of ten deerskins. No more was heard of the matter, nor was anything ever said of Henry's role in the affair. Even though no one else in the settlement knew how close to a pointless and futile war with their Indian neighbors they had come, the knowledge he might have saved the settlement helped him to crawl out of the dark hole he had been in since losing Margaret.

36

ST. CATHERINE'S REVISITED

June 1672

Two years before, Henry had made a vow to rescue Margaret from the Spanish at St. Augustine, no matter the cost. He had since realized Lord Ashley Cooper, now the Earl of Shaftesbury, would be of no help. He told the settlers that the Spanish ambassador had promised to return all of the prisoners taken at St. Catherine's. That was months ago, and nothing had happened. Henry had asked Yeamans, recently appointed as governor, to help; he declined. Henry Brayne had made repeated offers to stage a rescue of the prisoners, but when Henry had last asked about it, Brayne said he could do nothing without Charles Towne's permission.

It was time to act on his own, and he realized he should have done so long before. A raid of St. Augustine was out of the question. Searle and Pierre Piques had been able to rescue him only because Searle had a crew of bloodthirsty buccaneers, and St. Augustine had not been expecting an attack. Charles Towne had one ship and no more than fifty untrained men, even if the governor was willing to help. Also, St. Augustine was no longer unprepared.

He would have to rescue her by stealth, and he knew he could not do it by himself. He would need the help of his Indian friends, starting with the Kiawah cassique. After the trade agreement for three tons of corn, Henry expected the cassique, who was no friend of the Spanish, would agree to help him.

Meeting with him, Henry said, "You remember that when I first came here, the Spanish and Guale had taken our people from *The Three Brothers*. I am here to rescue one of them, and I need your help."

Considering Henry's request, the cassique replied, "I will be glad to help you, but you know we cannot attack St. Augustine."

"Of course not. I only wish for you to provide a canoe and two men to take me as far as the Escamacu town at St. Catherine's and wait there for a week. I won't put you at risk."

"We can do that. When do you want to leave?"

"Tomorrow."

<hr>

Several days later, Henry was meeting with Wommony at St. Catherine's. "Last we met, you helped me search for passengers captured by the Spanish from *The Three Brothers*. They were taken to St. Augustine and are still prisoners there. One of them, Margaret, is the woman I intended to marry. I've come to rescue her."

Wommony simply said, "How can I help you?"

"Are any of your men welcome at St. Augustine?"

Wommony replied, "We are required to furnish workers to the town, so our people are always coming and going from there."

Henry said, "This is my plan; two of your men will take a canoe to St. Augustine and deliver a letter I've written for Margaret. She is one of only two English women there, so she should be easy to find. The letter will instruct her that, on the morning after she gets it, she is to go to the riverbank at the south end of town where a canoe will be waiting for her. It will bring her back to St. Catherine's, where I will be waiting to take her to safety."

Wommony answered, "I think we can do that with little trouble. My men will pretend to be bringing fish to trade with the town. When they leave, they can cover her with deerskins so any guards who see the canoe will not be suspicious."

"How many days do you think this will take?"

Wommony replied, "It's at least a four-day journey to St. Augustine, so count on ten days or less."

Two days later, the canoe with two men and Henry's letter set out along the coast for St. Augustine.

Eight days later, the two men returned and went directly to Wommony's home.

Wommony told Henry, "I have bad news for you. Margaret died several months ago. A woman at the hospital said she became ill with a fever and did not recover."

Henry stood, staring out at the water, saying nothing for quite a while. Then he said to Wommony, "Thank you for helping me. I'm going home."

Finding the two Kiawah men waiting for him, Henry boarded their canoe and left for Charles Towne.

Wommony never forgot the look of cold fury he had seen on Henry's face.

37

ESPIONAGE

Carolina Colony, May 1672

Saying farewell to the ship that had taken him from St. Augustine to Port Royal, the grizzled stranger began the fifty-mile trek through marshes and across rivers, a journey that would seem too daunting for someone of his advanced age. But Antonio Camunas was a hardened soldier, used to far worse. Camunas was a spy sent by St. Augustine's governor to study Charles Towne and its defenses.

As he stood on the bank of the Edisto River, pondering how to cross, two Edisto Indians paddled their canoe to the river's edge and inquired what he was doing. After hearing he was walking to Charles Towne, they offered to take him.

At the settlement, a man stopped him at the palisade gate and asked him what his business was; he replied, "The governor of St. Augustine sent me to deliver a message to your governor about a peace treaty."

After a long wait, another man returned and told him to wait outside the settlement overnight. The next day, six of the town's militia, in full military dress, escorted Camunas to the governor's house. John Yeamans, just reappointed as governor the preceding month, and several of the council were waiting for him.

Camunas did not speak English, so Yeamans found an interpreter who spoke Spanish. The interpreter introduced himself as Brian Fitzpatrick, an Irish indentured servant. As Camunas handed Yeamans a packet of letters from the St. Augustine governor, he heard the sound of cannon fire; Fitzpatrick told him it was in honor of his presence.

Apparently pleased with the contents of the letters, Yeamans proposed a toast to the King of Spain; Camunas proposed one to the King of England, and Yeamans a third toast to the St. Augustine governor.

After the toasts were completed, Yeamans offered to take him back to St. Augustine by boat. Camunas demurred, saying English ships were not permitted there. Yeamans then offered to take him as far as St. Catherine's; again, Camunas said that would not be a good idea. Finally, they agreed that a boat would take him as far as Port Royal.

Yeamans, eager to show off the settlement, invited Camunas to stay longer; he accepted. Over the next eight days, Yeamans showed him every detail of Charles Towne, its fortifications, artillery, militia strength, and even a description of the harbor and what size of ships could enter it. Yeamans showed Camunas a boat he was building for himself and said that his ships were bringing more settlers, supplies, and cattle from Barbados.

After eight days of being well treated and very well informed, Camunas returned to St. Augustine, not having to slog through the swamps on his return, thanks to the governor.

❧

Six weeks after Camunas' visit, Henry received a summons to immediately appear at the governor's house. *Another secret mission*, he thought.

When he arrived at Yeamans' home, James Needham was also there. Yeamans handed them a document, a transcript of the council's meeting the previous day:

> *Forasmuch as Brian Fitzpatrick hath departed this province with an intent to go to the Spaniards and intelligence is given that he as yet hath got no further than St. Helena, it is advised that Mr. Henry Woodward and Mr. James Needham be dispatched to St. Helena in order to take said Brian Fitzpatrick and bring him back, but in case of opposition so as they cannot take and securely bring him alive then to maim, destroy or kill him as they shall find best to agree with their own safety.*

Henry knew that Fitzpatrick had served as the interpreter for Camunas. It was common knowledge that he was a troublemaker and was unhappy in Charles Towne. He had killed a Kussoe Indian a year earlier; only Yeamans' intervention had saved him from charges. Henry had wondered about Camunas' true intentions during his visit; it reminded him of his plan in St. Augustine four years earlier to be an unofficial spy. Apparently, Camunas came to Charles Towne as an official spy and, during his visit, had learned of Fitzpatrick's dissatisfaction and told him he would be welcome in St. Augustine.

140

Henry and Needham set out immediately. It was a three-day journey from Charles Towne to St. Helena; Fitzpatrick had a two-day head start. Henry knew their chances of overtaking him were slim. South of Charles Towne, they met two Kussoe men who said they had seen him earlier, heading south and in a hurry. Two days later, at the Westobou River, marking the boundary of Spanish-controlled Guale, they had not spotted him and knew it was not safe to continue.

Back in Charles Towne, Henry reported their failure. He expected Yeamans to be furious, but that was not the case; Yeamans was eager to sweep the entire incident under the rug.

⁓⁓⁓

A week after Henry and Needham returned from their wild goose chase, Needham told Henry he had something to say to him. "I've been thinking about my future in Charles Towne. I don't wish to become a planter; that's why I left Barbados. I was hoping for something more exciting, like our journey on the Indian Trading Path. But I don't see much chance for that to happen again if I stay here. I've decided to take up Abraham Wood's offer to us at Fort Henry to work for him as an Indian trader; I'm leaving this week."

Henry was silent for a few moments and then said, "I can't blame you. I had hoped to become a trader here and ask you to be my partner. But I've made little progress since arriving and can't promise you that I will be successful anytime soon. I wish you the best of luck; my only advice is that to be a trader, you must understand how your Indian trading partners think—we're in their country, and we have to be respectful of them and their ways of doing business."

After Needham had departed, Henry thought, *Now I truly have nothing; even my future trading partner has deserted me.*

38

SHAFTESBURY AND ST. GILES KUSSOE

England and Carolina Colony, 1674

Anthony Ashley Cooper was having a bad year. He had been Charles II's rising star—Chancellor of the Exchequer, member of the Privy Council, then elevated to Lord Chancellor, the highest post available to an English subject. As a reward for his services, in 1672, the King made him an earl, Lord Anthony Ashley Cooper, the Earl of Shaftesbury. From then on, he was known simply as Shaftesbury.

In his first year as an earl, Shaftesbury's political fortunes declined. He had been so outspoken in his distrust of the king's brother, James, who Shaftesbury believed was sympathetic to the Catholic Church, that Charles finally had enough. He dismissed Shaftesbury as Lord Chancellor and ordered him to leave London. Shaftesbury packed up and moved to his family estate at Wimborne St. Giles, a hundred miles south of London.

Now, isolated in the English countryside with few diversions, he again focused on Carolina Colony and asked his secretary, John Locke, to report the colony's status.

Locke found that, other than John Yeamans and one or two others, none of the settlers were wealthy enough to acquire indentured servants or slaves needed to clear fields, plant crops, and cut timber. Many were too poor to survive without support from the lords proprietors. He predicted that the colony would soon fail if the proprietors did not make a large cash infusion.

Shaftesbury, taking Locke's advice, got a commitment from each of them to contribute 100 pounds annually toward the colony, but only Sir Peter Colleton followed through—Carolina was not a high priority for the rest. Shaftesbury also wrote a lengthy letter to West and the Carolina Council bitterly complaining of their ingratitude and ineptitude and signed a commission replacing Sir John Yeamans with Joseph West as governor.

Having made his dissatisfaction with Charles Towne's lack of progress and ungratefulness clear, he turned to an idea he had been flirting with for several years—his own plantation in Carolina. The Fundamental Constitutions of Carolina provided that every lord proprietor was entitled to a 12,000-acre estate in each Carolina county, but so far, none had availed themselves of this right.

———

First, Shaftesbury needed to hire someone he knew and trusted as his manager. In April of 1674, he offered the job to Andrew Percival, a family acquaintance—*to make a plantation on his land in Carolina and to settle a trade there with the Indians, Spaniards, and others.* Percival would get his living expenses and one-fourth of the yearly profits. Presently at loose ends and looking for adventure, he accepted the job.

Shaftesbury fired off five letters to Percival, Joseph West, and Henry Woodward in a single day. He sent Percival instructions, including his plans for Edisto Island, which he renamed Locke Island—*You are to sail directly to the Edisto River and there choose a convenient place to settle in upon Locke Island. You are to understand that at present, you are no way under the Government of the plantation at Ashley River, and you therefore have the liberty to trade as you think fit with the Natives or any other, their Laws having no influence upon you. You are to endeavor to begin a trade with the Spaniards for Negroes, Cloths, or other Commodities they want wherein you are to take special care that it be so managed that they get no Intelligence of our strength, condition, or place of settlement.*

He also suggested to Percival that Governor West should consider setting up a new 12,000-acre plantation to be owned by the lords proprietors where the poorer Charles Towne colonists could move and become leetmen, that is, indentured servants, working for the wealthier colonists that Shaftesbury hoped to attract to Carolina.

———

After Percival had settled his affairs in England, carrying Shaftesbury's letters to Governor West and Henry Woodward, he sailed on *The Edisto*, a ship that Shaftesbury purchased and named for his new enterprise. Arriving in Carolina in the early fall of 1674, his first order of business was to meet with Joseph West. He introduced himself and handed West a bundle of documents, including Shaftesbury's letters and the commission appointing him as governor.

He told West, "Shaftesbury has hired me to set up a 12,000-acre estate for himself on Edisto Island. He has also fired Sir John Yeamans and appointed you as Carolina's new governor. He asks that the two of us work closely managing Charles Towne's affairs."

Hearing this, all West had to say was, "Yeamans died last month."

That evening, as West read Shaftesbury's letters, the more dismayed he became. He heard that Shaftesbury had fallen out of favor with the King and had been banished from London. It seemed that he was now taking out his frustrations on Charles Towne. His letters made it clear they could expect little future financial assistance from the proprietors. Not only would the colony have to make its own way, but it would also have to compete with Shaftesbury's new plantation on his terms. And worse, Percival was to become an unofficial governor of Charles Towne—Shaftesbury's final instructions were, *I would have your Dispatches concerning these matters come to me from you and Mr. Percival jointly.*

Percival delivered Shaftesbury's letter to Henry in person. "Shaftesbury speaks highly of you. He is establishing a plantation on Edisto Island and hired me to manage it. He wants you to be his agent and establish a trade with the Indians at the plantation."

Henry quickly read the letter—it instructed him to buy Edisto Island from the Indians there. He was also to *settle a trade with the Indians for furs and other commodities that are either for the supply of the Plantation or advantageous for trade,* for which he would receive one-fifth of the profits.

The letter continued: *You are to consider whether it be best to make peace with the Westos or Cussitaws which are a more powerful Nation said to have pearls and silver and by whose Assistance the Westos may be rooted out.*

Shaftesbury's proposal was everything and more that Henry could have hoped for. Four years after his attempt to make a trade agreement with the Cofitachequi, his hopes of becoming a successful trader like Abraham Wood might finally come to fruition. Shaftesbury, a wealthy man, could easily finance trade with any tribe, and Henry would finally be out from under the thumb of the Charles Towne government.

※

Percival's instructions were to sail immediately for Edisto Island. *The Edisto*'s captain was ready to leave; an hour later, Henry was also. Familiar with the coastline, Henry directed *The Edisto*'s captain through the treacherous inlets and sandbars to the mouth of the Edisto River. A group of Indians hailed them from shore; Henry recalled this was what had happened eight years earlier when the Sandford expedition anchored in the same spot. Now able to speak their language, Henry introduced himself and said that he and Percival had business with their cassique.

Edisto town was just as Henry remembered it. Shadoo, who he had met four years earlier, was now their cassique.

He told Henry, "We are again having problems with the Westo. Their scouts have been seen near our village, and I fear they are planning a raid. We are too far from St. Augustine for protection from the Spanish and too far from Charles Towne for protection from the English."

Henry replied, "I have been ordered by the chief of Carolina, a man named Shaftesbury who lives in England, to make peace with the Westo. When I meet with them, I will try to get their agreement not to molest any towns in Carolina."

Finally, Henry got around to the reason for his visit. "Shaftesbury wants to buy Edisto Island and put a plantation there. Would you be willing to sell it to us?"

Shadoo replied, "We have little use for the island and would be glad to sell it to him. Have you ever visited it before?"

When Henry admitted he had not, Shadoo said, "You should visit it first; you may find it unsuited for a plantation."

The following day, the three of them took the ship toward the island; Shadoo said the only way to get there was on the Edisto River, but he didn't think they could get through. He was right—logs and sand bars blocked the river. Shadoo said the only other way onto the island was by canoe or on foot through the marshes. Shaftesbury's Locke Island plantation was not to be—the island was useless if sea-going vessels could not reach it.

Percival was now homeless. His twenty-one-year contract with Shaftesbury provided he was to settle at Edisto Island. He had sold everything when he left England, never intending to return. Though not in as dire straits as Percival, Henry's hopes of becoming a successful Indian trader had yet again been dashed.

—⁓⁓⁓—

They agreed to look for another site before Percival wrote to Shaftesbury with the bad news. Henry said he had not been staying abreast of what land was available, but Governor West should know.

West had cringed when he saw Shaftesbury's orders to cooperate with Percival in setting up a competing settlement. But here Percival was, on his doorstep with Henry Woodward in tow. Percival was diplomatic, explaining that he had tried to carry out instructions from Shaftesbury to establish his plantation on Edisto Island but that it was not accessible by ship, so they were looking for another location. West said Maurice Mathews, Charles Towne's surveyor, had once been instructed to locate a 12,000-acre parcel for Shaftesbury. He didn't know what became of the request, but he would ask.

Mathews, arriving at West's home, pointedly ignoring Percival and Henry, told West that in early 1672, he had surveyed 12,000 acres at the headwaters of the Cooper River for Shaftesbury; he had no idea what, if anything, had happened to it. After Mathews left, Percival explained his rudeness -- Mathews was supposed to have been the manager for Shaftesbury's new plantation at Edisto but had abruptly been fired and replaced by himself.

The council's records confirmed that the land was still being held for Shaftesbury, who had apparently forgotten about it.

Percival and Henry sailed *The Edisto* up the Cooper River to view the potential site. Against an unfavorable tide, it took most of the day. The next morning, they walked the land along the riverbank -- there was good anchorage for ships, the land was suitable for cattle and crops, and its location would be ideal for trading with Indians north of the colony. But it was some thirty miles upriver from Charles Towne. Shaftesbury wanted a convenient location; this was too far away. Henry suggested that they look at the headwaters of the Ashley River instead as it was closer to Charles Towne.

Arriving at the Ashley River's headwaters in half the time it had taken on the Cooper, they anchored at a low bluff. The land was even better than the Cooper River site, with broad savannahs for grazing and cedar waiting to be harvested.

Percival said, "This seems a perfectly suitable site for a plantation. I can already see a house here on the bluff, overlooking the river."

"I agree," replied Henry. "I suggest we name it St. Giles Kussoe after Shaftesbury's estate in England since it's on the Kussoe Indians' land."

"Will that be a problem, taking their land?"

Henry replied, "It shouldn't be. Most of the Indians here are willing to let us live on their lands if we protect them from Westo raids."

Percival said, "I thought I might have to move back to England if we didn't find a new location. I'll write Shaftesbury with the good news. By the time he gets the letter, we should have the plantation up and running."

Henry added, "By then, he may have forgotten about Locke Island, and he should be pleased that his plantation will be named after his estate and on a river named after himself."

THE WESTO

Percival wasted no time settling in at St. Giles Kussoe. With borrowed servants, he set to work constructing two log homes and a barn, as Shaftesbury had directed.

Henry, staying for a few days to help design the building to be used for Indian trading, looked over the trade goods that Percival brought from England—hundreds of pounds of beads, looking glasses, brass kettles, wool duffle cloth, knives, hatchets, fowling pieces, shot, and gunpowder. Whoever had put the goods together knew their business; Henry thought it must be the same London merchant who supplied Fort Henry's trade goods. He was surprised to see guns on the list—Charles Towne was not allowed to give guns to its Indian neighbors; Shaftesbury apparently didn't intend this ban to apply to himself.

As Percival and his men were raising the rafters on his new home, one of the workers called out in alarm. Ten Indian men, faces painted black, were crossing the clearing toward them, several carrying loads of deerskins and furs. They did not speak English; all Percival could make out was what sounded like "Henry Woodward." Despite their terrifying appearance, they seemed peaceful enough and, by their gestures, pointing at their skins and furs and Percival's tools, they were here to trade. Percival immediately sent two of the workers to town to fetch Henry.

When the workers described the strange Indians, Henry's first thought was that they might be Westo, perhaps the same ones he had met on the Indian Trading Path three years before. He finished his business in town and headed upriver in his yawl, reaching St. Giles in the early afternoon. As he suspected, they were indeed Westo. They spoke neither English nor Kiawah but indicated they wanted him to go with them to their town, a week's travel to the northwest.

Communicating with gestures, Henry told them they could spend the night there and that he would accompany them the next day. But they did not want to stay and, even though it was late afternoon, insisted that he leave with them when they were finished trading. With beads, mirrors, and hatchets from *The Edisto*'s stores, Henry offered them the same terms for their skins and furs he recalled from his last visit to Fort Henry.

Telling Percival that he was visiting the Westo's town and would be gone for several weeks, he packed up more trading goods for gifts, including a fowling piece for their chief, and set out in a cold rain. Along the banks of the Ashley River, Henry saw that the Westo had carved tree trunks with symbols of a beaver, a man on horseback, and a gun to mark the way.

The weather continued cold and wet. They stopped for the night at a broad savannah a few miles from St. Giles; Henry dreaded the thought of sleeping with only a blanket for protection from the elements. But the Westo men showed their resourcefulness, building several bark-covered huts for shelter.

Even though out of the rain, Henry spent an uncomfortable night. It had been months since he had last traveled the backcountry on foot, and he found the ground hard and the cold cornmeal and dried venison unappetizing.

The weather for the rest of the week was no better, but at least the meals were. The Westo were excellent hunters; for the rest of the journey, they ate fresh venison and turkey.

At week's end, they met two men sent from Westo town to greet Henry. They accompanied him to the bank of a wide river where a group of Westo had laid out a meal of their favorite delicacies, waiting for him. When the weather finally cleared, the men took him upriver to their town on a point overlooking the river.

Once in sight of the town, Henry fired his fowling piece to announce his arrival and was answered with a volley of gunshots. His guides escorted him to their chief's house. The townspeople surrounded the building; several children climbed onto the bark roof and peeled away pieces to peer in. Through the translator, who spoke English, the chief introduced himself as Paytah. Greeting him, the chief made a speech about the Westo's strength.

That evening, the women spread bear oil on Henry's eyes and limbs as a greeting and presented him with deerskins. After an enormous feast, Henry gave the Westo his gifts, including the fowling piece for Paytah.

The Westo homes were unlike any Henry had seen before—longhouses with their sides and tops covered with bark. Many of the houses had poles festooned with scalps. Along the river banks were at least a hundred canoes; as Henry walked through the town, he observed it was well stocked with muskets, ammunition, and trade goods.

This was a town prepared for war.

Henry stayed another ten days exploring the surrounding countryside and meeting with Paytah.

Initially reserved, the chief began to open up to Henry and one evening told him his story:

"Twenty years ago, our home was far to the north, where we were part of the Erie people. We lived near a lake so large you could not see across it, along a river with an enormous waterfall called Thundering Waters. We were enemies with a large nation, the Iroquois. Both of us traded beaver skins, us with the French, and the Iroquois with the English and Dutch. The Iroquois declared war on us; we were brave fighters, but the Iroquois had more guns. After two years, we were defeated, and we moved to different places. The English call our war the Beaver Wars. About ten years ago, six hundred of us fled south and settled near the falls of the James River in Virginia Colony, out of the reach of the Iroquois. There, we were known as the Rickahocan."

After the evening meal, the chief invited Henry to his home and offered him Virginia tobacco which he proudly said was from Fort Henry. He then continued the story of his people:

"When we settled in our new home, there were English nearby, and we wished to trade with them. But the English and their friends, the Powhatan, did not want us there. They came into our camp with soldiers and told us to leave. We sent five of our elders to negotiate, but the English seized and killed them, including my father. Then they attacked us with one hundred soldiers and two hundred Powhatan. The soldiers were not good fighters, and the Powhatan were armed only with bows and arrows.

"We killed most of the Indians, including their chief and some of the soldiers; in Virginia, they call it the Battle of Bloody Run. After our great victory, we met with the new captain, Abraham Wood, and made a trade agreement with him. After my father's death, I became the chief of my people."

The chief reloaded his pipe and resumed his story.

"There were not as many beavers in Virginia as in our old home, so we also began trading deerskins. Wood told us that if we could capture other Indians, he would buy them from us. He said that they would become slaves on tobacco plantations in Virginia.

"In our old home, we tortured and killed enemies captured in battle or made slaves of them, and they did the same to us. Now, we began to capture Indians from nearby towns we are not at war with and sell them to Fort Henry. It is more profitable than trapping beaver and hunting deer.

"But Wood told us that these Indians would escape back to their towns, so we agreed to capture Indians from far away towns. He said there were Indians who lived to the south in a country called Guale, and they were friends of the Spanish. We could reach them by the Indian Trading Path, which begins at the Fort. Some of our men went to see these Indians and said the Spanish did not let them have guns and they were not warlike. We came back with more warriors to raid their towns and captured many young boys. Wood told us that the plantation owners were happy with the new slaves because they did not run away. But we had to travel far from our home to reach the Indian towns. Also, the people in Virginia did not want us living so close to them. So, we agreed to move to the south end of the Great Trading Path, far from the English and closer to Indian towns we raid. We now bring the captives along the Trading Path to Fort Henry.

"Then, a year ago, Wood told us that he had made a trade agreement with the Cherokee. They are our enemies; Wood betrayed us with this agreement. The Cherokee began using the Indian Trading Path to bring their goods to Fort Henry. We told Wood that we could not share the Trading Path with them; he told us we had to if we wanted to keep trading with him."

When the chief finished his story, Henry said, "As a child, I lived near Fort Henry; I still remember the Battle of Bloody Run." He didn't mention that his father had been a surgeon in Virginia Colony's militia during the battle.

Henry asked the chief, "Is it true that the Westo are cannibals as many of the tribes here believe?"

Paytah replied, "We are not, but because we take away the Indians we capture and they are never seen again, many believe we are." He added, "The scalps you see on our dwellings are from warriors we killed in battles with our enemies, not from the towns we raid for prisoners."

When Henry asked him how the Westo knew to find him at St. Giles Kussoe after he and Percival had just arrived there, Paytah said that, through their spies, they kept track of what was happening in the colony. "We did not trust the people there and were happy when we heard of this new settlement and that you are to be a part of it."

The next day Henry told Paytah that the chief of the new settlement was a powerful man named Shaftesbury, who lived across the ocean in England and had told him to make a trade agreement with the Westo. He said, "I propose that you stop trading with Fort Henry and trade only with us. We will pay you the same as Fort Henry for deerskins and furs."

Paytah asked if they would also buy captive Guale Indians as Abraham Wood did.

Henry replied, "Before I can agree, I need to talk to Percival, who is the manager of St. Giles."

Henry and Paytah agreed that the Westo would come to St. Giles several times each year, and their first visit would be in March. Henry asked if he could take the translator with him to St. Giles. He would send the translator back with the details of their agreement and whether they could also trade for Indian slaves.

As Henry was preparing to depart the following day, two strange Indians arrived, speaking a language nobody could understand. They identified themselves as Savannahs and, by signs, said they lived to the southwest and wanted to be friends with the Westo. Their leader gave Paytah some beads and other trade goods as presents, indicating that they got them from the Spanish, whom they did not like. Then he said that the Creek, Chickasaw, and Cherokee tribes were planning to attack Westo town.

The chief shrugged when he heard this news. Henry asked if he was concerned; he said that everyone was always threatening to attack them, but they were the only ones with guns.

The chief gave Henry a captive young Indian boy as a parting gift. Henry repeated he would ask for Percival's consent to trade for Indian slaves and send his answer back with the translator.

Ten men laden with deerskins accompanied Henry on the return journey. Henry used the opportunity to ask the translator the Westo words for the plants and animals along the way. The translator told Henry that he had been at Fort Henry when Abraham Wood said he had made a trade agreement with the Cherokee. He added, "Wood told us that the Occaneechi killed one of his men he sent to the Cherokee town."

When Henry asked if he knew who it was, the translator replied, "It was a man named James Needham."

Stunned, Henry told him that he knew Needham. The translator continued, "Needham and his companion were near the town of Sara several days from Fort Henry when their Occaneechi guide, Indian John, shot Needham. He cut out Needham's heart and held it over his head, saying he did not like the English. He said he had been paid to kill Needham and told the other

Indians to kill Needham's companion. But they spared him, and he made it back to Fort Henry after a long journey."

Henry was devastated when he heard this. He had not heard from Needham since he left Charles Towne for Fort Henry two years ago. At the time, he had been upset with Needham for taking Wood up on his offer to work for him. But he had harbored no ill will against him. He recalled when the two of them had visited Occaneechi town on their Virginia journey for John Yeamans. Needham had not gotten along with the Occaneechi, and Henry had admonished him about it. However, if what the translator said was true, his death was not Needham's fault but an attempt by the Occaneechi to thwart Wood's trade agreement with the Cherokee.

The translator added, "The Occaneechi are bad people. When we sent men to their town to agree to use the Trading Path peacefully, they were killed. The Occaneechi are one of the reasons we no longer want to trade with Fort Henry. If we trade with you, we do not need to use that part of the Trading Path."

The translator's mention of the Occaneechi on the Trading Path reminded Henry of the agreement he had tried to make with the Cofitachequi, also on the Trading Path, four years earlier. Since that time, the tribe seemed to have simply vanished. He asked the translator if the Westo had ever dealt with the Cofitachequi.

The translator replied, "We have. They were bothering us and demanding payment as we passed by their town on the Trading Path. Then we heard that they said we were afraid of them and that they were better warriors. So we attacked them, killing some of them; their scalps are hanging in our town. They fled to the north and have never returned."

⸎

With his Westo entourage, Henry was back at St. Giles in early November, where he found Percival putting the final touches on the buildings. Henry told him that he had made a trade agreement with the Westo on the same terms as they had with Abraham Wood at Fort Henry, but he did not want to commit to trading for Indian slaves without Percival's approval.

Percival thought about it and said, "Shaftesbury instructed me to make a trade agreement with the Spanish at St. Augustine to sell them commodities, including Negroes. He gave you instructions to trade with the Indians for furs and other commodities. To my mind, Shaftesbury considers slaves to be commodities."

Henry replied, "But the Temporary Laws he sent to Charles Towne say that Indians cannot be made slaves."

To which Percival said, "The instructions he sent me say that when I set up his plantation, I am not subject to Charles Towne's laws, and I can trade with the Indians as I see fit. He knows who the Westo are and what they do. I see no problem in trading with them for Indian captives."

Henry said, "We should not allow them to take captives from the towns near Charles Towne. They should be taken from the Guale lands; the Indians who live there are allies of the Spanish. The Westo are already taking most of their captives there, so they should be agreeable."

Henry told the Westo they would buy Indian captives on the same terms as Fort Henry, but they must be from Guale, not from Carolina. After trading their skins and furs, the Westo left with a promise to return in March.

40

RED BIRD

Carolina Province, 1674–1675

The next four months passed quickly. *The Edisto* left in early January with a load of lumber to be delivered to Barbados and a hogshead of deerskins for England. Percival put the Indian boy given to Henry by the Westo chief on *The Edisto* to deliver him to a slave dealer in Barbados.

As promised, in early March, fifty Westo men laden with deerskins and furs, and a file of captive Indians, hands bound, appeared at St. Giles. After setting up camp at the same clearing they had used before, they began ferrying loads of deerskins and animal furs to the newly completed trading building. The final tally was less than Henry had hoped for -- 800 deerskins, 200 beaver pelts, twenty bearskins, and an assortment of otter, fox, raccoon, and other furs. Finally, the Westo brought in the Indian captives, twelve young men and boys.

Henry spent the next few days training Percival's servants to sort and grade the deerskins and furs and bargaining with the Westo for St. Giles' trade goods. Their leader was unhappy about the price Henry offered for the slaves; Henry told him that selling Indian slaves in Barbados was a new idea, and he did not know what price they would fetch there, compared to African slaves. Finally, the accounts were settled, the Westo men loaded up their trade goods and promised to return in the late fall. The captive Indian boys and young men were sent to Barbados, and the skins and furs were crated for shipment to London.

The following October, the Westo were back with skins, furs, and captives, more than they brought in March but still less than Henry and Percival had hoped for—they would need to at least double the volume for this to be a profitable venture.

When the skins and furs had been sorted and graded and prices for the captives had been negotiated, Henry told the Westo leader he wanted to accompany them back to their town to meet with their chief.

The week-long journey was much more enjoyable than Henry's first visit. The weather was mild and dry, and the men seemed to be in no hurry to return home. He received a warm welcome upon his arrival; two of the men had gone ahead to tell their chief, Paytah, he was coming, so a feast was waiting for him.

The next day, after the obligatory speeches, Henry told Paytah the purpose of his visit. "Could the Westo provide more skins, furs, and captives? Abraham Wood at Fort Henry traded with several Indian tribes; we want to trade only with you but, to do so, we will need more deerskins and more captive Indians."

Paytah replied that he would discuss Henry's request with the other tribal elders.

While Henry was waiting for the chief's response, he recalled that several months ago, John Locke had written him, asking about the religious beliefs of the Indians in Carolina. He had pen, ink, and paper with him, so it seemed appropriate to reply. He would tell Locke about the Escamacu Indians he had first lived with at Port Royal and compare them to the Westo.

Sir,

I have made the best inquiry that I can concerning the religion and worship, origins, and customs of our natives, especially among the Port Royal Indians amongst whom I am the best acquainted. They worship the sun and say that they have knowledge of Spirits who appear often to them. One sort of these Spirits abuses their women when he comes upon them in the woods, after which the women never conceive. They acknowledge the sun to be the cause of the growth and increase of all things, and likewise the cause of all diseases. They have several feasts and dances every year dedicated to the sun. They have some notion of the deluge and say that only two people were saved in a cave, who after the flood, found a dead red bird. They pulled the feathers from its body and blew them into the air. From each feather appeared Indians, a separate tribe for each feather, each with their own language, manner of dress, and name. The two Indians knew that the flood waters had dried up by the singing of the red bird. The Indians claim to be able to tell, no matter how far they are from the river, whether the tide is ebbing or flowing by the varying of the bird's note.

They believe, to acknowledge the immortality of the soul in allowing those who live morally, there is a place of rest, pleasure and plenty, and contrarywise, to the others a place where it is very cold and they are fed nothing but nuts and acorns, sitting upright in their graves.

They say they had knowledge of our coming into these parts several years before we arrived and some of them heard at night a great noise as if it were the falling of trees.

Some sort of Indians pretend to cure diseases by sucking on the affected part of the body but this is a fallacy as they make their own mouths bleed, pretending to have sucked the blood from their patients. Another sort acquires a general knowledge of herbs and roots, and gives this knowledge only to their next of kin. Had I not been up in the mainland, I would have sent some, but shall do so at the next opportunity. Another sort has such power over the rattle snakes that he sent out a snake several miles over rivers and flood tides to bite a particular Indian who had been overbearing. And the doctor who sent the snake was killed by the relatives of the other Indian. At the doctor's death, several snakes came and licked up his blood.

The Westos among whom I now am, worship the devil in carved images of wood. They are seated in a most fruitful soil and are a far more ingenious people than our coast Indians. I hope before my return to accomplish my business here and shall give you a further account by the next.

Yours to command,
Henry Woodward
From Westo town November 12, 1675

The following day Paytah told Henry that they could provide more deerskins and conduct more raids for Indian captives. They agreed that the Westo would come to St. Giles Kussoe the following spring with a larger shipment.

41

ST. GILES WIMBORNE

England, 1676

Paytah kept his promise. The following April, a hundred Westo men laden with skins and furs and bringing twenty-five captives showed up at St. Giles Kussoe. They spent the next two days ferrying their goods to the storage building until it was overflowing with two thousand deerskins, a thousand beaver pelts, ninety bearskins, and stacks of other furs.

Since the Westo's last visit, Henry and Percival had been busy preparing a price list, based on costs of the English trade goods and London market prices for deerskins, currently about four shillings for a large skin. Abraham Wood had told him that he aimed to make a four- or five-fold profit; he would do the same. The most common trade items were hatchets which cost a shilling; they set the trade price at one deerskin for one hatchet. A firelock musket cost ten shillings; the price was set at twelve deerskins. The price to pay for the captives was the hardest to determine. Wood had sold them directly to Virginia planters; St. Giles Kussoe would be dealing in the Barbados slave markets, with transportation costs and a middleman's cut. An African slave there cost about twenty pounds; Percival decided to undercut that price and sell theirs for fifteen. So, they would give the Westo seven muskets, or other goods of equivalent value, for each captive.

By the time the trading was completed and a final accounting made, Percival had run out of trade goods to exchange, and Henry had to convince the Westo to take credit for the remaining balance.

Henry was pleased—with twenty percent of the net profit, he had just made a large sum, although not as much as he had as a buccaneer. He decided this would be an ideal time to accompany the shipment of deerskins and furs to England and meet Shaftesbury in person. Percival was now experienced enough to handle the Westo trade in his absence.

—✦—

The voyage was unremarkable. *The Edisto*'s captain was first-rate, with numerous Atlantic crossings under his belt. Henry, berthed in the cabin reserved for Shaftesbury and his friends if any of them were ever inclined to visit Carolina, had the most comfortable voyage of his nautical travels.

The Edisto docked at Gravesend in early September, eleven years since Henry, nineteen years old, with only the clothes on his back and his father's surgeon's bag, had convinced the captain of a ship bound for Jamestown to take him on as the ship's surgeon. Then the Thames had been at a standstill due to the Great Plague. Now it was bustling; *The Edisto* had to wait two days for a ship's pilot to take it upriver to London.

Henry barely recognized the city. When he had left, the buildings were ramshackle wooden affairs, overhanging narrow streets. The streets were as he remembered -- narrow, smelly, and strewn with garbage, but the buildings had been rebuilt with stone and brick after the Great Fire of 1666. He walked around his old neighborhood, visiting Merchant Taylors' School, where he had spent a tedious year. It had been destroyed in the fire and rebuilt. He knew nobody there, so he did not linger.

The fire had not touched the Tower of London. Henry stood outside the walls, torn as to whether he wanted to visit the Royal Mint and his family's former home. Realizing this might be the last time he visited London, he finally went through the gate. His old home was unchanged. Seeing a man at the front door, he introduced himself: "I'm Henry Woodward, the son of John Woodward. He was the former Assay Master."

In turn, the man introduced himself, "I'm John Brattle, the current Assay Master. I worked with your father; he was a good man, and I'm sorry for your loss."

Henry had been unsure how he would feel coming back here. He realized that curiously, he felt almost nothing. He remembered living here, how much he had disliked Merchant Taylors' School and other details, but the memory of his family's deaths and the circumstance of leaving London seemed so distant it was as if it belonged to someone else.

Realizing he knew nobody in London and after six years of living in Carolina and finding the congestion, noise, and smell intolerable, he returned to

The Edisto. Shaftesbury's steward, Thomas Stringer, was supervising the unloading and storage of the crates of skins and furs.

Henry introduced himself and said, "I've come to London to meet Shaftesbury and John Locke and tell them about our Indian trading at St. Giles Kussoe."

Stringer replied, "Shaftesbury recently sold Exeter House and now lives at his family estate, St. Giles Wimborne, south of London. Locke left for France last year and is not expected back for some time."

Pressed by Henry about visiting Shaftesbury, Stringer said he would ask him about the possibility.

A week later, Henry received a written invitation to St. Giles; Stringer arranged for a carriage to take him. The coachman was pleasant, but from his comments, Henry could tell that he thought he was there as a servant. Henry said it was at Shaftesbury's invitation; he could not do enough for Henry from then on.

As a teen in London, Henry had never traveled far from the city in his five years. This was a new world for him; it was not the crowded squalor of the city nor the vast wilderness of Carolina. The carriage roads meandered through endless small fields interspersed with simple cottages; the scattered villages were lucky to have a single inn. The almost complete absence of trees was striking. Except for the occasional copse of oaks, fields dominated the landscape.

When Henry commented on it, the coachman told him, "It is said that hundreds of years ago, the countryside was covered with forests which were cut down to make ships for the English navy."

Henry thought to himself, *Our biggest export from Charles Towne is lumber. Could we ever run out of trees as well?* He decided that was unlikely—there were only a few hundred settlers and many thousands of trees.

On the first day of the journey, Henry found the scenery tranquil; by the second day, the sight of endless small farms was becoming tedious, and the people working in the fields seemed a pitiful sight, gaunt and dressed in rags. The coachman told him that most of the farmers were tenants of large landowners such as Shaftesbury, and they had a hard life—prices for crops and wool had been falling for years; many farmers were on the edge of starvation. Henry began to understand the allure of Charles Towne—as hard as it was there, this was worse.

Arriving at St. Giles Wimborne, Henry had expected to see a castle. But instead, it was a tasteful and comfortable-looking home, two stories of brick and stone, surrounded by outbuildings and barns. At the door, the butler greeted him and said he would tell Shaftesbury of his arrival, adding, "You must address him as 'your lordship.'" Recalling his meetings with Governor Modyford in Jamaica and Berkeley in Virginia, he was prepared for a lengthy wait. But Shaftesbury met him almost immediately. Henry knew that he was in his mid-fifties, but the man before him seemed older, tired, and not in good health.

Shaftesbury invited Henry to dinner, suggesting that he might want to change first. Henry was too embarrassed to admit that he was wearing his best clothes. Shaftesbury said he would have his son Ashley give him a tour of the estate before dinner.

Ashley, six years younger than Henry, was nearly an invalid and, to Henry, seemed rather slow-witted. But he was friendly and eager to show Henry the grounds. Their first stop was the riding house, where he had the groom saddle two horses for them. Ashley didn't ask Henry if he could ride, apparently assuming that, of course, he could.

The estate reminded him of Green Spring, Governor Berkeley's Virginia estate, with a myriad of fruit trees surrounding the house. But instead of tobacco, wheat and barley fields reached as far as one could see.

Ashley was eager to talk about the estate. "We have over 5,000 acres of fields and a forest, a river, and a lake. We also own most of the nearby tenant farms."

Henry remarked that his father must be very wealthy.

Ashley replied, "His income is 6,000 pounds; my own allowance is 1,400 pounds yearly."

Henry recalled how excited he had been when Shaftesbury had given him twenty pounds as a reward for his services several years earlier; he now realized that sum was only a trifle for him. Henry asked why his father had sold Exeter House in London and moved to Wimborne. Ashley's answer was muddled, but it seemed that Shaftesbury had so annoyed Charles II over matters involving the King's brother James that he had been banished from London.

The dinner was sumptuous, laid out on several tables in the large dining room. The head waiter guided Henry to his seat at Shaftesbury's table, seated next to Ashley, who proudly explained that his father, always the organizer, had just come up with a new seating plan: "Family and important guests sit at the main table and are served first. The second table to be served is the Stewards' Table for the most important household members. Next, the Gentlemen Waiter's Table is served, then the Groom's Table, and last, the Maids' Table. Each table is served food left from the last table. Then, any scraps are given to the poor people waiting at the gatehouse."

Hearing this, Henry got a better sense of Shaftesbury as a person. His letters had made him seem obsessively detail-oriented. Indeed he was.

After six weeks of shipboard rations, Henry found the dinner menu over-whelming. Heavy meat dishes, followed by venison, ending with fruits, sweets, and cheese. Some of Shaftesbury's friends were also seated at his table; when they learned who Henry was and where he was from, he was peppered with questions about life in Carolina and the Indians there.

He almost told them about his trip to Westo town, and the scalps hanging from the lodges there, but decided it was not a suitable dinner topic. He also did not mention his brief career as a buccaneer as Shaftesbury wanted him to make a trade agreement with the Spanish upon whom Henry Morgan's ships had preyed. From their comments, Henry could tell the guests found it hard to grasp that Charles Towne was a tiny colony of a few hundred people, poised on a small peninsula with marshes on one side and endless forest on the other. They found it even harder to understand when Henry told them he was the most at home in that forest with only Indians for company.

After dinner, the men retired to the library for drinks, where Shaftesbury was now the center of attention. He spoke at length about his mining invest-ments, managing the Hudson Bay Company, developing the Bahamas, and his ownership interest in the Royal African Company, buying and selling slaves. He said it was profitable, but his poor relationship with its governor, Charles II's brother, made his continued participation difficult.

The conversation then drifted to politics. Shaftesbury went on a lengthy tirade about Lord Danby and his Test Bill. Shaftesbury had written a pamphlet attacking Danby, *Letter from a Person of Quality to his Friend in the Country*, that caused such a furor the House of Lords ordered it be publicly burned.

Henry had no idea what Shaftesbury was talking about, but it sounded com-plicated and tedious, whatever it was.

By the end of the evening, Henry felt very small. Shaftesbury's world was so complex compared to his life in Carolina that Henry realized that he was only an insignificant player in one of Shaftesbury's many interests. Lying awake that night, thinking over the evening's conversation, he wondered how Shaftesbury would take to spending a week in Westo town.

Shaftesbury had invited Henry to stay at St. Giles as long as he wished, but he was starting to grow restless—entertainment on the estate was mainly riding and hunting, and in the evenings, drinking. But *The Edisto*, docked in London, wasn't to return to Carolina for another two weeks, and Henry decided that he would rather be bored at St. Giles than return to London to wait.

The day after the dinner party, Shaftesbury finally brought up the topic of Carolina. "I am very pleased with the trade agreement you have made with the Westo. This is the first profit I've seen on my investment in Carolina."

Henry thanked him and said that he planned for it to be even more profitable in the future.

Shaftesbury then asked, "Can you get more Indian captives? If you can, selling them in Barbados will be more profitable than deerskins and perhaps even more than my investment in the Royal African Company."

Henry remembered him mentioning the Company at dinner and asked him what it was.

"I am a major investor in the Company; it brings thousands of African captives each year to be sold as slaves to the sugar plantations in Barbados and Jamaica. It even sells some in Virginia Colony. But many die during the lengthy voyage, and many others are too ill to fetch a good price. The voyage from Carolina is much shorter, and few of the Indians will die or arrive in poor health. The demand for slaves is greater than what the Company can supply, so I can take as many Indian prisoners as you can provide."

Shaftesbury said he agreed with Henry's decision to take slaves from towns far away from Charles Towne. The tribes near the settlement provided an essential source of food, labor, and information; for that reason, it was important they not be mistreated. But it was clear to Henry that Shaftesbury saw all Indians as a resource to be exploited.

Shaftesbury brought up his wish that Henry could make a trade agreement with the Spanish at St. Augustine; he considered Spain an important ally and trading partner and wanted to expand the relationship to include St. Augustine.

Henry replied, "I spent almost two years in St. Augustine as their prisoner. It was once an important fort to protect the Spanish silver fleet but is now poor and run-down. It has few resources and has to import much of its food and supplies from Havana or neighboring Indian towns. Since Searle's raid, its governor has been determined to destroy Charles Towne and will never make a trade agreement with it or your plantation, even if he could afford to. I believe that St. Augustine will always be an enemy of Carolina even if England and Spain are at peace."

He added, "Just as the Indians around Charles Towne are important to us, the Guale Indians are important to the Spanish, especially as there were few soldiers at St. Augustine and the Guale are expected to support any attacks it makes against Charles Towne. So it is in our interest to have the Westo take captives from the Guale towns to weaken the Spanish." Henry did not feel it prudent to include his personal feelings about the Spanish and the Guale.

Shaftesbury reluctantly agreed with Henry's assessment and told him he need not pursue a trade agreement with them.

Henry had been given the informal role of keeping Shaftesbury's son Ashley entertained, a role he found tiresome but informative—Ashley seemed unable to keep any secrets about his father. Henry learned that, except for John Locke, Shaftesbury eventually turned against everyone in his life if he perceived that they had crossed him or his ideas. This even included Charles II, who he had so offended that he was within inches of being thrown in the Tower of London.

Henry was bored with life at St. Giles. He did not understand the world that Shaftesbury lived in, nor, he had to admit to himself, did he have much interest in it. His role as Ashley's companion was tedious—he had by now told him as much about his father as he could.

He began to explore the countryside on horseback; one afternoon, just outside of a small village, he saw a young woman, tall, plainly dressed, with long dark hair, on the road standing next to a horse, inspecting one of its hooves. Coming alongside, he greeted her; she replied by aiming a pistol at him, ordering him to stay back.

Laughing, he assured her he had no ill intentions toward her.

She looked him over—clean-shaven, well dressed, riding a beautiful horse; she lowered her pistol and said her horse had gone lame.

Henry said, "I'm not an expert on treating animals, but I trained as a surgeon and would be glad to take a look."

The problem turned out to be simple—a rock had lodged in its hoof; he removed it with his pocketknife. Introducing himself, he said he was staying at St. Giles Wimborne; he couldn't tell from her expression if she was impressed or not.

She said her name was Margaret; she was a servant at an estate not far from St. Giles. When she gave him a direct look with her brown eyes, Henry wavered for a moment. *Margaret.* Was he back on *The Three Brothers* or on a country lane in England?

"I do apologize for pointing a gun at you; several travelers were recently robbed on this road." She said it was her day off and, as she often did, she was exploring the countryside on horseback.

Henry, quickly recovering, asked if she minded him riding with her. He spent the next hour telling his life story. By the time they had reached her master's estate, all he had learned about her was that she was twenty, single, and bored with life in rural England.

Before turning his horse toward St. Giles, he asked if he could see her again. Smiling, she said, "Yes."

For the next week, he could not stop thinking about her. She had little free time away from her duties; he spent as much of it as possible with her. Then he heard *The Edisto* would be setting sail in several days. He had been looking forward to returning to Carolina; now, he found himself dreading the thought. In just a few days, Margaret had become the center of his world, and he did not want to leave England without her. He decided that, before *The Edisto* sailed, he would ask her to marry him. If she accepted, perhaps he could persuade her to return with him; if she wanted to stay in England, he would ask Shaftesbury for a job at St. Giles. He hoped she would want to leave with him.

He rode to her master's estate the following day, planning what he would tell her. When he arrived, she was outside in the garden.

His prepared speech deserted him; all he could get out was, "Margaret, will you marry me?"

Before he could say more, she said, "Henry Woodward, of course I will marry you, and I will go to Carolina with you if that is your wish."

They were married in the Parish Church of St. Giles two days later. Henry told Shaftesbury and sent a note to Stringer that there would be two of them returning to Carolina.

⁕

The day before Henry was to leave, Shaftesbury took him on a tour of his gardens and fruit orchards. In addition to the usual English fruit trees—apples, pears, plums, there were rows of peaches, figs, and nectarines, all laden with fruit. There were also acres of grapevines and mulberry, even some olive trees. These last three were the plants that Shaftesbury had been pushing the Charles Towne settlers to grow, so far unsuccessfully.

Shaftesbury, warming up to one of his favorite topics, money, explained his reasoning for these unusual plants: "Much of my income comes from the crops on my estate and rents from my tenant farmers. We grow mostly wheat, barley, and oats, but their prices have fallen for years. I'm trying different crops that could thrive here and be more profitable."

He continued, "I've been urging the settlers in Charles Towne to plant grapes, mulberry, olive, and silk trees for the same reason. I see this as the colony's future—large plantations with crops that don't compete with tobacco or sugar cane, worked by slaves, and owned by wealthy men who can afford to pay rent to the lords proprietors."

Shaftesbury said he had no interest in being personally involved in owning a plantation and had established St. Giles Kussoe only to recoup some of the funds he had poured into Carolina. The quickest way he had found to do this was to harvest timber, raise cattle, and trade with the Indians.

He then asked Henry what his plans were beyond the Indian trade, now that he was a married man.

When Henry admitted he had none, Shaftesbury told him that being an Indian trader was a way to make money to buy land and slaves and become a planter, but it was not what he should be doing once he had a family.

Knowing he needed to stay on Shaftesbury's good side, he thought it wise not to say that he had no love for plantation life after his experiences in Virginia and Jamaica. Instead, he said, "I'm working full time to build the Indian trade at St. Giles Kussoe and haven't had time to think beyond that."

The next day as Henry and his new wife prepared to board the coach for London, Shaftesbury handed him a small but heavy leather pouch, telling him it was a wedding present. He thanked Henry for the time he had spent with his son and that he was delighted with his efforts at St. Giles Kussoe. His parting words were, "You can shortly expect something further from me, showing my appreciation."

As the coach pulled away, Henry could not resist looking in the bag—it contained what looked to be at least a hundred golden guineas, more than enough for them to set up a comfortable home in Carolina.

Before *The Three Brothers* sailed, Henry stopped by Stringer's office in London to say goodbye. Stringer congratulated Henry on his marriage and added, "Did you know that John Godfrey arrived from Charles Towne earlier this week?"

Henry had not heard and asked if he knew what he was doing in London.

"He was quite secretive, but I understood that he is here to meet with Sir Peter Colleton."

Henry knew Colleton was one of the only lords proprietors, other than Shaftesbury, who had shown any interest in Carolina Colony and that both he and Godfrey were Barbadians. Were they going behind Shaftesbury's back about something? Either he would find out later, or he wouldn't. Shrugging, he thanked Stringer for the information and departed.

42

LONDON

April 1677

Sir Peter Colleton looked around the lords proprietors seated at the table—Albemarle, Craven, Clarendon, and most important, Shaftesbury. Three of them were not in attendance.

"Gentlemen, I called this meeting to discuss the Carolina Colony. As you know, any hopes we may have had of making a profit from the colony have not been realized. The settlers cannot afford to pay rent to us, and some are still asking us to support them. But that is not why I called this meeting—John Godfrey, a friend of mine from Barbados and one of the settlers, recently visited me. He said that Shaftesbury has established a 12,000-acre plantation near Charles Towne and now has a profitable trade with the Indians. He told me that the only way for us to make a profit from the colony at present is the Indian trade."

Shaftesbury interrupted—"Why is this anyone's business other than my own? The Fundamental Constitutions allow each of us to establish a plantation of our own in Carolina and what we do with it is up to us."

Colleton replied, "I agree with you in part. But Charles II awarded Carolina to us as a reward for our help in putting him on the throne. He intended that we all benefit from the colony; at present, only *you* benefit. I remember you saying that Governor Yeamans was the only person in Charles Towne making money at the expense of the other colonists. I believe you are now doing the same. Godfrey tells me you profit more from selling Indian slaves in Barbados than from your interest in the Royal African Company. I believe that, just like the Company, any of us should be able to invest in the colony and share in the profits."

Shaftesbury, now red in the face, shouted, "None of you have lifted a finger to develop Carolina—it has been my effort alone. Why should you now share in

166

the fruits of my labor? Also, almost all the profit comes from trading with one Indian tribe, the Westo, and my agent, Dr. Henry Woodward, is the only one who can deal with them."

Colleton responded, "Godfrey suggested that I establish a 12,000-acre plantation and set up an Indian trade there. I would hire a manager, just as you did, but I agree that, at least for now, nobody else has Woodward's skills in dealing with the Indians. So, I propose that he be the agent for any of us who wish to participate in the Indian trade. We would each honor his agreement with you that he receive one-fifth of the profits from such trades. You can keep your trade agreement with the Westo; but there are other tribes we can trade with. Any of us that wish to participate would contribute funds to an account managed by our treasurer."

Shaftesbury asked, "So, who among you is interested in having your own plantation and Indian trade in Carolina?"

Only Colleton answered: "I am."

Shaftesbury then said, "Well, that's a different matter. There isn't room in Carolina for each of you to set up your own Indian trade. But, if it's only Sir Peter, we can work something out. The only Indians I know of who are worth the trouble of making a trade agreement with are the Westo and the Creek. They are good hunters and warriors who can bring us deerskins and Indian slaves. There may be other tribes distant from Charles Towne to trade with as well. The Indians around Charles Towne are peaceful farmers and fishermen who are not profitable trading partners. I propose that Sir Peter and I keep the Westo, Creek, and other distant tribes for ourselves. Charles Towne can trade with the tribes who live close to the settlement. We can tell them this is for their own good."

After further discussion, Colleton said, "Let's put it to a vote."

The proposal passed unanimously. The proprietors agreed to put it in writing and send an order to the Charles Towne governor notifying him of the terms.

10 April, 1677
Whereas we have thought it necessary for the safety and good of those people that are planted and our Government in Carolina upon Ashley and Cooper Rivers to take into our hands during the space of seven years the whole trade and commerce with the Westo, Creek, and other Nations that live at a great distance from the said Rivers, and whereas it is absolutely necessary that trade be carried on with these nations, that so they may be supplied with commodities according to agreement made with us, by which means a firm and lasting peace shall be continued, and we become useful and necessary to them, it is agreed that before the 24th day of June next,

we shall each pay into the hands of Mr. William Saxby, our Secretary and Treasurer, one hundred pounds, and if any of us shall fail in paying, then it is agreed that the benefit of the trade shall accrue to such of us as have paid. And it is further agreed that the agreements already made by the Earl of Shaftesbury with Dr. Henry Woodward, whereby he is to have one fifth part of the clear profit of said trade, shall stand firm and good.

In witness whereof we have hereunto put our hands and seals, the 10th day of April, 1677.

Before they adjourned, Shaftesbury said, "We need to keep Woodward on our side for this to work. He's the only person in Carolina who knows how to trade with the Indians and is only paid one-fifth of the net profits. Unless you object, I propose that we award him 2,000 acres of land in the colony; it would cost us nothing and will give him the incentive to keep working for us."

The weather was uneventful for Henry and Margaret's Atlantic crossing. Once again, the captain had given Shaftesbury's cabin to Henry, so the voyage, her first, was pleasant.

She spent hours on *The Edisto's* bow, silent, gazing into the distance. Henry finally asked, "What do you see?"

"Nothing and everything. In Dorset, I could only see as far as the distance across a field. It was always the same fields, day after day. Here, I can see to the edge of the world. Like the fields, every day it's the same. But it's also never the same."

⚬⚬⚬

Arriving in Charles Towne, *The Edisto* unloaded its two passengers, supplies, and trade goods for St. Giles Kussoe.

Henry's yawl was tied up where he had left it, now with a foot of rainwater in it, nearly submerged. As he bailed it out, he wondered, *What will Margaret think of my home?* He had replaced his daub and wattle shack with a one-room log cabin, but it had a leaky roof, a dirt floor, no windows, and no fireplace. Henry knew she was used to far better in England, even as a servant.

But he needn't have worried—as they sailed up the Ashley River, she was so taken with a school of dolphins following them, white egrets under the moss-covered oak trees along the riverbank, and even an alligator basking in the sun, that she barely noticed his home when they arrived.

Henry tied up his yawl and ran up to the cabin, several sheets of parchment in hand. Margaret was outside, working in their garden.

"Exciting news for us! Shaftesbury has awarded me 2,000 acres of land and appointed me as his deputy for Charles Towne. He also sent me a copy of an order to Governor West—Charles Towne is prohibited from trading with the Westo and Creek for seven years. He calls me 'Dr. Woodward' and credits me for discovering those tribes."

> *To the governor and Grand Council at Charles Towne:*
>
> *Whereas the discovery of the Country of the Westo and the Creek, two powerful and warlike nations, has been made at the charge of the Earl of Shaftesbury, one of our number, and by the industry and hazard of Dr. Henry Woodward, and a strict peace and amity made between those nations and our people in the Province of Carolina, which will conduce very much to the peace and settlement of our people there and encourage others to come and plant there when these fierce and warlike nations are not only at peace with us but become a safeguard to us from the injuries of the Spanish and other Indians.*
>
> *We therefore command that no person under our government there have any commerce, trade, and traffic or correspondence with any of the Westo, Creek, Spaniards, or other Indians that live beyond Port Royal or at the same distance from our settlement that the Westo and Creek now inhabit, without such persons having license from the Earl of Shaftesbury and one more of the lords proprietors for seven years.*
>
> *We leave all trade free and open north along the coast as far as the Santee Hills and south as far as Port Royal and not less than 100 miles in any other direction, it being fit that we should not be interrupted by you in our treaties and transactions with these Nations that inhabit those distant countries by charge from his Majesty only we have the authority to treat or intermeddle. We expect exact and punctual compliance with our order and shall cause any who break it to be severely prosecuted and punished.*
>
> *Given under our hands and seals this 10th day of April 1677.*

Henry spent the next month looking for the perfect 2,000-acre tract, finding that the most desirable lands along the rivers had already been claimed. Finally, he turned to his Kiawah friends for ideas; they suggested he look along the Stono River south of Charles Towne. Taking their advice and one of them as a guide, he sailed up the Stono but found most of the land too marshy. Frustrated, he anchored at the mouth of a creek emptying into the river.

His guide told him, "We call this Abbapoola Creek. I think it is deep enough for your boat if you want to explore it."

They sailed upstream until his yawl began to touch bottom, where he tied up at a point on the north bank. The land was every bit as fine as St. Giles Kussoe—open savannahs mixed with oak and cedar forest. He decided that if it was available, he would take it. But he remembered he was now married—he needed Margaret's approval.

Standing on the same point as he had the day before, he asked her, "What do you think of it? Our house would be on the hill overlooking the creek. We would graze cattle on the open land and cut timber from the forests."

Margaret agreed. "You've found a wonderful location. Could we put a horse pasture over here, next to where the house will be?"

Having Margaret's blessing, Henry asked the Charles Towne surveyor if the land along Abbapoola Creek was available. It was; Henry told him to issue a warrant for the 2,000 acres.

Other than Shaftesbury, he was now one of the largest landowners in Carolina.

44

ABBAPOOLA CREEK

1677–1678

It was July in Charles Towne, miserably hot and humid. Margaret, who had never been away from Dorset with its cool summers, suffered in silence. She had taken it upon herself to put in a large garden behind the cabin, but it was too hot to work by mid-morning, and it got worse as the days progressed.

She had vowed not to complain about her new home, but finally, she asked Henry, "Is it always like this in the summertime?"

Henry, like most settlers, paid scant attention to the summer weather, simply enduring it. "What do you mean?" he said.

"It's so hot I can't work outside most of the day."

Henry replied, "Well, yes, it is hot in the summer. But it will be cooler by October."

"Oh."

By August, she was beginning to wonder what she had gotten herself into. She loved Henry but, when she agreed to come to Carolina Colony with him, she thought she would be escaping to a world of excitement and adventure. Charles Towne was not that world, at least for her. Margaret's days were spent alone at their cabin while Henry was miles away at St. Giles Kussoe, or even farther. She knew no one in the settlement and missed her family. She thought, *I shouldn't feel sorry for myself; at least I don't have to work in the heat like the indentured servants.* But that was little consolation to her—at least they were busy; this was the first time in her life she had more time than she knew what to do with.

She tried to put on her best face, but she became more withdrawn day by day.

Finally, Henry asked, "Margaret, you seem unhappy. Is something wrong?"

"Nothing, dear. The heat must be getting to me."

"I've been thinking—you must get bored here with me gone all day and you knowing nobody here. Why don't we start building our house at Abbapoola Creek?"

Margaret's face immediately brightened. "Henry, that's a wonderful idea. My father built homes before he died; I think he had always wanted a son to go into business with him, but he did teach me a lot. I would love to help you with our new home."

<hr>

"I want us to have the grandest home in Charles Towne. With the funds Shaftesbury gave us as a wedding present and what I've made in the Indian trade, we can afford to build a home like Shaftesbury's at St. Giles Wimborne."

Margaret laughed. "I saw his home once; it's a brick mansion. Even though we could afford it; there are no bricks or stone here, only trees. Our home will have to be made of wood, and it won't be a mansion."

She threw herself into the new project; two weeks later, she told Henry what she had planned. "It will be post and beam construction, two stories tall with a stair tower in the back and a parlor and porch in front. There will be a fireplace on either end of the house, and the kitchen will be outside to keep the house cooler in the summer. It must have glass windows and wood floors."

Henry realized he was out of his depth—he had never lived in anything other than the small house at the Royal Mint in London and even smaller dwellings in Virginia and Charles Towne. "I'll leave the design up to you. I can get started clearing the lot and cutting trees for lumber."

<hr>

Their new home kept Margaret and Henry busy. He hired a crew of indentured servants to fell trees and cut lumber for the house; Margaret was designing the home, working with a carpenter in town who was more than happy to put his skills to something other than making barrel staves.

By November, the lot had been laid out; they were ready to begin construction. Henry's crew had cut a stack of twenty-foot-long oak logs for the upright posts. The carpenter said to Henry and Margaret, "I know that digging the posts into the ground is how it's been done for years, but I heard about a new method they're using Virginia. When the posts are buried in the ground, they begin to rot within the year. But if the sills are laid on wooden blocks and the posts set on top of them, the posts don't touch the ground."

Henry added, "We can use cedar for the wooden blocks—we have a forest full of cedar; it never rots."

Finally, the enormous oak posts had been set in place with the help of a pair of borrowed draft horses. Then, the workers attached the horizontal girts and plates to the posts, creating the frame for the two-story home. Next, joists were added to carry oak plank flooring.

Margaret was so engrossed in the building process that she spent more hours at Abbapoola Creek than Henry was spending at St. Giles; she was the happiest Henry had seen her since their voyage to Charles Towne.

The roof rafters and laths were in place by February, and the workmen were busily splitting cedar logs for the shingles. When the exterior wall studs were set in place, Margaret said, "It's starting to look like a real home. When can we spend the night?"

"Let's wait for doors and windows," replied Henry. "There are still wolves and bears here."

⸺◈⸺

Two months later, the glass casement windows, specially ordered from England, hadn't yet arrived, so work was at a temporary standstill. Margaret, back at their cabin with nothing to occupy her time, was becoming dejected. One evening she said to Henry, "You never talk about work. What is it that you do at St. Giles Kussoe? There must be more to it than trading deerskins for glass beads."

Henry got a sinking feeling—he realized that, intentionally or not, he had not been very forthcoming about what he did for a living. "Well, I trade a lot more than just beads—cloth, iron tools, even guns."

"Guns? The Indians here don't have guns. Who are you trading with?"

It all came out. Henry told her about the Westo capturing Indians and bringing them to St. Giles. Andrew Percival then sent them to Barbados to be sold as slaves to work on sugar plantations. He got twenty percent of the profit from the sales.

Margaret was horrified—first speechless, then angry.

"How could you do such a horrible thing? I thought the Indians were your friends."

"Some of the Indians are; the ones we are capturing are allies of the Spanish at St. Augustine; they are not my friends."

This did not satisfy Margaret; Henry found himself trying to justify how he made his living. "I never thought much about it. At Fort Henry, where I grew up, Abraham Wood traded in Indian slaves with the Westo. When Shaftesbury

174

hired me to develop an Indian trade at St. Giles Kussoe, I took over Wood's trade with the Westo, including buying their Indian captives. Both Shaftesbury and Percival knew and approved of it. I don't allow the Westo to take any Indians who are our friends."

"Henry, I'm ashamed of you. I don't even know what to think about this. It's not right for someone to own another human being; it's even worse to sell them.

"Look at how many people in England, including Shaftesbury, are getting rich selling slaves from Africa," Henry defended.

"That is also wrong, but you're doing it here and now. Couldn't you stop trading in slaves and just trade for deerskins?"

"Percival and Shaftesbury would immediately fire me. They make a lot more profit from selling slaves than deerskins. I have no other way to make a living here."

⸻ ∾ ⸻

A week later, Margaret was still barely speaking to him; glares were her primary method of communication. Henry, who had never before spent a lot of time thinking about the morality of how he made a living, finally realized that she wasn't going to change her mind about how she felt. He thought, *We can't continue like this; there must be something I can do.*

Then he remembered when they had picked out their land on Abbapoola Creek, Margaret pointed out where she wanted a horse pasture. Why not buy the horses now? She loved to ride; that should take her mind off their problems. *What were those horses he'd seen at Governor Berkeley's plantation in Virginia? Quarter pathers.* The plantation manager had told him that Berkeley and his friends raced them on the path to Jamestown. Perhaps he could buy a pair. Henry knew that his old friend, Henry Brayne, captain of a ship sailing between Charles Towne and Virginia Colony, was in town.

"Henry Woodward, I haven't seen you in for ever. What are you up to?"

"The Indian trade business is keeping me busy. I recently married a woman I met in England; we're building a home south of Charles Towne. Do you know anything about horses?"

"No, why do you ask?

"I'd like to get my wife a riding horse as a surprise. She loves riding, and there is little to keep her busy here. I saw a kind of horse in Jamestown they call quarter pathers; Governor Berkeley races them at his plantation. Would you be willing to see if you could buy a pair for us?"

"Of course. I'm going to Jamestown next week and returning here after that. I'll see if I can find some to bring back then."

—∾∾—

Henry was meeting with Andrew Percival at St. Giles Kussoe when he saw a ship tie up at the wharf. It was Henry Brayne, and he had company, two beautiful horses tethered on the deck.

"Here's your quarter pathers from Jamestown. I bought them at a good price from someone who won them in a card game. I had a horse expert look at them; he said they're fine animals."

One was a sorrel mare for Margaret, the other a taller chestnut gelding for Henry.

Brayne added, "You didn't mention anything about saddles, so I took the liberty of buying two; one is a woman's saddle."

Thanking him, Henry paid him from the shrinking pile of guinea coins Shaftesbury had given him and took the animals to the stable at St. Giles Kussoe.

—∾∾—

Henry thought briefly of bringing Margaret to St. Giles to surprise her with the horses but decided that was probably not a wise idea. Instead, he saddled both horses, mounted his, and ponied the mare behind him back to their cabin. Tying them up, he asked Margaret to come outside.

"Do we have company?" she said when she saw the two saddled horses.

When he told her the horses were theirs, he saw her smile for the first time in weeks. She climbed onto the mare immediately and disappeared down the trail, returning five minutes later. "I love her—what is her name?

Henry realized he'd forgotten to ask Brayne. "You get to choose it."

"My favorite horse in Dorset was Molly; that's what I'll call her."

As Henry hoped, Margaret's horse carried her out of her dark mood. She rode every day, with or without him, to Abbapoola Creek to check the progress on their house, into town for supplies, or just for pleasure. In the evenings, the two would often ride together. Henry never understood why she preferred riding with a side-saddle; her explanation was that's how it was done in England. It didn't seem safe to him, especially as Molly was a little skittish.

—∾∾—

One summer evening, heading back to their cabin, Margaret called out, "I'll race you!" and, with that, took off at a gallop.

Henry's horse was faster, and he quickly pulled ahead. Out of the corner of his eye, he saw a snake coiled along the side of the path; it looked like a rattlesnake. As he turned to call out to Margaret to watch out, Molly, also seeing it, bucked; Margaret was thrown.

Henry turned back to help her to her feet; she wasn't moving. Dismounting, he saw her lying on her back, seemingly uninjured. But her neck was at an impossible angle. He immediately knew she was dead.

45

SORROW

Summer 1678

Henry buried his wife on the overlook at Abbapoola Creek. The next day, he took the two horses to St. Giles Kussoe.

"Henry, you look terrible. Is something wrong?" the foreman asked.

"My wife just died. Please tell Percival that he can have these horses. I'm going to be gone for a while; I don't know when I'll be back."

"What happened? Where are you going?"

"Her horse threw her; she broke her neck. I don't know where I'm going."

⁕

Henry indeed had no idea where he would go; all he knew was he wanted it to be far away. The next day, he was deep in the wilderness, his brain in turmoil. *How could I have killed the two women I loved? The first, because I insisted we stop at St. Catherine's; now my wife dies because I bought her a horse to try to keep her from being angry with me.*

But solitude failed to bring Henry escape from the most profound sadness he had ever experienced; he couldn't keep Margaret out of his thoughts—the first time they met in England—Margaret pointing her pistol at him, then claiming his heart and mind. Margaret, watching for hours at the bow of *The Edisto* on the voyage to Charles Towne. Margaret, seeing Abbapoola Creek for the first time, showing him where she wanted their horse pasture.

Was he cursed? Everything he touched turned to ash.

After three days, he realized that if he continued further into the forest with no food, he would not have the strength to return. He didn't know if he wanted to return or not. But he owed the women who had died something; he didn't know what. He turned back toward St. Giles. When he arrived, the foreman, upon seeing him, said nothing. Instead, he instructed a servant to lay out a meal for him.

His cabin reminded him of Margaret every waking and even sleeping moment. He decided to move into the unfinished Abbapoola Creek home, but the memories were even stronger there. He instructed the workmen to do no further work and board it up. St. Giles Kussoe was worse—after the Westo delivered a group of Guale captives, all he could think of that night was Margaret's horror when she found out he dealt in Indian slaves.

Having nowhere else to go, he returned to where he had stayed when he first arrived ten years earlier—Kiawah town. He felt welcome there; they were always kind to him, and their simple life of farming and fishing was exactly what he craved. By that fall, his world began to seem brighter.

Finally, feeling ready to face fellow settlers, he went into Charles Towne. One of the first people he saw was John Godfrey. "I'm very sorry to hear about your wife's death. That was a terrible tragedy," Godfrey said. "I don't know if you've heard, but my daughter Mary also lost her husband last month."

Henry replied, "I don't know her very well, but please give her my condolences; I know how hard it is."

"Yes, she does have her daughter as comfort, but the loss is still difficult for her."

Hearing that made Henry realize how alone he was in the world—no family, no close friends. It came to him that he needed to find some happiness where he could—his fondest memories were his childhood with his family in Virginia Colony, Bella at Port Royal, telling him the story of the red bird, of his brief time with Margaret Tuder on *The Three Brothers*, and the few happy months he spent with his wife. He needed to hold on to them.

46

MARY GODFREY

Charles Towne, 1678–1679

Henry saw John Godfrey in town at a council meeting a month later. As Shaftesbury's deputy, Henry was supposed to attend all of the meetings but hadn't for a long time. Godfrey said, "My wife and I were talking about you the other day; she asked me to invite you for Christmas dinner."

A home-cooked meal sounded wonderful; also, Godfrey was someone Henry wanted to get to know better. One of the original Barbadian investors in William Hilton's 1663 exploration of the Carolina coast, he was the former acting governor and Lieutenant Colonel of the militia. He was also reputed to be wealthy.

"Thank you; I would be delighted to accept."

"Wonderful, we'll see you Christmas afternoon. By the way, my daughter Mary will be there as well."

Why would he mention that? Henry thought to himself, *I don't even know her.* Then he remembered—she was a recent widow.

Henry grew increasingly nervous as Christmas day approached. He wanted to make a good impression on Colonel Godfrey and his wife, but he hadn't been to a formal dinner in years. His clothing was nearly in rags, so he went into town to buy a new shirt, pants, and shoes. He knew he was expected to bring the hostess a gift but found nothing appropriate in the small shop.

Returning home, he saw an orange tree laden with ripe fruit, a survivor from the days of the Spanish, and remembered that his mother always gave him and his brother oranges for Christmas.

Freshly bathed and shaved, wearing his new clothes, and a bag of oranges in hand, Henry knocked on the door of the Colonel's residence. A Negro servant answered and ushered him inside. The house was filled with Godfreys—John introduced his wife, two sons, his daughter Mary, and an assortment of grandchildren. It was also filled with the smells of Christmas dinner. The remains of a yule log blazed in the hearth with cut greens surrounding the chimney.

Henry had not seen such a lavish table since Shaftesbury's estate in England. The centerpiece was a boar's head decorated with sprigs of rosemary, accompanied by mincemeat pies, two roast turkeys, venison, sturgeon, oysters, and other dishes Henry couldn't identify, all to be washed down with flagons of spiced wine.

The Godfrey adults were excellent conversationalists, and the children were well behaved. Henry found himself talking more than he had in a long time, and as the evening progressed, directing his tales toward Mary. A few years younger than him, she was pretty and self-assured. She had a daughter about ten, also named Mary.

By the end of the evening, Henry did not want to leave. All that was waiting for him was his cold, dark, and lonely cabin. As he said his goodbyes, Mary gave him a basket of leftovers and said, "I very much enjoyed meeting you and look forward to seeing you again."

That comment brightened his way home.

Henry and Mary did meet again, repeatedly, and were soon married. Mary, who had already been a wife for almost ten years, settled quickly into a domestic routine; Henry moved from his one-room cabin into Mary's home.

But it was falling apart—almost ten years old and poorly constructed. Henry had put his uncompleted and abandoned home at Abbapoola Creek out of his mind after Margaret's death, but it now seemed the logical solution to their problem. He told Mary about the house's history and what had happened to Margaret. The story didn't seem to bother her, and he found that talking about it made him feel better.

The Abbapoola home had been nearly completed when Henry boarded it up. Other than a family of raccoons that had taken up residence, it was as he had left it; Mary pronounced that she thought it was a fine home. The long-awaited windows had arrived from England and were waiting to be installed, and the second-story flooring had not been laid.

The workers finished the home in July, and, by the end of the month, Henry, Mary, and her daughter were comfortably settled.

Abbapoola Creek was isolated; the nearest neighbor was some two miles away. Henry spent much of his time at St. Giles Kussoe; Mary, now five months pregnant, was bored and lonely. One morning over breakfast, she said to Henry, "Have you considered making a plantation here? You have 2,000 acres of good land; we could grow crops, raise livestock, and harvest timber. You're only thirty-three, but someday you'll be fifty-three, and being an Indian trader will seem a hard life."

Henry laughed. "Shaftesbury told me the same thing when he gave me this land. You are probably correct, but I find the life of a planter boring."

"I know you're happy as a trader and would never ask you to stop," replied Mary. "But I have an idea—I could develop and manage Abbapoola Point as a plantation; you continue as a trader. If you ever decide to settle down, it would be waiting for you."

"Mary, do you have any idea how much work it is to clear forests, plow fields, build fences? We would need a team of laborers which I can't afford."

Mary responded, "When we arrived in Charles Towne from Barbados, we had five indentured servants and a slave. I'm used to managing workers."

If Henry thought Mary would give up on the idea of turning Abbapoola Point into a plantation, he was mistaken. Almost every evening, she had new plans and ideas to tell him about; he realized she had a knack for planning and organization that he lacked. Finally, he gave in.

Mary was prepared. "I've been talking about this with my father and brother. They both agreed that we would need five or six workers to develop a plantation of this size. Indentured servants are hard to come by and too expensive; we would need to buy Negro slaves."

Henry knew that most of the successful settlers in Charles Towne now had African slaves, but even though he was the agent for St. Giles Kussoe's

Indian slave trade, he had never considered being a slave owner himself. He recalled Shaftesbury telling him that his vision for Carolina Colony was large plantations owned by wealthy planters with Negro slaves. Was this going to become his future?

He told Mary, "Andrew Percival recently bought several slaves through his uncle in Barbados; I could ask him to find some for us as well. He's in Bermuda now; I could write him there. I have enough credit with him at St. Giles to cover the cost."

Mary replied, "That seems a good idea. Ask him to buy a Negro or mulatto girl who speaks English for the house; the others will work outdoors."

"I'll write him."

⎯⎯∾⎯⎯

To Mr. Andrew Percival

Sir,

Pray buy me three Negro lads, two Negro girls, all of them, if possible, under twenty years of age, and one native-born Negro or Mulatto girl about the same age, if to be had. If you pay a premium rate, make sure that they are, in your judgment, choice likely slaves. If you are not in Bermuda, please give me credit with Mr. Joseph Harbin in Barbados for the like number of slaves to be sent at the first opportunity. If they are of different countries, the better, but by no means to be all of one language. If you do not have the opportunity to buy the Negroes, then leave the above-mentioned credit with Mr. Harbin.

Oct. 17, 1679

Yours, Henry Woodward

47

GOOSE CREEK MEN

Spring 1679–1680

On a gloomy February evening at Yeamans Hall Plantation, Maurice Mathews, well into his third mug of rum, was bitterly complaining to his friend James Moore. Two years earlier, when John Yeamans's wife died, her daughter, now Moore's wife, inherited the property, a thousand-acre plantation located along Goose Creek, north of Charles Towne. Boasting the only brick home in the colony, it was a favorite meeting place for a group of disgruntled former Barbadian planters known as the Goose Creek Men. Mathews was their de facto leader, Moore, his lieutenant.

"When Peter Colleton hired me last year to manage his new plantation, Fairlawn, he promised I would be paid as much as Andrew Percival at St. Giles Kussoe. I'm barely making enough to put food on the table. I can only trade with the northern Indians for deerskins; Percival has a monopoly on trading with the Westo for Indian slaves. Also, Henry Woodward is supposed to be the agent for both plantations but refuses to make any effort to help me expand my business."

Moore, known for his bluntness, replied, "So what are you going to do about it?"

Mathews had only intended to complain, not propose a solution. But Moore, in addition to the rum, got him thinking. "Percival is in England, not to return for months. While he's gone, perhaps I could persuade the Westo to start trading with me."

Moore said, "We've taken a hard line against them in the past, barring them from coming into town. Why should they trust you now?"

"I get along well with our Indian neighbors, but I don't understand the Westo. All I know is that I can't make a living as an Indian trader without dealing

184

in slaves, and Percival, Woodward, and the Westo control the business. Maybe I should visit them while Percival's away. But it's a long journey, and my health does not allow me to travel that far."

Moore asked, "Are you looking at me?"

"I wasn't, but that's a good idea. Would you be willing to do it?"

Moore replied, "The lords proprietors barred us from dealing with the Westo. But if we can get permission from Governor West and the council, I would consider it. John Boone might be willing to go with me; he's always looking for an adventure, and he's no fan of Percival or Woodward."

Mathews said, "I think we have enough friends on the council to agree to let us visit the Westo; I'll ask West to set up a meeting."

⸺〰⸺

A month later, back in Charles Towne, Moore and John Boone met with Mathews to tell him about their visit to Westo town.

"That was quite the experience," Moore said. "I believe we're lucky to have our scalps still. The Westo are every bit as fearsome as we've heard. They must have as many guns as we do and are suspicious of everyone except Woodward. They seemed to have been expecting us; perhaps he tipped them off. I believe they would die before abandoning him."

Mathew replied, "Perhaps it will come to that someday. In the meantime, I'll think of something we can do while Percival is still in England."

48

HENRY AND PAYTAH PLOT

February 1679–1680

My father stopped by while you were out and said that you need to see him right away," Mary told Henry as he walked into the house. "Did he say what it was about?"

"No," she replied, "Only that it's important."

"Well, dinner is important also. It will have to wait until tomorrow."

Henry was at his father-in-law's home the next day.

Godfrey said, "I'm not sure what to make of this information, but it's important you know about it. Maurice Mathews and James Moore recently met with the council; Mathews said he had heard that the Westo were planning to attack our Indian neighbors and that he was working on a plan to stop them from ever being a threat to our security again. The council approved Moore visiting Westo town to spy on them, but nothing further."

After hearing the details of Mathew's plan to deal with the Westo, Henry replied, "Thank you for warning me; this is indeed concerning. Mathews has been angry recently; he believes he's not getting a big enough share of the Indian trade. With Percival in England, he may have decided it's a good time to do something about it. I'm going to have to go to Westo town to warn them. I don't want to leave Mary and the children alone at Abbapoola Creek, especially now that she's expecting another child. Could I leave them with you?"

"Of course, we are always delighted to see them. Be careful; I don't trust Mathews or Moore."

⌘

Henry and his two Kiawah guides were on the trail the next day. As always, the chief, knowing they were on the way, had a feast ready for him when they arrived at Westo town.

After exchanging gifts and listening to the chief's speeches, Henry said, "I told you earlier that Andrew Percival is in England and not expected to return for several months. You know there is a new plantation, Fairlawn, set up to trade with the northern Indian towns. Maurice Mathews manages it. He is angry because those towns are only providing him a few deerskins and no captives. I heard that Mathews told the leaders in Charles Towne that he is sending two men here to spy on you and see how powerful you are. He said he then plans on inviting you and the other Westo leaders to negotiate but instead will take you prisoner and sell you as slaves. He would then organize a raid to destroy Westo town. I believe he plans to take over the entire Indian trade."

Paytah replied, "We will watch for them. You told me that you heard of the Battle of Bloody Run. The Virginia militia tried to do the same to us twenty years ago. They killed our leaders, including my father, by trickery, but we defeated them in battle. The Charles Towne leaders are too few to attack us by themselves, and none of their Indian neighbors are strong enough to help them with such a raid."

"Be careful. If what I heard is true, Mathews and Moore are our enemies. While Percival is gone, there is little I can do to stop them."

Paytah replied, "There is a town elder named Ariano here who is unhappy with me and some other elders because we did not allow him to become our chief. I have never trusted him; he is the kind of man who might plot with Mathews for revenge, so watch out for him."

Changing the subject, Paytah said, "I told you last fall that it is getting harder for us to capture Indians in the Guale towns. Many of them are moving closer to St. Augustine for protection; soon, we will have trouble bringing you enough captives. We are planning an attack on the town of Santa Catalina de Guale at St. Catherine's. It's the most important Spanish outpost in the Guale lands. Several hundred Guale Indians live there, and it only has a small force of Spanish soldiers. We could easily destroy it in a single day and be gone before more soldiers arrive from St. Augustine. With the town gone, we would have new lands to raid for captives."

Paytah now had Henry's undivided attention. He had vowed to avenge Margaret Tuder's death in St. Augustine but had never had an opportunity to do so. Attacking St. Catherine's would be the perfect answer—this was where, ten years ago, the Spanish and their Guale allies had seized her and the other settlers when *The Three Brothers* put ashore for supplies. He told Paytah, "Not only do I think well of your idea, but I would also like to accompany you. Have you decided when?"

"Before summer, perhaps in two months."

Henry replied, "That would be a good time for me. Percival won't be back from England yet, so I won't need to tell him about it. He would probably approve, but I think it best if he doesn't know about it beforehand."

<hr>

Henry and Paytah spent the next day planning the raid, agreeing that a force of one hundred warriors would be adequate. Henry said, "Several years ago when I helped you make a peace treaty with the Creek Indians, I promised their chief that I would bring them into the Indian trade at St. Giles Kussoe. I never did, and he recently asked me about it. They are strong warriors; why don't we include them in the raid? They would be good allies for both of us to have."

Paytah thought for a while and then said, "We've always done raids alone, so this is hard for me to consider. But the Creek are neighbors of ours, and I agree that it is better to have them as friends than enemies. Why don't I ask their chief to meet with me to discuss it?"

Henry replied, "I will return by mid-April to work out details." With that, he headed down the trail on the long trek back to Abbapoola Creek and his family.

ARIANO AND THE GOOSE CREEK MEN

April 6, 1680

M r. Mathews, there's an Indian at the edge of town to see you. He said his name is Ariano and that he met your friend Moore in Westo town last month. He wants to talk to you, but our rules don't allow him to come into town."

Mathews thanked the servant and then stopped at James Moore's home. "There's someone from Westo town who wants to talk to us. Perhaps your trip last month did some good after all."

They found three Westo men patiently waiting for them. The oldest, who was very old indeed, introduced himself through their translator, "My name is Ariano; I'm an elder in Westo town. I heard what you said when you visited us last month."

Moore said, "I remember seeing you. What brings you here? It must be important for you to make a week's journey."

Ariano replied, "Both you and I are not happy with the trade agreement between our people and St. Giles Kussoe. Our leaders keep most of the trade goods for themselves but do little of the work. Perhaps there is something you could do to change this."

Mathews interjected, "I'm not sure what we could do. Your chief seems very happy with the trade agreement and loyal to Henry Woodward. I don't see how we could change his mind."

Ariano said, "Henry Woodward is much of the problem; Paytah will do almost anything he says. Do you know that he came to our town before you arrived and warned Paytah that you were coming?"

"No. What did he say?"

"That you were going to spy on us and that if our leaders came to your town, they would be captured and sold as slaves and that your people are preparing to travel to our town and destroy it."

Mathews thought to himself, *Godfrey must have told him I said that at the last council meeting—he's his father-in-law. Could I somehow use what Woodward said against him?* Then he said, "Would you be willing to talk to our town leaders and tell them what you heard Woodward say? It might help to change the trade agreement with St. Giles Kussoe."

Ariano readily agreed; Mathews added, "Did he say anything about harming the men who were coming to visit you?"

"I don't think so."

"Think about it again; it's very important. Are you sure Woodward didn't say for you to hurt Moore and Boone?"

"Now I remember; he said that we should knock them on the head when they arrived."

"Does that mean to kill them?"

"Yes."

—∞—

Six days later, Governor West and the Charles Towne Council met in an emergency session called by Maurice Mathews. He opened it saying, "Gentlemen, as you know, with the council's consent, James Moore and John Boone traveled to Westo town to gather information about them. Since then, we have heard alarming news that requires the council's immediate attention. Three Westo leaders have come almost two hundred miles to give you their testimony about this matter."

The Westo men entered the room, and Mathews introduced Ariano: "He is an important elder in Westo town and has information about Henry Woodward that we need to hear."

With that, Ariano, through the translator, told his story: "Two months ago, Henry Woodward came to our town to meet with our chief and the elders. He said he had heard two men, Captain Moore and Mr. Boone, were coming from your town to spy on us to destroy us and that if our elders came here, they would be captured and sold as slaves and that your people would then destroy our town. He said that Moore and Boone were bad people, and we should knock them on the head when they came."

Mathew then said, "Mr. Moore and Mr. Boone visited Westo town shortly after Henry. The chief was not friendly, and they believed Woodward had warned him before they arrived, and they felt that their lives were in danger."

Governor West then asked, "What are you asking that we do?"

Mathew replied, "Woodward is plotting to have two of our citizens murdered. I believe that the council should arrest him and order that the Westo are not permitted in our settlement."

West said, "As I recall, there is already an order from 1677 that the Westo not come to our settlement. We can reaffirm that order. As far as Dr. Woodward, do you have any other witnesses to testify against him?"

Mathew answered, "No. But I believe we could find some if we had more time."

West replied, "I can't recommend arresting him based solely on the testimony we've just heard."

After further discussion, the council issued its findings:

Carolina, April 12th, 1680, at Captain Walley's plantation.

A conference was held on the above date with the governor, council, and several Westo leaders in attendance for the purpose of informing the Westo that they should not come to any places except where they have usually traded. If they did, they might come in contact with local Indians whose acquaintances they had killed and for which no reparations had been made. We informed them that we do not believe it wise to destroy many for the offenses of a few. The Westo were informed that they should not interfere with or disturb our neighboring Indians. After being so informed by our interpreter, they agreed. Ariano, an important Westo elder, then stated that Henry, meaning Doctor Woodward, said that the people of Charles Towne were bad and that they should therefore knock Capt. Moore and Mr. Boone on the head, meaning the Westo should kill them while they journeyed to the Westo's country. This journey was made with the authority of the governor and council to preserve the lords proprietors' lands and to maintain the peace and security of its settlers. Henry further told them that Mr. Moore and Mr. Boone were traveling to Westo country to spy on them to determine their strength and how they might easily be destroyed. He also told them that if they were invited to Charles Towne, they would be captured and sold as slaves overseas, and in the meantime, the Charles Towne settlers are preparing to come to their town and destroy them.

50

ST. CATHERINE'S

Spring 1680

On a late April day, seventy-five heavily armed Westo warriors dressed in battle gear and with faces painted black glided silently down the Savannah River in their war canoes. Henry was a passenger in one.

It was a 120-mile voyage from Westo town to the coast and another thirty miles to their intended target, the Indian town of Santa Catalina de Guale on St. Catherine's Island. Four days later, north of St. Catherine's, they met up with their Creek allies, twenty-five strong, who had arrived on foot. The Creek warriors were armed with bows and arrows, not guns, but were as equally fearsome a sight as the Westo men.

Seeing the assembled force, Henry briefly sympathized with the town's unsuspecting residents—until he remembered why he had vowed to destroy their town.

Henry told the Westo leader that, before the raid, he wanted to pay a visit to the nearby Escamacu, who had moved from Port Royal years ago, not mentioning they had done so to escape Westo raids. "They are my friends, and I do not wish to alarm them with our presence."

⸙

It had been eight years since he last saw Wommony, now middle-aged. Henry told him, "The last time I was here, it was to rescue the woman I loved. When I learned she had died in St. Augustine, I swore revenge on both the Spanish and the Guale; I've returned to keep that promise. I have seventy-five Westo

192

with me to raid Santa Catalina de Guale. But they know that I am friends with the Escamacu and will not harm you."

Wommony replied, "Once, I would have been upset to hear you plan to attack the Spanish—they let us move here to escape Westo raids. But we are no longer on good terms with them. They want us to send more workers and more food to St. Augustine every year. We get very little in return; they do not even give us tools, only glass beads. Some of my people have been talking about returning to Port Royal. Few of us will miss the Spanish if you defeat them."

Wommony was quiet for a few moments, then said, "I need to discuss something with the other elders. Could you return tomorrow?"

Henry was back the next day; Wommony had unexpected news for him. "If you are willing, we would like to join you in the raid. I know that we are not warriors like the Westo, but we know St. Catherine's well and can help you. If you are successful, we will be free of the Spanish. If you are not, we may have to move back to Port Royal."

Henry replied, "I would welcome your help. We have one hundred armed warriors to carry out the attack; you would advise us and help manage captives."

Wommony added, "I have one request. When we lived in Port Royal, a group of Indians moved near us to a town called Colone. They were not Guale and not from any of the tribes I knew. The Spanish called them the Yamasee. We became friends with them. Before we moved here, they moved again, to a town also named Colone on St. Simons Island, a day's travel from here. Like us, they never became Christians. Before you start the raid, I would like to visit them and find out if they are as unhappy with the Spanish as we are. If they are, perhaps they would want to join us."

With an agreement that Wommony would provide ten men for the raid and first visit Colone, Henry returned to his temporary camp.

⁓✠⁓

On April 28, Wommony, accompanied by his men and three Westo warriors, arrived at St. Simons Island. He had been reluctant to bring along the Westo men until Henry pointed out that the Spanish soldiers had guns; he did not. Seeing no sign of soldiers, they entered Colone unimpeded.

Introducing himself to the town's chief, he said, "Years ago when we lived at Port Royal, we were neighbors. You knew my father, Nisquesalla; I am now the cassique. We are here with an Englishman, Henry Woodward. We are unhappy with the Spanish and will drive them from St. Catherine's. I wanted to first talk to you and see if you are getting along with them. If you are, we will leave you in peace; if not, you could join us."

The chief replied, "I remember your father well; he was always very kind to us. I am sorry to hear that you are having trouble with the Spanish. There are only thirty of us here, so they pay little attention to us, and we are content here. There is a friar who watches over us; we ignore him. But he will know that you and your men are here. When he realizes some of them are Westo, who are enemies of the Spanish and Guale, he will ask Captain Fuentes to send soldiers to drive you out."

The chief was correct; Captain Fuentes had been only a short distance from the town when the friar gave him the news. Gathering a small group of Guale warriors, he immediately set out to defend the town from what he believed was a Westo attack. But the Westo had guns, the Guale, bows and arrows. Before Wommony even had a chance to let Fuentes know this was not a raid, Fuentes ordered the Guale to attack. The three Westo warriors opened fire, and in moments, there were three Guale warriors on the ground. The remaining Guale retreated. Wommony called out to Captain Fuentes that they did not want trouble and departed with his men.

———~~~———

Three days later, Henry's force was ready. By moonlight, Westo canoes ferried the warriors across the river to St. Catherine's. At sunrise, with the seventy-five Westo warriors leading the way, they approached the town from the north and swept through the Guale dwellings, killing anyone who opposed them. The Creek warriors followed, taking the remaining inhabitants prisoner.

Captain Fuentes, who had heard from the friar in Colone that Woodward and his men were planning an attack on Santa Catalina, was already in the town with five soldiers. But, seeing the approaching wall of Westo warriors, shrouded in a veil of gun smoke, he ordered his men, along with all the Guale men he could muster, to barricade themselves in the missionary convent.

The Westo immediately attacked the convent. But, in an act of desperation, Fuentes had given guns to the Guale men. The resulting fire from twenty guns drove back the Westo attack, killing several warriors. When Henry saw what was happening, recalling his buccaneer days when Searle, and later Morgan, had unsuccessfully attacked fortified buildings and suffered heavy losses, he ordered the Westo to leave the convent alone. Then he called out to Captain Fuentes to cease firing, or he would burn the convent to the ground with his men inside.

By midday, the fighting was over. The Guale townspeople who did not flee had been killed or captured in the first twenty minutes of the battle. Fuentes and his men were still holed up in the convent, not daring to come out.

Henry, fulfilling his promise to destroy the town, ordered that all the homes be burned. By afternoon, there was nothing left of Santa Catalina de Guale except for smoldering heaps of ashes and the convent.

Henry and his force regrouped on the other side of the river. He told the assembled warriors, "I'm pleased with the raid. We did what we had planned. Santa Catalina is no more, we captured a large number of Guale, and I believe those who fled are too terrified ever to return."

Henry's prediction was correct—within a year, St. Catherine's Island, Spain's most northerly outpost in La Florida, was deserted.

The Westo took thirty Guale prisoners destined for St. Giles Kussoe and Barbados. Wommony bade Henry goodbye, having no way of knowing this was the last time they would meet. He still remembered Henry's look of cold fury eight years before when he heard Margaret was dead. Henry had finally gotten his revenge, but Wommony saw no look of satisfaction. Instead, all he could see in Henry's face now was loss and sadness.

51

WAR CLOUDS

Charles Towne, June 1680

While heading into town for a meeting, Mathews saw three Indians working in his neighbor's field. He thought, *That's odd; I don't recall that he had any Indian workers. He must have just hired some Kiawah.* But they didn't look familiar. When he called out to them, they replied in an unfamiliar tongue.

Puzzled, Mathews went up to his neighbor's house. "William, I'm curious about the Indians working in your field. Who are they?"

William replied, "Oh, I bought them at St. Giles Kussoe. Percival's foreman said the Westo had just delivered thirty captives from a recent raid. Because Percival is in England, he can't arrange to send them to Barbados to be sold. He asked if I wanted to buy any; I told him that we couldn't own Indian slaves. But he said that only applied to Indians living close to the settlement. These are from much further away, so the order does not cover them. He would sell me as many as I wanted for fifteen pounds each; I bought three. They have been good workers, better than indentured servants."

Mathews asked, "Did the foreman say anything more about the raid?"

"No, just that it was not in Carolina, but closer to St. Augustine in the Guale lands. He said the Westo had also killed some Indians during the raid."

Mathews bade him good day and rode on.

James Moore and John Boone were also in town for the meeting; seeing them, Mathews said, "We need to talk."

Once they were alone, Mathews said, "I might have the answer for dealing with the Westo." He repeated what his neighbor had just told him about buying three Indian slaves at St. Giles Kussoe. "William thought that he was allowed to buy them because they were from far away, not from neighboring tribes, but I believe this violates the lords proprietors' orders that we not deal with the Westo and cannot own Indian slaves, no matter where they come from."

Moore replied, "As I recall, those orders are pretty confusing, but you may well be correct. What is your plan?"

"We need to call another council meeting and tell them the warnings I have made about the Westo are coming true. They are attacking, killing, and capturing our Indian neighbors and selling them as slaves."

Moore replied, "But aren't these Guale Indians, the same ones the Westo have been capturing for St. Giles Kussoe for years?"

"Maybe, maybe not; with Percival gone, who's to say? I will tell the council that they need to take immediate action to protect us from the Westo threat."

⸎

Mathews told the council what he had heard from his neighbor about the Guale slaves he had purchased and said that the Westo were an imminent threat to the settlement. Governor West and council members who had been skeptical at the earlier April meeting were now more sympathetic to Mathews' claims.

Governor West asked, "So, Mr. Mathews, what do you want us to do this time?"

Mathews replied, "I'm asking the council to enter a declaration of war against the Westo. They are a serious threat to our safety; I'd like to remind the council that, in the past, it has declared war on other tribes for far less. The council should also detain Woodward and find out his role in this affair. We know the Westo do nothing without his participation."

Governor West said, "Mr. Mathews, all we've heard is your testimony about what your neighbor told you. You've presented no witnesses with first-hand knowledge of what you claim. The Westo may well be violating our orders about dealing with the settlement and may even be a threat to our safety. However, I cannot recommend what you are seeking—the Westo have a close relationship with St. Giles Kussoe, which Shaftesbury owns; we cross him at our peril. However, I will recommend that if Indian slaves are being held in the settlement, they be freed immediately."

Mathews replied, "I ask that the council hold a new hearing immediately; I will present witnesses to testify about the grave threat the Westo pose to us."

After agreeing to set a new hearing for June 4, the council entered its orders:

Charles Towne, June 1, 1680.
The grand council, being fully informed that certain Westo Indians and their confederates have recently, contrary to their agreement with our governor, have killed and captured several of our neighbor Indians and that they intend to continue to hostilities, to our settlement's detriment. Also, certain persons in our settlement have purchased several of the captured Indians as slaves, contrary to the orders of the lords proprietors and the agreement made with us. Therefore, it is ordered that Capt. William Fuller and Mr. John Smith bring these Indians safely to Charles Town on Friday, the 4th, where their freedom shall be restored to them. It is further ordered that no persons shall sell ammunition or other instruments or provisions for war to the Westo or their confederates, nor repair their guns until further order. It is further ordered that Dr. Woodward be given notice to attend the grand council meeting on June 4th. It is also ordered that Captain Fuller take into his care and custody the public gunpowder under Mr. Andrew Percival's care, and the Provost Marshall is authorized to obtain a boat and people to assist him in discharging this order.

***

Three days later, Mathews was back in front of the council, this time with witnesses. Having realized the council was not going to risk Shaftesbury's wrath by declaring war on the Westo, he decided to go after the weak link, Henry Woodward, who had alienated many in Charles Towne by allying himself with Shaftesbury and St. Giles Kussoe. He saw that Henry was present in the room; the hearing would boil down to the word of his witnesses against Henry's.

Mathews had convinced Ariano that it would not be safe for him to return to Westo town after his testimony in April and had tucked him away outside the settlement just in case he needed him for another hearing.

Having spent several hours being coached by Mathews, when Ariano was called as a witness, he went even further than he had earlier: "When Woodward came to our town, he said that the people here are bad and that Westo warriors should come here and kill Mathews, Moore, and Boone, and any other of the leaders they can find before they try to kill us. He said we should also take the Indians who live closest to this town prisoner, and he will sell them as slaves. He bragged that, while Percival is away, he can do as he wishes, and no one can stop him."

The hearing was continued until later that month, and the foreman for St. Giles Kussoe testified. He said that the Westo brought captured slaves to St. Giles Kussoe to be sold as slaves, that Woodward was its agent and got twenty percent of its profits from Indian trade, most of it coming from the Indian slave trade. He admitted that he had recently sold Indian slaves to several settlers but denied they had been captured near Charles Towne. He also admitted that Woodward only answered to Percival, who was in England and not expected to return for several months.

Several of the settlers then testified that Woodward had a hostile attitude toward Charles Towne, that he only cared about St. Giles Kussoe, and that it was no secret that he did not get along with Mathews, Moore, and Boone.

Governor West then asked Dr. Woodward if he had anything to say in his defense.

"Andrew Percival would testify in my favor if he were here; he is not. All I have to say is that I have never told anyone to harm members of this settlement and have not told the Westo to seize prisoners from the towns near here. My feelings about Mathews, Moore, and Boone and their feelings about me are not relevant. Everything I do in the Indian trade is at St. Giles Kussoe, with the approval of Andrew Percival."

The council adjourned and reconvened the next day.

Governor West said, "I believe we have heard enough evidence to show that Dr. Woodward's relationship with the Westo is a threat to our settlement, especially in light of Andrew Percival's absence. We previously entered orders prohibiting anyone from selling weapons to the Westo. I think it now appropriate to order that Dr. Woodward cannot be at St. Giles Kussoe or have any contact with the Westo until further order. I believe he should also be required to post a bond to ensure his compliance with this order."

The council then voted, and with only Henry's father-in-law, John Godfrey, dissenting, entered the following order:

> *The grand council, having considered the safety and defense of the settlement from the Westo and also having considered the allegations, proofs, and affirmations made against Dr. Henry Woodward, hereby resolve and declare that, as matters presently stand, it is not safe for the Settlement for Doctor Woodward to remain at St. Giles Kussoe or trade, act, or negotiate with the Westo or their confederates until further order. The general peace of the settlement is in peril as it is under the apprehension that Woodward is encouraging the Westo to destroy certain persons in this Settlement and destroying and enslaving our Neighbor Indians. It is therefore ordered that*

Doctor Woodward shall give a security bond in the sum of one hundred pounds, that he not negotiate or correspond with the Westo or stay in any places where the Westo or their confederates should happen to come until further order.

On the way back to Abbapoola Creek, Henry thought about whether the hearing had been a complete disaster for him or not. *I can't have any contact with the Westo or even go to St. Giles. That puts me out of business. But the council did say its order was based on "as matters presently stand" and that the terms are subject to further orders. That's not so bad—when Percival gets back, he can straighten this out with the council; if the council doesn't fix it, Shaftesbury certainly will.*

When he arrived, he kissed Mary and said, "I'm finally going to be able to stay home for a while."

WAR PLANS

Summer 1680

Well, how do you think that went?" Moore asked Mathews after the hearing.

"Not so well. We've stopped Woodward and the Westo but only momentarily. The council refused to declare war on the Westo or arrest Woodward. Percival will have no problem getting the order changed when he returns, and it will be business as usual for them. We need to come up with another plan."

Moore replied, "Since the council won't do anything further, we're going to have to act on our own before Percival's return. The way I see it, we need to make either Woodward or the Westo go away. Percival could probably continue trading with the Westo even without Woodward. But if the Westo were to disappear, that would end the Indian trade."

"I don't see how that helps us; we would have won the battle but lost the war. I want to take the Indian trade away from St. Giles, not end it."

"That's true," Moore said. "We would need to find another tribe to replace the Westo. This may sound harsh, but perhaps we can find one powerful enough to destroy them if we promised they could take over the trade."

Mathews replied, "That is a drastic solution even to consider. How could we get away with it?"

Moore answered, "The Westo have no friends in Charles Towne, so our problem would be Shaftesbury. But, with Percival gone and Woodward out of action, he has no eyes or ears here. And besides, I heard he is having problems of his own in England; he was even imprisoned in the Tower of London by the

King recently. If we act while Percival is gone, by the time Shaftesbury learns the Westo are no more, it will be too late for him to act. And remember, the lords proprietors no longer have any real power over us."

"But even if nobody likes the Westo, I don't want to be seen as a murderer."

"We'll set it up to make it look like the Westo were attacked by another tribe, and there was nothing we could do to stop it," Moore replied.

"What tribe?"

Moore said, "How about the Occaneechi? They are enemies with the Westo and once killed some of their leaders."

Mathews replied, "That would be an excellent idea, but they were slaughtered in Bacon's Rebellion. They are no more."

Moore said, "I remember the Cofitachequi bragging that the Westo were afraid of them, but they seem to have disappeared."

"Yes, I heard the Westo drove them away."

"Maybe the Creek? Woodward once said that they were enemies of the Westo."

Mathews replied, "He got them to make a peace treaty; now they are friends."

"Well, I don't have any other suggestions; I'll think about it. But we need to move quickly while Percival is gone."

❦

Moore did think about it. The next day, he told Mathews, "Ariano told me something that may help deal with the Westo. He said that four days' travel to the northwest from Westo Town, there is a tribe called the Savannah. He said their warriors are as fierce as the Westo, although they do not have guns. The Savannah once wanted to join the Westo in trading with the English, but it did not happen. Perhaps we should pay a visit to them."

"James, that must be three hundred miles from here. That seems like a lot of effort."

"You wouldn't be going; John and I could do it with some Kiawah guides. We need to either get serious about what to do with the Westo or forget about it."

"Very well, let's plan a journey to their town."

❦

On the banks of the Chattahoochee River, Savannah town looked much like Westo town. There were at least a hundred homes, long and covered with bark, and a large meeting house in the town center. But unlike Westo town, they saw no scalps hanging from lodgepoles. The townspeople were friendly and curious; one introduced himself as their chief. Like the other men in the town, he was tall with red paint on his face, a shaved head with a long lock on top, and a silver ring in his nose. He greeted them in an unfamiliar tongue and spoke no English. Finally, with the aid of the Kiawah guides, they were able to communicate.

Moore asked the chief to tell him about the Savannah people. He replied, "That is your name for us; we call ourselves the Shawnee. About thirty years ago, we lived far to the north. The Iroquois wanted our land and began to attack us. We are brave warriors, but they had guns, and we did not. Finally, a group of us fled and settled here."

Moore said, "That sounds like the story of the Westo Indians who live near here. Do you know of them?"

"Yes, both of our tribes came to this area because of the Iroquois. Several years ago, I went to their town where we gave them beads and other gifts that we got from the Spanish. I warned their chief that the Creek, who live near here, planned to attack their town. We hoped to become friends with the Westo and agree to share in the Indian trade with the English. But, since then, they have ignored us."

Moore said, "That is why we are here." He explained that he was from an English settlement named Charles Towne, a week's travel to the southeast, and was looking for a partner for the Indian trade. "An Englishman named Henry Woodward has a trade agreement with the Westo, and he refuses to let anyone share in the trade. The Westo are bad people; they attack our Indian friends, and Woodward is telling them to kill us. Our leaders ordered the Westo to no longer come to our town, and Woodward could not trade with them. We want to take their place in the Indian trade and want to talk to you about becoming our trading partner."

The chief replied, "I remember Woodward—he was at the Westo town when I first went there. Let's talk about trade tomorrow. Now, you are our honored guests and will stay with us."

The following day Moore and the chief met again. The chief said that Pay-tah, the Westo chief, was being challenged by younger warriors who were more aggressive. Because the Westo had guns and the Shawnee did not, he worried they might attack his town someday. He added, "I heard the Westo have made an alliance with our neighbors, the Creek, and together they raided a town controlled by the Spanish. It is said that Woodward led the raid. If the Creek also get guns from the English, it will no longer be safe for us here."

Moore replied, "I believe both of us would be pleased if the Westo disappeared. We can talk about that later, but for now, I want to propose a trade agreement. The Westo capture Guale Indians and take them to Charles Towne, where Woodward and his people sell them to become slaves. They also bring deerskins and furs to trade. Woodward gives them guns and other trade goods. Now that Woodward cannot trade with the Westo, we want to take over the trade. I propose that you replace the Westo and we replace Woodward. We would pay you the same as he paid them."

"Would you give us guns?"

"Yes, guns, gunpowder, all of the trade goods that the Westo got."

The chief said, "But as soon as the Westo learn we have made a trade agreement with you, they will certainly attack us. Even if we had guns, we might be able to defeat them, but it would be a bloody battle, and we would lose many warriors."

Moore replied, "What if we attack them first?"

"They are skilled fighters; we would still have heavy losses."

"Perhaps not. If I can think of a plan, would you be willing to consider it?"

The chief replied, "I will have to talk it over with my people, but if it is a good plan, I will recommend it."

• ∿ •

"We're going back to Westo town," Moore told Boone.

"Whatever for? They were not friendly when we were last there."

"That was before the council shut down their trade with Woodward. This is my plan. I have copies of the council's orders barring them from Charles Towne and ordering Woodward have no contact with them. I will read those orders to the Westo and tell them they are out of business unless they find a new trading partner. They don't need to know that the council orders are only temporary. We will propose becoming their trading partners, replacing Woodward and St. Giles Kussoe."

"But don't the Westo want to kill us?"

"I don't think so—I had Ariano make that up for the council hearings. I will tell them that we would need to negotiate a trade agreement between their leaders and ours and that our leaders are afraid to come to Westo town, and I know they don't want to meet in Charles Towne. I will propose that we meet in a neutral place, Savannah town."

"I don't see how that helps us."

Moore replied, "We will have agreed with the Savannah; they will not be neutral. When the Westo leaders arrive in Savannah town, they will be killed. The Savannah will then raid Westo town before it learns their leaders are dead."

"That sounds ruthless."

"Exactly. But we don't yet have the Savannah's agreement; we need it before going to Westo town."

53

THE WESTO WAR

September 1680

Everything was going as planned. Unfortunately for the Westo, they did not know there was more than one plan. Paytah and two other Westo elders arrived, accompanied by three younger Westo who did not trust Paytah to negotiate in their absence. Moore and Boone had arrived the day before. Contrary to what they told the Westo earlier, they were alone; no Charles Towne leaders had been invited or even knew about the meeting.

The Savannah chief greeted the Westo men and said they would be in the town's meeting house. As previously arranged, he told Moore, Boone, and the Westo men to leave their guns outside. Moore and Boone appeared to protest and then reluctantly agreed. Seeing this, the Westo let down their guard and handed over their weapons as well.

Moore said to Paytah, "It is our hope we can settle our differences today and get along in the future. As I told you the last time I visited your town, Woodward has been ordered to have no contact with you, and you are forbidden from going to Charles Towne. But if you can make a new trade agreement with us, you will be able to continue your trade as before. The Savannah chief and his translator are here to serve as mediators."

Paytah said, "Where are the other leaders from Charles Towne that you promised?"

"They're already in the meeting house waiting for us. I'll introduce you to them."

Feigning politeness, Moore gestured for the Westo men to enter first. They entered; he did not. Instead, ten of the fiercest Savannah warriors, in full war paint and carrying their hatchet axes, went through the doorway.

It was over in seconds before Paytah and the other men had a chance to realize they had been tricked. The Westo were now leaderless.

———❧———

As Moore and the Savannah chief had earlier planned, the ten Savannah warriors, joined by Moore, Boone, and over a hundred more warriors armed with bows and arrows and hatchet axes, immediately set out on the 150-mile trek for Westo town.

At first light, the Savannah men, masters of moving through the forest undetected, crept up to Westo town until they could see its sentries. Then, three of their best archers dropped the sentries without a sound. The townspeople, having no warning of what had happened in Savannah town or what was about to befall them, were utterly unprepared when over a hundred Savannah warriors rushed into their town. A few of the Westo braves were able to pick up their guns, but at close range, the Savannah's bows, arrows, and axes were more effective than Westo guns.

The Westo were fierce fighters; even the Westo women and the older children fought, so the battle lasted longer than Woodward's recent raid of St. Catherine's, which was over in twenty minutes.

Finally, deciding they had inflicted enough destruction on the Westo, the Savannah's war chief ordered his men to stop, ending the battle.

———❧———

Moore and Boone were elated—their plan had worked perfectly. The Westo had been destroyed as a fighting force, and St. Giles Kussoe had lost its trading partner. The Charles Towne Council would probably be unhappy, and Shaftesbury would be furious when they finally realized what had happened. But it would be months before Shaftesbury would have even an inkling of what had happened, and the council should be grateful once they realized that St. Giles would no longer be able to dominate them.

54

HIGH CRIMES AND MISDEMEANORS

The Goose Creek Men's plan had succeeded—the Westo leaders were dead, and their town left in ruins. The way was now clear for Mathews, Moore, and their allies to take over the Indian trade from St. Giles Kussoe. But, a month after the raid, Mathews was still worried. "There is nothing to stop Woodward from setting up trade with another Indian tribe; he has better connections than we do," he told Moore. "We need to ask the council to take further action against him."

Moore replied, "I don't think the council has the power to ban him from the Indian trade. And, in any case, now that the Westo are no longer a threat to the settlement, I doubt if the council will do more."

"Maybe we could get the court to bar him from further trading and perhaps even imprison him."

"I don't know a lot about the law," Moore said. "But it's not as if he stole a neighbor's cow. What would he be guilty of?"

Mathews replied, "He must have done something wrong; I'll think about it."

⌁

Mathews wasn't as ruthless as Moore, but he was the shrewdest of the Goose Creek Men. In November, he again brought up the subject with Moore. "What you told me last month that it would be hard to prove Woodward committed a crime is probably true. But in England, Parliament can impeach a royal official for his actions by charging him with high crimes and misdemeanors. The official can be removed from his position, fined, or even imprisoned, even if what he did was not a crime."

"How does that help us? Woodward's not an official, and we're not Parliament," Moore replied.

"But he is—he's Shaftesbury's deputy for Ashley Creek under the Fundamental Constitutions. He seldom attends council meetings, but he's still an official. We might be able to persuade the council to bring charges against Woodward in county court for endangering the safety of the settlement and ask that he be barred from further Indian trading and perhaps even imprisoned. The next court date isn't until February, so we have plenty of time to plan what to do."

On a December afternoon, two men came up to the Woodwards' home at Abbapoola Point; one knocked on the door. Mary answered it; the man introduced himself, "I'm the Sheriff of the Craven County Court, and I have a paper to deliver to your husband."

"He's not available; I'll give it to him."

The sheriff grudgingly handed it to her, adding curtly, "Make sure he gets it."

When Henry arrived home that evening, Mary told him the sheriff had delivered a document for him; she didn't understand what it was.

He looked it over and told her, "It's a summons. The Charles Towne Council is claiming I imperiled the safety of the settlement when the Westo raided Santa Catalina de Guale because the St. Augustine governor has threatened to raid Charles Towne in retaliation. It also says I gave aid to the Westo when I warned them about Mathew's and Moore's trip to their town. There's to be a court hearing in February. The summons says that these are high crimes and misdemeanors and that if I'm found guilty, I can be barred from trading with the Indians, fined, or imprisoned. It sounds like something Maurice Mathews cooked up to keep me out of his way."

Mary said, "What do you have to do?"

"There's going to be a trial in early February; I have to appear and defend myself in front of a jury. As I recall from the last time I read the Fundamental Constitutions, it only takes a majority of the twelve jurors to convict me."

Mary asked, "Will Percival be back from London by then?"

"I don't think so. I wish he would be; I don't have a lot of friends in Charles Towne; he'd be an important witness."

In no time, it was the trial date; Henry was unsure whether he was glad the ordeal would soon be over or nervous that he might be in jail by week's end. He'd survived the plague, hurricanes, and battles, but this was different—his fate would be decided by twelve men who probably did not think well of him, and there was little he could do about it. It was still dark when he left; the children were asleep. He kissed Mary goodbye, said, "Wish me luck," and pointed his yawl downriver toward Charles Towne.

The tide had turned against him before he reached town, and he was almost late. The trial was being held in the town's meeting hall; Mathews and Moore were already there, and the court's sheriff was seating the jurors. The justice entered the room; the sheriff said, "All rise," followed by, "Be seated."

The justice, not a real judge, rather one of the settlers, read the charges against Henry and said, "These are serious high crimes and misdemeanors; do you understand them?"

Henry replied, "I do, Your Honor."

The council then presented its witnesses—Maurice Mathews and James Moore; Moore testified first. He told the jury the details of his journey to Westo town and said that Henry Woodward told the Westo the settlers planned on raiding their town and that the Westo should kill him and Mr. Boone.

Mathews then testified. "This is a letter the council recently received from the governor at St. Augustine. He states that on June first of last year, Mr. Woodward led the Westo Indians on a raid of one of the Indian towns under Spanish protection, Santa Catalina de Guale, on St. Catherine's Island. They destroyed the town and killed or captured many of its inhabitants. The governor states that he may attack Charles Towne in retaliation."

The justice asked Mathews if he had any other witnesses. "No, Your Honor."

"Mr. Woodward, do you have anything to say in your defense?"

Henry replied, "Yes, Your Honor. But first I would like to cross-examine Mr. Mathews and Mr. Moore."

"Your request is denied; proceed with your testimony."

"Mr. Mathews claims that I aided and abetted an enemy of Charles Towne by warning the Westo that he and Mr. Moore were plotting to raid their town. I did tell them of my suspicions; Mathews and Moore did visit the town and were responsible for the Savannah killing the Westo leaders and destroying their town, just as I warned them might happen. I deny ever telling them to kill Mr. Mathews or Mr. Moore. The Westo were not our enemy; they have traded with our neighbor, St. Giles Kussoe, for years."

Henry continued, "I admit that I was present during the Westo's raid at St. Catherine's last June. I would remind the court that it was at St. Catherine's in

1670 when the Spanish and their Guale Indian allies seized ten of our people from *The Three Brothers* on their way to settle this town. Since then, the Spanish have been plotting to attack us, and the Westo have been raiding Guale towns. We have written letters of protest to them, and they have written letters to us. This is an old conflict, not one that I started."

The justice interrupted, "Mr. Woodward, did you have the council's permission for the raid?"

"No, Your Honor."

"Did you notify the council, or at least Andrew Percival, in advance of the raid?"

"No, Your Honor."

"Do you have anything further you'd like to say, Mr. Woodward?"

"Yes, as you know, I am St. Giles Kussoe's agent for its Indian trade. The plantation is owned by Anthony Ashley Cooper, the Earl of Shaftesbury, one of the lords proprietors for Carolina Colony. This court has no jurisdiction over St. Giles and therefore has no jurisdiction over its agents."

The justice asked, "But you are Shaftesbury's deputy on the council?"

"Yes, I am."

"Members of the jury, please retire to the waiting room until you reach a verdict."

⁓෴⁓

Two hours later, the jury announced it had reached its verdict; the justice asked the sheriff to read it.

"We, the jury, by a vote of seven to five, find the defendant, Mr. Henry Woodward, guilty of the high crimes and misdemeanors of aiding and abetting an enemy of Charles Towne and endangering the lives of certain of its citizens and also of imperiling the safety of Charles Towne by participating in the attack of St. Catherine's."

The justice then spoke, "Mr. Woodward, in deciding what punishment to impose on you, I have considered Mr. Mathew's and Mr. Moore's testimony as well as your own. I find that due to your actions, while not as much of a threat to our settlement as they claimed, you must face some punishment. I cannot remove you as the Earl of Shaftesbury's deputy or bar you from further Indian trading. Also, I do not believe your acts were serious enough to imprison you. Therefore, I order that you be fined the sum of one hundred pounds."

55

HENRY APPEALS

London, 1681

Henry, arriving home, gave Mary, very pregnant, a hug and said, "Well, at least I'm not in jail."

"What do you mean? Tell me what happened."

He explained the court's verdict and that the justice, rejecting harsher punishment had only fined him one hundred pounds.

"That's not so bad, is it?"

Henry replied, "It could have been a lot worse, but I don't have a hundred pounds. Also, I've been found guilty of committing high crimes and misdemeanors against Charles Towne. You know that I don't much care what the town thinks of me, but my days at St. Giles Kussoe may well be over and I do have to start thinking about our future life here."

"So what can we do about it?"

"I don't know," he replied, "but there might be something in the Fundamental Constitutions about appealing the court's ruling."

There was. Henry, reading the sections that created Carolina's courts, said "This is nonsensical—there must be ten different kinds of courts. There's a chief justice's court, constable's court, admiral's court, treasurer's court, on and on. Here's a provision forbidding lawyers from appearing in any of these courts. Ah—this might be it. There's a palatine's court that can issue pardons; it's made up of the lords proprietors."

"Are you saying you would have to go to England?"

"Well, yes. They aren't going to come here."

Mary replied, "Wouldn't it be easier to use my money for the fine?"

"That still doesn't clear my name—only the lords proprietors could do that."

—✳—

Mary and Henry's child was born two weeks after the trial; a healthy baby boy. Both her mother and a midwife attended her; Henry stayed outside. They named him John, after their two fathers.

—✳—

Henry couldn't find any ships sailing for England for several months. One day, while he was waiting, a messenger came to the house and told him the slaves he had arranged to purchase through Andrew Percival over a year earlier finally arrived in Charles Towne. He had completely forgotten about them, including that they would need shelter, something he had neglected to take care of. He immediately took the boat into town to bring them back to Abbapoola Point.

His father-in-law was waiting for him in town. "Where have you been? There are six slaves at the wharf; nobody knows who they belong to and only one of the girls speaks any English. I spoke to her and realized they must be the ones you bought last year. The girl was born in Barbados so speaks English; the rest arrived in Barbados directly from Africa. They are terrified and have no idea where they are."

Henry admitted they were the ones he bought through Percival and that he had no idea what to do with them.

"Why not? You're a slave trader."

Henry explained that he actually had little to do with the captive Indians sold as slaves at St. Giles Kussoe. The Westo brought them there and Percival arranged to ship them to Barbados; he never had any direct dealings with them.

Godfrey replied, "I've got a lot of experience managing slaves. I'll go back to the house with you and help you get them settled in."

When they arrived at Abbapoola Point, Mary and her father immediately took over. The horses were put out to pasture, the horse stall cleaned out and fresh straw laid down. Mary had a long conversation with the one girl who spoke English; when they were done, Henry was sent back to town with a shopping list for clothing, bedding, and cookware.

Mary had earlier promised him that she knew how to manage servants and slaves; she did. Within the week, she had the young men constructing simple cabins for themselves and had already made the English-speaking girl her house servant.

Finally, a ship arrived in Charles Towne from Barbados, on its way to New York and then London. Henry spoke to its captain, Mr. Ward, who said the ship was owned by a business associate of Shaftesbury's and that he could send the bill for Henry's passage directly to him when they arrived in England.

On June 11, the day the ship was scheduled to sail, Henry wrote out a power of attorney in favor of his wife and father-in-law and packed for the voyage, thinking, *the last time I did this was ten years ago for John Yeamans when I went to Virginia for him. I hope this trip has a better ending.*

Kissing Mary and hugging the children, he told her he expected to be back by year's end.

56

HIGH TREASON

London, Summer 1681

On the morning of July 2, Henry was in the middle of the Atlantic. He had no way of knowing that 2,000 miles away in London, two men, Francis Gwyn, a Clerk of the Privy Council, the other, the Royal Sergeant-at-Arms, were presenting themselves at the entrance of Shaftesbury's London home, Thanet House, and asking the butler to summon his lordship. He asked them to wait outside and went to wake Shaftesbury.

Shaftesbury greeted Gwyn, "Francis, it's rather early for a social call. I assume that's not why you are here."

"I'm afraid not your lordship; I have a warrant for your arrest on charges of high treason and to seize your papers."

Shaftesbury, who had been expecting this for weeks, was unfazed, giving Gwyn his keys and telling him where he could find his papers.

At eleven that morning, Shaftesbury was brought before the privy council. Twenty years earlier, he had been president of the council and the king's favorite; now, he was appearing before him and seventeen others, some of them Shaftesbury's close friends. Lord Chancellor Nottingham read the charges of treason against Shaftesbury.

Shaftesbury responded, "While I have not always acted as some close to his majesty wished, everything I have done has been in the crown's best interests. I hope the councilors do not believe that I conspired with the Irish and the Papists to subvert the government. If I was capable of such actions, I should be sent to Bedlam, not prison."

When the warrant to confine Shaftesbury to the Tower of London was presented to the council for signatures, four members asked to be dismissed. Charles angrily exclaimed, "Sign it one and all"; they did.

Shaftesbury ate his last meal as a free man in the lobby of the council chamber—two roast chickens with a bottle of Madeira. He was then taken by barge through the Traitor's Gate and began his confinement, his second in four years, in the Tower of London.

The king ordered that Shaftesbury be allowed no visitors other than family. The following days were controlled chaos at his residence, Thanet House. Stringer organized a team to collect evidence, protect assets, and file motions with the court. Shaftesbury's allies unleashed a propaganda war with a series of pamphlets and editorials defending him; the crown did the same, attacking him. Shaftesbury's repeated motions for bail or an early trial were denied.

Arriving unannounced in London in late July, Henry tracked down Stringer, finding him in the same offices where he had visited him five years earlier. He knew something was wrong the moment he saw him.

"Dr. Woodward, I'm afraid that, whatever reason you're here for, you've come at a terrible time. His lordship was arrested in early July, charged with high treason, and is being held in the Tower of London. We're spending all our time working on his defense and trying to get him released before his hearing in November. If you need anything from his lordship, it will have to wait until he is freed."

"I'm sorry to hear that—I just went through a similar experience in Carolina Colony, which is why I'm here." Henry briefly filled him in on the parts he thought Stringer should hear, adding, "I was found guilty of imperiling Charles Towne's safety and fined one hundred pounds. I'm here to appeal the court order to the palatine's court."

Stringer replied, "I don't even know what that court is. You should talk to John Locke; he might know what you're talking about. I'll see if I can set up a meeting with him. Why don't you check back tomorrow afternoon?"

The following day, as soon as Henry walked into his office, Stringer said, "Mr. Locke can see you today at his lordship's home where he is staying. Do you know where it is?"

"No."

"It's the Thanet House on Aldersgate. Inigo Jones designed it; very modern looking, you can't miss it."

Never heard of him, Henry thought to himself. "Thank you, I'll go there now."

Henry had often thought of John Locke ever since writing to him some five years ago from Westo town, describing the Indians he lived with. He had never heard back from him after his letter. All correspondence, orders, and instructions from the lords proprietors passed through Locke's hands; it was widely believed in Charles Towne that he was responsible for Carolina's Fundamental Constitutions. Henry knew that, unlike himself, Locke was an actual doctor with a degree from Oxford.

Locke was very different than Henry expected. About fifty, tall, stooped, with a long face, he did not seem in good health. Most surprising was that Locke seemed more nervous than he himself felt, not meeting his gaze when Henry introduced himself.

When Locke called him "Dr. Woodward," Henry told him it was an honorary title; he had trained as a surgeon under his father but had no formal medical training so "Mr. Woodward" would be fine. Locke replied that at one time he had hoped to practice medicine as a career but never did, so he preferred not to be addressed as "Doctor."

Locke filled in more details about his employer's situation. "We've not been able to get him released on bail but, because of his health, he has been moved out of the Tower and into a house on the Tower grounds. The King is determined to see his lordship hang so we are mustering all of his friends and allies to support him. The evidence against him is weak and I expect he will be acquitted."

Changing the topic, Locke said, "I understand you are quite the adventurer. Mr. Percival has told me stories about you, some of which I can scarcely believe. You'll have to tell me about them sometime; but for now, what brings you to London?"

Henry repeated what he had told Shaftesbury earlier about seeking a pardon. "His lordship said that I'm to talk to you about appealing my case to the palatine's court. He said I am its first case."

"That is true. You also have the dubious honor of being the first in Carolina Colony to be convicted of high crimes and misdemeanors. Nobody has ever asked for a hearing in the palatine's court before; I'm going to have to think about how to handle your appeal. In any case, we can't convene the court until after the November hearing. In the meantime, I'll send a notice of your appeal to the Charles Towne County Court so that everyone has had an opportunity to respond."

"That will take months. I had hoped to be able to return home this year."

Locke replied, "Perhaps by next spring."

⸎

In late November, Shaftesbury's case was finally set for a grand jury indictment hearing in the Old Bailey. In an unusual move, counsel for the king moved to hold the hearing in open court; the chief justice granted the motion. Henry, deciding to attend, got one of the last remaining spectator seats. Shaftesbury was not present, although his supporters were.

The court first read the indictment, which accused Shaftesbury of having made statements attacking the King and gathering armed men to depose him.

The crown then presented its witnesses who testified about statements Shaftesbury had allegedly made attacking the king. After hearing their rambling testimony and the jury members' brutal cross-examination, Henry had little doubt that Shaftesbury would not be indicted. He was correct; shortly after the hearing was over, the grand jury entered a verdict of *ignoramus*—insufficient evidence.

⸎

That evening, the streets were filled with mobs, drinking, lighting bonfires, and shouting "God Bless the Earl of Shaftesbury!"

Several days later, Shaftesbury was released on bail. The king had banned further public demonstrations celebrating his freedom so his triumphant return by boat from the King's Bench at Westminster was uneventful. His supporters issued a silver medal with his bust on one side, the sun shining through the clouds over the Tower of London, and the word *laetamur*—"rejoice," on the other.

Again, Henry was reminded of what different worlds he and Shaftesbury lived in—no celebrating mobs or a medal for him and he had sailed home alone after his conviction.

HENRY AND SHAFTESBURY CONVERSE

More than half a year before, Henry had left Carolina Colony to appeal his conviction of high crimes and misdemeanors. All he had accomplished so far was to see Shaftesbury acquitted of high treason.

Shaftesbury hadn't forgotten about him. In mid-December, Stringer sent him a note—Shaftesbury wanted Henry to meet him the following day to discuss his request for a pardon.

He looked older than their last meeting four years ago, gray, more stooped, and now using a cane—his months of imprisonment had taken a toll on his health.

"Dr. Woodward, I apologize for putting you off for so long, but I've been busy trying to keep my head attached to my body. I understand that you've had a similar experience in Carolina Colony."

Henry replied, "Your lordship, I attended the grand jury hearing and congratulate you on the result. I was found guilty of high crimes and misdemeanors, not punishable by death, so I was in no danger of losing my life as you were. But I feel strongly that I didn't get a fair hearing and was wrongfully convicted."

"Remind me what happened to you. It's been a while, and I've heard so many conflicting accounts from Charles Towne that I have no idea what occurred."

Henry replied, "I can only tell you what I believe happened; much of it was kept secret from me. The Indian trade business at St. Giles Kussoe was very successful; our Westo partners brought many Guale captives to sell, as well as deerskins. The Carolina Fundamental Constitutions prohibit the colonists from buying or selling Indian captives; some of the settlers saw St. Giles is profitable and were angry they couldn't share in the trade. Maurice Mathews, James Moore, and their allies, known as the Goose Creek Men, decided to get rid of the Westo and take over the trade for themselves despite the ban. They made allies with the Savannah Indians and arranged for the Westo leaders to meet in Savannah town to discuss a trade agreement with Charles Towne. It was a trick; the Savannah murdered the Westo leaders at the meeting. Mathews then claimed that I told the Westo to kill him and Moore and that I put the colony in danger when we had raided a Guale town near St. Augustine earlier. They convinced the Charles Towne Council to bring charges against me for high crimes and misdemeanors. I was not allowed to present witnesses or ask questions of theirs, was found guilty, and fined one hundred pounds."

Shaftesbury replied, "That sounds much like what happened to me. But fortunately, most of the jury members were my allies, not the king's, so I was acquitted. Going back to your case, months ago, I told the governor and Charles Towne Council to send documents and affidavits that supported their version of events; I've received no response. I'll ask Mr. Locke to look into how we should deal with your request for a pardon. You're the first person to bring a case to the palatine's court, so we don't have a formal procedure in place."

Shaftesbury added, "By the way, where are you staying? I recall you've no family here; you've been here some four months and may well be here a lot longer."

"I've been renting a room."

"Thanet House is enormous, and there is only my myself and my wife, as well as Mr. Locke living here. I'm sure we can find a spare room for you. Please ask Mr. Stringer to take care of it."

⸻ ❧ ⸻

Mr. Stringer introduced Henry to the butler. "Dr. Woodward will be our guest here for a while; his lordship asked that you set up a room for him."

"Sir, I'm afraid it will have to be on the third floor. Will that be acceptable to you?"

Henry laughed; the butler gave him a puzzled look. He explained, "I'm glad just to have a roof over my head. In Carolina Colony, I often sleep outdoors with a fire going all night to keep away the wolves and bears." That was only a slight exaggeration; the butler looked suitably impressed.

"Will you be taking your meals in your room?"

"What do you mean?" Henry asked.

The butler replied, "We serve three meals daily; Mr. Locke generally takes meals in his room; do you wish to do the same?"

I thought Shaftesbury would be furious with me over losing the Indian trade, Henry thought. *Instead, I'm staying in his mansion with prepared meals brought to my room. I don't understand him.* "That will be fine; thank you."

58

JOHN LOCKE

London, 1681

Life began to return to normal at Thanet House after Shaftesbury's acquittal. At first, Henry felt out of place, but everyone was friendly, and it was an enormous improvement over the room he had rented since arriving in London.

In early January, Henry received a note from John Locke—Henry was to prepare a formal petition listing the grounds for his request and he would give copies to the proprietors and the Charles Towne Court. They would hear his request for a pardon on May 1 in a closed session; Henry would not attend.

He had been looking for a chance to talk to Locke about Carolina Colony's Indians ever since they had corresponded about the Westo and Escamacu Indians—he had always been an enigmatic figure. His note was the perfect opportunity. From Henry's perspective, four thousand miles away, Locke always seemed in Shaftesbury's shadow.

❧

Several days later, after breakfast, when Henry knew Locke was at work in his rooms, he knocked on his door. "Mr. Locke, I'd like to talk to you about my request for a pardon in the palatine's court. Would this be a good time?"

Locke, appearing calmer than he had in months, replied, "As good as any, I suppose; I finally have some time of my own."

Locke reaffirmed what his note said and explained to Henry that the May date for the hearing, almost four months away, was based on having to send his petition to Charles Towne and then wait for a response. Henry realized there wasn't anything he could do about it and changed the subject.

"I reread the Carolina Fundamental Constitutions this summer and wonder who drafted them. It is an impressive document and must have taken a lot of time. Mr. Percival told me that you wrote it."

"The first version was drafted by his lordship in 1669. He had taken on Carolina Colony as his pet project and spent countless hours planning it. My interests are more along the lines of science and philosophy than politics, but I made certain changes and edited the whole of it. I've since been involved in its subsequent revision and expect to work on a new revision sometime soon.

Henry asked, "Has anyone ever told you that they are perhaps too complex for such a small colony?"

Locke replied, "I can't count how many letters I've received from the governors and council members complaining that either they are impossible to apply or that the colony isn't following them. I'm not to blame one way or the other. His lordship seldom takes my advice, especially on matters involving Carolina. The Constitutions might be suited for a colony the size of Barbados or Jamaica but not for one with a population of a few hundred."

"Mr. Locke, I was homeschooled and only had a single year of formal education, so I don't have your knowledge and experience. But I've lived in Carolina since its beginning and believe I have insights into the colony that no one here has. As you know, the Fundamental Constitutions prohibit anyone from criticizing them, and I have no wish to get into more legal trouble than I already have. Could you and I agree to have a friendly discussion that doesn't leave this room?"

"I suppose we can, but I'm not sure that you can add anything that his lordship has not already considered."

"I know what he thinks; I'm more interested in your views about the Constitutions than his. He claims he has created a republic, but the reality is that Carolina is an aristocratic republic. The lords proprietors have absolute power and authority over the colonists, but other than his lordship and perhaps Peter Colleton, none of them have any interest in the colony or the ability to govern it. The settlers are either actively taking advantage of this or have given up and are simply trying to survive. Unless Carolina is allowed more say in its future, I fear that it will not succeed."

Locke replied, "When the settlers came to Carolina and were given land, they signed a document promising to abide by the terms of the Fundamental Constitutions. They consented to follow its laws, and they receive the benefit of the lords proprietors protecting their property rights."

Henry responded, "Many of the settlers don't know how to read or write and few have even read the Constitutions. I don't see how they knowingly consented to them. If they were to design a government that fit their circumstances and needs, it would look nothing like the Fundamental Constitutions. It's difficult to appreciate without being there, but Charles Towne is nothing more than a few hundred people who were dropped into an unfamiliar world. They have simple but real and immediate needs that I don't believe the lords proprietors understand."

Locke replied, "His lordship believes that most of the settlers who are complaining are lazy and ungrateful. He has used his funds to support them with little to show for it. The only profit he has made from Carolina has been from the Indian trade at St. Giles Kussoe."

Responding, Henry said, "I'd like to tell you a story about what I did before arriving in Charles Towne. You might find it helpful in understanding my views. For almost two years, I served as the surgeon on a buccaneer ship out of Port Royal, Jamaica, as one of forty ships sailing in Henry Morgan's fleet. Most of them were under the absolute control of the ships' owners and captains, not unlike Carolina Colony under the proprietors. But some were not; instead, the ship's crew, a hundred or so men, elected their captain who could be voted out of office for mistreating the crew, poor judgment, or any other reason if the crew wasn't happy with him. The captain had absolute power only during battles; the rest of the time, the ship's quartermaster, also elected by the crew, had more power than the captain—day-to-day management of the ship, distributing loot, settling disputes among crewmembers, and deciding on punishment for offending crewmembers. The crew voted on what targets to attack; if a crew member was dissatisfied, he was free to leave at the next port. The captain, quartermaster, and crew members signed articles that set out this agreement. Unlike the Fundamental Constitutions, this document was written more for the benefit of the crew members than the captain or quartermaster.

"The buccaneers were usually content while at sea, at least while they were accumulating loot, because, as much as was possible under the brutal circumstances of their lives, they were free. The lives of the Charles Towne settlers are not unlike those of the buccaneers—a small group of men far from England, amid a vast expanse of trees instead of water, trying to make a living. If they had the same form of government as the buccaneers, I believe they would be at least as content with their lot."

Locke retorted, "The Fundamental Constitutions give the settlers a great deal of freedom, more than they would have at home. They have their own governor and the grand council to protect their interests and property."

"But those freedoms are mostly illusory—the lords proprietors appoint the governor, and the settlers can't vote him or the proprietors out of office."

"Be that as it may, I'm only his lordship's secretary; I can't change how the colony is governed, and he doesn't care to hear my opinions. Speaking of that, I need to get back to work."

Henry finished their conversation on a friendlier note. "I enjoyed our discussion; it's been a long time since I've been able to talk about anything other than the price of deerskins. I hope we can talk again when you have more time."

Henry and Locke continued their conversation later that week.

Locke began. "Thinking over our last discussion about the Fundamental Constitutions, I believe it is important to give his lordship credit for the religious freedom they give the settlers and even slaves."

Henry replied, "I agree the Constitutions give some religious freedom but not as much as they should. They require that every settler acknowledge there is a God who must be worshipped and that there is an afterlife. They also state that only religions following the Church of England can use public funds to build and maintain their churches. But it hardly matters—in Carolina, few pay much attention to religion at all; rather, they are either hard at work trying to survive or else plotting how to get rich."

He continued, "This does bring up something I'd like your opinion on— slavery. The Constitutions state, Every Freeman of Carolina shall have absolute power and authority over his Negro slaves, of what opinion or religion soever. I've never thought much about this before, but last month, I heard a lecture by Thomas Tryon, a merchant who once lived in Barbados, and Richard Baxter, a preacher. They were strongly opposed to slavery and had persuasive arguments supporting their views. What are your thoughts on the matter?"

Locke replied, "That is one provision in the Constitutions where I did have some say. An earlier version said that settlers had absolute and arbitrary power over their slaves and their children and could punish them with death for any reason their owner saw fit. I talked his lordship out of such extreme language, and he agreed to replace it with the current version."

Henry responded, "But does it reflect your personal views?"

"I have thought a lot about the topic and am writing a treatise that discusses slavery, among other topics. Someday I may publish it, although I think it is too controversial for these times. I believe that all men are, by the law of nature, free. But when they enter into a society, they are bound by its rules, including the rules of warfare—a conqueror has absolute power over the lives of those he captured in a just war waged against him. He can kill them or make them his slaves, at his pleasure. This is the long-standing rule of many civilizations. I have expanded upon it—I believe that this right does not extend to the children of the captives nor their property."

"I suppose that makes some sense," Henry replied. "But, in my experience, that is not how slavery works in the real world. For example, I think you would agree that the Indians in Carolina live in a state of nature. Under your argument, they have not consented to the laws of our society and therefore are not bound by its rules. I expect this is also true for Africans. But even more importantly, we are making slaves of those not captured in a just war. Most of them, Indians and Africans alike, were peaceful hunters and farmers who had no quarrel with us, and even if they were to declare war against us, by your rule, we could only enslave the warriors. Yet, we often kill the warriors because they make poor slaves; we are capturing the women and children who are more docile and better slaves."

Locke responded, "To be frank, I intended the just war theory apply only to European nations, not Africa or Carolina Colony. However, Carolina's Temporary Laws prohibit settlers from enslaving Indians or selling them as slaves."

"Mr. Locke, we both know that provision was included so that Charles Towne would stay on friendly terms with its Indian neighbors; the Indian slave trade business was reserved for his lordship at St. Giles Kussoe."

Locke had no response.

Henry added, "Baxter rejects the just war doctrine, saying that Christians may by their wickedness, forfeit their life or freedom but to take Negroes or others who have never done so is one of the worst kinds of theft in the world, and those who do are the common enemies of mankind, more devils than Christians. Tryon added to this. He said he was appalled by the cruelty and violence he saw on Barbados plantations; those who enslave others claim they have a right to do so, but there is no right, only power, expressed as violence. They are not defeating enemies in a just war but going to remote regions to buy captives taken in imaginary feuds or by treachery."

Again, Locke was silent.

The next day, picking up where he had left off in his conversation with Locke, Henry said, "There's one other thing I'd like to hear your views on—the Fundamental Constitutions say how land is to be granted to the proprietors, settlers, and others. But when we arrived in 1670, all of the lands were inhabited by Indians; we're taking it from them by trickery or force."

Locke replied, "That is a simpler matter than slavery—ultimately, it is God's will."

"How is that?"

"God gave the world to men in common, in particular to the industrious, who acquired ownership of it by their labor."

Henry said, "I'm not following you."

"I'll use Carolina Colony as an example—in the beginning, all was America; the earth and its creatures were in a state of nature and commonly owned by all mankind. But every man has a property right in his own body that belongs to him alone, and his labor is thus his as well. When, with his efforts, he removes something from the earth provided by nature, he has mixed his efforts with it, thereby making it his property so long as there is enough left behind for others. This does not require the consent of others. For example, if an Indian kills a deer to feed his family, it becomes his property alone. This also applies not just to the earth's bounty but to the earth itself. As much of the common land as a man can cultivate and use the products of, so much is his property."

"So why do my Indian neighbors not own the land that they hunt and fish on?"

Locke answered, "Because they are not putting it to its best use. God intended the industrious to own property by their efforts; cultivating crops is a better use of the land than hunting or fishing."

"I understand your argument, but I'm not sure I agree with it. You say that a man can only claim ownership to as much land as he can cultivate with his labor and can use the crops from it. His lordship gave me 2,000 acres of land that belonged to the Indians. I can't possibly cultivate that much land and, even if I could, I can't use all of the corn or squash from it. His lordship has even more than that, 12,000 acres at St. Giles Kussoe alone. How can claiming that much land give a man ownership of it?"

Locke responded, "I have developed a theory of how that can be justified. Society has agreed to use gold and silver as money; one who has more land and produce than he can use by himself may sell the surplus produce and save the money or use it to buy more land. By this means, one can properly possess more land than he can use for his own purposes."

"Mr. Locke, I've never met someone who can argue as well as you, but that seems a bit too clever. According to your theory, I can come onto my Indian neighbor's land, plant and harvest corn on it that I do not need for myself, and sell the corn. The Indians lose their land without receiving anything of value from me, and I become richer. You would argue that they never owned the land since they didn't cultivate it. I expect that if they knew how to argue as well as you, they would say that it is their land by their rules of society, not ours, and our rules do not bind them. Then it simply becomes a matter of who is more powerful. The settlers have guns; the Indians do not."

Locke answered, "We became owners of the land by the will of God; if the Indians became Christians, they would understand this and perhaps become farmers themselves."

"I've never been attracted to the life of a planter, finding it dull," Henry responded. "It appears to be immoral as well—we took the Indians' land, believing it was God's will because we used our labor to improve it, but it is largely slave labor, not our own, that develops and maintains our plantations. You might argue that because the planter owns the slave, he owns their labor as well. But your only justification for slavery is the just war theory; we know few if any slaves are taken in wars, so a planter has no legal or moral claim to the slave or his labor. As you say, a man's labor is his property, so a slave's labor is stolen property. Not only are we stealing a slave's labor, we are then using that stolen property to claim ownership of the Indians' land. I can understand why Baxter said plantation owners are more devils than Christians."

Locke responded, "You should have been a lawyer; you argue well. But I would remind you that you are responsible for many Indian captives ending up as slaves on plantations. If owning slaves is wrong, then selling them is at least as wrong. You are not in a good position to criticize."

Standing, Henry said, "I know. If Tryon and Baxter are correct and there is a hell, I have no doubt I will be there someday. I can't justify what I did, but perhaps I can explain it. I never captured and sold Indians living in Carolina Colony, or any Indians I considered my friends. I only allowed the Westo to capture Guale Indians, allies of the Spanish who are our enemy. This was partly revenge for what the Spanish and the Guale did to us, taking prisoners from *The Three Brothers*. I've since realized that revenge is not an excuse for harming innocent people. My other reason was less personal—it was a way to make a living. I didn't invent the Westo Indian slave trade; I took it over from Fort Henry, at his lordship's and Andrew Percival's direction."

PARDONED

London, May 1682

When the day of Henry's hearing before the lords proprietors, May 1st, finally arrived, he was thoroughly tired of London and wished he had followed Mary's advice just to pay the hundred pound fine and move on with his life. The day passed without any word about the hearing, as did the following days. Finally, Henry asked Locke what had happened.

"I know that four of the lords proprietors, including his lordship, met and considered your petition. I don't know what their decision was, only that it will be in writing, probably later this month."

On the last day of May, Shaftesbury's butler informed Henry that his lordship wanted to meet with him in the library. Descending the two flights of stairs, Henry was apprehensive—he knew it was about the hearing and had no idea what to expect. When Shaftesbury entered the room, he was smiling; Henry knew he had been pardoned.

"Doctor Woodward, congratulations. Here is a copy of your pardon. Not only have you been pardoned for the high crimes and misdemeanors, but for any other acts you may have committed in Carolina. We have also released you from the fine. I know that your trading days with the Westo at St. Giles Kussoe are over as the Savannah Indians vanquished them. But I believe you are still a valuable asset to the colony; no one has your experience exploring and dealing with the

Indians. With that in mind, I convinced the other proprietors to issue a commission appointing you to explore the inland areas of Carolina, and report to us all discoveries you make. The commission states that no government officials or other persons are to molest or hinder you. I could not get the other proprietors to agree to a payment schedule for you, but you know from our past dealings that I reward those who do their jobs well. Also, you must be low on funds by now, so I'm loaning you thirty pounds. Finally, after reviewing your petition for a pardon and letters from various Charles Towne settlers, including one from your father-in-law, we issued an order banning the taking of any Indians as slaves within 400 miles of Charles Towne."

⚬∿⚬

May 18, 1682

William Earle of Craven Lord Lieutenant of the County of Middlesex and Borough of Southwarke, one of his Majesty's most Honorable Privy Council Palatine and the rest of the true and absolute Lords and Proprietors of the Province of Carolina.

To Henry Woodward, Greeting.

Whereas it may be much for the honor and profit of our sovereign Lord the Kind and for the good and benefit of us, the Lords Proprietors, to have the Inlands of our province of Carolina well discovered and what they do contain and also a passage over the Appalachian Mountains found out. We, reposing great confidence in the loyalty, conduct, and prudence of you, Henry Woodward, do hereby appoint and empower you to take with you as many persons as you think fit and are willing to go with you and to search and make discovery of those parts of our Province where you shall think any mines are or other things fit or useful for us to know about. You are, from time to time, to give us an account of what discoveries you have made and what kind of country the Inlands of our Province are, and how qualified for planting of vines and inhabitants. We do further grant power and authority to you to erect a house and reside in any part of our Province from whence you judge the aforesaid discoveries are most likely to be made. We require all governors, magistrates, military officers, and all other persons whatsoever not to molest or hinder you in your aforesaid discovery. You are to observe such instructions as are herewith given you and such as you hereafter receive from us.

Given under our hands and the great seal of our Province this 18th day of May, 1682.

Henry believed so strongly that the Charles Towne Court had wrongly accused him that the pardon was almost anticlimactic; no other outcome seemed possible. He was intrigued by the commission. It was as if his time working for Shaftesbury at St. Giles Kussoe had never happened. There was no mention of continuing to work here in any role or finding new Indian trading partners to replace. Instead, it reminded Henry of his first months in the settlement when Shaftesbury encouraged him to explore for gold and silver. Was the commission an offer of a fresh start or a demotion? In the past, Shaftesbury had encouraged him to settle down as a planter; the commission was as far from that as one could imagine. Again, Henry realized he didn't understand him.

Henry booked passage on the next ship to Charles Towne, almost exactly a year after he had sailed for London, not knowing this was the last time he would see or hear from Shaftesbury.

CAROLINA COLONY

1682

During the voyage home, Henry spent hours thinking about his commission from the lord's proprietors to explore Carolina Colony. It was broad—explore Carolina for a passage through the Appalachians and for mines and other valuable things, taking as many men as he wished and not answerable to anyone but the proprietors. He could live wherever he chose in the colony, and nobody could disturb him. Back in Shaftesbury's good graces, but now without his financial support, he was on his own, with a family to provide for.

He recalled what Abraham Wood had done decades earlier at Fort Henry in Virginia Colony. The government gave him a surplus fort and permission to explore and trade with the Indians, which he did on his own. *I could do the same,* he thought, *and only work for myself.*

He didn't know what his reception would be like when he arrived home at Abbapoola Creek. He'd promised to be home by year's end, but it was now August, and Mary had been alone with an infant and a ten-year-old for more than a year.

But her reaction was not what he feared; instead, it was as if he had only been gone a few weeks. Little Johnnie, now two, didn't recognize him, clinging to his mother's skirts. Mary's daughter gave him a shy hello. Mary said, "Get cleaned up; I'll have the servant set an extra place for dinner."

Henry was prepared to recount his time in London but realized it wouldn't be a good idea to tell them about being served breakfasts in bed at Shaftesbury's mansion. Instead, he said, "Mary, the place looks remarkable. Tell me what you've done with it."

—⁂—

Abbapoola Point's transformation was remarkable. The slaves had cleared new fields, planted them in corn and squash, and built cabins for themselves. It looked like an actual plantation.

Mary said, "We're making a small profit. I'm sending most of the corn to Barbados, along with lumber we cut clearing the fields. When the field hands aren't busy, I rent some out to other settlers. Even my daughter has a job, feeding the chickens and gathering their eggs."

Henry soon realized he had a family and a comfortable home. Why would he want to go out into the wilderness for weeks on end, sleep on the ground, and eat dried cornmeal? Their son Johnnie was becoming a little person; it wouldn't be many years before he could teach him how to hunt and fish and start bringing him to the local Indian towns. Perhaps he should ignore the lords proprietors' commission to explore and instead take the advice Shaftesbury had given him years earlier—settle down as a planter and raise a family.

That idea still seemed attractive the next day, so he broached it to Mary.

She commented, "It would be wonderful to have you at home, but have you thought about what you would do all day? The field hands do all the hard work, clearing trees, cutting lumber, and tending the fields. My servant and I do the housework and cooking."

"Your brothers are always busy. What do they do?"

Mary replied, "Both of them still have businesses in Barbados. Their servants and slaves take care of the fields and the house, just as we do. Speaking of businesses, almost all of our income came from the Indian trade at St. Giles Kussoe. We would need to be very frugal without it."

"We have 2,000 acres of prime land. Maybe we can cut more timber and raise more corn to sell," Henry said.

"That's a lot of work for a small profit. In Barbados, plantations were only profitable growing sugar cane; in Virginia, tobacco. Carolina has no such crops—olives, vines, mulberry trees for silk; all have been failures here. A planter's life will always be hard until we find a successful crop."

"Perhaps I can come up with a plan, but for now, I just want to be at home."

But, after a year at home, Henry's free moments were now filled with memories of his days as an Indian trader. Sleeping on the hard ground and eating dried cornmeal seemed a small price to pay for the solitude of the forest, visiting Indian towns that had never seen an Englishman before.

But that October, Henry was also a father again, another boy, named Richard. He tried to ignore thoughts of returning to his former life as a trader, to no avail.

Finally, he decided to confide in Mary. "You were right when you said there would be little for me to do here as a planter. I want to get back into the Indian trading business; it's the only thing I enjoy and am good at. But I want to be here as well. I've been thinking of putting together a crew to start trading again; once they learn enough about the business, I can spend much of my time at home."

Mary replied, "We could use the income; we're barely making any money now. But who would you trade with?"

"I'm not sure; possibly the Creek Indians in Apalachicola Province along the Chattahoochee River. They've wanted to trade for years, but I always put them off when I was trading with the Westo. The main problem is that they're three or four hundred miles west of Charles Towne; that's a long journey. Also, the Spanish consider that area to be theirs; they would not be happy to see me there. But, for now, I'll talk to some of the men in town who might want to work with me."

THE SCOTS

Carolina Colony, 1684–1685

Half-heartedly chopping firewood on a cold early January morning, Caleb Westbrooke wondered if it had been a mistake to move to Carolina Colony. Life had been hard in England, but at least he had friends to commiserate with in the taverns; at St. Helena, he was fifty miles from the nearest one. All he had to show after three years was 260 acres of marsh and forestland awarded to him for moving here and the loss of his three indentured servants who were to clear the land but that he'd been forced to sell.

His ruminations were interrupted by a group of Indians disembarking from a canoe. They looked friendly; one was holding a letter in his outstretched hand. He had learned none of the local Indians' language in his time here, but one spoke some English. The letter was from the governor of St. Augustine, addressed to the governor of Carolina Colony; he couldn't get a coherent explanation why they were delivering it to him. He was able to make out that they came from far to the west, near the Creek Indians' lands, and moved to St. Helena, where they had relatives. He said that they were called the Yamasee by the English.

One of them asked if he knew a man named Henry Woodward; Caleb knew of him but had never met him—he was the Indian trader the Charles Towne government had recently convicted for his dealings with the Westo. The Indian said they hoped to meet him because they wanted to trade with the English.

Thinking there might be something in it for him, Caleb said he would see what he could do and for them to come back later. But first, he needed to get the letter into the hands of the governor. So far, he'd had little luck making his mark in the colony; he'd never even met the governor. Then he recalled that last November, a large group of immigrants from Scotland, fifty in total, had settled at Port Royal, practically in his backyard, and had named their settlement Stuart's Town. Its leaders were William Dunlop and Lord Cardross. He'd heard that the lords proprietors had granted them the same rights as Charles Towne, including rights to trade with the Indians. He needed to talk to them.

———〰———

Stuart's Town reminded Caleb of Charles Towne's early days—crude huts scattered among the trees. However, it was a much better location on a high bluff overlooking the river. Caleb introduced himself to William Dunlop, explained why he was there and gave him the letter from St. Augustine. When Dunlop asked why he was not delivering it to the governor himself, he said his boat needed repairs.

When Dunlop thanked him and promised to deliver the letter, Caleb interjected, "The Yamasee Indians said they were interested in trade with the settlers, and I promised I would look into it. Is this something that you and I could discuss?"

"You should talk to Lord Cardross; he knows more about business than I do. He's around somewhere; why don't you wait for his return?"

Lord Cardross was very interested in what Caleb had to say. It had only taken him a few weeks to realize that it would be difficult for Stuart's Town to survive economically; Charles Towne had a big head start on trade with England and Barbados. "Mr. Westbrooke, please explain the Indian trade business to me; I'm afraid it's an area I know nothing about."

Caleb explained that St. Giles Kussoe and its trading partner, the Westo Indians, formerly had a monopoly on the trade for deerskins sent to England and Indian captives sold to Barbados plantations. The lords proprietors barred Charles Towne from this business. A group known as the Goose Creek Men resented this monopoly and arranged to destroy the Westo and discredit St. Giles agent, Henry Woodward. Since then, the Goose Creek Men had taken over some of the trade, but there should still be room for others.

"Your town is well placed to trade with the Indians to the west, especially now that some Yamasee are moving from there to St. Helena. One problem might be with the Spanish—they consider the lands south and west of Charles Towne, including where we are now, to be theirs."

Cardross listened thoughtfully to all of this and then replied, "Stuart's Town is independent of Charles Towne. We can do as we please and are only answerable to the lords proprietors. But it is a lot of effort to set up a trade for deerskins, and I don't have the connections to sell them in England. Tell me more about selling slaves."

Caleb admitted he was not an expert on how that business worked but recalled that after banning the Indian slave trade for several years, the proprietors had relented in the face of pressure from the Goose Creek Men. He promised Cardross he would find out more. When he finally left for home, he and Cardross had an informal agreement to negotiate a trade agreement with the Yamasee for captive Indians, as the Westo had done for St. Giles. Caleb would receive one-quarter of the profits.

March 21, 1684
To Col. John Godfrey, Deputy Governor
Honored Sir,
John Chaplin has returned to Port Royal and told me that he saw arms and other things delivered to the Yamasee and that they have gone against the Timucua Indians. Last Monday, Lord Cardross, Mr. Dunlop, Mr. Hamilton, and Mr. Westbrooke went to Amacaraw on the Savannah River. He does not know who or where the Timucua are nor why Cardross and his men went to Amacaraw, but the reason is evident as he was told that a great booty is expected from the Timucua. Mr. Chaplin said that he believes that Mr. Westbrooke persuaded Cardross to undertake this raid, which I consider unadvised. Since I last wrote you, Antonio has been with me from St. Helena and others who also complain that Mr. Westbrooke is responsible for the Scotch and Yamasee going on this venture.
I rest your obedient son-in-law,
Henry Woodward

62

CHARLES TOWNE

April/May 1685

When Henry arrived home, Mary said to him, "My father asked that you stop by his home this week; he has something he wants to tell you."

Henry had wondered if he would hear from Godfrey about his letter warning him about a possible raid by Lord Cardross and the Yamasee Indians. Since then, he'd heard from his friends in Kiawah town that a large group of Yamasee warriors, led by their chief, Altamaha, were seen leaving St. Helena and that Cardross and Westbrooke were still at Amacaraw on the Savannah River. If they were planning on attacking the Timucua as Chaplin claimed, that was alarming. The Timucua towns were no more than a hundred miles from St. Augustine; attacking them would almost certainly result in retaliation by the Spanish, not only against Stuart's Town but probably against Charles Towne.

When Henry told Godfrey of his concerns, he replied, "It may well be too late for Charles Towne to act, but at the least, we need to know what Cardross and Westbrooke have done so we can prepare for the consequences. Could you go to Amacaraw and learn what you can? We need to keep good relations with Stuart's Town, so I don't want to let them know that I'm asking you to do this in my role as deputy governor. If asked, you should say you are exploring for the lords proprietors under your commission."

"I can do that; I don't know that area so it will indeed be exploration. I'll take some of my men with me; we can leave in a day or two."

———⌘———

This was the first time Henry had taken his newly-assembled crew out of Charles Towne. He had planned a trip to Creek country in May, but this mission took precedence. Four of his men were available; two days later, they set sail in Henry's yawl for the mouth of the Savannah River, a hundred miles down the coast. All he knew about Amacaraw was that it sat on a bluff, not far from the ocean and downriver from the former Westo town.

Reaching the bluffs, and, seeing no sign of Cardross's men, they went up the hillside. Almost immediately, they were accosted by at least ten men, all with guns. Woodward recognized one as Caleb Westbrooke. Another, clearly their leader, introduced himself as John Hamilton. When Henry introduced himself, Hamilton brusquely replied, "I have a warrant to arrest you and take you to Stuart's Town."

When Henry asked to see the warrant, Hamilton refused. Henry showed him his commission from the lords proprietors; he replied, "I don't care about your commission; we are taking you prisoner."

Seeing as they were outnumbered two to one, it seemed to Henry a wiser course of action to comply and sort it out later. Hamilton confiscated their weapons and put Henry and his men in a boat. Westbrooke was in the same boat, so Henry took the opportunity to ask him about the Yamasee's raid.

Westbrooke was not shy in bragging about it. "The Yamasee's chief, Alta-maha, and fifty of his men attacked Santa Catalina de Afuyca in the Timucua's lands. They killed twenty of the townspeople, took twenty more as slaves, and burned the town to the ground. The slaves are being brought to our town to be sold."

Henry replied, "That was foolhardy—the Spanish won't ignore this attack on people under their protection, especially so close to St. Augustine. They are going to sail a fleet up to your very doorstep and destroy Stuart's Town."

Westbrooke retorted, "You did the same thing four years ago at Santa Catalina de Guale, and the Spanish did nothing."

"Their governor promised to destroy Charles Towne if we ever did anything like that again. I don't believe they will let this attack go."

Westbrooke said, "We will see, but I predict that Stuart's Town will replace St. Giles Kussoe, and I will be its agent. Cardross won't allow you to cross the lands the proprietors granted to him, so you won't be able to trade with any Indians to the south or west of Charles Towne."

By day's end, they were in Stuart's Town and Henry was brought before Lord Cardross. He repeated what he had told Hamilton—he had a commission from the lords proprietors to explore anywhere in the colony without being disturbed by others.

Cardross replied that the commission was meaningless to him—the Scots were an independent nation from the English and would control all trade on the lands granted to them. He held Henry and his men another four days until releasing them with a promise from Henry that he and his men would stay off the land Cardross was claiming as his own.

⁕⁕⁕

As soon as he was freed, Henry told his father-in-law what had transpired with the Scots. Godfrey seldom showed emotion, but Henry could tell he was furious when he told his story. Godfrey said, "I know you were planning to leave on a trading mission shortly, but please stay here for another week or so while I talk to the grand council. Cardross has not heard the last of this matter."

⁕⁕⁕

Two weeks later, Henry was summoned to give his deposition regarding Cardross's actions. The council also called several Yamasee Indians who were familiar with the raid. When the depositions were completed, the council immediately issued arrest warrants for Cardross, Westbrooke, and Hamilton. Cardross claimed he was ill and could not turn himself in; Westbrooke and Hamilton fled into the wilderness.

Henry's prediction about the Spanish response to the raid was correct. The following year, three ships from St. Augustine burned Stuart's Town to the ground before sailing toward Charles Towne to repeat their performance. Once again, the town dodged a Spanish bullet—an unexpected hurricane damaged the fleet, and Charles Towne was spared. But Henry had no way of foreseeing the ultimate consequences for his crew.

COWETA TOWN

Apalachicola Province, 1685

When Matthews and Moore had orchestrated Henry's conviction for high crimes and misdemeanors, it took him over a year to clear himself. But, watching Shaftesbury, a master politician, demolish the crown's case against him, Henry had learned his lesson. This time, it only took him a few weeks to turn the tables on Lord Cardross and Caleb Westbrooke.

In June, Henry and his crew set sail for Apalachicola Province on the Chattahoochee River. Ruben Willis, at forty, the oldest of Henry's six-man crew, asked, "It's been some time since we've talked about the plan. Could we go over it again?"

Henry said, "We're going to Coweta, the largest town in Creek country. We could make the entire journey by land, but it's almost 400 miles. It will be easier to sail from Charles Towne up the Altamaha River. Then it's only 100 miles west by land to Coweta. We're taking two Yamasee guides who lived in Coweta and are familiar with the journey."

"I don't know a thing about the Creeks. Who are they?" Ruben asked.

"The Creeks are the largest tribe within hundreds of miles of Charles Towne; they've wanted to trade with me for years. We're only going to trade for deerskins and furs, not Indian captives. After my experience with the Westo, I've decided that's too much trouble even though it is more profitable than deerskins. Half of the profits will be divided equally between the six of you." If Henry's decision was based in part on any moral qualms about the slave trade as a result of his earlier conversation with John Locke about slavery, he did not say so.

———◦∿◦———

Bidding Mary goodbye, Henry said, "I should be back by fall. I promise never to be away from home this long again."

"I'm worried about you. It seems everyone is after you—first the Goose Creek Men, then the Scots; I expect the Spanish won't be happy with you either."

"They won't be, but they will never catch me."

———◦∿◦———

One of the Yamasee guides who had lived with the Creeks told Henry and his crew about them. "They do not call themselves Creeks, rather the Muscogee. They live along the Chattahoochee River. Their towns are either red towns, symbolizing war, or white, for peace. Coweta is the most important red town; Cussita is the largest white town. The most important thing in their world is the clan. Men and women live almost completely apart, and each family has a hut for the man and another for the woman. Every morning the men meet in the town square to talk, smoke and drink. The leader of each town is called a mico; one of his jobs is to greet visitors so you will meet him."

———◦∿◦———

After five days on the river and four on foot, the men arrived at Coweta. Four buildings surrounded the town square; their guide said all of the Creek towns were arranged this way, representing the earth's four corners. Henry was escorted to the mico's building on the west side of the square. He did not speak the Creek's language, nor did the mico, named Quiair, speak English, so one of the Yamasee translated.

Henry began, "I am honored to meet you at last. I hoped to do so earlier, but there were obstacles in our path. I believe our two peoples can now make a trading agreement that will benefit both of us."

Quiair responded, "We have been friends of the Spanish at St. Augustine for many years. But some of us have become unhappy with the Spanish. We want to trade with them and to be able to look to them for protection, but they offer us only their religion."

"I can promise you trade goods and that we will not tell you how you should live. In turn, we will take all of the deerskins and furs you provide."

"Can you promise we won't suffer the same fate as the Westo if we trade with you?" Quiair asked.

Henry answered, "If the Westo had heeded my warning, they would still be here. In any case, they were destroyed because the Goose Creek Men wanted to control the Indian slave trade business; they have little interest in skins or furs. I have no interest in trading for captives. But, since you mentioned the Westo, tell me what you thought of them. I worked closely with them for several years but never truly understood them."

Quiair replied, "We believe that everyone has two parts. One is the soul that speaks to us in our dreams. It is part of the Upper World, where it returns after death if the person has led a good life. The other part is the ghost, which is responsible for feelings of good and evil and is part of the Lower World. It can leave the body during sleep; if it does not return, the person can become ill or even die. I believe that the Westo allowed the ghost part of their being to rule over their souls, leading them on a bad path. The end they met was to be expected."

⸺◊◊◊⸺

Henry and Quiair spent several days discussing a trade agreement. Explaining the importance of clans to the Creeks, Quiair told Henry that his, the Wind Clan, was the most powerful, and promised that Henry's success as a trader would be assured if he joined it. Henry readily agreed but was not prepared for what the Mico said next.

"You will have to marry into the Wind Clan. My niece Talisa is unmarried; I will arrange the wedding."

All Henry could say was, "But I'm already married."

"That is not a problem. Men are allowed to have more than one wife in our tribe."

"But the English are not."

"Even if your first wife agrees you still cannot take a second wife?"

Henry finally realized that Quiair was not going to relent—if he were to establish a successful agreement, he would have to marry Quiair's niece. "If I do marry her, do we have to live together?"

"No; you can each live in your separate house; what you do in your marriage is up to you."

Henry and Talisa were married in a small ceremony; he did not invite his crew. He told himself, *there's no reason that anyone other than the Creeks needs to know about this.*

⸺◊◊◊⸺

Quiair began to act on his promise immediately. Within days, Henry's crew, assisted by Coweta men, were building a blockhouse to hold trade goods. The Coweta hunters killed twenty deer on their first day; the women were busy skinning them. Several other Creek towns were asking to join the trade agreement; Henry's dream of his own Indian trading business was succeeding.

CAT AND MOUSE

Apalachicola Province, 1685

If Henry was pleased with the success of his trade agreement with the Creeks, the Spanish were not. They had long considered the Creeks their allies and, in recent years, a buffer between themselves and the English at Charles Towne. It was bad enough that Coweta town had made a pact with Woodward, but now their spies reported that other Creek towns were joining it. He had been a thorn in their side for too long, and the St. Augustine governor could not let this latest incursion go unanswered.

❧

From Juan Cabrera, governor of St. Augustine
To Don Melchor Portocarrero, Viceroy of New Spain
Most Excellent Sir,
Last September 1685, I was informed by Lieutenant Antonio Mateos that seven Englishmen sailed from Carolina some 350 miles to the province of Apalachicola, whose natives had been obedient to us.

The leader of these Englishmen is Captain Enrique. He has a large income from England granted by his monarch because he was the discoverer of the province of Carolina. At the time of the discovery, he remained among the Indians, and in two years, his companions were to come for him. He had a great deal of information about the Indians, and he spoke five languages of these provinces and others. At the end of the appointed time,

245

no ships came for him, and he wrote a letter in Latin to Don Francisco de la Guerra, then governor of St. Augustine. He came here and asked the priest Don Francisco de Sotolongo to baptize him. The latter became his godfather and kept him in his house until the night the enemy entered this province, at which time he fled and went back to England. He then returned to Carolina, where he still resides. Because of his income in England, his mastery of languages, and his great intelligence, he seems to be popular, and he has stirred the said provinces.

I ordered Lieutenant Matheos to go to Apalachicola to apprehend the English but he had no success. The Indians have taken a great fondness for them because of the offers the English have made them, and have concealed them in the mountains. From there, Enrique wrote a message to us whose translation to Spanish is enclosed.

The English overran these provinces again a few days after the Lieutenant returned to Apalachee. This second attempt brought about another raid by the Lieutenant, a report of which is also enclosed.

If we had been able to capture Enrique, it would have been a great help toward maintaining peace in these provinces.

God preserve your Excellency many years in his greatness.
Respectfully, Juan Marques Cabrera
March 19, 1686

By late August, the Creeks had provided enough deerskins and furs for Henry to return to Charles Towne. As he was settling the trading account, Quiair approached him. "A group of Spanish soldiers accompanied by Indians is headed toward our town. Our scouts say they are coming for you and your men."

"Should we be alarmed?"

Quiair laughed. "We've hunted in this country for hundreds of years and know every bush and tree. My men will take you north into the mountains; the Spanish will have no more chance of capturing you than they would the birds in the sky."

The mico was correct. He had his scouts spread out across the hills; whenever the soldiers got within a few miles, the Creek men would take Henry's crew in a different direction. Henry found it amusing once he realized they were in no real danger; the only annoying part was having to eat cold meals because they could not light fires.

One day, when they stopped for their midday meal, Henry took a sheet of parchment, wrote a note, and pinned it to a tree trunk with his knife. When Ruben asked him what it said, Henry read it aloud:

I am very sorry that I came with so small a following that I cannot await your arrival. Be informed that I came to get acquainted with the country, its mountains, the seacoast, and Apalachee. I trust in God that I shall meet you gentlemen later when I have a larger following.
September 2, 1685. Vale.

Having seen no sign of Henry and his men for several weeks, Governor Cabrera called off the chase. But a week later, Henry was back at Coweta, and it was business as usual. Cabrera sent his forces back to Apalachicola Province; Henry and his crew again fled into the mountains. But this time, Cabrera, reverting to the ruthless tactics of earlier St. Augustine governors, told the Creek towns that they could pledge loyalty to the Spanish and turn over Henry and his crew or face destruction.

The strength of the clan system in Creek society now came into play. The Wind Clan controlled Coweta and several of the neighboring towns. Henry had become a member of the clan by marrying Quiair's niece, and the clan would protect him at all costs; their towns refused to comply with the Spanish demands. Lieutenant Matheos destroyed Henry's blockhouse in January, seizing 500 deerskins and furs. Four of the Creek towns refused to cooperate; Cabrera carried through on his threats, burning Coweta and three adjoining towns to the ground the following month.

⁓⁓⁓

Henry and Quiair met to decide how to deal with this disaster. Henry knew the Creeks had paid a heavy price for their trade agreement with him, and he expected the Mico to be furious. He was angry, but not at Henry. "The Spanish have declared war on us," he said. "They refuse to trade with us for tools and other goods that we need, then destroy our towns when we deal with you. I'm unhappy that our towns to the south did not support us against the Spanish, but that was to be expected—they are not in the Wind Clan."

Henry replied, "I've been fighting the Spanish for almost twenty years now; I hoped it would end after the Westo were destroyed. I was wrong. You could have turned your backs on me and made peace with the Spanish, but you did not, and I will do everything within my power to help you. I'll ask my government in Charles Town for assistance; they are no more a friend of the Spanish than I am."

The Mico agreed with Henry that there was no reason for him to stay longer—the townspeople would be busy rebuilding and would have no time to gather more deerskins and furs. He promised to return in March, with whatever aid he could persuade the Charles Towne government to provide.

ABBAPOOLA CREEK

Henry told his wife he would be back in a few months; that had been six months ago. As he tied up at the wharf, a young boy ran to the house, calling, "Mother, there's a stranger outside."

It wasn't until Mary came outside that Henry realized it was his son Johnnie, who didn't recognize him.

Mary seemed more amused than upset with him. "I was certain the Spanish had captured you and taken you back to St. Augustine one more time," she said.

Over the evening meal, Henry told his family of his exploits, being chased by Spanish soldiers through the mountains. The two older children were fascinated; Richard was too young to understand. What would his wife think if she knew he had married the niece of a Creek chief, even if in name only?

The next day, Mary took him on a tour of the Abbapoola plantation. There were more fields cleared than when he had left; she had since replaced the cows he had sold to Percival, and they had calves. If he had ever had doubts about her ability to manage the plantation in his absence, they were now put to rest.

Henry finally worked up the nerve to tell his wife that he was only home for a week or so and then he would be returning to Creek country to bring back deerskins and furs—the Spanish had seized the last shipment. He promised that this time he would only be gone as long as it took to collect them.

Mary said nothing.

Henry told his crew that he realized they were upset over not being paid for the expedition, especially since they had risked their lives. "We had agreed to divide the profits, but there were none. We're going back to Coweta shortly; any of you who wish to accompany me are welcome, and I will advance each of you five pounds toward the profits from that trip."

One of the men asked, "How do we know the Spanish won't seize our goods this time as well?"

Henry replied, "I've been thinking about that. When I was trading with the Westo, no one dared to interfere with us for years as the Westo were better warriors than anybody. The Creek are brave, but they are more concerned about their clans than the Spanish seizing our goods. We need to have someone on our side paid to fight for us if necessary."

"Who?" asked Ruben.

"Perhaps the Yamasee. Hundreds of them have moved to Carolina Province, and since Stuart's Town was destroyed, they have no allies here. I'll ask their chief if we can hire some of their warriors."

The Yamasee chief accepted Henry's proposal eagerly—this seemed an excellent opportunity to ally with Charles Towne. He agreed to provide Henry with forty-five warriors, many of them armed with guns that Lord Cardross had provided, to accompany him to Coweta.

Henry's next visit was to the Carolina governor. He realized he no longer knew who the governor was and asked his father-in-law. When he explained to Godfrey that he wanted to ask the Carolina government to supply him with guns to arm the Creeks to protect themselves from the Spanish, he expected a negative reaction. But Godfrey surprised him. "Joseph Morton is again our governor, for the second time. I heard he is planning a raid against the Spanish at St. Augustine, so should be receptive to your idea."

By week's end, Henry had a force of Yamasee warriors and twenty-six guns plus swords from the governor to give to the Creeks and more trade goods. He also rented a second ship large enough to carry the additional men.

Once again, he bade his family goodbye; this time, he didn't make a promise as to when he would return.

1686

During Henry's brief absence, the Creeks had been busy rebuilding their towns. Quiair was delighted to get the firearms and other weapons; the Yamasee instructed them how to use and care for the guns. Henry explained that the Yamasee were there as his soldiers; the Spanish and their Indian allies should be reluctant to chase armed Indians who knew the wilderness far better than they did.

The Creeks spent the following months amassing deerskins and furs. By the end of July, they had collected 3,000 deerskins in addition to beaver and otter pelts, bearskins, and even a few buffalo skins, more than the forty-five Yamasee could carry back to Charles Towne; Henry sent one of them back to ask the Yamasee chief for another hundred men to help. When they arrived in early August, Henry told Quiair he was ready to return to Charles Towne.

Before they left, Henry went to look for Talisa. She was in their garden, tending to the corn. "I'll be back in a month or two," he said in the Creek tongue which he was still mastering.

"Safe journey," she replied.

Walking back to the partially rebuilt blockhouse where the skins and furs were being loaded, he heard a rattle and immediately felt a sharp pain in his calf. He knew what it was even before he saw the rattlesnake slither into the brush. By the time he reached the blockhouse, his leg had begun to swell. As he said to Ruben, "A rattlesnake has just bitten me," he realized his lips and face were going numb, and his vision was fading away.

"I'm going to sit here for a while until I feel better."

For the next three days, Henry was in a delirium; the only thing keeping him conscious was the intense pain. Finally, he began to improve but couldn't put weight on his leg. He realized there was no way he could cover the hundred miles overland from Coweta to the river where their boats were moored.

"No problem," said the head of Yamasee the crew, "We'll build a litter of deerskins and carry you."

And so they did, arriving at their boats four days later. Henry was no better; he couldn't keep food down, and his limbs were beginning to swell. The Yamasee, reinforced with ten Creek men, all burdened with skins and furs, headed back toward Charles Towne on foot. Five of Henry's men with two Yamasee took one of the boats. Henry, Ruben, the Creek chief's son, and two others took the smaller boat. The chief's son told Henry and Ruben he knew of a different river that would be faster to Charles Towne, but it was too shallow for the other boat. Agreeing it was essential to get Henry home as quickly as possible, the boats split up. Several Creeks said they had to turn back, so the extra deerskins and furs were loaded in the larger vessel.

Henry's condition continued to worsen as they sailed downriver. He became sluggish, confused, drifting in and out of sleep.

A day later, he fell into a coma and died.

He would never learn the fate of his crew at the hands of the Guale Indians.

The Deposition of an Indian from Santa Catalina de Guale
St. Augustine, September 27, 1686

I am Juan Cabrera, the governor of St. Augustine; this is my interpreter, Alonso Garcia. I will ask you some questions about what happened to you last month. Do you promise to answer the questions truthfully?

"Yes."

"Please tell me your name, your age, and where you are from."

"My name is Matheo, twenty-two. I am a Guale Indian from Santa Catalina de Guale. About six years ago, the town was attacked by the Westo Indians and the English, led by Captain Enrique. We fled to the island of Santa Maria. Then

I went to the province of Carolina with some Yamasee Indians because I wanted to see the English town."

"What did you do there?"

"Very little; I did not like it. In early August, I was returning home when I met Spanish ships carrying Indians from my town. I asked them what they were doing. They told me they were helping the Spanish who were going to attack Stuart's Town near Santa Elena, where English people called Scots lived. In late August, we destroyed their town and were on our way to attack Charles Towne when a storm struck, sinking one of the Spanish ships. I and some other Indians were told that there was no room for us on the other ships, and we would have to return home by land."

"What did you do next?"

"We found an abandoned canoe which we took to a river from Apalachicola lands. We were stopped by five Englishmen and two Creek Indians in a boat. They tied us up and asked if we were Christians. We said that we were. They said, 'Well, later on, we will kill you" and left us for the night."

"What happened then?"

"Four of the English were sleeping, the other and the two Indians were awake. One of us found an oyster shell on the ground and used it to cut his bonds. When we had freed ourselves, we used their guns and a stick to strike the four sleeping Englishmen, killing them. The other Englishman and the two Indians escaped but the Indians returned when we promised not to kill them."

"They told us that the Englishmen were from Carolina province and had been with the Creek Indians in Apalachicola for many months. They were returning to Carolina from Coweta. They said that their leader, Captain Enrique, was ill and he, one other Englishman, and several Creek Indians were returning on a different river. We took their guns and went home in their boat."

67

THE YAMASEE WAR

Carolina Province, 1715

In the early morning hours of April 15, 1715, Good Friday, the devil appeared at the Yamasee town of Pocotaligo.

Thomas Nairne, William Bray, Seymour Burrows, and several other traders had spent the night as guests in the Yamasee's lodge after delivering a letter from Governor Craven that he wanted to meet with them and the Creek Indians from Coweta to discuss claims of abuses by the Indian traders. The governor and his militia stopped briefly at John Woodward's (Henry's older son) plantation ten miles to the south. Yamasee scouts reported their presence to the Yamasee chief who decided that the governor's true intent was to attack and destroy Pocotaligo.

Nairne and his men were awakened by the sound of warriors armed with hatchets and adorned in red and black war paint bursting through the doorway. The braves seized and bound them; Burrows broke free and fled. Despite being shot twice, he managed to escape, running and swimming five miles to John Barnwell's nearby plantation, warning him of the attack.

Other warriors invaded the Indian traders' homes in the town, capturing and killing men, women, and children alike. Nairne, South Carolina's official Indian agent and most prominent of the traders, was singled out for special attention. He died after being cruelly tortured for four days.

The other Yamasee towns joined in the massacre of the Indian traders, sparing only those they felt had treated them well.

Thanks to Burrows' warning, the Port Royal settlers had time to flee to Charles Towne; two hundred of them crowded onto a ship anchored in the Beaufort River and sailed to safety. Yamasee warriors pillaged the region throughout the weekend, burning buildings and killing or capturing any families who had not fled. Governor Craven hastily constructed a fort at John Woodward's plantation and manned it with two militia companies; as a result, he and his family were unharmed.

The following week, Creek Indians from Coweta joined the raid. Within days, the English presence from Coweta almost to Charles Towne had been decimated. By the following Sunday, with few exceptions, only smoldering buildings and roving war parties remained.

⁕⁕⁕

The Yamasee War permanently changed Carolina Colony, as the Powhatan War changed Virginia Colony almost a hundred years earlier. The Woodward family survived and prospered. Carolina Colony eventually flourished after the crown took control from the lords proprietors. The power of the Yamasee and Creeks was crippled, and by 1728, they were gone from Carolina Colony.

The glory days of the Indian traders faded away as the colonists finally discovered a crop that would fulfill Shaftesbury's dream—large plantations owned by wealthy men and worked by African slaves.

The crop was rice, and Carolina was soon one of the wealthiest of the English colonies.

The Red Bird and the Devil
AUTHOR NOTES

Abbreviations:
BPRO—British Public Records Office
CSP—Calendar of State Papers
CEB—Colonial Entry Book
JGC—Journal of the Grand Council of South Carolina
SP—South Carolina Historical Society, The Shaftesbury Papers (Tempus Publishing, 1897, 2000).

CHAPTER:

One. Falling Creek Ironworks

Christopher Woodward was Henry Woodward's great-grandfather and the first of the Woodward family to emigrate to America. See John Hotten, *Musters of the Inhabitants of Virginia, The Original Lists of Persons of Quality* (London 1874), 206, and Fontaine & Kirby, 1991 *Tidewater Ancestors* (Lewis Kirby and Plumer Printing Company, 1991), 406.

The Ironworks, now a Chesterfield County park, is located ten miles south of present-day Richmond. It is unknown whether it ever became operational before being destroyed in 1622. See fallingcreekironworks.org for further information.

The Powhatan massacre of 1622 is well documented in the historical literature. See Ben McCary, *Indians in Seventeenth-Century Virginia* (The University Press of Virginia, 1957).

Christopher Woodward, Jr. followed his father from England to Virginia Colony. See Louise Niemeyer Fontaine, *Some Descendants of Christopher Woodward...* (The Society of Genealogists, London, 1952), 405-406, and Merle Safford, Woodard Footprint (Lulu Publishing, 2016), ch. 5. Christopher's letter to his wife is imagined.

Two. London, 1646

Thomas Woodward, Henry's grandfather, was fired from his position as Assay Master of the Royal Mint for his loyalty to Charles I. Like many other royalists, he fled to Virginia Colony around 1649. See *Tidewater Ancestors*, above, 408 and John Woodward's petition in *Calendar of State Papers, Domestic Series of the Reign of Charles II: 1660s,* 137. Thomas' letter to his brother is imagined.

Three. London, April 1649

Henry Woodward's father, John Woodward, married Mary Kirkman, in London, February 11, 1645. See *Register of St. Botolph Without Bishopgate,* London, vol. 1. He served briefly as a "chirgiun" (surgeon) in John Merrick's Regiment in the Parliamentarian Army. See Edward Peacock, *The Army Lists of the Roundheads and Cavaliers* (J. C. Hotten Pub., 1863), 28.

Henry Woodward was baptized in the Church of St. Stephen's Coleman St., on October 16, 1646; his brother John was baptized on April 2, 1644. See Charles Robinson, *Register of the Scholars Admitted Into Merchant Taylors' School from A.D. 1562 to 1874, Vol. 1* (Farncombe & Co., 1882), 248

Four. Virginia Colony, 1650

The story of the voyage of *The Virginia Merchant* was actually worse than portrayed, including one of the only recorded instances of cannibalism in the colonies. See Col. Henry Norwood, "A Voyage to Virginia" (Force's Collection of Historical Tracts, vol. 111, no 10.) and Sharon Himes, *Cavalier's Adventure, the Story of Henry Norwood* (Arcadia Publications, 2000)

There is no primary source documentation that the Woodwards were on that voyage but see Jeff Carter, *Ancestors of Jimmy and Rosalynn Carter* (McFarland & Company, 2014), 144, stating that Thomas Woodward bought passage on *The Virginia Merchant* in 1649. There is also no primary source material proving that John Woodward and his immediate family emigrated to Virginia at this time. But see Lyon Gardiner Tyler, *The Cradle of the Republic: Jamestown and James River* (Heritage Books, 2007), 62, stating that both John and Thomas Woodward were in Virginia "at or before the restoration" of 1660. Also, there is ample evidence that other family members were in Virginia at this time. Assuming the Woodward family traveled to Virginia together, it seems that John kept a low profile there.

Shirley Plantation, Virginia Colony's first plantation, is located on the James River between Richmond and Jamestown. The oldest family-owned business in North America, it is open to the public for tours. Pagan Point, on the Pagan River, was located at the present-day location of Smithfield, Virginia.

Five. Virginia Colony, 1652

William Woodward, John's cousin, owned land near Fort Henry and later become an official interpreter. See "William Woodward, Indian Interpreter", *The William & Mary Quarterly*, Vol. 14, no. 2 (April 1932), 178 and *Jamestowne Society Magazine*, Vol. 40, No. 2, Fall 2016, 7, He was granted 2,100 acres in 1664 by the queen of the Pamunkey tribe who petitioned the Virginia governor, stating she wanted him as a neighbor and as a translator for her people. See Patricia Brady, *Martha Washington, An American Life* (Penguin, 2006), ch. 1.

Other details of his life, including whether he knew Henry Woodward's family, are imagined by the author.

Six. Fort Henry, Virginia Colony

Fort Henry was located in present-day Petersburg, Virginia. For details about Abraham Wood and Fort Henry, see Scott and Wyatt, *Petersburg's Story: A History* (Wittet & Shepperson, 1960). Details about the Woodward family at Fort Henry are imaginary; descriptions of the Indian trade business and relations between Virginia Colony and the Powhatan are more or less accurate. See generally, Ethan Schmidt, *The Divided Dominion: Social Conflict and Indian Hatred in Early Virginia* (University Press of Colorado, 2015).

Seven. The Battle of Bloody Run

Unsurprisingly, there is little published information about this battle, fought near Richmond, Virginia; it was not the Colony's finest moment. See *Church Hill People's News,* December 2, 2014, at https://chpn.net/2014/12/02/the-battle-of-bloody-run/. John Woodward's role, if any, in the battle is imagined.

The Rickahocan Indians, key characters in this novel, were a warlike tribe that had a large impact on the southeast colonies in the seventeenth century and then disappeared from the historical record. They had different names at different times and places; when they moved from Virginia Colony to Carolina Colony, they became the Westo. They originally settled on the James River near the falls and later moved to a location near present-day Augusta, Georgia. The best source of information about the Westo is Eric Bowne, *The Westo Indians: Slave Traders of the Early Colonial South* (The University of Alabama Press, 2005).

Eight. An Unholy Alliance, Virginia Colony

Abraham Wood did make a trade agreement with the Rickahocan/Westo Indians, including trading for Indians captured in Spanish-controlled lands in present-day Georgia to be sold as slaves on the Virginia tobacco plantations. See *The Westo Indians*, above.

Nine. Paradise Lost

Merchant Taylors' School in London was founded in the sixteenth century and still exists. Enrollment records show that Henry's grandfather Thomas was a student there as a young man. It was common for Virginia colonists who could afford to do so to send their children to England for schooling as educational opportunities were limited in Virginia at that time.

Ten. London, 1659

John Woodward and his family were in London in 1659. He enrolled Henry and his brother in Merchant Taylors' School and filed a petition to get his father's former position as Assay Master at the Royal Mint. See *CSP, Domestic Series of the Reign of Charles II: 1660's,* 137 and Charles Robinson, *Register of the Scholars Admitted Into Merchant Taylors' School from A.D. 1562 to 1874, Vol. 1* (Farncombe & Co., 1882), 248. The latter document shows that John Woodward was working as a surgeon at this time.

Eleven. London, 1661-1664

Henry and his brother only attended Merchant Taylors' School for a single year; see above school records. John Woodward's petition to take his father's job as Assay Master at the Royal Mint was finally granted. See *CSP*, 137, above.

William Hilton's account of his exploration of the Carolina coastline was the impetus for the exploration and settlement of South Carolina but he played no further role in the colony's development, other than naming Hilton Head Island after himself.

Twelve. The Ship Rat and the Flea, London 1664

The details about the Great Plague of London are largely accurate, other than John Woodward's role, if any, and were taken from Moote and Moote, *The Great Plague* (Johns Hopkins University Press, 2004, the definitive work about one of London's greatest disasters. For a more colorful and less accurate account, see Daniel Defoe's 1722 work, *A Journal of the Plague Year* (Penguin Books).

Thirteen. Lord Have Mercy on Us, London 1665

Henry's immediate family died of the plague in 1665. See London Metropolitan Archives, London, England, Church of England Parish Registers, 1538-1812; Ancestry.com, London, England, Church of England Baptisms, Marriage and Burials, 1538-1812. The account of their deaths is imagined, other than dates and burial details. There is no record of how Henry survived and made his way to America.

Fourteen. Carolina Colony

The details of this chapter are imaginary.

Fifteen. Sir John Yeamans

This chapter is based on actual events. For Yeamans' life in Barbados, see http://www.stnicholasabbey.com/The-Plantation/Owners-History/.

Modyford's letter to the lords proprietors: see *SP*, 10-12.

Hilton Expedition: Yates, et al., *History of South Carolina, Volume 1* (Lewis Publishing Co., 1920), 44-50.

The lords proprietors letter to Modyford has been revised for clarity and brevity—see *SP*, 13-14.

Lords proprietors commission to Yeamans: see *History*, above, 51-52.

Sixteen. Cape Fear

Yeaman's Cape Fear expedition: see *History*, above, 55-56; Robert Sandford's report, *SP*, 57-81.

Robert Sandford's role: see *History*, 56-57.

Captain Stanyon: see Robert Sandford's report, above.

Seventeen. Port Royal

Henry Woodward's role before joining the Sandford expedition is speculative. Sandford's mention of him in his report is Henry's first documented appearance in America. See *SP*, 65. The author believes that the only plausible way he could have been a member of Sandford's crew is that the major events in his life as portrayed in the preceding chapters are more or less accurate. His grandfather Thomas and Sandford were both government officials in the same region at the same time and would have known each other.

Edisto Indians: *SP*, various pages.

Escamacu Indians: *SP*—Sandford report, Port Royal Indians.

Eighteen. Henry Among the Escamacu

St. Augustine governor's order for Escamacu to relocate to Guale lands: see John Worth, *The Struggle for the Georgia Coast* (Anthropological Papers of the American Museum of Natural History, No. 75, 1995), 22, 76.

Nineteen. St. Augustine

The letter from the Spanish Treasurer to the King about Henry is from Gene Waddell, *Indians of the South Carolina Low Country* 1562-1751 (The Reprint Company, for the University of South Carolina, 1980) 189-190. Also see letter from Juan Cabrera, governor of Florida, to Viceroy of New Spain, March 19, 1685, reference: Seville, Mexico, 61-6-20 (South Carolina Department of Archives and History, Josephine Pinckney files).

Twenty. Pierre Piques

Pierre (Pedro) Piques was a mysterious figure in St. Augustine's early history, only identified as a French surgeon, with "an excellent professional reputation" who was badly treated by the governor and in revenge, aided Robert Searle in attacking St. Augustine. See Diana Reigelsperger, "Pirate, Priest, and Slave: Spanish Florida in the 1668 Searle's Raid" (The Florida Historical Quarterly, Vol 92, No. 3, Winter 2014), 579-580. However, there was no plausible reason for a French surgeon to voluntarily be in St. Augustine at that time. Spain and France were at war in 1668 and there was little reason for him to have been in the region except as a surgeon on a French corsair, attacking Spanish targets. l'Olonnais was an actual corsair, whether Piques ever sailed with him and if and how Piques ended up in St. Augustine is speculative.

Twenty-one. Revenge

The broad details of Searle's 1668 raid of St. Augustine are accurate. The raid, which was responsible for the subsequent construction of Castillo de San Marcos, the oldest existing masonry fort in America, fueled the flames of animosity between the English and Spanish in America for decades. See "Pirate, Priest, and Slave", above. Also see Jean Waterbury, ed., *The Oldest City, St. Augustine Saga of Survival* (St. Augustine Historical Society), 193. Piques was rescued by Searle as he was being taken to Havana and provided Searle with a plan for the raid.

The official Spanish account that Piques was a respected French surgeon who seemed to have snapped due to mistreatment by the governor and returned solely for revenge is not credible (See William M. Straight, "Medicine in St. Augustine During the Spanish Period" (Journal of Florida Medical Association, 1968, vol 55) and should be seen as a whitewash by the government of an extremely embarrassing event—Piques was apparently a wolf in sheep's clothing allowed into the St. Augustine fold. No books or articles this author is aware of have ever made a connection between Henry and Piques but there must have been one. Both were surgeons and foreigners in the small and remote town of St. Augustine. Henry was being held against his will; Piques most likely was as well. There is nothing in the record to suggest Woodward was taken by Searle as a prisoner, the fact that he later became a surgeon on a buccaneer ship suggests the contrary. There is every reason to believe that the Searle raid was driven by Piques' dream of a share of 133 silver bars and, hopefully, his friendship with Henry.

Twenty-two. Jamaica

The broad details about Jamaica are accurate, including the relationship between Henry Morgan, one of history's most famous buccaneers, and Governor Modyford. There is no primary source documentation showing Henry was ever in Jamaica but Searle returned there after the St. Augustine raid and presumably both Henry and Piques were with him. Recommended reading: Thibault Ehrengardt, *The History of Jamaica from 1494 to 1838* (The Jamaica Insula Series, 2009); Michael Pawson & David Buisseret, Port Royal, Jamaica (The University of the West Indies Press, 1974).

Twenty-three. A Buccaneer's Life

The broad details about Henry Morgan's activities in the Caribbean are correct; Henry Woodward's role is imaginary. However, we know that he served as a surgeon on a buccaneer ship here during this time. (See letter to lords proprietors, *SP* 190-191). Morgan controlled all of the English buccaneer activity operating in Jamaica at this time so presumably, Henry's involvement as a ship's surgeon was similar to what is described. See Jon Latimer, *Buccaneers of the Caribbean* (Harvard University Press, 2009); Stephan Talty, *Empire of Blue Water* (Crown Publishers, 2007); Terry Breverton, *Admiral Sir Henry Morgan, King of the Buccaneers* (Pelican Publishing Co, 2005). Alexandre Exquemelin was real, as is the quote from his famous book, *The Buccaneers of America*.

Twenty-four. Shipwrecked

See notes for Chapter 25, below.

Twenty-five. Nevis, Fall 1669

The total loss of a large English buccaneer ship in a hurricane off the coast of Charlestown, Nevis was reported on August 16, 1669; the ship was not identified. See Victoria Sandz & Robert Marx, *Encyclopedia of Western Atlantic Shipwrecks and Sunken Treasure* (McFarland & Co., Inc., 2001), 169. Henry survived and joined the fleet headed to Carolina. See letter to lords proprietors, *SP* 190-191 and Childs, "The First South Carolinians" (South Carolina Historical Magazine, Vol, 71, No. 2, April 1970), 101-108. The details of his time in Nevis are fictitious.

Twenty-six. Nevis, December 1669

The ship *Carolina*, captained by Henry Brayne, along with *The Three Brothers*, did arrive in Nevis in December 1669, and in an almost unbelievable coincidence, found Henry there, eager to leave. See above letter in SP (which misspells the island as Meavis). It is unknown whether he left Nevis on the *Carolina* or *The Three Brothers*. The issue becomes important later in the novel; for several reasons the author believes he was on *The Three Brothers*. Brayne, the captain of the *Carolina* was familiar with the Carolina coastline from his presence on the 1666 Sandford expedition. Henry was the only other person with that familiarity; it makes little sense to put them both on the same ship, leaving *The Three Brothers* without a guide if it separated from the *Carolina*, as did occur.

Twenty-seven. The Voyage of *The Three Brothers*

The difficulties faced by *The Three Brothers* on its voyage are largely accurate. Margaret Tuder was a real passenger on the ship and was taken prisoner by the Spanish. The relationship between Henry and Margaret is imaginary. She is the subject of an early romantic novel, Annie Colcock, *Margaret Tudor: A Romance of Old St. Augustine* (Dodo Press, 1901).

Twenty-eight. St. Catherine's, Guale Land

The details of the capture of passengers from *The Three Brothers* by the Spanish and their Indian allies are generally accurate, other than Henry's participation, which is imagined. See *SP*, 169-171. There is no evidence that any of them were ever released by the Spanish.

Twenty-nine. Albemarle Point

The broad details about the settlers' eventual arrival in Carolina Colony are accurate. The original name of the settlement was Albemarle Point, later Charles Towne, then Charlestown, and finally, in the late eighteenth century, Charleston.

A detail that has puzzled students of early Carolina history is the three-and-a-half-month gap between the arrival of the *Carolina* and the later arrival of *The Three Brothers*. The novel offers a plausible, although rather complicated, answer, based on an analysis of the available information—Brayne may have been a competent coastal captain but apparently had little experience in the open sea.

Today Albemarle Point is a beautiful state park, Charles Towne Landing, with a seventeenth-century replica ship, eighty acres of gardens, guided historical tours, and displays, including several about Henry.

Thirty. Silver and Pearls

Henry's visit to the town of the Cofitachequi (also spelled "Chufytachique") was the beginning of his career as an Indian trader/emissary/scout. Unfortunately for him, it was not a propitious beginning (See Corn chapter.) He didn't leave a detailed account of his journey so most of the details in this chapter are taken from other sources. (See *SP*, 186, 181.) The Cofitachequi were, by all accounts, once the most powerful tribe in the region; in a few years they had mysteriously disappeared. The most probable explanation is that the Westo Indians drove them away. (See Eric Bowne, *The Westo Indians* (University of Alabama Press, 2005),86.

It is generally believed that their town was located on the present site of Mulberry Plantation, near Camden, SC, about thirty miles north of Charles Town. For further information about the Cofitachequi, see Chester DePratter, "Cofitachequi: Ethnohistorical and Archaeological Evidence" (Anthropological Studies, vol 9, 1989), 133-156; Gene Waddell, "Cofitachequi: A Distinctive Culture..." (Ethnohistory, Spring 2005, 52(2)), 333-369; Charles Beck, et. al, "On Interpreting Cofitachequi" (Ethnohistory, summer 2008, 55(3)), 465-490.

Thirty-one. Henry Woodward, Indian Trader

Governor West did send *The Three Brothers* back to St. Catherine's to demand the release of the passengers seized by the Spanish and lost two more men. Perhaps Henry, based on his prior experience with St. Augustine, could have talked him out of it if he had been there. See *SP*, 173-174. It was this time in Charles Towne's history that cemented Henry's place in early Carolina history. The settlers, with no experience surviving in the wilderness, were running out of food, despite the abundance of fish, fowl, and deer surrounding them. Henry's trade agreement with the local tribes put enough food on their tables to get them through their first year. See *SP*, 191.

Thirty-two. The Very Short Battle of Albemarle Point

The general details of the attack by the Spanish are accurate; Henry's role, if any, is imagined. The attack is briefly described in *SP*, 170 and 187. It is surprising that the settlers seemed to have not considered this to be a potentially serious attack; perhaps they didn't want to alarm the lords proprietors about how precarious their situation was.

Thirty-three. Henry and Lord Anthony Ashley Cooper

Henry realized early on that if he were to prosper in Charles Towne, he needed a patron. He selected John Yeamans, who was at that time, the most important individual associated with the colony. Unfortunately, he was also the most devious. Henry wrote to Yeamans, describing his trip to Cofitachequi town and the aborted attack by the Spanish. The letter has been edited for clarity and brevity; the original is in *SP*, 186. But Yeamans blindsided him, writing to the Lords Proprietor Ashley Cooper that Henry had made a major discovery that he wanted to disclose in person in England, but that Henry was needed in Charles Towne and that he would extract the secret from Henry and tell Ashley Cooper what it was. However, a subsequent letter from Ashley Cooper to Henry was all Henry could hope for and more—Ashley Cooper was a far more powerful man than was Yeamans. The letter has been summarized and edited; the original is in *SP*, 315-317.

Thirty-four. Woodward's Secret Mission

Woodward's secret overland mission to Virginia in the summer of 1671 has always been a mystery to historians and probably would have gone unnoticed if Governor West had not caught wind of it and complained bitterly to Ashley Cooper (see following chapter.) This chapter is largely imaginary; the details about their probable route and the Indians Henry would have encountered, as well as Berkeley's Green Spring plantation, are essentially correct. The trip was almost certainly an effort by Yeamans to get Governor Berkeley of Virginia Colony on his side in the battle for the governorship of Carolina Colony. Its governor was selected by the lords proprietors and Berkeley was not only the most senior but the only one living in America. The journey would not have been considered particularly perilous by the standards of Henry's later expeditions, but it was one of the longest treks by an Englishman at that time in the southeast. It is unknown whether James Needham accompanied him or not; later events suggest that he did.

Thirty-five. Corn

The Grand Council's order declaring war on the Kussoe Indians for stealing some corn from settlers' fields is set forth at *SP*, 341-2. The follow-up order is in *SP*, 344-5. Henry's participation in this event is imaginary.

Thirty-six. St. Catherine's Revisited

The events of this chapter are imaginary; there is nothing in the record of Margaret Tuder's fate or any relationship between her and Henry.

Ashley Cooper wrote to Governor West that the Spanish ambassador had promised the prisoners would be released. The letter showed that he seemed more concerned that the ungrateful settlers had supposedly found and kept 200 pounds of ambergris that belonged to the lords proprietors than he did about the prisoners. See *SP*, 209.

Thirty-seven. Espionage

This can be viewed as clever retribution by the Spanish for Henry's coming to St. Augustine under false pretenses six years earlier. Unlike Henry, Camunas didn't hide his intentions and Yeamans seemed more than eager to show off Charles Towne's defenses to him. Camunas returned to St. Augustine and gave his deposition in July of 1672 with a detailed account of his visit and the layout and defenses of the town. A month later, Brian Fitzpatrick, a troublesome indentured servant who had served as the translator for Camunas' visit, fled to St. Augustine; Henry and James Needham were ordered to track him down and kill him if necessary (*SP*, 411). They were unsuccessful and Needham also gave his deposition, detailing Charles Townes' defenses. See Archives of the Greater Indies: Mexico 61-1-18 containing a letter from Manuel de Cendoya of December 15, 1672. This is described in Stanley South, *Archaeological Pathways to Historic Site Development* (Plenum Publishers, 2002). These depositions are the most detailed contemporary descriptions of Charles Towne for that time and show that the Spanish often collected and kept the best records extant of Charles Towne's early days, including Henry's adventures.

Thirty-eight. Shaftesbury and St. Giles Kussoe

Anthony Ashley Cooper, the First Earl of Shaftesbury was one of England's most intriguing political figures in the second half of the seventeenth century. The best account of his complex life is K.H.D. Haley, *The First Earl of Shaftesbury* (Clarendon Press, Oxford 1968). The details of his involvement with the Carolina Colony are accurate, as are most of the general details about Andrew Percival and Henry finding a 12,000-acre plantation for Shaftesbury and naming it St. Giles Kussoe. Shaftesbury's instructions to Percival are in *SP*, 441; his letter to Henry on page 445. The letter was beyond Henry's wildest hopes—Shaftesbury was asking to set up a trade with Indians for "furs and other commodities," for which he would receive a fifth of the profits. This would be the true beginning of his career as an Indian trader.

St. Giles Kussoe was located on the Ashley River, just upstream from present-day Middleton Plantation. A historic map of the plantation, also known as the Signiory of St. Giles or Ashley Barony, is at https://digital.tcl.sc.edu/digital/collection/sclmaps/id/823/.

Thirty-Nine. The Westo

The appearance of the Westo warriors at St. Giles Kussoe and Henry's subsequent journey to Westo town, also known as Hickauhaugau, is one of the most written about events in Henry's life. His lengthy letter of December 1674 to Shaftesbury describing his visit to their town is a treasure trove of information about the Westo and the Carolina wilderness. *SP*, 456-462.

For a quarter of a century, the Westo, known as the Rickahocans in Virginia and the Chichimeco by the Spanish, were a highly disruptive force in Virginia, Carolina Colony, and the Guale lands (present-day Georgia) after Virginia traders began buying captive Indians from them to be sold as slaves. Hardened by the Beaver Wars (the French and Indian Wars), in the Great Lakes region, the Westo, the only tribe with guns at that time, ravaged the more peaceful tribes of the southeast. When they shifted their trading alliance from Virginia to St. Giles Kussoe, Henry's career as an Indian trader began in earnest. The best account of the Westo's role in early Carolina is Eric Bowne, *The Westo Indians: Slave Traders of the Early Colonial South* (University of Alabama Press, 2005). The Westo Chief's, whose name is invented, story about his people is taken largely from it.

The scope of Indian slave trading on Shaftesbury's plantation is a matter of dispute. That the Westo made their living selling Indian captives to the English was no secret. Henry states in his above letter to Shaftesbury that they traded for "young Indian slaves" and that they gave him a young boy they had captured. While there are existing account books reflecting the trade in deerskins and furs between the Westo and St. Giles, there are no corresponding documents detailing trade in Indian slaves. However, skins and furs were shipped directly to England to be sold; Indian captives were transported to Barbados to be sold as slaves. Presumably, this would have resulted in two different sets of accounting records. Documents reflecting the details of slave trading, whether involving African or Indian captives, have largely disappeared from the historic record; that appears to be the case with St. Giles as well, with only a few exceptions, including a cryptic reference in the June 29, 1677, St. Giles account statements—"By Indian slaves bought of them and sold." (Microfilm copies of the account statements for Andrew Percival and Henry Woodward with Shaftesbury are in the South Carolina Department of Archives and History.) Also, see a letter of March 9, 1680/81 from Shaftesbury to Andrew Percival, sent just after the Westo War, asking for an accounting of "all skins furs slaves, etc." and to have Henry sign off on the list so that "we may better know how to even accounts with him." *BPRO CEB*, vol. 20, 164. The Westo traded exclusively with St. Giles Kussoe for almost six years; there is nothing in the record showing that Shaftesbury forbade trading in Indian slaves at St. Giles; his only prohibition was that the Charles Towne settlers could not trade in Indian slaves, solely to preserve the peace.

Forty. Red Bird

The title of the novel comes from Henry's famous letter to John Locke about the Westo, who worshipped the devil, and the Escamacu, to whom the red bird (cardinal) was sacred. The letter, which went unnoticed for many years, is in *Correspondence of John Locke, vol. 1*, #305 (Clarendon Press, 1976-199), 431-433.

Forty-one. St. Giles Wimborne

The prices for trade goods are speculative, based on an analysis of existing account records for St. Giles, price schedules from the early eighteenth century, and the literature. See Kathryn Braund, *Deerskins & Duffels* (University of Nebraska Press, 1993), 88-90. Copies of the account statements are kept by the Shaftesbury Estate Office, Wimborne St. Giles, Dorset, England. There is anecdotal evidence that, in at least one instance, an Indian captive was traded for one musket. More realistically, the price must have been much higher as African slaves were selling in Barbados for about twenty pounds at the time. The trader Thomas Nairne reported that "one slave brings a Gun, ammunition, horse, hatchet and a suit of Clothes, which would not be procured with much tedious toil a-hunting." *Deerskins*, above, 33. Henry's trip to England is speculative, based solely on a September 28, 1676 entry in his account statements of six pounds "for his own passage home." This was the price of passage from Carolina to London at that time. Copies of the account statements are kept by the Shaftesbury Estate Office, Wimborne St. Giles, Dorset, England. The description of Shaftesbury's life at St. Giles Wimborne comes from *The First Earl of Shaftesbury,* above. Margaret is an imagined character. However, Henry was at least briefly married to a woman named Margaret in 1677, based on January 3, 1677 order signed by Governor West granting Henry and his wife Margaret 250 acres. Nothing else is known about her.

Forty-two. London

Colleton's meeting with the other Lords Proprietors is based on a letter Governor West wrote to John Locke complaining about Godfrey. De Beer, *Locke Letters, vol. 1,* #318. The April 10 Lords Proprietors' Agreement and Order have been edited for brevity. The unabridged documents are in BPRO, CSP 1677-80, 60-61.

Forty-three. Carolina Colony

The letters awarding Henry 2,000 acres and appointing him as deputy are in *BPRO CEB* vol 20, 123. The April 10 Order is in William Rivers, *A Sketch of the History of South Carolina* (McCarter & Co., 1856), 388-389

Forty-four. Abbapoola Creek

This chapter is imaginary although the building styles and techniques of the period are accurate. Quarter pathers, today's quarter horses, are real and were supposedly ridden on Berkeley's plantation. It is unknown what happened to Margaret, who was Henry's wife at least through 1677 (see above.) The Abbapoola Creek plantation was real. An archaeological investigation in 1980 identified the property, located on John's Island. See Stanley South and Michael Hartley, *Deep Water and High Ground: Seventeenth Century Low Country Settlement* (University of South Carolina Scholar Commons Research Manuscript Series, Book 159, 1980), 28, 94-96.

Forty-five. Sorrow

The details of this chapter are imagined.

Forty-six. Mary Godfrey

Mary Godfrey, John Godfrey's daughter, was real and was married to Henry by no later than 1680. Henry's letter directing Andrew Percival, the manager of St. Giles Kussoe, to buy six Negro slaves is real. It is in Susan Bates & Harriott Leland, eds., *Proprietary Records of South Carolina, Volume Two* (History Press, 2006), 55 The portrayal of Mary having successfully run their plantation during Henry's frequent absences is imagined but not unheard of at this time. See Cara Anzilotti, *Autonomy and the Female Planter in Colonial South Carolina* (The Journal of Southern History, vol. 63, No. 2, May 1997), 239-268.

Forty-seven. Goose Creek Men

The historical background of the Goose Creek Men is more or less accurate; the details of the chapter are imaginary.

Forty-eight. Henry and Paytah Plot

The details of this chapter are imagined; the historical background, and the events leading up to the Westo raid of St. Catherine's in Guale lands (modern-day Georgia), are more or less accurate.

Forty-nine. Ariana and the Goose Creek Men

This chapter is a more or less accurate portrayal of events. Moore's trip to Westo town is set forth in Verner Crane, *The Southern Frontier, 1670-1732* (University of Alabama Press, 2004), 19 and *The Westo Indians*, 99. The Council's findings of April 12 are in A.S. Salley, ed., *Journal of the Grand Council of South Carolina* (The State Company, 1907), 83-84.

Fifty. St. Catherine's

Historians are vague about the identity of the Englishman or men accompanying the Westo on their attack of St. Catherine's Island. The author believes without a doubt, it was Henry; he may have had other English with him. Revenge may well have played a part in his participation—he was most likely at St. Catherine's in 1670 when Spanish soldiers seized passengers from *The Three Brothers* (chapter 28). An excellent discussion of the raid is by Charles Philips, Jr., "Capitan Enrique: Dr. Henry Woodward and the World of the Early Carolina Indian Trader," Master's Degree dissertation (The Citadel, 2001), 22-28.

Fifty-one. War Clouds

The sale of Indian slaves to Charles Towne settlers is taken from the Grand Council order of June 1, 1680. *JGC* 83-84. Its order regarding Henry is at *JGC*, 85.

Fifty-two. War Plans

The leadup to the Westo War is murky and the few surviving records do little to clarify it. The author believes it is best explained by the Goose Creek Men doing whatever they felt was necessary to take the Indian slave trade business from the Westo and St. Giles Kussoe/Henry Woodward and covering their tracks in the process. See *The Westo Indians*, 99.

Fifty-three. The Westo War

The Goose Creek Men and the Grand Council did a good job concealing the details of the Westo War from the lords proprietors who didn't learn what had happened until later. See letter from lords proprietors to the governor, March 7, 1680/81, *BPRO CEB*, vol. 20, p. 165. Initially, the Goose Creek Men's efforts to blame Henry for the war were at least partially successful. See February 21, 1680/81 letter from Shaftesbury to Andrew Percival, instructing him to conceal this matter from Henry and others until peace was concluded with the Westo. *BPRO CEB* vol. 20, 164. (This letter was apparently never sent to Percival.) After destroying the Westo, the Goose Creek Men, who now dominated Charles Towne's government, fulfilled their plan to become the biggest Indian slave traders in the colony. See *The Westo Indians*, 101-108.

Fifty-four. High Crimes and Misdemeanors

There is no record of the Charles Towne proceedings against Henry; the only mention of his conviction for high crimes and misdemeanors is the pardon he received from the lords proprietors in May of 1682. (As the Charlestowne Council's actions became more outrageous during this time, its records of the events became correspondingly scantier.) In eighteenth-century England, charges of "high crimes and misdemeanors" were directed almost exclusively against public officials as part of a parliamentary impeachment proceeding and included charges of negligence and improprieties while in office. Punishment was usually banishment, imprisonment, or a fine. It was a stretch to bring such charges against Henry but the court system in Carolina at that time was rudimentary at best.

Fifty-five. Henry Appeals

There is little historical documentation for Henry's journey to England to seek a pardon. He signed a power of attorney in favor of his wife and father-in-law on June 11, 1681 (a copy is in the South Carolina Department of Archives and History, Josephine Pinckney files); he was also reimbursed for his voyage to London on that date.

Fifty-six. High Treason

Ironically, at the same time Henry was seeking a pardon from Shaftesbury for his conviction for high crimes and misdemeanors, Shaftesbury himself was the target of a similar charge brought by the Crown. The description of his trial is taken from *The First Earl of Shaftesbury*, above.

Fifty-seven. Henry and Shaftesbury Converse

The details of this chapter are imaginary.

Fifty-eight. John Locke

Locke was living at Shaftesbury's home, Thanet House, at this time; Henry almost certainly would have met him in London. Although this chapter is imaginary, it raises important issues of the time: the enslavement of both Africans and Native Americans and the taking of the latter group's lands in the American colonies. Locke's involvement with Carolina Colony has been the subject of numerous scholarly articles. See James Farr, *"Absolute Power and Authority": John Locke and the Revisions of the Fundamental Constitutions of Carolina* (Locke Studies, vol. 2020, October 29, 2020).

The most discussed issue about Locke's involvement in Carolina Colony has been his role in drafting the Carolina Fundamental Constitutions and his views on slavery. A recently discovered five-page anonymous memoir about John Locke helps answer some of these questions. See Felix Waldman, "John Locke as a Reader of Thomas Hobbes's Leviathan: A New Manuscript" (The Journal of Modern History, The University of Chicago, June 2021), 245-282. Waldman, describing the find as "the holy grail" of Locke scholarship, identifies the anonymous author as James Tyrell, a close friend of Locke's. The memoir gives a blunt and uncomplimentary assessment of Locke. Tyrell wrote that Locke did not speak familiarly about important matters with his employer, Lord Shaftesbury, did not enter into political intrigues with him, and did not give him advice. This assessment should help answer whether or not Locke was an active participant with Shaftesbury in drafting Carolina's Fundamental Constitutions.

Henry's discussion with Locke about the near "absolute power and authority" the lords proprietors have over the settlers was written to showcase the gap between the real world of Carolina Colony and the basis of much of Locke's future fame—personal liberty versus the power of the government.

This chapter makes the suggestion that Henry's story about life as a buccaneer might have influenced Locke's views of the role of government and personal freedom as he finished the Second Treatise. Certainly, if Locke was exposed to the details of Henry's life as a buccaneer, frontiersman, and Indian trader, it must have been something new to him.

Locke knew that St. Giles Kussoe was a slave-trading outpost for captured Native Americans as he handled all of the correspondence between Shaftesbury and St. Giles. If he had any moral qualms about the business, he never expressed them. Locke's views on slavery ascribed to him in his conversation with Henry are essentially the views he sets forth in Chapter IV of his Second Treatise of Government. Commentators have pointed out that his view had nothing to do with the realities of slave trading and he seems to have had a disconnect between what he said and what he did. See James Farr, *"SO VILE AND MISERABLE AN ESTATE" The Problem of Slavery in Locke's Political Thought* (Political Theory, Vol. 14 No. 2 May 1986), 263-289. Again, Tyrell's memoir helps explain this discrepancy. He wrote that Locke believed that principles of morality were relative to the different countries of the world and that what was a crime in one place was not in another. This flexibility would help explain his justification for slavery in the Second Treatise which was totally at odds with the enslavement of Native Americans and Africans at this time. His theory of slavery apparently only applied to European nations, not Africa or America.

Thomas Tryon and Richard Baxter were actual people and were some of the earliest abolitionists in England. Their views are real. Henry hearing a lecture by them is imagined.

Henry points out the logical flaw in Locke's theory of property ownership (set forth in Chapter 5 of the *Second Treatise*), at least as applied to the American colonies. Locke argues that men can acquire land because their labor, which belongs to them alone, improves the land. Henry points out that much of the land (virtually all, in future years) in the colonies is worked by slaves. The slaves weren't taken in just wars so a planter has no moral claim to them thus he can have no claim to the property worked by them on his behalf.

Fifty-nine. Pardoned

A full copy of the pardon is in *BPRO CEB*, vol. 20, 198.

Sixty. Carolina Colony

As a side note, Shaftesbury, fearing for his safety, fled to Holland in November 1682 where he died shortly thereafter.

Sixty-one. The Scots

Henry's letter to his father-in-law is in *BPRO CEB* vol. 21, 49; it is perhaps the last written communication from Henry in the historical record. For the early history of Stuart's Town, see George Irish, "The Carolina Merchant: Advice of Arrival" (Scottish Historical Review, v. 25, no. 98, Jan. 1928), 98-108.

Sixty-two. Charles Towne

The circumstances surrounding Henry's journey to Amacaraw, or Yamacraw, also called Amercarais, on the Savannah River are unclear. The location is in present-day Savannah, Georgia. At that time, the river was generally called the Westo River, but it is referred to in the novel as the Savannah for clarity's sake. The author believes the sequence of events in this chapter is more or less accurate. The Scots, teamed up with the Yamasee, did attack the Timucua Indian town as described. Henry probably did plan on seeing what Cardross was up to when he traveled to Amacaraw; he and his men were seized and held prisoner by the Scots. The depositions are in *BPRO CEB*, vol. 21, 61-68. This is the first verifiable instance of Henry having a crew of men working for him.

Sixty-three. Coweta Town

Henry's greatest triumph as an Indian trader was his trade agreement with the Creeks; unfortunately, it was short-lived. The Creek Indians in the novel were not called the Creek by the settlers until the early eighteenth century; they were known as the Upper Creeks, who lived along the upper Chattahoochee River, and the Lower Creeks, who lived along the lower part of the river which forms part of the Alabama-Georgia border. They considered themselves part of the Muscogee Confederacy. For simplicity's sake, the Lower Creeks, who Henry traded with, are referred to as the Creeks.

Henry had helped them make a peace agreement with the Westo and the Creeks years earlier but had never pursued a trade agreement with the Creeks until now. The description of their culture and beliefs is more or less accurate, although greatly simplified. See Bill Grantham, *Creation Myths and Legends of the Creek Indians* (University of Florida Press, 2002). Quiair was a real person; he apparently was a Coweta Mico, and Henry did reportedly marry his niece, whose name is invented.

There is nothing in the historical record showing he traded for Indian slaves with the Creek. Whether this was based on moral or practical reasons, or neither, is unknown. By the early 1700's, years after Henry's death, the Creeks were heavily involved in Indian slave trading with Charles Towne traders. For details of the Creeks and Henry's involvement with them, see Steven Hahn, *The Invention of the Creek Nation*, 1670-1763 (University of Nebraska Press, 2004) Also see Kathryn Braund, *Deerskin & Duffels*, University of Nebraska Press, 1993).

Sixty-four. Cat and Mouse

The Spanish soldiers' unsuccessful pursuit of Henry through the Georgia mountains and destruction of his trading blockhouse is described in Eric Bowne, "Dr. Henry Woodard's Role in Early Carolina Indian Relations;" LeMaster & Wood, eds., *Creating and Contesting Carolina* (University of South Carolina Press, 2013), 73-93. A translated copy of the original letter from Juan Cabrera, governor of Florida, to Viceroy of New Spain, March 19, 1686, is in the South Carolina Department of Archives and History, Josephine Pinckney files. The original is in the Seville, Spain Archives, A.G.I. 58-4-23. Henry's famous "letter on a tree", taunting the soldiers is also in A.G.I. 58-4-23 and is set forth in Herbert Bolton & Mary Ross, The Debatable Land (Russel & Russel, 1923), 50.

Sixty-five. Abbapoola Creek

Henry did return to Coweta with forty-five Yamasee warriors, as well as firearms. See *Early Carolina*, above, 88.

Sixty-six. Apalachicola Province

Henry's return to Coweta is documented; see above sources. His departure is described in a letter dated August 21, 1686, from Lieutenant Antonio Mateos to Governor Cabrera. A translated copy of the original letter is in the South Carolina Department of Archives and History, Josephine Pinckney files. The original is in the Seville, Spain Archives, A.G.I. 61-6-20. The rattlesnake bite is based on Spanish reports that he was ill; some historians believe it was from a snake bite. If Henry did die of a rattlesnake bite, apparently some days after he was bitten, it was possibly from kidney failure, uncommon but not unheard of with rattlesnake bites.

The last contemporary information about Henry is the Guale Indian's deposition given in St. Augustine stating that Henry left Coweta with an Englishman and several Indians. Whether the Englishman was in fact Ruben Willis is unknown but of all of Henry's crew, he is the only one known to have survived as he is named in a South Carolina land warrant dated April 2, 1694. The entirety of the unedited deposition is in John Worth, *The Struggle for the Georgia Coast* (American Museum of Natural History, Anthropological Papers, No. 75, 1995), 154. The story is generally told that Henry returned to Charles Towne on a litter, accompanied by 150 braves laden with deerskins. The above Spanish sources only state that he, his crew, and the braves left Coweta separately. Presumably the braves were on foot, and Henry was in a boat. There is no evidence he made it home alive.

Sixty-seven. The Yamasee War

The Yamasee War was much larger, longer, and more complex than just the Good Friday attack. For a general account of the War, see Lawrence Rowland, et. al, *The History of Beaufort County, South Carolina, Vol. 1* (University of South Carolina Press, 1996), 95-110. For a more detailed account of the war, including the events in this chapter, see *This Torrent of Indians: War on the Southern Frontier, 1715-1728* (University of South Carolina Press, 1996). A final irony in the Henry Woodward saga is that the governor's visit to his son John's plantation was misinterpreted by the Yamasee chief, which triggered the start of the war. Both the Yamasee and the Coweta Creeks were Henry's close allies at the time of his death thirty years earlier.

Henry Woodward's descendants were influential in South Carolina's affairs for many years. These included three state governors, four U.S. Senators, six Representatives, four judges, three state attorney generals, and many more. See Joseph Barnwell, "Dr. Henry Woodward, the First English settler in South Carolina and Some of His Descendants" (South Carolina Historical and Genealogical Magazine, Vol. 8, No. 1, Jan 1907), 29-41.